Hell
has its
Demons

Book 1 of *The Sotil and Savage Adventures*

MARK LORD

ISBN: 1495982858
ISBN-13: 978-1495982859

Published by Alt Hist Press
www.althistpress.co.uk

Edited by Lyn Worthen, Camden Park Press,
http://www.camenparkpress.com/

Also by Mark Lord, http://marklord.info:

Novels
By the Sword's Edge (Historical)
The Return of the Free (Fantasy)

Short Stories
The Honour of Rome (Historical)
Forged in Blood (Fantasy)
Demon River (Fantasy)
Vulture Returns(Fantasy)
The Vulture, The Giant and The Flea(Fantasy)
Two Lives for the Sea God(Fantasy)
The Human Factor (Science Fiction)
Little Boy Found (Science Fiction)

Short Story Collection
Tales of Mayhem and Madness (Historical & Fantasy)
Through a Distant Mirror Darkly (Medieval Historical &
Fantasy)

Non-Fiction
The Court in English Alliterative Poetry, 1350-1450

PROLOGUE

Here follows a fragment of a letter discovered on the reverse of manor rolls for Chislehurst manor, Great Wopping. The original parchment has been dated to the late fourteenth century.

To Master Roger Sotil, Professor of Astronomy, Merton College, Oxford; from Peter, Abbot of St. Brett's.

For months now I have not slept, worrying about the fires of hell. Some days it seems as if the very maw of hell will open in its mouth below our town and swallow it up in one belch of fire. Ever since the feast of Christmas and the New Year's celebrations enjoyed by the burgesses and common folk of the town, a sort of madness has descended upon them. I took it at first for drunkenness or some new onslaught of the plague. But the strange actions and words coming from the people of this vill can only be a result of witchcraft, sorcery and the influence of daemons.

I have been a member of the Benedictine order ever since I was a boy, and was ordained a priest twenty years ago, yet never have I encountered such devilry in one place. In fact, apart from some examples of deadly sin that one might put down to the devil's influence, I have never seen anything that, in certitude, could be given the name of witchcraft. Indeed I do not deny that the devil's handiwork is all around us, in the temptation laid before us to sin; whether it be through greed, lust or pride, all of these are around us every day. Yet for people to act as if possessed and under the direct authority of a daemon and even to speak as if with a daemon's voice, or to commit a heinous crime and afterward deny memory of it, thus showing at the time they were possessed of a daemon, is far outside the ken of this humble servant of the Lord.

So that is why I must turn to you, Master Roger. Although you are young and, I hear, not an ordained priest, yet your travels both geographically and intellectually have taken you to places where other men fear to walk. You step in your tutor's footsteps, and I wonder perhaps if you have surpassed him. He told me, before he died, that you had what the Greeks called a genius, and that already your theorising was beyond his own, as if you were touched with divine inspiration.

I hope that this is true, because I fret that only a miracle can save the souls of our folk.

I ask that you come with all swiftness to our Abbey, but I also beg of you to maintain utmost secrecy of the purpose of your travel. For the love that there was between your tutor and I, please attend to my request.

May the grace of God protect you. Written in my own hand, this day, the fifth Sunday of Easter, at St. Brett's.

Peter de Maudville, Abbot.

CHAPTER 1

Oxford, 1376

"Pass me your helmet and I'll piss in it for you, you old fool," said Jake Savage. "Come on give it here, or do you want to watch my bladder explode?"

"You can drink your own piss before I'll give you my helmet," said Hugh. "And who are you calling a fool?" The man-at-arms swayed over Jake, then put an arm out to steady himself against Jake's shoulder and fell over into the middle of the tavern. Jake leant over and helped him onto a chair.

"Right, that's enough; all of you get out," shouted the innkeeper. With a few shoves and curses the three men — a soldier by the name of Hugh, Jake, a servant, and John, a student — stumbled into the bright sunshine. Jake put his hand to his forehead and blinked. Now where had he put his horse? He knew he was meant to go somewhere this afternoon. He had something to do for Master Roger, but what was it?

"What was it?" he shouted at Hugh and John.

Hugh and John both laughed. Hugh replaced his pot helmet and grabbed his halberd from the innkeeper. Taking John by the arm, the pair lurched up the street singing songs about football and glory. Every time that Jake met them it was the same: boasting about their glorious football exploits while drinking too many pints of ale. Sometimes when he woke up the next morning to a furry tongue and throbbing head, Jake wished that King Edward's attempts to ban the sport had succeeded.

"Hey, Jake, you old git, don't forget this." The innkeeper passed him a wax-sealed letter, slightly wet from ale, but the address still legible. That was it. Roger wanted him to find a messenger to despatch the letter. Where was it going again? Jake squinted at the envelope. To St. Brett's, to Abbot Peter. Yes. St. Brett's was a Benedictine house, which meant he must ride south to Abingdon Abbey to send it by one of their riders. Jake looked in the stables for his horse and after tipping the stable-lad a penny asked for a foot up into the saddle.

"Are you right enough to ride, sir?" said the boy.

"I've ridden with a bigger ale-stomach than this," said Jake. He nudged his mare, Lois, in the flanks with his boots and let her trot off. Turning back to the boy, he shouted, "next time you mock your elders, I'll give you a beating."

"Watch the tree," shouted the boy. But it was too late. The branch of the tree hanging over the wall of the inn's yard whacked Jake hard on the head. He fell forward over the mare's neck and whispered to her: "Come, take me away from this shameful place." Another nudge and Lois was trotting down the road, towards the Grandpont and onto the road south to Abingdon.

Lois's fast trot, combined with the rush of fresh air into his lungs, had the effect that Jake both expected and dreaded. After a mile, he reined Lois to a halt, half fell out of the saddle, and vomited into a drainage ditch by the side of the road. A peasant with his cart passing in the other direction crossed himself and hurried on.

"I haven't got the plague, you idiot, it's just the drink," muttered Jake.

Despite the pain in his guts and the taste in his mouth, Jake's head felt clearer. Recent memories came flooding back like excrement from an open drain. St. Brett's was it? Bugger that. No wonder he had been in a mood to drink that afternoon. He hadn't needed much persuading. After Roger passed him the letter, he had gone to find Hugh to tell him that he couldn't play that Sunday. The man-at-arms had cursed him. He would miss the final against Oxford borough, and although he wasn't as fast as he used to be, Hugh and the others regarded Jake as a wily player. Jake had promised to buy Hugh a drink in recompense, but he also wanted a drink to help him forget about the prospect of returning to St. Brett's. They had met John at the pub. He'd just been leaving, with a plan to attend one of Master Roger's lectures by happenstance, but had been easily convinced to stay for another round. That had been at sext, when the sun was at its highest, and now it was past vespers, so the three had drunk full and fast at the White Hart for upwards of six hours.

Of all the towns in the kingdom of England, why did it have to be St. Brett's? Jake had told Roger that the Abbot's letter was wrong-headed and pure monkish make-believe. Daemons indeed! Such spirits were the fancy of the Church, lies concocted to keep people fearful. But the danger with such lies was that there was always the chance that some idiots would decide to believe them and think they or others were possessed. But for the people of St. Brett's to imagine such a thing? Jake knew the inhabitants of that town well. The largest and most prosperous vill owned by the Abbey of St. Brett's, the town was a small but growing trading centre north of London; though not recognized as a borough, despite its pretensions. He knew that those people cared more for throwing off the yoke of the Abbey's lordship than they did for religion. Some of the richer bastards might fret about the affects of avarice upon their souls and pay for the monks' prayers, yet they were not a pious lot. But daemons? Smelt of dabbling in witchcraft. Smelt of the fragrant Isabel perhaps? Smelt of her bullshit.

Jake gritted his teeth and decided that once he returned to Roger's rooms at Merton College he would confront his master and refuse to travel with him to St. Brett's. Master Roger would have to travel without his manservant, and if he wasn't happy with it, then that would be the end of their time together. Roger was his master and not his friend, he must remember that. No use becoming sentimental. So if he wanted to dismiss him then that was fine. But what then? Either thieving or soldiering, Jake supposed, but somehow he would get by. There were always wars to be fought, and there were places where men could disregard the law and turn a profit. He had been a fool to think he could be in the same country as that woman again and forget her remembrance.

Jake and Lois came to a junction where the road from Cirencester joined the road to Abingdon. Three men on horseback were approaching at a fast trot from the direction of Cirencester, each with a laden sumpter in tow. He would have companions it seemed for the last mile into Abingdon. Three different-looking men you could never expect to see. Despite not wearing any armour or carrying weapons openly, they were accoutred like soldiers. Jake knew the type. He had been that type.

He could see the bulge of helmets covered in cloth and hear the clink as they bounced on their horses" harness. He could see their padded jerkins, stained by the rust from mail. The swords at their sides were not unusual (any careful traveller would wear a sword), but on their sumpters he could see long, cloth-wrapped poles — he had seen poles wrapped like that before to protect against their elements, amongst the baggage of men-at-arms, or their cursed lighter brethren, the hobelars.

One of them looked too young to be a soldier, not yet thirteen, while the man who rode in the middle was old enough to be anybody's great grandfather, with his thin wispy beard and bald liver-spotted head, but something about his build spoke of strength in his body's scrawny muscles. The third was so fat and bloated like a bull frog that it seemed impossible his horse could bear his weight.

Jake proffered a greeting. "Well met gentlemen. Do you ride for Abingdon?"

But the old man, the boy and the man the size of a whale only glanced at him and carried on without a word. They hurried their horses and set off in a canter down the gentle hill toward Abingdon. Jake wanted to call after them to tell him what utter ungentle fuckwits he thought they were, but knew better. The odds were against him, despite the motley appearance of the three soldiers. Foolishly, he had travelled with only a dagger at his side, while they carried the full equipment for war.

"Let's hope they aren't stopping in Abingdon," he said to his horse Lois. "I don't fancy sharing a tavern with them."

He rode onwards through the gloom of dusk navigating by the lights of village settlements until in the low valley below he saw the silhouettes of the Abbey and town of Abingdon, with its large stone bridge straddling the broadening flow of the Thames.

At the Abbey a helpful young monk showed him into the Prior's office, who as well as being second in command to the Abbot was also comptroller of the Abbey's messenger service. A small fire and a single candle on the man's desk provided the only light, and Jake glanced with concern at the growing darkness outside the single small window.

"A letter, at this hour?" said the Prior once Jake had stated his business. After glancing up as he came in, the monk had not looked away from the rolls of parchment that lay on the desk in front of him. "Where is it bound?"

"To Abbot Peter at St. Brett's," replied Jake.

"And who sends it?" asked the monk, still not looking up.

"Does that matter?" said Jake.

"It will to the rider. You'll need to agree on your price with him."

"Fine," said Jake. "Where can I find him?"

"I would like to know as well. He was expected today."

"So will he come tomorrow?"

"Who can say?" said the monk. "Let me have the letter and 10 marks and I will arrange everything once the rider comes."

"I thought I had to agree my price with the rider. I think I'll pass on your offer," said Jake. "I'll come back tomorrow."

"Wait," said the monk. As Jake turned he saw that the man had actually stood up. "You may think I am trying to swindle money out of you, but that is not my intention. We have our own letter to go to St. Brett's, so I know yours will go straight there and quickly; the rider won't be stopping in London first. I can also swear to you on the Bible that his price will be 10 marks. That's what we will pay him, as well."

Jake sighed. His head hurt and he needed to rest, perhaps another drink as well. He wanted rid himself of this letter and rid of Roger and the madness of returning to St. Brett's. He reached into his jacket pocket and drew out the folded and sealed letter. The monk extended his hand, and in the flickering light Jake could see underneath his black cassock the edge of his shirt's sleeve, and there unmistakably were two letter Ss intertwined, silver stitching on a black cuff. He was one of the Duke's men.

Jake himself had worn that badge while on campaign in France, as a member of the retinue of a baronet from the Duke's affinity. After the King and his eldest son, the Duke was the richest man in England, and could afford to spread his largess far and wide. At home in England the Duke retained a wide network of officials and other influential men — judges, financiers, wardens of forests, castellans, many local gentry and even it seemed members of the clergy.

He knew that Abingdon, like many Abbeys, received donations from the nobility. John of Gaunt, the Duke of Lancaster, was known to patronise several religious houses, including St. Brett's. But for a monk to wear John of Gaunt's livery hidden beneath his habit? That was unusual. Why would the Duke retain a monk like the prior, and why would the Abbey accept it?

The fact that the monk hid his allegiance — or at least made an effort to not flaunt it — made Jake more suspicious. Was it a sign meant only for him?

The monk's hand closed around the letter, but Jake didn't let go. They stood for a moment both gripping the letter. "I have changed my mind. I will come back tomorrow and speak to the rider myself," said Jake.

But the monk would not let go of the letter.

"Did you hear me?" said Jake.

"As you wish," said the monk, letting go at last. "You had better be here early. If the rider comes and your letter is not here, he will not wait."

Jake left the Abbey and walked his horse down the High Street of Abingdon, looking for an inn where he could spend the night. Abingdon attracted several traders as well as pilgrims who visited the Abbey, so there were a few places to choose from. Jake walked past the two biggest inns, which were right on the marketplace and near the Abbey, and instead found a smaller establishment on the street leading towards the river.

Jake ordered a pint from the bar. He had found a nice little tavern. The food on offer looked good, a roast pig was being turned over a fire in the open kitchen behind the bar, which was not too busy, and the pot-girl had a friendly look about her. He hoped he could spend a pleasant evening there. A bit of time on his own might be good for him, let him get his head around things. St. Brett's and Isabel. St. Brett's, Isabel, and his father.

"Peace be with you pilgrim," said a shuffling man in a long habit who walked past Jake's table. The man's staff clacked on the hard earth floor, not yet muffled by fresh reeds, as he walked a circuit of the room, repeating the same phrase to each person there, yet not looking any of them in the face. The man stopped at the bar and bowed to the pot-girl.

"Boiled water if you please," he said in a soft, clear voice. Jake and the other men in the bar all looked at him. He was stooped and wore a cleric's habit, and could have been a friar, but he lacked a tonsure, instead boasting a full head of bushy hair.

A couple of men drinking by the small window onto the road chuckled to themselves.

"Stupid beggar," said one of them, a stout ape with a loud-voice. His friend, as well built but with a weasel thin face and greasy black hair snickered and glanced over at the robed man.

Jake considered getting another ale, then with a grunt stretched out his legs and levered himself off his bench. Too long sitting in one place did that to him now. He nodded at the beggar with the staff who stood blowing on his cup of boiled water as he approached. The beggar looked up and stared at Jake with a fool's smile on his lips.

"Go with peace in these troubled times, and go ye not to war, my son," he said.

"I have no plans to go to war, father," said Jake.

"We are all God's children, you should call me brother," he said. Jake shook his head and walked back to his table by the stairs.

He supped on the warm beer and felt a glow of pleasure flood his throat. Lovely stuff this Abingdon Ale, he would have to ask the tapster for the recipe.

"Horsemen, where is your fourth rider?" exclaimed the beggar, still standing at the bar, pointing at the stairs behind Jake. The three soldiers he had passed earlier, the youth, the old man and the fat man had, at that moment, walked down the stairs and entered the room behind Jake.

Jake didn't have a mind to talk to them again, so turned away, but the loud-mouth by the window laughed and said, "Meet our madman, friends." His weasel-faced friend laughed through his nose with a high-pitched squeal.

Jake heard one of the soldiers behind him mutter something as they walked past his table and went to sit at the far end of the bar. The beggar swivelled to watch them walk past and nodded at each as they did so. "Yes, yes, three have come, and a fourth will join them. Is it you?" He pointed at Jake. Jake scowled and got up to leave.

The tapster waved him to sit again. "I'll get rid of him. Look you, there is a church just a few steps down the way; why don't you get alms there, and stop disturbing my patrons."

The beggar bowed low to the tapster and withdrew, bowing to Jake and then to the three soldiers, who talked quietly amongst themselves over pints of ale and chunks of bread and cheese the pot-girl had brought them. Jake returned to his beer and thought about whether it might be worth ordering some food. He also thought about whether he might take himself and Lois to another tavern, but the horse's board and his were paid for the night. He could pay extra and get a room, but he felt daft even thinking about paying more just to be away from these three soldiers.

Another beer would help. *Where was that pretty pot-girl?* Over by the door, busy talking and smiling to a young man who had just walked in, a bundle of leathers over his broad shoulder. He walked with her to the bar, one hand holding his merchandise and the other on the girl's plump arse. He hurled the sheets of leather onto the bar with a slap and put his other hand round the girl's waist and kissed her. The tapster was smiling and didn't seem to mind.

"Been better market days," said the young man in answer to the tapster's question.

"Trade still bad, my love?" asked the girl.

"Too many taxes and too little money I'd say. Means people make do for as long as they can with their old leather — bit of a repair here and there, but won't buy new unless they need to," said her young man.

"Been that way since Gaunt started fucking up the wars with the French," said the tapster. "Always seems to be more money for no return, and then the purveyors take what they want for the army."

Moaning about war and taxes; what a monotonous barroom topic, thought Jake. He caught the eye of the pretty pot-girl and ordered another ale and told her to buy one for herself, too. She shook her head with a smile and a blush and fetched his order. He was old enough to be her father, but she was a pretty young thing and looked like no stranger to the ways of love as she kissed the broad-shouldered leather-maker again full on the lips. Jake wondered if the young man might be the tapster's son. Tall and handsome where the tapster had a full belly and sloping shoulders, but the facial features were there; the tapster might have been almost as handsome once. And that would explain why Sir Broad-Shoulders didn't pay for any of his drinks. He kissed the pot-girl once more and took his leathers over to the table where Loud-Mouth and Weasel sat by the window. All three knocked their ale cups together and shared a toast to their friendship and against all taxes and purveyance. From what Jake overheard of their conversation, Loud-Mouth and Weasel were craftsmen, too, who had fallen back to the tavern being fed up with the slow trade at the market. Jake heard the odd snatch of debate from them bemoaning heavy taxes, the avarice of their landlord (the Abbey of Abingdon) and the greed and incompetence of those running the war against France.

As they drank more their words became louder; Loud-Mouth managed to boom with more noise than before. Jake wished they would shut up. He glared at their table and at Loud-Mouth in particular, but they paid him no mind. But he did see that they were also getting the attention of the three odd-looking soldiers at the far-end of the bar. The young man, the old man and the fat-man all cast long glances at the noisy, opinionated table by the window, then turned to talk again amongst themselves. They didn't seem the type of men to welcome loud company.

"Better hope that Parliament will stop the taxes. Every year like pissing in the river, we don't know where it goes, do we?" said loud-mouth.

"Gaunt won't let them get out of London without granting a fifteenth at least. He'll fix them with his dark eyes and they won't be able to deny him. Their knees will tremble and their coin, and ours, will spill all over the earth at his feet," said Weasel.

"Gaunt's back now, isn't he, from Flanders," replied loud-mouth. "They say he got a treaty that will give away the whole of Gascony to the French, but in return they'll help him help himself to Spain. That's what he really wants."

"That's bullshit," said the broad-shouldered young man, whose girlfriend buzzed around their table keeping them all well supplied with ale, roast port and bread. Occasionally her hand would rest on his shoulder and he would slap her bottom gently, but without breaking conversation with his friends.

"Gaunt," continued Broad-Shoulders "wants nothing more than the crown of England itself. His father's dying, his elder brother, too; and then there's only young Prince Richard, a boy of nine in his way. Be easy pickings for him. That's why we're going to be paying more taxes and he's making a truce with France, so he can build an army to take over here."

"Doesn't need an army," said Weasel. "Just kill the boy and put it down to the plague and that's it, done and gone."

"Excuse me please, if you can drag yourself away, could I get a beer over here," asked Jake, standing as the pot-girl brought the craftsmen more drinks. Woah! His legs were a bit shaky. He steadied himself against the bar and waved at the girl. She nodded with a blush in his direction. Nice piece of young bird she was and no mistake, and it didn't seem like her man had much time for her tonight. But it looked like those soldiers were interested in them and more so, after those words about Gaunt. The soldier-boy had stood up and was striding over to the craftsmen's table, a glove clutched in one pale, thin hand; the other on the pommel of a long dagger or short sword that hung from his fine leather belt.

"What would you like? Sure you don't want something to eat?" asked the pot-girl, as Jake approached where she stood by the bar. He steadied himself and smiled at her.

"Well what you got," said Jake. He winked and looked at where her breasts peeked over the top of her blouse.

The girl blushed. "There's suckling pig turning on the spit, still some good bit of haunch left."

"Give me some of her rump then," said Jake, moving closer. He was about to put out a hand to touch the girl's blushing cheek when broad-shoulders stood up and shouted "what the fuck!"

But Broad-Shoulders hadn't cried out against Jake's pass at his wench. He was clutching his cheek which was bleeding from a thin cut, and was red and sore all over from where the boy-soldier had slapped him with a metal studded leather glove.

"I call you on your honour, sir," said the boy-soldier. "Stand by your words like a man, or withdraw them."

"I'll grind you into the dust for that, you little runt," roared Broad-Shoulders.

"Hey come back you hussy," said Jake, as the pot-girl rushed up to the side of her man. But he brushed her aside with his strong arm.

"Get me a poker from the iron. I'm going to teach this boy a lesson."

The boy had drawn a short stabbing sword from its sheath and held it in a guard position ready to duel with the broad-shouldered craftsman.

"What's this, what's this," blustered the tapster. He came out of hiding from behind the bar, a large rolling pin clutched in one hand and a frying pan in the other. "What do you argue for? You, young lad," he said turning to the boy-soldier, "just a pup, and you, my son" he turned to Broad-Shoulders, "a man of peace, why do you want to fight?"

"Can't you see what that evil little thing did to my Hugh?" screamed the pot-girl passing a poker into his hand. She had wrapped the scarf from her head round the bottom of it to form a grip for her man to hold. Her hair was let free, soft and blonde. But Jake preferred Isabel's darker locks. The little tart, she wanted her man to kill that boy, lusting for his blood like that. She should be lusting for him instead, thought Jake.

He shook his head. *Get those thoughts out of there now, or you'll end up in this fight too.* He glanced over at the other soldiers. They sat at their table, watching, but showing no emotion.

"A man must defend his honour and the honour of his liege lord. You outraged the honour of mine, so for that I demand recompense," said the boy. The sword, although short and thin, looked like a full-sized broadsword in his slender hand. His thin arms must be strong to wield it so freely, thought Jake.

"You one of Gaunt's brood then?" said Loud-Mouth. He had stood along with Weasel, outraged at the attack on their friend. Now he stood behind Broad-Shoulders, happy to throw insults at the boy, but not happy to get near his sword. The boy didn't reply to Loud-Mouth, but addressed Broad-Shoulders:

"Are you ready?"

Broad-Shoulders waved the heavy poker in the air to get the feel for it. It was longer and fatter than the sword, and if it connected would do much damage with the power of that man's large frame behind it.

"I'm ready," he said, and lunged forward the poker high above his head. The boy ducked aside and sliced at the man's side as he flew past. A long cut opened down the man's jerkin and blood began to well from it. With a gasp, Broad-Shoulders clutched his side to ease the pain.

"You fucker, you'll pay for that!" He attacked again, but this time with more care. The boy dodged and parried with ease, using the tables and chairs of the bar to his advantage. Jake saw his own pot of beer go flying. It was an interesting fight. The boy was no novice. He had the experience of a good swordsman, he could see that, and must have fought in similar places, bar-rooms or houses before. He glanced at the other soldiers. *Was it part of a con trick?*, he wondered; the other soldiers seemed unworried and almost bored. They had a good view of the fight, though as did he, but they paid little attention. The pot-girl had gone scurrying back behind the bar, as had the tapster, watching his furniture take some punishment as Broad-Shoulders chased the boy around the room. A poker smashed through the back of a chair, demonstrating the damage that the man might do the boy if he got hold of him. Jake shook his head and laughed quietly to himself. It was like a childhood game of a youngster playing with an adult, teasing him to do his worst, but the adult was full of anger and spite and the boy was calm, controlled and in deadly earnest, rather than a cheeky scamp trying to bait an elder.

Loud-Mouth had withdrawn to the stairwell, where he thought he might be safe. But Weasel hadn't fled the fight. Jake saw him skulk in a corner. He'd gone to fetch something. And now he returned with a long stick, with a cruel hook on the end, most likely used for lifting up bales of wool. It was sharp, though, and could do some hurt to flesh if it was used with malice. He crept up behind the boy, who parried and occasionally jabbed at the enraged craftsman. Jake guessed that Weasel was looking for the right moment to strike out at the boy and cut his throat.

That's not fair, thought Jake.

"The skinny one's behind you," Jake shouted at the boy. The boy pushed a table in front of Broad-Shoulders to buy some space, then lunged behind him where Weasel stood. The sword cut Weasel's hand and he dropped the hook with a gasp of pain.

"Whose side you on, you old drunk?" said Broad-Shoulders to Jake, as with a roar he jumped on the table and swiped at the boy again.

"Fat old lecher! Are you on their side?" shrieked the pot-girl at Jake.

"It's not right, not chivalrous, two of them against one boy like that," replied Jake.

She shook her head and cheered as her man swung his poker, but he missed the boy and hit a tall cupboard instead, which then fell, knocking the boy of his feet. The boy still held his sword, but Broad-Shoulder's foot was on his hand in an instant and the boy let go with a whelp of pain. Weasel and Loud-Mouth hurried to help Broad-Shoulders hold the boy down.

"Now we'll see about what's right and wrong," said Broad-Shoulders.

The boy grunted and struggled to get out of the grip of the three men. Many boys his age would be in tears by now. So would many men, thought Jake.

"Aren't you going to help him?" he shouted to the two soldiers. At least they had stood up now, and had walked over to get a better view of what was happening on the ground. The fat man raised an eyebrow and shook his head at Jake.

"Call yourselves soldiers, men of honour. That's not how we did things when I was at war. We always stood together, or we were nothing." Jake spat out the words. The pot-girl glared at him hatred in her eyes.

"You're one of them aren't you?" she snarled. "Always the same. They pass through here on the way from the wild places up north where they breed hard cruel men like these on their way to Hampton or another port, and they leave violence and suffering in their way."

Jake pushed the girl aside, and drew his dagger. "Turn you caitiffs! You're all cowards. I'm here to fight you, so turn, damn you!" he shouted at the scrum of three men and a boy that struggled on the floor of the bar. "Ahh! He bit me," cried Weasel.

Broad-Shoulders stood up. "Keep the boy still, I'll deal with this fat old git." Poker in hand he faced Jake. Then he thrust at Jake with it. Jake had never been much good at sword-craft, always better with a bow or swinging a mace or pole-arm, but he easily twisted his own long dagger around the craftsman's improvised weapon and sent it spinning across the bar to thud into a wall. He jabbed at Broad-Shoulders forcing him back through the bar.

"Get him, he disarmed me," called Broad-Shoulders to his friends. Loud-Mouth let go of the boy and went to stand by his friend, but they both cowered away from Jake, as they had no weapons other than the broken chairs held before them for protection.

That was enough. The boy wriggled out of weasel's grip, scooped his sword from the floor, and smacked the man across the face with the flat of the blade. The man fell stunned to the floor.

"Let's go," said the old soldier.

The boy brushed the dust off and cast a hateful glance at the three craftsmen. "I should finish what I started," he said.

"You should have, yes, but now we go," said the fat soldier. He tossed the boy his knapsack and the soldiers strode out of the tavern. The fat soldier stood by the door, hands on hips, while his two comrades went round the back to fetch their horses.

Jake looked around the bar. "I had better be off then," he said.

No one tried to stop him leaving, but a chorus of insults, mostly about the size of his paunch and the lack of his virility, sent him on his way into the dimly lit street. He gathered his own small bag and went back to the stables. The boy and old soldier passed him leading their own mounts.

"You're lucky," said the boy.

"Pardon?" said Jake. "You're lucky I came to help you. Your friends here would have let you be killed by all accounts."

"Lucky? I didn't ask you to fight. You prevented me from gaining my satisfaction with those men."

"What? You ungrateful bastard!"

The boy drew his sword and pointed it at Jake's throat.

"Put it away, that's enough for one night," said the old soldier, moving the blade aside with a gloved hand.

"You will have to excuse this one," the old soldier said to Jake. "As you can see, he wants to test his mettle. You are a soldier I can see that; you talk of honour, but you are not gently born."

"I know about killing, if that's what you mean," said Jake.

"Which lord do you fight for?" said the old soldier.

"No lord, and I don't fight, not anymore if I can help it; I work for a Master at the University," replied Jake.

"A clerk?" The old soldier laughed and the boy curled his lip in contempt. "It is a sad world when men of war lose all pride and courage. Good luck in your dotage." The soldiers turned their backs on Jake, mounted and rode off. Without a word of thanks, and another insult! That ancient must have been twice his age and he was calling him old!

Jake led Lois by the bridle down the street looking for another tavern.

"Come on girl, let's go and get drunk."

CHAPTER 2

Roger was very happy. He was on his own at night in the middle of the countryside, seated on an old barrel in almost complete darkness. Only the stars provided any illumination. All the villagers of the nearby settlement had long ago dowsed their torches and fires and gone to bed. For the first time in what seemed like weeks since he had discovered this place, he enjoyed a perfect conjunction of phenomena. No clouds obscured his vision of the night sky, the moon had not risen to drown out nearby stars with her milky glow, and furthermore he was away from Oxford with no fear of interruption from drunken undergraduates. The constellations of the spring sky surrounded him in a magnificent circle. Perhaps on a night like this Spurinna had foreseen the death of Ceasar, or his old mentor Ashenden the end of the French army at Crécy?

He was on the upper floor of an abandoned manor house, open to the elements and to the heavens, high enough for an excellent view over any tree; because of the building's broken roof and wall, he benefited from an expansive vista. Only the top of a church tower would be a better place. He had once tried asking a village parson for such a favour, but the prospect of being summarily lynched had put him off that idea forever.

His instruments were arrayed around him. Now that he had seen that his view of the sky was as good as it could be, it was time to start the initial mappings; then the real work could begin. But first he must fix the position of Polaris and each of the constellations in turn. He reached for a quill and his parchment roll and scratched the time without the need of a candle, as after several hours here his sight was attuned to seeing only by the light of the stars.

Roger worked quickly to make his preliminary observations and notes, as he would not have another night like this for weeks. The moon would not properly enter her waxing crescent phase for another two nights, yet Roger had, by his own hand, ensured that he had lost those nights of study. It would be another twenty seven days until he had such good conditions again, and then there would still be a sliver of moon in the sky. If he could only call on some spirit to clear away the clouds when he wanted ... He shook his head. Those were blasphemous thoughts. To summon any sort of spirit, even if he knew how, was akin to necromancy. But what of Ashenden, his old mentor? Roger knew that he had not gained his mastery of knowledge through observation of the stars alone. The man was dead, but his spirit haunted his student and successor. Could Roger turn that apparition to his own purpose?

Roger yawned with fatigue as he remembered the encounter with Ashenden's spirit. The day had started early for Roger with a meeting at the chambers of the Warden of Merton College. He had gotten up very early that morning in anticipation, excitement, and not a little fear at the prospect of what he must ask the ruler of the college. Merton College was one of the oldest, largest, and most renowned of the Oxford Colleges, yet in recent years the buildings and fixtures of the place had fallen into disrepair. Endowments were down and there were fewer undergraduates due in part to twenty years of plague, while others had been lured away by the new colleges, such as the Queen's College where the faculty wore dashing blood red cloaks and participated in a glorious ceremony every feast day. Such attractions could easily turn the head of an impressionable undergraduate looking for a home. Last year the faculty of Merton College elected a new Warden, John Bloxham. Bloxham had never been much of an academic, but he had a head for numbers and a mind full of plans and drawings; and most important of all, a vision of how he saw the college in the future. Some said that he wanted a memorial to his own greatness, but his champions amongst the masters saw him as a saviour who would restore the fortunes of the college and bring students with fresh supplies of coin for their teachers.

Roger knocked on his door at prime and waited for a reply. But instead the muffled voice he'd expected, the door opened and Bloxham glared out at him.

"Make an appointment with my secretary," said the Warden as he slammed the door.

Roger did as he was bid, yet the clerk who acted as the Warden's notary gave him no time or date even for his appointment. "You will be summoned," he said.

Later that morning Roger was half way through a lecture on Ptolomy's *Tetrabiblios* when a college servant interrupted with a message from the Warden.

"Now?" asked Roger.

"The Warden says this minute or not at all," replied the servant, looking at the lecture hall and maintaining a straight face.

Roger looked up at the rows of seats, and realising that they were all empty, followed the servant to the Warden's chamber where Bloxham stood talking to a man wearing a leather apron covered in dust. The stone mason looked up as Roger entered the room, and started to roll up a set of plans.

"No, don't mind him," said Bloxham, "explain to me how high you propose to raise the height of this wall again, I can't see it on the plans." He frowned at Roger for a moment, then carried on his conversation with the mason.

Roger waited by the door, moving his weight from one foot to the other as Bloxham and the mason talked. He glanced at the door and was thinking about leaving when a shiver of cold air groped his neck, and his whole body shuddered in response.

"Don't let him treat you like this," said the voice of Ashenden from somewhere above and behind him.

Roger stood still. "Go away," he whispered. He kept his eyes fixed on Bloxham, and the Warden seemed at last to notice him there, looking up with a smile of distaste. Perhaps he had sensed Roger's eyes boring tunnels through his skull in an effort to avoid looking around the room. He would not, absolutely not, try to catch sight of Ashenden's spirit. No.

"But I can help you," said Ashenden, his voice now coming from the floorboards near where Bloxham stood.

"Be quiet," said Roger, not whispering for a moment, and then hushing his voice again. "He'll hear you."

Bloxham looked again at Roger and the mason, noticing his distraction, stopped talking. Bloxham did not smile anymore. "You may go now," he told the mason, who hurried from the room.

Bloxham poured himself a glass of watered red wine and sat down in a high-backed chair with grand carved wooden armrests, not dissimilar to a throne. On the table in front of him his battle plans for a glorious building campaign lay flattened or furling as they preferred.

Behind Bloxham, and resting a spectral hand on his shoulder, floated the ghost of John Ashenden, once a reputed Professor of Astrology, dead the past nine years a "victim" of suicide. A "victim" he kept reminding Roger, although the Church would not allow him to clothe himself with the name victim, of unrequited affection for a student who rejected him and fled to Italy to avoid him. Ashenden had taught him a great deal about science, but even more about the bitterness of human nature. What amazed Roger was how much Ashenden enjoyed his ghosthood. He wallowed in it, a pig happily rolling in his own faeces; happy, too, to throw it in the face of the one who he claimed had forced him to mortal sin.

"Well?" asked Bloxham.

"I ...," said Roger, before stuttering to a stop as Ashenden interrupted him.

"Now young Sotil, remember that you are a Professor and therefore an important member of faculty. Don't let him bear you down with his pretence of power and authority."

"It would be better if you just stayed quiet and stopped interrupting me," said Roger, looking over Bloxham's shoulder at Ashenden's ghost.

"There's no need to take that tone," said Bloxham. "What's the matter with you?"

"Uh, I'm sorry. I didn't mean anything by it. I was talking to, well ..." mumbled Roger.

"To the Warden of Merton College and don't you forget it. And I should remind you that one of my duties is to ensure discipline is maintained amongst faculty as well as the student body. It is not proper for you or any of your peers, or me for that matter, to speak to another in that manner."

"Of course not, but you see I wasn't talking to you."

Bloxham smiled, got up and turned in a complete circle. One of his arms parted the smoky form of Ashenden's ghost for a moment. Ashenden grimaced as he did so and waved a finger at Roger.

"Will you listen now boy?" the ghost said.

Bloxham made a great show of looking around the room, peering under a table and behind the curtain. "Can the Merton Professor of Astrology see anyone else in this room except I?" said Bloxham.

Roger tried to get a hold of himself. "We are the only two living creatures here, I grant you. Please forget my earlier words, my mind was transported elsewhere and I indeed forgot myself and found myself having imaginary discourse with a rather annoying character. In my head I was framing the conversation I mean to have with him later. I hope you can excuse my impertinence, those words were not directed at you, nor would I ever wish to insult you or any of the other living faculty of this College."

"A pretty speech, but I don't like your tone," said Ashenden, as Bloxham replied simultaneously so that Roger could hardly make his words. (Somehow everything Ashenden said was quite clear no matter who living might be speaking in the same moment.)

"Go on then, I said that I accept your apology, but I haven't got all day," repeated Bloxham.

"Of course, well here's the thing. I received a letter from the Abbot of St. Brett's yesterday, and ... well ... you see ... he has asked for my assistance in a matter of some delicacy." Roger had not brought the Abbot's letter, but found he could relate it all to Bloxham by heart now. He had read and reread the missive a dozen times since receiving it.

There was silence from Bloxham after his speech yet a deep frown creased his forehead. The ghost of Ashenden had gone from behind his chair to stand next to Roger. It stood looking at Roger proud and expectant, but thankfully quiet.

"I would like to see the letter," said Bloxham. His words were clipped and loud. "But before you go and fetch it, tell me: do you know why the Abbot has asked for your help, in getting rid of his town's ... demons?"

"No doubt he has read my recent opus on the nature of astral spirits, where I hypothesise that Thomas Aquinas's supposition relating to the ruling of the planets was mistaken."

"What has star-gazing have to do with demons?" asked Bloxham.

"I see you dare to question the Angelic Doctor, St. Thomas Aquinas," said the ghost of Ashenden, his words overlapping Bloxham's. *"I only lived to such a ripe old age,"* said the ghost as he fingered his spectral beard, *"by not making all my thoughts known in writing, and here you go publishing a refutation of Aquinas? Are you possessed yourself?"*

"Not mad, but right," said Roger

"Pardon," said Bloxham. "I didn't call you mad."

"No you didn't, I'm sorry. Look I don't want to take up any more of your time. If it is alright with you I plan to leave tomorrow. I will have a message sent to my students informing them that my lectures will resume in two weeks time. I am sure that will be enough time to help the Abbot with his problem. Although whether I can really help I'm not sure, more likely just diagnose I would think."

Bloxham muttered and shook his head. As he did so the ghost approached near to Roger and laid a fatherly — yet cold and insubstantial — hand on his shoulder.

"Don't sell yourself short, Roger my boy," he said. *"You veer from intellectual arrogance to misplaced modesty. You know the regard I had for you. It was I who told the Abbot about you, before I died of course. He knows what I taught you; well some of it."*

"Just tell me in simple words what use could the Abbot have for you?" demanded Bloxham. Are you a saint who can banish devils? Or an inquisitor of the Holy Office. You're not even in minor orders are you?"

"No, I have never been tonsured."

"Then what can he want from you, if you can't exorcise his spirits? Does he want a horoscope to foretell when it will all end? If so, can't you just write it up here and send it to him?"

"No, it's not that. He has heard about my research and my theorems regarding the governance of the stars."

"Well God governs the heavens, doesn't he, so what has that got to do with the devil and his demons?"

"But you're mistaken, as was Aquinas. My research has shown that it is impossible for God's angels to command the powers of all the circles of heaven, and that our conception of the 'top to bottom' nature of the universe is all wrong. My studies of the horoscopes of men possessed to do evil acts show that they were under the influence of certain combinations of stars that could only be aligned by the working of demonic powers. My master believed the same."

"I did not!" shouted the ghost.

"Your own work proved it!" said Roger to the ghost.

"What!" said Bloxham. "I'm a rhetorician."

"You wouldn't know it would you?" muttered the ghost. *"You could get more sense out of a donkey's arse."*

"Shut up!" said Roger to the ghost, but again Bloxham thought the words intended for him.

"How dare you! Who do you think you are talking me in that way?" Bloxham screamed. There was a knock at the door. "Can I help sir?" said the notary who entered the room. He was a rather tall and stocky man, and cast a concerned glance in Roger's direction.

"Master Sotil will need escorting back to his quarters, where I think he should start packing his belongings immediately!" said Bloxham.

"Listen to me boy," said the ghost. *"Tell him that the Abbot has offered money if you can help him."*

"But ...," said Roger.

"Get out!" screamed Bloxham. The notary grabbed Roger's skinny bicep in his large paw and started to pull him towards the door. He could see his tenure at Oxford ending very quickly after this meeting, and although he could afford to maintain himself perhaps by independent teaching he knew his family could withdraw his annuity or, worse, carry out their plan to have him ordained and placed on the road to a position of political influence within the Church. It pained him to listen to Ashenden, but he was desperate.

"The Abbot has offered money...," Roger said.

"How much?" said Bloxham. The notary stopped tugging Roger towards the door. The ghost of the old man had been very astute.

"Tell him that the Abbey has plans to endow one of the Oxford colleges with at least four manors and a one-off sum of 10,000 marks," said the ghost. *"That should be enough."*

Roger repeated the ghost's suggestion. The Abbot had mentioned no such reward or financial payment, yet Bloxham believed him and told the notary to leave the room and to take his hand off Roger's arm, he wouldn't be leaving Oxford for good after all.

"Sit down," he gestured to a chair. "You should have told me this from the beginning." Bloxham asked more questions about the Abbot's proposal, and Roger replied as best he could with the ghost feeding him tall tales about the Abbey's current financial prosperity and desire to support academic endeavours at Oxford, but also making clear that they had not decided on where to place their proposed endowment, there being a number of options available.

"Hmm, and we will most likely need to get rid of Wyclif soon too, the monks hate his words about the avarice of the Church. But tell me, Roger, you mentioned that your research involved questioning the nature of demonic powers and the stars? How many people know about this?"

Before Roger could reply, Ashenden's ghost gripped him by the shoulders with his cold hands. *"Tell him that it is merely a footnote to your main investigations into the stars and their influence on men, these are not your theories. Tell him that you only recount the theories of other scholars; that should satisfy him."* Roger wanted to reply that this was a lie and that he would not tell falsehoods about the research that was so precious to him. But he knew that his dead Master was right.

"No one, they are just ramblings in my notes, some ideas I have been working upon," said Roger.

"It would be best if you kept them that way," said Bloxham. "Would you care for some wine?" Roger nodded his assent and Bloxham poured a cup of red for each of them. "I would like you to send the Abbot a letter about the endowment; my notary will draft it for you from my dictation and you should send it today under your seal. I would like them to receive it before you arrive. As soon as you get there and speak to the Abbot, you are to write to me and relate whether the Abbot agrees or not."

Roger had read through the letter written by the Warden's notary as he collected together his equipment for that night's stargazing. He wondered how he had got into this mess. The letter accepted the Abbot's invitation most briefly and then over several pages of vellum described at great lengths the merits of Merton College and the building programme that Bloxham had begun. Particular stress was laid on the planned improvements to the collegiate church, the places that would be made available for monks from St. Brett's to study at Merton; there was a hint, too, that the current Abbot would be remembered in the prayers of the College for many years to come. Roger was relieved that Bloxham had not asked for the Abbot's letter, for now the lie would continue. Jake could arrange for this letter to go, but it might be best if he did not wait for the Abbot to send a reply before setting off for St. Brett's.

The sky's blackness was turning to yellowing dawn. Roger was satisfied with a good night of mapping the stars, but even so the task before him seemed gigantic. He dared not think of how many more nights it would take him, and then there were the calculations to make and the evaluation of those calculations. Perhaps a life's work. Yet for what? The Warden had told him not to publish his theories. And yet while they remained only theories he was right. Somehow he needed proof, actual physical phenomena that he could record.

The dawn chorus was beginning and Roger could now see the outlines of the village before him, the church, the rectory, and its small orchard. Fires were being lit in the village. Small puffs of smoke came out of roof-holes and from the chimney of the rectory. He could smell cooking on the wind. Roger sniffed the air . Someone was grilling bacon, and what also smelt like eggs, but eggs that smelt rotten. Roger winced and coughed.

There were two rather large birds on the roof of the rectory. Too big for crows, thought Roger, but surely not eagles, not here away from their preferred mountain eyries. He remembered his childhood and the eagles that his father and uncles would sport with, taken at an early age from nests in the fells. Those birds had seemed so massive when he was small and he had always been frightened of them, but he respected them. Yet though these creatures were as large as eagles, they were ungainly and lacked the nobility of birds of prey.

He pulled a large thick convex disc of glass from his pocket and held it several inches from his eye and looked at the large birds on the roof of the rectory. Through the lens, which magnified his view, he could see that the creatures had only very small wings, curled on their black shiny backs. They were not birds. They each had two legs and two arms that were as long and thin as spider's legs. One of the creatures turned towards him and he could see the face close-up, magnified by his lens, doglike but with longer fangs, black sheen of skin, and with two goat-horns protruding from its crown.

"Demons," whispered Roger, fearful lest he be heard. He reached for his bag, knocking over his astrolabe as he did so, and produced a fine pencil of charcoal and some old vellum for mark-making. Quickly he tried to sketch the creatures with one hand while holding up the lens to look with the other. They moved with fast and jerky movements, hopping across the roof of the rectory; sometimes it was difficult to say they had moved, but rather they seemed to disappear and reappear at different places on the roof.

Now they hung like bats over the main door of the rectory, which like the manor house was on the upper story at the top of stone steps that descended to the ground. A man, a pastor by the look of his tonsure, walked through the door, and one of the demons jumped down to perch on his shoulder. The man walked down the steps, pulling his robes around him and tightening a belt oblivious to the winged creature sitting crouched on his back. The thing seemed to be whispering in his ear. Then a woman appeared at the door. Even though the daylight was still dim, Roger could see that her hair was loose and not covered and neither was the flesh of her shoulders and neck. The second demon jumped onto her back now. The priest turned and started shouting at the woman, who shouted back, shaking her fist.

Roger looked down at his vellum again, and made a few marks with his charcoal. He saw a movement behind him. His only thought was that he hoped it was not a demon. And then he was knocked by a heavy force to the ground, something sharp and cold shoved into his neck, and a large clammy hand closed over his mouth.

CHAPTER 3

Jake opened his mouth and bit down hard on Isabella's leg. Blood flooded his mouth as he chewed on the flesh of her leg muscles. He pulled his head back to rip her flesh away, a chunk of skin flapping loosely off her leg covering a gap where muscle used to be. Thick red blood welled out of the wound to fill the gap and spread rapidly over the white sheets.

Isabel did not move. She lay like a fey princess, motionless and naked, her soft brown hair spreading across the pillow, longer than he had ever seen it. Next to her lay his father, a huge broadsword impaled into his groin, splitting his manhood in two. His skin was blue where Isabel's was still white, and no blood flowed from his body. Jake knelt on all fours on the large bed and dove towards Isabel's breast to take another bite out of her. As he chewed on her breast and tore off a nipple with his teeth, he felt something growing underneath him. He looked below him and saw her stomach expanding rapidly, growing outwards like a ripe fruit ready to burst. He leapt back just in time as her stomach burst covering him with blood and sticky fluid.

The dream ended abruptly, replaced with blackness, hands gripping him in the dark. He couldn't see. Someone had dragged him out of his bed and was struggling to restrain him on the floor; a hand covered his mouth. Jake couldn't breathe. He struggled and tried to twist and elbow the person aside.

He bit down and there was a man's scream as the hand jerked away from his mouth. "Get the fuck off me," shouted Jake. He got enough room to loosen the man's grip. He kicked down and by the sound of the man's yelp connected with his balls. Jake smashed his elbow into the man's face. He got up and reached for his knife. He could see it on the low table by the window. The door was open, faint light from the corridor that led to his room. The intruder wasn't a burglar then, but must have come from inside the Abbey, thought Jake.

The man was just getting up. Jake saw a glint of metal at his side and didn't think anymore. He lunged out with his blade and sliced at the man's throat. Blood spurted out drenching him in warm liquid. He jumped aside and looked at the open door. The man had collapsed to the ground, blood hissing from his throat. He would be dead soon. Jake fetched his bag, jerkin, and boots, and then remembered Roger's letter. He tugged it from under the mattress and ran for the door.

This was very bad. Having accepted the hospitality of the monks, he had now been attacked in his room in the Abbey's guest-house and murdered his attacker. Last night had been a blur. After the fracas between the soldiers and the craftsmen, he had wandered the streets and taverns of Abingdon, a jar in one hand and Lois's halter in the other, offering her sips of his ale as he looked for a place that might shelter a drunk and his horse. The inns were happy to sell him ale, but none of them wanted him staying there longer than it took to pass a new jug of ale across the counter. Then, as he stumbled along a dark street, a holy man had shown him the way to the Abbey, offering him a bed for the night. The holy man had told him that the monks had a place where a weary traveller like him could find comfort and peace.

But now Jake had murdered peace.

He looked up and down the corridor. A lantern burned by the guest-house gate, lighting the inner courtyard below. He remembered seeing a servant guarding the entrance when he had been shown in. What time was it? How long had he been asleep? His tongue was still thick with the taste of ale. He would have to get past that door-keeper, fetch Lois who was in the stable block just outside the guest-house door, and then find a way through the gate to the Abbey compound, which was sure to be shut and guarded by at least one of the Abbey's servants. He was no thief or sorcerer, escape seemed impossible.

"You shall go in peace if you follow the light," said a voice he recognized.

"Who the fuck," he whispered and spun round. Had he been discovered already?

"The lamb returns to the fold to lie down with the lion. The oath-breaker returns from over the sea and the land lies in darkness." The speaker stood a few yards down the corridor from Jake, a cowled figure. Jake could not see his face, but he recognized the voice. It was the beggar from the inn, the mad man the tapster had thrown out. All he needed.

"Yes father, as you say, but I must be on my way. God be with you," said Jake and made for the stairs down into the courtyard. He would try to bluff his way past the doorkeeper, tell him he had to make an early start and pray that no one found the body in his room before he was beyond the Abbey walls.

"Follow me if you want God's grace," said the beggar.

"I have no time for prayers." Jake walked away from him and began to descend the stairs. He could see the doorkeeper at the courtyard's entrance sitting on a stool and leaning against a wall by the door. The door was closed and he would most likely need to wake the doorkeeper to unlock the door.

"Do you know me not? You spurn me, yet the one who gave you entrance to this place can also gain your exit. Follow me and I shall deliver you."

Jake carried on down the stairs, trying to keep quiet and wishing the beggar would shut up. He needed the doorkeeper to stay asleep.

"You came in peace to find rest for your weary heart," said the beggar.

Jake stopped walking. *Come in peace and rest your weary heart.* Those were the words the holy man had used last night when he offered him a place to stay at the Abbey.

Jake went back up the stairs, looking around as he did so. He walked up to the beggar and looked him in the face. "Who are you?" said Jake.

"Peace, brother," said the beggar, genuflecting with exaggerated motions in the air above Jake's head. The man laughed and drew back his cowl. "Do you not know me still? Have you not guessed yet? Perhaps still as muddled by drink as before in the inn?"

Jake's ears vibrated with the pulse of blood. "Hereward?"

"Who else?"

"But you were dead. In Gascony. Hung for desertion."

"Like you should have been?"

"I just wanted to get home."

"And murder, rape and pillage were a nice diversion along the way?"

"I only took food when I was hungry, and only killed when I was attacked, and I would never touch a woman."

"Not a son of Sodom are we?"

Jake swung a fist at Hereward, but the man's arm came up to block it and then he tripped Jake, but caught him before he hit the ground. The disguise of a harmless beggar hid a soldier with quick wits and strong limbs.

"Stop it you fool," Hereward whispered, dropping the speech of the holy man and kneeling down, his face close to Jake's. "I saw the blood and the body. Someone wants something from you. I'll help you out of here, like I helped you in here. Lucky I felt sorry for you — been watching out for you after I saw you ride into town. You keep getting yourself into trouble, but you don't know how to get out of it again."

"Not like you, you fucking eel."

"Slippery ain't I?"

Hereward's hand clamped over Jake's mouth and he nodded his head down the corridor. A door opened and a man walked out onto the gallery. He walked towards them along the gallery. Hereward loosened his cowl and spread it over the crouching Jake as he himself lay on top of him. Hereward started moving his body back and forth. He grunted with pleasure as the man came nearer.

The man saw them and shook his head. "Don't mind me ladies, I have man's work to do." The man laughed and entered another door just past the stairs, the door to the guest-house lavatory.

Hereward smiled and released his hand from Jake's mouth.

"Prick," said Jake.

"Now now, got you out of another scrape then didn't I? Don't be so sensitive, he didn't clock you." Come quickly before anyone else decides to get up for a piss or decides to tell the prior that there's a monk fucking a servant in the guest-house."

Hereward took Jake to a spiral staircase that led directly to a locked door in one corner of the guest-house. He produced a key and opened it.

Outside the Abbey precinct was still quiet. Dawn had not yet begun to lighten the sky. They found Lois asleep and unhappy to be woken in the stable, but Jake calmed her with a handful of oats and some soft words.

Hereward then led Jake to the Abbey gate. The door-keeper here was awake, but he just nodded at Hereward and then they were through and into the town. Jake mounted his horse and thought about which way to go. It was dark still, which meant the roads would be difficult riding, but he didn't fancy hanging around in Abingdon after what had happened.

Hereward offered his hand to shake. Jake shook his head. "Thanks, but you're not my friend, never will be."

"That's so sad, I could help you. You look like you need help."

"Not yours, I am happy, comfortable even. Tonight was just a mistake."

"As I said, someone's after something of yours, and they won't be stopped by tonight. You had best watch out."

"Who are you these days, Hereward?"

Hereward laughed. "I'm but a poor beggar with a few observations about the world. The monks trust me, you see. I do errands for them in the town, keep an eye on things for them, and listen to the townspeople. No one cares what they say in front of a beggar. They're well used to me coming and going by night. I gave my report to the prior after I found you a bed, and got my silver coins in return, a hot meal, a good bed, and a novice to warm it."

Jake's face flushed.

"You were a handsome young man once, too," said Hereward. "There's going to be a lot of cleaning up to do, and I'm happy to do it for you. We're even now, do you reckon?"

"Spare me," spat Jake. "You know your sort disgusts me, especially amongst soldiers. It's despicable. You claim you have saved my life, but I could have got out of there on my own. I put my body on the line for you in France; tonight wasn't any comparison."

"Memories of bad times fade faster don't they?" Hereward winked. "God speed to you." Hereward slapped

Lois's rump and she jerked into a canter down the paved road.

A few hundred yards out of Abingdon the road petered into a muddy track. The moon was not in the sky, and it was hard to see where he went. The stars were bright and he could see a few lights in the distance. The lights of Oxford he hoped. Lois could see better than he and she would know her way back. He was happy to let her follow her nose.

Hereward reported to the prior, yet who else knew he had a letter for St. Brett's? He reached into the bag at his side. The letter was still there. What could be so important about a damn letter? He should have challenged Hereward on it. He worked for the prior; had it been the prior who wanted his letter? But why try to kill him for it? He would have delivered it into the hands of the prior's courier the next day, after all. Jake felt muddled. Better give up the ale and the wine then. But the ale and the wine had their uses. They washed away all the memories.

§

Jake woke up just before he hit the ground. He'd fallen asleep in the saddle and when Lois stopped in front of a building he had lost his balance and fallen. He managed to tumble onto his back so he didn't smash his face or sprain his hands.

It was still dark. Lois puffed over his head and nuzzled him.

"You can say sorry, but that still hurt," he said.

Jake stood up and looked around. It was dark, but he could see that he was in the middle of a village. There were a number of single story houses, a church, and a stone rectory. In front of him was a manor house. One end of the top story had fallen into ruin, like a loaf of bread with the top corner bitten off. The ground floor was an under-croft used for storage. A large door, big enough to drive a

wagon through was locked in place, a large padlock
securing it. Probably used as storage by the monks and
their reeve and secured to keep the villagers out, thought
Jake. The lord's living quarters would have been upstairs,
and stone steps led up to a smaller wooden door on the
upper floor. The lord was long gone though. Probably a
lone esquire, with large debts, who had sold up to the
Abbey of Abingdon. The monks had no need of such a
large property except for storage.

He could really do with some more sleep, he thought,
and if there was no one occupying the manor, then there
would be no harm bunking down here for what was left of
the night was there. Jake tied Lois to a nearby tree,
hobbled her, and took the saddle with him up the steps. If
someone stole old Lois, at least they would get a sore arse
riding her away.

Jake was relieved to find the door at the top of the
steps unlocked. He came into a hall and looked around,
but could see very little, although some light did come
from the ruined end of the building. Some of the roof and
the top of the wall were gone, no one bothering to repair
the ravages of time before it was too late. He moved
carefully towards the light.

Something sharp and solid made sudden contact with
his shin.

"God's teeth," he hissed, dropping his saddle as he
leapt back, his dagger out in an instant. A dog barked in
the distance. Jake kicked out with his boot and made
contact with something that made a dull metallic sound as
it rocked against the floorboards. *Sounds like a bloody anvil,*
he thought. He came closer and felt the shape, and as his
eyes became accustomed to the dim light he saw that it
actually *was* an anvil. And now he could see other tools
littering the floor of the hall. A plough here, numbers of
shovels and picks, and what even looked like a scythe.
Imagine if he had walked into that. Elsewhere he could see
more normal-looking barrels and sacks, no doubt full of

produce ready to be taken away by the monks' agents for market or for their own cellars. Thieving shits. He wondered for a moment if any of them contained ale, but he didn't fancy his chances of not dipping into something disgusting by mistake, better just to find a place to bed down. And if he made any more racket blundering around in here, that dog might start at it again and wake someone up.

So he made his way to the end of the hall, careful to avoid anything made of metal or hard, injury-inducing wood. There was an entranceway to what would once have been the lord of the manor's private chambers. Beyond it he could just glimpse the night sky through the opening in the upper wall. He laid his saddle and his coat down inside the hall, better to keep out of the draft from the wall's opening, and managed to find an empty sack to use as blanket. This was all more complicated than it should have been. If only he had maintained some of the discipline he'd had when he was an archer. In those years of campaigning, he would never have been without a flint and a wick, a blanket — and something to drink, of course. Next time he would be more careful, he thought as he lay on his back and regarded the small square of night sky that was visible. Was that the Draco or the Ursa Major? Those maps that Roger showed him made no sense, and that connivance of a mechanism he carried around with him everywhere was worse still.

He fell into a deep sleep, but woke after what seemed like only minutes to feel something running over his face. He prayed it was not a rat, but spat out anyway in case the foul vermin's feet or nose had been near his mouth. Rats and plague always went hand in paw. He heard a squeak to his left and stabbed his dagger at the floor at his side, but made no contact. The squeak didn't come back. He settled down again and realised how sore his left shoulder was. The floor was damn hard.

There was another sound, a shuffling from inside the ruined chamber a few yards from where he had been sleeping. *Sounds like a big bloody rat.* He drew his dagger again and with great care lifted his body off the ground and crept up to the doorway to the chamber.

A LETTER

Here follows a modern English translation of the contents of Sloane MSS. XIIV, Folio 27. The cipher used to hide the content of the letter has also been interpreted and the true meaning of the letter transcribed. Translation in Early English Texts Society, Vol. 35.

To the most privy eyes of the Duke of Lancaster, greetings,

Your humble servant has grievous news to impart. Edmund, your retained monk, Infirmarian at the Abbey of St. Brett's, has caused, I believe, much strangeness to occur this past month. Yet for the moment the cause of said strangeness is not known to any except him and your humble servant, and as my presence is unbeknownst to Edmund, in his own belief he is the only one in St. Brett's with knowledge of his acts. I suspect he believes that you are not aware of his acts, even though he is your servant and retained man.

On Sunday last, fourth after Easter, said Edmund did, I conceive, conjure a demon again and allowed it permit to dally with the townsfolk of this town, in particular with a woman during the service of mass in the parish church of St. Peter's, a parish of the town of St. Brett's. You will recollect my Lord the events of New Year gone that I recounted to you in some depth. The revelries, the obscene orgies practiced by groups of the townsfolk, and indeed some of the monks of the Abbey. I have reason now to believe that these were inspired by demons summoned at that time by your aforementioned servant Edmund. Although less common, such events have been repeating themselves, and the Sunday of third after Easter, one the Lord's most holy of days, was marred in the parish church of St. Peter's by a most heinous possession of a woman. St. Peter's parish, is, for the remembrance of your grace, one of the parishes of the said township of St. Brett's. It occurred thus:

On receiving the host from the priest, for she has been known as a most pious and Godly woman before that Sunday, she did spit the body of Christ into her hand and in full view of the priest and the congregation of St. Peter's she tucked the host into her clothes, even between the flesh of her bosoms and had no qualms with showing that flesh and baring herself in a most disgusting and lascivious manner. She did then proceed to swear at the priest, calling him a false priest and a whoreson of Satan. The congregation was outraged and were not able to prevent her actions because they were dumbfounded, and I suspect that this to be caused by a spell cast by the demon inside her. Out of the hands of the priest she took the bowl of hosts and the goblet of Christ's blood, and with these in her hands went from the church, and from there it is not known where she took them.

The name of this woman is Elizabeth Hamond, she is the wife of a baker of the town, and one of the congregation was heard to make light of this horrible event and say that she wanted to copy the Lord's recipe in order to recreate his body. But this tale about the recipe can be given little credence as the bread used by this priest is baked by her husband. Despite this terrible crime and sin being committed, and despite the tears of anger of the priest as he wept on my shoulder that evening, no actions were taken to punish or question her. The woman was not approached by the town's bailiffs, the Abbot deigning to ignore all protestations from the priest and the holy parishioners of the congregation. In the town there are whispers that this is because the woman is a part of a group called the Company of Good Women, and that the mistress of this group, Isabel Haukwake, is herself a witch, but that she is above reproach as she is wife of John Haukwake, the richest man in the town and also the town's bailiff, appointed by the Abbot.

Although the Abbot will not publicly talk of his concerns about Edmund, I read a letter that was sent from him, as you have ordered for all letters sent from and to the Abbey of St. Brett's to be read. In this letter, his deep anxiety about Edmund is revealed. The letter does not name Edmund as the cause of the manifestations of sorcery in St. Brett's, but it does recount at length some of the examples that I have previously informed you of, including the example of the crime against the Host as detailed in this very letter of mine to you. The Abbot's letter is addressed to a certain Master Roger Sotil of Merton College in Oxford. I do not know of him, but it seems that Abbot Peter respects Master Sotil's guidance in this matter and even requests his presence at his earliest convenience at the Abbey of St. Brett's. The Abbot notes that his own attempts at exorcism have been for naught, and I can testify to this having witnessed these attempts myself. However, as you yourself are aware, the Abbot is not the holiest of monks, having accepted indeed certain monies for his silence from your good self for many years in respect of the said Edmund. His letter to Sotil threatens to uncover the scandal of Edmund in this town and widen the notoriety of sorcerous events that are already becoming well known within the vills of St. Brett's, and now threaten to be the talk of scholarly discourse further afield.

A faithful copy of the Abbot's letter accompanies my own. I remain your humble servant and await your further instruction in this matter.

The letter is unsigned. No accompanying letter is found with the transcript from the Duke's register. The letter itself is thought to be a fake written during the era of the War of the Roses to discredit the Lancastrian dynasty.

CHAPTER 4

After knocking him to the ground and kneeing him in the stomach, Jake clamped his hand over the man's mouth and slipped the cold blade of his knife under the man's Adam's apple.

"Who are you?" whispered Jake.

"Mphmugh!" came the reply.

Jake didn't see any reason to loosen his hand over the man's mouth. He could do without him calling to any of his friends who might be nearby. It was not at all beyond the ken of man that he might have been followed here, and while he stupidly slept rather than finishing his journey to Oxford, they had caught up with him and even now were closing in to ambush him. These fucking priests must have thieves coming out of their ears. They certainly had coin enough to pay them.

Jake looked around the rest of the ruined manor house chamber. It would have been the lord's solar once upon a time, a place to relax with his family and to count his ill-gotten monies. But now, in the dim light of dawn, Jake could see only a few rotten old barrels, a piece of masonry that this man had been using as a seat, and some astronomical instruments very much like his master's.

49

He looked again at the figure he held in a grip that must be causing quite a bit of pain, especially as his knee was still trying to push his victims guts through the cracks in the man's spine.

"Mamimphighuh!" said the man again. He was a young man, thin and anaemic-looking, damned bony this close up, he was glad he wasn't a whore who had to fuck him. He'd never thought about his master like that before though, a shiver passed through him as he suddenly recognized him. This was even worse than he thought. He was going to resign from this man's service and now he had nearly killed him.

Jake let go of Roger and pushed him away with a shudder. "What the fuck are you doing here? You gave me a fucking fright!"

Roger dabbed at his neck where Jake's blade had nicked the skin. "Look at that roof. Can you still see the imps, here take my lens," said Roger passing Jake a thick disc of glass.

Jake did as his master bid and held the disc up to his eye and looked towards the rooftop he had indicated, a two story parsonage half a bow-shot away. He moved the lens back and forth until he got a clearer view, just as his master had shown him how many times before. The roof came into focus. There was nothing there, but he could hear two people arguing, a man and a woman. He adjusted his gaze and then took away the lens as he tried to find the source of the disputers. They stood at the foot of the steps and he could make them out well enough without the lens's aid. A priest and his "housekeeper" no doubt arguing over the amount of the tithe she should get for servicing him.

"I can see the priest and his whore well enough without your lens, master," said Jake. "I am sorry for hurting you. What strange coincidence this is, I thought you were out to murder me, it has been a strange night."

"Oh that, no matter, I read of conflict between us in the horoscopes I cast yester-morning. The combination of the Mars in Sagittarius and your phlegmatic blood made an attempt to kill me not unlikely. Let me look at the roof, are the imps gone?" Jake handed back the lens, but Roger was already looking, shielding his eyes from the bright low rays of the morning sun.

"They have gone, your noise must have driven them away," said Roger.

"Forgive me, but when you say 'imps,' do you mean demons? Roger, have you seen them again?"

"Yes, two fine specimens were loitering on that roof and then dove upon those two sinners you see and hear. If only you had seen them, Jake," said Roger.

"I'm always in the wrong place aren't I, but are you sure they just weren't crows or some other bird?"

"Look at these," Roger thrust a sheet of parchment in front of Jake on which were scrawled in black coke images that might be taken off the wall of a church, to frighten sinners.

"Perhaps you dreamt it?" said Jake.

"No, I never see them in my sleep. I dream very little."

And sleep very little, thought Jake. *No wonder you don't have time for dreams at night, your head spins with enough of them by day.*

"We should go back to Oxford and back to our beds. I don't think you have lectures today, do you?"

"No lectures, but today's the day that we must leave for St. Brett's. The Warden of Merton commands it. I was lucky to have last night to myself. I managed some quite excellent observations, Jacob."

"You want to go there today? But I haven't been able to deliver the letter," said Jake.

"That might be a good thing. It was a collection of drivel dictated by Bloxham that I was forced to put my name to. Embarrassing the lengths that man will go to for money."

"Do you know why I was so jumpy last night and why I was inches away from cutting your throat?"

"I think the measurement you want is *lignas*, inches would have meant cutting right through my neck I think, which would be quite unnecessary."

Jake sighed and started again. "Master, there's something about that letter and about St. Brett's that's dangerous. I don't think we should go."

"Demons are dangerous. According to the Church Fathers, their only aim is to tempt men into sin and win their souls for the devil. I am not so sure that things are as black and white as someone like Peter the Lombard makes out. Did he ever meet a demon, or an angel for that matter? There's nothing like firsthand evidence and experimentation, that's what made Aristotle so great, he based his thoughts on his own observations, and more recently Roger Bacon did the same with optics, and ..."

"Master, someone tried to kill me last night for your letter."

"If someone has something to protect, then they will to go to any lengths to do so. So perhaps the Abbot isn't mad or deluded, perhaps there really is sorcery in St. Brett's and *someone* doesn't want it known about?"

"So this person wants to kill us in order to stop us finding out about a dangerous happening in St. Brett's? I'm all for avoiding the place altogether if that's the case."

"Didn't you come from that part of the country? Aren't you at all curious or worried about your kinfolk?" asked Roger.

Jake shrugged. "What happens if you can't solve the Abbot's problems or get rid of whatever's haunting his town? He won't be happy and then Bloxham won't be happy because the College won't be paid, and you'll be out on your arse. What will your family say to that?"

"I hate teaching and the students never listen anyway."

"There aren't any students prepared to listen to you, you mean. We only survive on the money your family sends to you. I think we only had two students who paid anything last term, and one of them now wants his money back."

"Then I'll become a wondering scholar," said Roger.

"A poor wondering scholar, disowned by his family for giving up his prestigious career at Oxford, with a bedraggled servant trailing behind to keep him from being murdered by vagabonds. I don't very much like the future that you're dreaming of," said Jake.

"I have a good feeling about St. Brett's. I think we will find all that we desire there."

"Did you see that in the stars?"

"No, I feel it in my stomach. I can't say why, but when I read Abbot Peter's letter, at that moment it was like my life began, like this was what I was meant for."

"You were meant to chase around after market traders pretending to be insane? The one thing I do know about St. Brett's is that the people there aren't stupid, and they aren't superstitious and what you would call prone to visions and being touched by spirits, whether holy or unholy. All they want is a way to earn more money, and if that means getting one up on the Abbey, then they'll do anything. Maybe this is what it's all about?"

"You told me someone tried to kill me for your letter," said Roger. "Who'd want to do that, if the townspeople are just making it up? I think an important man is trying to hide something."

"Gaunt," said Jake.

Roger shrugged his bony shoulders. "He gives generously to a number of Benedictine houses, including St. Brett's, and its proximity to London makes it a regular pilgrimage site and stopping point for the nobility with estates in the north, so I am sure he visits there on a regular basis. He may not want scandal attached to the monks, although if he is anything like my father I am sure he could use the situation to his advantage to extract a favour from the monks. But tell me Jake, do you remember Ockham's razor that we once talked of?"

Jake nodded, but wasn't paying Roger much heed. The smell of breakfast cooking somewhere in the village reached his nostrils. He was starving. He'd not eaten anything last night except beer, and his stomach growled with emptiness. The White Hart did a good breakfast, and it would only take them half an hour to be there.

"Master let us be gone from this place, I need to eat," said Jake.

Jake helped gather up Roger's instruments and they went to find their horses. Roger's mare had been hobbled only yards away from Lois, and the two stood grazing next to each other seemingly as unconcerned as their owners at meeting in this place.

Jake and Roger mounted and rode past the ruined manor house and along a track past the parsonage that would take them to the Abingdon road that passed through the village and then to Oxford.

"Look, the parson's housekeeper," said Roger, pointing at a peasant woman carrying a large basket on her back full of turf. Behind her a male peasant walked with mattock in one hand and a flask of ale in the other. They were walking from an area of common land that bordered the manor house, and were making for the main street of the village as well.

"I am going to ask her about the imp, whether she noticed anything," said Roger, who nudged his horse so that he would catch them up.

Jake kicked Lois harder and grabbed the bridle of Roger's horse. "No," he said. "Leave these people alone." Roger glared at Jake and then to one side. "I'm sorry, master," said Jake. "I just don't want you to get in trouble. We're like to get chased out of here if you ask people such things, and be burnt at the stake for our troubles talking about demons so openly."

"That doesn't happen in England," Roger looked away from Jake. "But I saw it once in Italy. I never want to smell or hear that again." Roger sighed. "You're right. In any case the victim of possession are most likely unaware or would deny any knowledge of it, being under the influence of the demon. But that is what will be so refreshing about St. Brett's. At last I will have license to ask these questions."

Jake clenched his jaw and let go of Roger's bridle and they rode back towards Oxford in silence. They stopped at the White Hart and ordered two trenchers full of cooked meats, with eggs scrambled and blended with milk to form a soft paste that bound the pork meats together.

"The Abbot's letter told of many cases of demonic possession, Jake," said Roger. "This could really be the basis of a comprehensive opus, don't you think?"

"Maybe," said Jake. He didn't want to talk about St. Brett's. He didn't want to think about it. Certainly didn't want to go back there. But Roger was set on it. And he was indebted to him. He couldn't desert him could he? And if Roger was walking himself into danger then shouldn't Jake set aside his concerns and make sure he was alright? Perhaps if he stayed in the Abbey? Perhaps if he went in disguise?

"I said what route do you think we should travel? You look tired Jake, perhaps the night without sleep has taken away your senses, I do believe you've stopped listening to me," said Roger, patting Jake on the arm.

Jake looked up. He'd been sitting with a spoon full of egg in one hand and a knife with sausage skewered on it in the other staring out of the window. He was tired and he didn't know what to say to Roger. But he couldn't go with him. He didn't want to see Isabel and his father ever again. He had sworn to himself that it would only to see their graves.

"I'm sorry Master. I can't go with you to St. Brett's."

"But Jake, why?"

"You don't know much about my past except what I told you of in France — and most of that I kept vague, and I thank you for never prying. You're right: my family are from around St. Brett's. In fact, the only family I have now is my father, and he lives in St. Brett's. He's the leading burgess of the town, the Abbot's right-hand, his bailiff, keeping law and order and head of the confraternity of leading townsfolk."

"Then our work will be all the easier. Your father can smooth the way for us, help get the confidence of the people there? He may know something perhaps."

Jake grunted, not knowing how to go on, to tell the whole truth.

"But I'm stupid," said Roger. "You must have great fear for your father given what has been happening according to the Abbot's letter. I am sure the Abbot would have mentioned an important man like your father by name if he had been involved in any of the demonic occurrences, so I don't think you need worry on that score. But surely it means that we must make haste, your only family member is in danger."

"I hate my father, he could die and I wouldn't care."

Roger paused. "Jake, I too hate my father. He wants me to join the Church. To give up my life's calling of research and investigation. But I am sure if he was ill or under threat he would thank me if I visited, to be reconciled before death."

"That old bastard isn't going to die anytime soon, not with that witch looking after him," replied Jake.

"Witch? Has he been enchanted by a sorceress?"

"Hah! First me and then him, she didn't take long to get her claws into him?"

"Now you're saying she's some type of were beast?"

Jake looked at Roger and smiled. His Master was so willing to believe in the most fanciful of things, yet he closed his thoughts to the savage realities of life, such as how to earn enough money to eat. Perhaps that came of being born of noble blood. Jake wished he had the luxury to float through life as if it were a fair laid out to amuse him. But he had the misfortune to be born amongst the grafting classes, where selfishness and money were the only things that mattered. And they mattered more if they determined if you could eat that day, or find a dry warm place to sleep. How could he blame his father for what he was? He was a survivor and he had passed some of those traits onto his son, for which Jake knew he should be thankful. But family was family, and all of their neighbours would look after their own, helping sons and even cousins to get on in life. His father had once, helping him with his tavern, but when Isabel came along that all changed. She'd turned him into a wolf, ready to take what he wanted with no thought for his son.

"Aren't all women close enough to beasts?" Jake said. "When you become a priest," Roger shuddered when Jake said the word, "that's what they'll tell you. Steer clear of women because they'll lead you into sin, into animal passions."

"I hope that day never comes," said Roger. "But tell me about your father and the woman you mentioned. Does she practice magic?"

"Someone once told me that she did, but I'm not so sure. Her name is Isabel."

"Are you going to tell me anything more?" asked Roger.

What could Jake tell his master? How his father who ran the brewing business in St. Brett's and acted as arbiter for all the other trade in the town, had treated his only son as a business rival and done his best to put him out of business? Even after Jake's Edith had died of plague, John Haukwake had shown no sympathy for his son. Jake had considered leaving St. Brett's to get out from under John's shadow, but then he found Isabel and her mother huddled on his doorstep one frosty winter's morn. That had been the start of what he thought would be the rest of his happy life. But his father had denied him that as well. She was a whore, and his father was a thief, and Jake was the victim of them both. They deserved death. If he hadn't been so drunk that night he would have gone through with it. But instead he had fled and tried to find death in France. Going back to St. Brett's after all these years would be like going back to his own hell on earth.

Jake stopped looking out of the window and looked straight at Roger. "She's a whore who broke my heart. She lives with my father now, that's all there is."

"Oh really?" said Roger. "It sounded like it might be more complicated than that?"

"Isn't life?" said Jake.

"But that doesn't mean we should shy away from life from complexity, that's what being human is," replied Roger.

"You think me a coward?" said Jake.

"Although you won't talk about it, I think I can understand why you are reluctant to return. I, too, would be reluctant to return to my father's seat in Westmoreland. But do you want to live the rest of your life with these thoughts of ill-will? They will become demons that haunt your every day. I sleep less than you, and often while I study the stars and you are asleep in your cot, I have walked past and seen you mutter and turn in your sleep. I can tell that you are deeply troubled by something — and now I guess it must be with St. Brett's, your father, and this woman Isabel?"

"Another ale?" asked a pot-girl. They both nodded. Jake watched her as she walked away. She was a new one and very pretty. Jake looked at her long dark hair, not bound under a wimple, and noted the dress that showed some of her shoulder and the top of her breast. The landlord wasn't stupid and didn't care if his serving girls looked somewhat immoral in their attire. It brought the business in. Jake had never stooped to that, but when Isabel had helped him with his tavern she didn't need to dress like a slattern to attract more customers. Her beauty shone out of her no matter what she wore. She would be seven years older now. Would age have diminished her beauty?

"Perhaps my demons are worse than the ones you seek in St. Brett's?" said Jake.

"Perhaps," said Roger. "So you'll come with me?"

Jake sighed. "Someone's got to keep you out of trouble."

CHAPTER 5

Roger was grateful to have Jake as his travelling companion. His manservant knew the roads of southern England much better than he and was also an expert on the inns where a weary traveller might rest and not be afflicted by bed bugs or scandalous prices. After packing a few things that morning they had set out from Oxford on the road towards London. They reached the market town of High Wycombe towards evening. From there, on the next day, they would need to turn off from the London road and proceed across lesser-used ways through villages and small towns unfamiliar to Roger to reach St. Brett's located in Fordingshire north of London. All roads might lead to London, but not all roads lead *around* London.

Jake found them a good, comfortable inn for the night and managed to negotiate a good rate for a room. They retired early, exhausted from the previous sleepless night and long day's travel. Roger took the bed while Jake curled on a straw mattress by the door guarding the entrance like a loyal wolf-hound, falling asleep immediately. Roger could hear the steady breathing turn into snores. He sat up, lit a candle and reached a copy of Aristotle's *De Caelo* from his bag, but before he opened the pages he watched Jake sleep for a moment. The angry features of the older man were relaxed and softened. He had shaved before retiring for the night and his smooth face looked like a boy's in the dim light. *I hope you can find peace,* thought Roger.

Peace had been utterly absent when Roger and Jake first met. Roger had been returning from a period of study at the University of Bologna, an institution renowned for legal scholarship and for the study of astrology. After a brief commission at the Papal court at Avignon, Roger had joined a group of French clerics and merchants who travelled together for their protection up the Rhone valley and into Burgundy. None of them had expected to encounter *routiers* that far East. The Kingdom of France, and especially the Duchy of Burgundy, were a good deal more secure than they had been in earlier years during the war with England that had left much of the French realm devastated. Roger's nationality was not a problem to his fellow travellers. Some of them had joked that he was an English spy who had planned to collude in their robbery with the Duke of Lancaster. They would be fine pickings if he had been. A Cardinal, two Bishops, an Abbot and three rich Parisian merchants travelled in that cavalcade.

But the instance of disorder and banditry that befell them on their journey never appeared in any monk's chronicle and barely made it to a footnote in the records of the local justice. They had been in an area of high country bordering the Auvergne. A bleak plateau at that time of year, the Aubrac had been virtually depopulated in the twenty years since the great plague. Humanity had retreated from the marginal lands it had once been forced to exploit due to the increase in population in the first half of the fourteenth century after Christ. So there was no safe castle, monastery or fortified inn where they could rest. That night they sheltered along a high river valley where the river meandered past cliffs and formed a shallow beach along sand and stony banks. The travellers could see caves in the cliffs overlooking their campsite that might shelter bears, so a careful guard was kept and fires lit to ward off any animal intruders. That moon was full that night, and the moonlight shone off the limestone rocks and the pebbles of the beach to create light that almost seemed as bright as day once the eye became accustomed to it.

Roger couldn't sleep. The light was much too bright for him. And he couldn't help wondering about their exposed position. The moon shone down on a landscape that might be the very image of the moon itself.

When it came, the attack was clumsy and desperate. Most of the travellers had time to get away. The English had come creeping out of the caves and splashing up the river thinking that they would be invisible to dozing guards. But the whole camp seemed to be sleepless and jumpy and their attackers were quickly spotted. Roger had run for his horse, but found that a bishop had jumped on it instead, taking the first mount that he came on. One of the bishop's guards waved a sword at Roger as if he was a bandit trying to steal the horse. He was left on foot with a few other unfortunate members of the travelling band who were too slow to mount up. None of the travellers or their guards had considered defending the camp, but only of flight, and that was easily achieved although in a haphazard manner. Some of them were shot down by the English, who found it easy to find and kill their targets in the bright moonlight.

Roger had not been reticent in expressing his thoughts. "You fools. What sort of inept ambush was that? Why didn't you wait until the moon had at least gone down? We all saw you coming!"

He had been lucky not to get his throat sawed through at that point. But a stocky, thick-haired fellow had put his arm up to keep the blade from his throat.

"He's an Englishman. He's one of us no matter what company he might keep." That man, who called himself Jake Savage, had saved his life. All the other travellers, minor people like him, were slaughtered and their possessions taken. None of them had been worth a ransom. Jake and the rest of the gang were a mix of English soldiers who had deserted the army of John of Gaunt in Bordeaux following his disastrous march from Calais to Bordeaux in the Duchy of Aquitaine. Gaunt had claimed the march as a victory. They had ridden across French lands and challenged the ability of the French king to protect his subjects. In reality they had been chased south with French armies at their heels, taking what they could steal from the land. Many of Jake's comrades had died on the way either from disease or starvation or the assaults of the local population who preyed on the English as their foraging parties spread across the countryside like the contents of a broken drain. Those that reached the English held Duchy of Aquitaine were required to stay and form the heart of an army to defend the province. The French had been knocking on the door ever since the illness of Aquitaine's Duke, Edward, the Black Prince and son of the king of England, Edward III. With the fearsome Black Prince brought low by a crippling and mysterious disease, John of Gaunt, the Duke of Lancaster and Edward III's second eldest surviving son, was de facto the most senior military commander available. The old king himself had put himself in charge of an expedition to rescue the Earl of Pembroke's army in La Rochelle the previous year in 1372, but the fleet had stood at anchor at Winchelsea for seven weeks trapped by the winds, and by then it was too late.

Although they were only indentured to fight for the period of six months, Fearing the dissolution of his forces, Gaunt had declared it a treasonable offense for any English soldier to return to England from Bordeaux without special permission from him. But Jake had been one of many who'd had enough. He, like many others, hadn't been paid, and there had been little opportunity to grow rich through ransoms or pillage. But for Jake, Roger thought, there was something more to it. It had been

Jake's first campaign. He had joined up hoping to find something, or perhaps to forget something. But whatever bothered him did not disappear with going overseas or with the experience of war.

Jake had let Roger go, and he had made it back to England. Roger thought he would never again see the common archer with the heart of a chivalrous knight, only to discover him in a cage in the back of a cart being led through Hampton docks to the gaol at Winchester Castle.

"We claimed that we were free mercenaries who had been released from service in Brittany," Jake told him later, "but those bastards wanted proof and asked for names. Seems Gaunt's captains had sent on lists of names of those who'd left when the money ran out. One of the Bretons dobbed us in — he'd heard one of the men using his real name and talking about Bordeaux whores. After that we were all assumed guilty."

Roger had surprised himself by his quick thinking. Waving his staff and making the most of his clerk's robes he stopped the carter and addressed the guard who rode next to him. "You have my servant up there! I have been looking for him for two weeks since we were taken by pirates in the channel." The guard had been further swayed with the offer of a bag of coins and Jake was released. Once out of earshot, Jake swore to serve Roger in any capacity. Roger had said 'no, you are your own man,' but Jake was insistent, he was in Roger's debt. "But I am only repaying my debt to you," Roger had told him.

As he lay by the door, Jake propelled a loud snort out of his nostrils and rolled over onto his other side. Time to get to sleep himself, Roger realized. He put down the book he'd been holding without reading and blew out the candle.

They left early the next day. Roger woke with the dawn. "Come, let us get some bread and ale from the landlord and break our fast while we rise."

"I could sleep for another day," Jake replied as Roger passed him his boots.

Jake didn't talk much as they rode. Roger put it down to their early start. Some mornings he never heard more than a word from Jake at least until terce. They reached a crossroads at the village of Crokkingham, and Jake pointed towards the Eastern road, which was no more than a narrow track leading out of Crokkingham into some wooded hills. Roger thought about asking one of the villagers whether that was the best way to St. Brett's as it didn't look like a great road, but held his peace. Jake seemed definite that they must go that way.

The road got worse as they went up higher into the hills. Rocks and holes in the ground made their horses tread so carefully their pace was slower than walking on foot. Eventually they passed the stone shell of an abandoned farmhouse, which seemed of particular interest to Jake, who kept his eyes on it as they rode by.

"What's wrong?" asked Roger.

"Things have changed," was all Jake said.

The road lead up a steep wooded hill and then the trees opened out to reveal a valley of farmland, with a sizable stream running through it. Delvings in the hillside showed where miners had once worked, cutting stone for building projects many miles away. At the end of the valley, before it turned north and became a narrow tangle of forest and cliffs, stood a clutch of village buildings. Jake quickened the pace of his horse, and Roger nudged his own to keep up with him. Jake turned round in the saddle, glaring at Roger as if he were his direst enemy. Roger reined in his horse to a slow walk, and let Jake go on ahead. Whatever was the matter, Jake didn't want him anywhere near him.

Jake could be moody sometimes; often after a few drinks he would become morose, but he would never talk about his problems. Not that Roger wanted to discuss his servant's emotional life, but he could tell that Jake was not keen to delve into the past. Roger knew that he was not the most considerate of the feelings of others. He was often caught up in his own researches and speculations, and oblivious to those around him. So that when he had made a new discovery he would immediately have to share it with another person, whoever that might be — and because of his lack of students and the unfriendliness of the other Merton *magisters*, Jake's were often the only human ears available to listen.

Roger often found it remarkable that a man of such lowborn status, a commoner of no family wealth and little formal education beyond a year of grammar school, could not only understand the theories and observations of natural and astral science of which he spoke, but also question and challenge his theories. If he ever finished (or properly began) his magnum opus, he must find some way to acknowledge his debt to Jake.

Roger carried on along the track through the valley leading to the small village. On either side were fields, lying fallow. Even with his own limited understanding of estate management, Roger could see that was unusual. Two-thirds of these fields should be growing crops of some sort. Jake stood in the centre of the village, which consisted of about a score of stone-built dwellings, sturdy looking structures whose builders had made good use of the stone found in the surrounding hills. His horse was untethered and moved around the Common's centre, greedily cropping the abundant grass.

Roger approached cautiously and slowly, and jingled his reins and spurs to make sure Jake would hear him coming. As Roger neared him, Jake glanced up and wiped tears away.

"This is Sipsley, where you were born," said Roger.

"Yes, forgive me Master," said Jake, turning his head as he wiped his face dry. Roger nodded and rode over to recover Jake's horse for him, holding it steady as Jake remounted.

He knew better than to ask. The village was empty, abandoned since the ravages of plague had reduced so many marginal settlements like it to a state so poor that their inhabitants simply moved to where there was better pasture. Wherever these refugees went, there were the empty houses left by families who had not been so fortunate. They rode on in silence.

They came down from the high hills and came to a gently rolling landscape of small river valleys and farmland. Sheep grazed as they might anywhere else on the hills, and peasants tilled the fields in the valleys. At Buckstead they came to a larger north-south road that cut across their path. The grass was well cut back from the verges and the surface even laid with stone in places.

"North or south?" asked Roger, breaking the silence that had lain between them since leaving Sipsley.

"South from here a few miles is King's Langley, where the royal family have a hunting lodge; to the north is the Black Prince's castle of Berkhamsted," said Jake. "For St. Brett's, we must climb this hill and then cross another valley, then we'll be in sight of the Abbey." They rode through the village of Buckstead, and Roger felt his stomach groan at the sight of a group of peasant men and women taking an afternoon meal of bread, cheese, smoked ham and pies, served up to them at a stall outside a larger house where the smell of fresh cooking came.

"Perhaps one of these serfs might sell us a pie?" he said to Jake.

"As you will," said Jake.

"Goodwife, serve us two of your biggest pies, and wrap them well. We still have far to travel today, I think."

"Where you be bound?" asked the pie-woman.

"St. Brett's," replied Roger.

The woman wrapped their pies in cloth and passed them over without another word. Roger reached out his hand and offered her a couple of pennies.

She accepted the money, but without a smile of thanks. "Enjoy the pies, for what good they'll do ye."

Roger shook his head at her rudeness and passed a pie to Jake.

"Word travels fast," said Jake once they had ridden out of the village.

"Pardon?" said Roger.

"You told her that we are going to St. Brett's. The peasants don't like the Abbey and town at the best of times, and now they have no doubt heard something about the witchcraft the Abbot wrote you of. Good of them to think we're doomed."

"Peasant superstition," replied Roger.

"Is it? I thought you believed in these things: destiny written in the skies, the influence of spirits malign and benign on the lives of men?"

Jake must be in a better mood, thought Roger, if he could poke fun at him.

"You don't believe in anything of course," replied Roger. "Doesn't that mean you live without hope, without wonder in your life?"

"Oh I wonder alright. I wonder how you lot at Oxford get away with it. What did I read somewhere?"

"I don't know what? Can you read Jake?"

Jake even smiled.

"I read — and in Latin actually, though only a few words and slow, but my school master would have been proud of me — that a doctor of the Church wrote a whole opus on how many angels might dance upon the head of a pin."

"That's a myth and you know it, no one ever wrote such a thing."

"But it is ... what is it? A Greek word I think. I know, a *metaphor*, a metaphor for the pointlessness of academic enquiry?"

"Well not quite the right word, but I see what you mean. But I disagree, enquiry is not only of academic utility. *A verbis ad verbera.* Where there is an effect there must be a cause."

"Listen, is that screaming?" said Jake.

"A woman and a child I think," replied Roger. They had gone over the high ridge above Buckstead and were now approaching the small river that wound along another low valley. The screaming and the sound of men shouting carried down the winding lane banked on both sides by grassy slopes, bushes, and trees as the track cut down the gradual slope of the hillside.

Jake reached for his scabbarded sword from one of their sumpters and strapped it to his side. "Best be prepared," he said.

Roger's felt the blood drain from his face and his heart beat ice around his body. It was like France again, ambush and death awaiting around any corner.

Jake was already several yards ahead of him, having kicked his horse into a trot. Roger crossed himself and did the same. They plunged down the muddy lane, partly flooded by the overflowing ford ahead of them. Just upriver from the ford, stood a watermill, a weir and channel that moved most of the water under boards by the side of the river and thus created shallower water, a few inches deep, for people, animals, and carts to cross. There was a cart in the ford at that moment, pulled by two oxen that protested with deep groans as a young woman sitting atop the cart flicked the cart's reins at them to move, her task was not made easier by three men armed with billed polearms who were shouting at her to move the cart out of the river. Roger could see a rock that had stuck underneath one of the cart's wheels, holding it fast. The cart was full of sacks, barrels, and furniture, with a crate of chicken, a lamb and a small child screaming its lungs raw.

Another man lay face down in the shallow water of the ford, blood forming a red aura around him in the slow water.

Jake drew his sword and charged his horse at the three men. They turned in shock as he came at them. One of them tried to put up his bill to defend himself, but Jake knocked it aside with his sword as he swept past, and let Lois knock over another one of them, who was too slow to defend himself. Jake slipped from the saddle and with a word sent Lois back to the side of the ford, where Roger sat on his horse watching. Jake had the element of surprise and was able to dismount unhindered. One of the men was kneeling in the water winded from Lois's charge, another was trying to stop his bill floating away, while the last of the three men held his weapon out towards Jake, but his face was a crease of anxiety compared to the mask of fierce determination that Jake wore. Jake swung his sword to test the man's reactions, and he simply dropped his bill and ran. The weaponless man did likewise, and the man struggling to get up received a kick from Jake that spurred him to make the best of his escape as he stumbled after his friends to the other side of the ford and down a track into the distance.

Roger broke from his trance of inaction, dismounting and wading into the ford, hoping that he might help the man who lay bleeding in the river. His studies had included at least the theory of medicine if not its application. Once the fight was over, the woman, too, was kneeling by the man's side, cradling his head in her lap as her skirts floated around her in the river. As he drew closer, Roger didn't need his book knowledge to realize that the man was dead, anyone could have seen that from the way his head lay limply in the woman's lap; that and the paleness of his face and his unmoving, staring eyes, coupled with the amount of blood that had spilled from the gaping wound in his chest and into the river.

Yet the woman cradled her man's head in her arms, and whispered words to him as if he might hear, willing him back to consciousness.

"Mistress," said Roger, "I fear he is dead."

She ignored him. Jake came over and addressed her. "Joan Metcalfe, I remember you when you were a girl, and now meet you here in these dire circumstances. It is a sad day, but what my master says is right."

She looked up at this, and studied Jake's face for a while. "John's son, yes I remember, you played truant with my brother, and after that you would beat him once or twice every year after you'd had a drink."

Jake shrugged. "He knew he deserved it. Here let me carry him to the bank." Joan had calmed since recognising Jake and let him take the man's body from her. He struggled under the weight. The man had been young, of moderate height, without fat, but still heavy with all the water soaked into him. The paleness of his face didn't hide his handsome features.

"We could take you home to St. Brett's," said Roger. "Jake here will keep you safe from any more vagabonds along the way, and your man can have his burial."

Jake nodded. "My father is bailiff and can raise the hue and cry to capture those who did this."

"They were Abbey men like your father. Are you in their employ? Don't trick. I won't go with you and I won't let you have take back his body to raise more devils. I'll bury him myself before taking him back there." She crossed herself and made another sign with her fingers, crossing them and touching them to her ear, and tugged at the body of the man on the bank of the river.

"We're not Abbey men, don't be foolish. Look he's too heavy for you, let us help you," said Jake.

"Stop," said Roger. We want to rid the town of evil spirits. Please stay and tell us what you know."

She listened to neither of them, but dragged and pulled the body through the ford and onto the back of her cart. Her child and animals still screamed with the strife all around them. The child broke into sobbing tears as the corpse of the man who had once been her father was rolled onto the back of the cart next to her.

Frantic, the woman loosened the rock from in front of the cart's wheel and tugged the oxen and cart out of the ford herself, refusing all offers of assistance. Despite the protestations of Jake and Roger, she never looked back and never said another word to them.

CHAPTER 6

The Abbey's L-shaped profile loomed massively over the landscape around it, sitting on a low hill over the surrounding plain. It was clearly visible to Jake and Roger as they reached the hill crest above the ford.

"It's beautiful," said Roger.

"Built on the blood and misery of thousands of good Englishmen," replied Jake with a scowl. Jake felt guilt for his bitterness, but then again he was only here because Roger willed it, so why shouldn't he be bitter.

As they rode nearer, the square towers that formed a cross of stone and brick could be more easily discerned. Jake had seen bigger churches, and ones more elegantly constructed with more daring feats of architecture, but few in the low, dying sunshine of a May evening could match St. Brett's for the power of its first impression. The sunlight seemed to turn the walls a brassy brown, which twinkled with flashes of starlight as the sun reflected off glazed windows.

They passed fields and small farms and farm-buildings that would belong to the richer inhabitants of the town, those who might keep their agricultural work separate from their trade in the town. "My father spoke of buying a

73

grange in the valley along the river Varn, near where the Abbey's mills are."

"Or perhaps one of these is his. No one is working in them though, isn't that strange?"

"What date is it?"

"It's the 28th of May," replied Roger.

"St. Brett's day, they'll all be in the Abbey Church. This is one of the few days the monks let all the villeins of the township through their doors; normally they keep all out except the gentry and the wealthiest burgesses, as they're the only ones who can afford to join the Charnel Brotherhood."

"I don't know much about this St. Brett's. He's not a commonly worshipped saint elsewhere is he?"

"Oh don't worry I can tell you quite a bit about him, but you'd be better off talking to the monks, they'll bore you to death with his legend. It's all written down as well, of course. No doubt they'll scribble you off a copy, even illuminate it for you if you have a year to wait. They're desperate for patronage and money, despite their lands and the taxes and tithes they gather, always looking to attract more patrons and pilgrims."

"Some works require great expense. The monks here write many chronicles, and there was an Abbot who lived here more than fifty years ago who was famous for his mechanical clock. Art and science on that scale is costly," replied Roger

"And for what end Master? What I see you working on is pretty pointless, but at least it doesn't cost the earth."

"It would cost more if I could get someone to fund me. I could build some sort of device for creating a clearer image of the stars, using lenses."

"Become a monk then! Their ambitions don't seem to be bound by concerns over money." Roger grimaced and shook his head.

"I wish you wouldn't talk about money all the time. It's all I hear, from you, from the Provost, from my family."

Jake felt like telling Roger that only those who didn't *want* to worry about money could afford *not* to worry about it, but he held his tongue.

"I'm sorry. The closer we have come to this place, the greater has been my feeling of disquiet."

"I can understand that. I myself have experienced a darkness descending upon me after the battle of the ford. Yet I wonder if we also feel the malignity of the dark forces located in St. Brett's spreading their claws across the land to our souls."

"My soul certainly dreads the prospect of this place, but I have reason. All that I hate lives there."

"It is a pity that we do not have time to pause and consider and take readings of the stars to determine the possible combination of factors. It would make an interesting study on its own."

Jake shook his head. To him the combination of events was obvious.

Their track now joined a larger road, paved as it came towards the town. "Watling street, the old Roman road from London, puts St. Brett's less than a day's ride from the city," said Jake.

"Very handy," said Roger.

They rode past townhouses, but there were no people. "It'll be the end of the mass and then there will be celebrations as the sun sets on the Romeland field."

"Rather late for a fair isn't it?" said Roger.

"These are not those sorts of celebrations," said Jake. "There will be singing, dancing, eating, and a mystery play put on by the monks telling the life of St. Brett's to those who won't understand the Latin spoken in Church, all to the light of a hundred torches and a great bonfire."

The road rose up the steepening hill, on one side of which ascended wattle and daub townhouses, their upper floors elbowing each other for space like old women at a hanging. On the other side of the road, the wide Abbey compound expanded at its leisure where a hundred houses might have happily found room. Along with the massive structure of the Abbey Church positioned at the very crest of the hill at the most northern end of the Abbey's compound, there rose a number of stone built structures. Two huge cloisters stood like miniature walled forts, one just to the south of the church and the other to the south and east of it, separated by other large buildings from which tall chimneys stoked smoke into the heavens, keeping their hearths warm for the monks and cooking their evening repast. Clusters of wooden outhouses for stabling, animals, stores, farming equipment and servants' quarters dwelt alongside their larger stone brethren. Yet despite this multitude of buildings, there was still room for a large orchard, a walled garden that adjoined the smaller cloister complex, and a large field in which were pastured the numerous horses for riding and burden owned by the Abbey, as well as an area set aside to enfold sheep and cattle.

The whole was enclosed by a stone wall, which, although not as mighty as a castle wall, was still strong and tall enough to keep most intruders out. The Abbey could only be entered by a small gate to the east, which faced the road on which Jake and Roger now travelled, or by a larger, more impressive entrance on the north wall, just to the west of the Abbey Church itself, where a huge gatehouse dwarfed the walls to either side and the town buildings nearby.

§

Roger shook his head when he saw the huge bloated toad that hung around the gatekeeper's neck. He looked over at Jake. Jake had pulled a hood over his head, and tugged his collar up around his cheeks, hanging back behind Roger as they rode up. *So he had seen the demon as well,* Roger thought, assuming that this toad was a demon and not either a wizard's familiar (a more common-looking wizard than the gatekeeper he could not imagine), or perhaps a bizarre pet, but he rather doubted either of those options to be true.

"Do not be afeared of this foul creature," he whispered to Jake. "I wear a charm that will protect us both, just stay behind me and do as I do."

Thus leaving Jake reassured, Roger dismounted his horse. Behind him Jake did likewise and gathered the reins of their sumpters.

The toad spat a globule of black bile at Roger's feet. The gatekeeper, a fat man with wide, greasy cheeks underneath a bald pate that he insisted in keeping uncovered, opened his eye-slits to regard them. He had been leaning against the wall apparently asleep.

"I'm ..." started Roger.

"You're late, they're at mass. The Abbot's being dancing 'round like he's been needing to piss his pants all morning. He thought you'd arrive yesterday."

"Yesterday? But I came as soon as I could," said Roger.

"Don't talk to my master like that," said Jake, stepping forward. The toad around the gatekeeper's neck snarled and spat again, this time a bigger globule of black bile passed close by Jake's face, but he didn't flinch.

The gatekeeper held Jake's gaze for a moment, then he looked away and smiled. "Inside, gentles. As I said, they're all at mass, so you'd best be going to the big church, I am guessing you can find it yourselves. I'm staying here." The gatekeeper opened the gate. Roger walked through and Jake followed. The door slammed behind them, and Roger thought he heard a croaking laugh as the door shut.

"How dare he be so insolent to you," hissed Jake.

"But Jake, were you not scared of taking on that monster, you didn't flinch," said Roger.

"Low life scum like that, he's one up from a cess-pit cleaner."

"I meant the toad, that demon," said Roger.

"That's a bit harsh maybe," replied Jake.

Roger bit his lip until it hurt. Had Jake not seen the demon then? Was it happening again? The visions? He looked around, but there were no other people visible for him to test his fears.

Wherever there are people there is devilry.

Those had been the words of Ashendon in the suicide note he had left him, and since then he'd had reason to believe those words quite, quite literally.

§

Jake gritted his teeth and took a deep breath as they approached the main doors of the church. They were open to allow a spill of townspeople to overflow onto the grass beyond. The crowds who couldn't get inside nudged and pushed each other to hear or even see something of the mass of their patron saint. Jake remembered these days well. Each year had been something to look forward to, although it often fell during the calendar of the Passion, St. Brett's day was special for the monks and the town, perhaps the only day of the year that both parties came to an accord and called each other brother under the roof of one church. Other feast days allowed for similar festivities, but St. Brett's day was the only one where the whole town attended the Abbey Church rather than one of the three parish churches, which was truly the only place to be to celebrate the life and martyrdom of St. Brett's. And everyone came. For many of the people it was their only chance to the see the monks at their work and to gawp at the riches of the church, but that wasn't the only draw. The feast of St. Brett's attracted gentry and nobility from far afield to the abbey. And on more than one occasion a member of the royal family had attended the service. Both Gaunt, his older brother, the Black Prince, and a variety of Earls had come over the years, bringing along with them a lesser constellation of famous and rich knights and ladies.

And for the richer townspeople as well, especially the ladies, St. Brett's day was the day to show off their finery.

Jake had only seen Isabel at the service once before he left St. Brett's, and he'd had the pleasure of sitting next to her that day, near the front on a bench his father had reserved for them, his hand clasped in hers, and her scent in the warm spring day wafting over him like a drug. His last happy day? One of the last perhaps.

"We'll never get in this way," said Jake looking at the crowd pushing and shoving to get a better view. "We could just wait until they're done and then see the Abbot afterwards."

"Yes you're right. We would need a full army of angels and the saints to fight our way past these witches and their demon familiars," replied Roger.

Jake looked at the younger man standing next to him. Had Roger completely lost it? He was staring with what looked like a mixture of awe and abject terror at the crowd of townspeople, normal men and women, dressed as well as they could, but mostly from among the more common folk of the town, but at least they wore their newest woollens, more brightly coloured than their everyday wear. Jake watched in disbelief as Roger began to make the sign of the cross and drew out of his bag a book and a small silver cross. He held the cross before him and began to stride towards the crowd.

"With me Jake! I will make my observations and I want you to note them as best you can." Roger thrust the book into Jake's hands, together with a wooden box, which Jake knew contained his quill and ink.

"But I need a flat surface on which to write," said Jake. "And," said Jake, thinking how to save his master and himself untold scorn from the town's villeins, "would it not be best to find a vantage point better suited to observe these creatures? What about inside the church. I know steps that will take us to a gallery high in the nave."

"Jake, some days I don't know how I could live without you," said Roger. *Neither do I,* thought Jake. "Take me to this place high in the nave," said Roger.

Jake wondered where he was going to take Roger. It would mean entering the church via the monk's apartments to get to the spiral stair that led from their dormitory to the corner where the nave met the transept. There a small window opened in the wall in the eyes of a carved saint and allowed the viewer to lean forward and stare through the eyes of the statue itself and see the whole nave. Although all the monks would be at the service, the doors might be locked; furthermore, there would be difficult questions to answer if they were caught. Jake could hardly claim they lost their way and found themselves in a secret passageway, especially when its discovery twenty years ago had resulted in his expulsion from St. Brett's grammar school.

Without consulting Roger, he took them instead along the north side of the Abbey to a door leading into the other side of the transept. Here the more honoured guests of the Abbey would be allowed entry so that they might walk undisturbed to benches at the front of the nave, nearer to the music and chanting of the mass, and nearer to God and his saint, St. Brett. Here at least they might make themselves known to the novice who would be holding the door and a message could be relayed to Abbot Peter of their arrival. The door was shut as they approached. From within Jake could hear the sonorous chanting of the monks. He knocked gently.

"Devil, or demon, won't you let me in," sang Roger in a childish voice behind him.

"What?" said Jake.

"I wonder if a beast of the pit will open the door for you?" said Roger.

Instead, as Jake predicted, a novice eventually opened the door a crack. Jake smiled and the door shut in his face with a slam. He knocked again. Again the door opened, and the novice whispered: "Back to the nave, knave." The door was slammed shut again.

"Did you see his scales?" asked Roger.

"No? What are you talking about?" replied Jake.

"Scales. His black, lizard-like hide."

"You're mad or making fun of me again. The boy had nothing but skin, not even a hair on his lip yet."

Jake knocked once more and the door was opened again. This time Jake put his hand against the door and pushed it open enough to insert his heavy riding boot into the gap. "We are here to see Abbot Peter, at his order. This is my master, Magister Roger Sotil of Merton College, Oxford."

The novice didn't look happy. He curled his lip, and hung his head. "Come then inside, but you must keep quiet, the mass must not be interrupted. The Abbot will see you after its conclusion, but not before. Wait here in the wings."

He gestured them to an area of floor that was hidden from the nave by the corner of a wall, but gave a view past the rood screen to the altar. They could see the monks sitting in their choir, with psalm books in their hands, lifting their voices in a polyphonic plainsong.

"How long until it finishes," asked Jake of the novice before he wondered off.

"Oh an hour I would say."

"Do we get a bench to sit on?"

The boy looked as if he'd just been asked to do the washing up for the whole monastery

"I'll see." He sloped off and exited a door in a dark corner of the Abbey's north wing.

§

A church full of demons — and no small church, either. The Abbey of St. Brett's dwarfed the collegiate churches of Oxford for size and the glory of its decoration. On its

81

painted walls and its windows, and the more temporary wooden boards and curtains that served to section off certain areas or to hide areas of stonework under repair, scenes of the Bible were retold. Roger's eyes were particularly drawn to the scenes of the life of St. Brett himself, which were given the most prominent position of all, with special boards that had been wheeled in front of the rood screen for the common laypeople to view. He noticed that demons were portrayed in these scenes. St. Brett casting out demons from the heads of pagan kings. St. Brett tempted by a devil in the form of a beautiful woman as he lay sleeping. St. Brett martyred by a pagan king inspired to evil by Satan himself.

Roger watched now as the priest at the altar raised the host up to the cross. As he did so a huge black-scaled creature (another demon!), twice the size of a man took the wafer from him and popped it into his mouth and chewed. The creature flapped its black leathery wings and laughed. The stink from his breath reached Roger who stood at least fifty paces away. Roger watched aghast as the demon grabbed the priest in his claws and began to chew his head from his body, twisting the man's limp torso to break the neck and tear it from the body. The demon threw the body to another demon, one of a line of twelve who had formed an orderly queue walking from the nave past the rood screen and choir to the altar.

Roger looked at Jake, who sat on the bench the novice had provided and seemed to be asleep. Roger shook his arm. "Are you bewitched? Do you not see?"

Jake looked up and Roger pointed across to the scene at the altar, where now each of the twelve demons took their turn to eat chunks of the priest's flesh.

"Yes I see the old bastard," said Jake. "But how did you know that was my father?"

Roger shook his head. That arch-demon was Jake's father? What was the man saying? Roger got up from the bench and strode over to the choir where the monks of the Abbey sat as if nothing out of the ordinary was happening. "Which one of you is Abbot Peter?" demanded Roger. The monks hushed and waved Roger away with angry looks. The novice from before ran to Roger, but he knocked aside his efforts to grab his arms. Then he was knocked to the floor from behind, and dragged kicking and screaming back to his bench in the darkness. Jake had him in a strong grip that he could not resist.

"Traitor!" shouted Roger. The whole of the church was in uproar. There was shouting and Roger could swear he heard swords drawn. Yes at last they had seen the demons for what they were and would either flee or fight. He was not mad after all.

He struggled still. Jake tried to clamp a rough skinned hand over his mouth. He tried to bite it but couldn't get a grip with his teeth. And then, looking down on him, he saw a woman, or perhaps she was an angel. Her hair was a lustrous brown, the colour of chestnuts, but with streaks of blonde so that it appeared bound with gold. Her eyes were clear and hazel and her skin like clear marble. She laid a cooling hand on his brow and wafted a small vial under his nose.

"There, that will do it," she said.

§

When Roger awoke, he was sitting next to Jake at the side of the nave, propped up against a number of prayer cushions that acted as pillows for his head and body. The service was reaching a conclusion. A procession of monks dressed in their finest priestly-garb lead a line of well-dressed laypeople draped with Brotherhood surcoats, with huge red crosses stitched into their white material.

"Who was she?"

"Be quiet ,will you," said Jake.

"What happened to them Jake? Are you one of them, a witch?"

"Stop it, or I'll take you to the top of the tower and throw you off it." Jake snarled those words at Roger so viciously that he did as he was bidden and fell silent. He looked up as the procession went past. The congregation cheered as the image of the humble-looking saint carried high on the arms of well dressed lay people in ornamental robes was carried past. They threw flowers at the statue of the kneeling man with his hands lifted up to heaven and stretched out their own hands as it passed, hoping to be nearer the aura. "Bless me, St. Brett," was mumbled or sometimes pronounced with more conviction by those around him. He even heard Jake say it.

Roger glanced around the nave. There was no evidence of the earlier disturbance. The house of God seemed clear of any devils. Yet as he glanced around, he noticed several people staring at him, but when he met their gaze they looked away. All except one. The woman who had lulled him to sleep with her soft words and beautiful looks. She stood on the opposite side of the aisle, in the front row, a bouquet of flowers ready to throw in offering to the saint. She was staring at him, and after he looked back at her she kept looking, her mouth opened her lips in the shape of a slight smile. But then the saint and his carriers came between them and he lost sight of her.

A wail of pain broke the festive hubbub, and the statue of the saint dropped suddenly as one of the six bearers fell to the ground. Roger stretched on his toes to get a better view, but suddenly the crowd was lurching forward, and he got knocked against a bench and bashed his knee. He clutched the bone as if holding it would take away the agony.

"Stop pushing me!" he shouted at a middle-aged woman behind him, who was shoving to get a better view of the commotion in the aisle. She looked up at him, made the sign of the cross, and hurried to give him some room. After that no one pushed in his direction.

"What's happening?" Roger asked Jake.

"Let's see." Jake grabbed Roger's arms and pushed with his strong shoulders through the crowd. "My master is a physician, let me through. Let me see the injured man." Roger realized that Jake must mean him.

The crowd reluctantly parted and they reached the aisle. The statue of the saint had fallen on its side, and the eyes of St. Brett seemed to glare at Roger with reproach. "How dare you ruin my day," he seemed to say. Roger stared at what had happened. One of the bearers had collapsed on the ground, but no one had come near him. He was not surprised. After all, who'd want to lend medical aid or comfort to a man with a foot long black tongue lashing out of his mouth, who seemed to have sprouted bat's wings from his neck, and was in the process of making sex actions to the floor of the nave?

The members of the congregation were alarmed, but didn't look as scared as Roger thought they might be. Roger was fascinated. "Jake, help me with him."

"You're joking," said Jake.

"I want to study him. Perhaps the monks can lend us a cell in which to keep him, and we can talk to the devil inside him."

"You are mad. It would be kinder to kill him," said Jake.

"He's my husband, don't you dare talk of killing him," said a middle-aged woman, well dressed in furs and silks.

"He's a witch, and brought this on himself," said a man who stood next to her. The woman looked up at him.

"If you weren't my brother I'd take my hand to you," she replied.

"You be a witch, too, and all these women of the company," screeched a female voice from somewhere behind Roger.

The middle-aged woman's mouth stretched wide in an angry shout. She roared. "May Beelzebub curse you! Bitch!" And then she opened her mouth again but instead of her normal high-pitched voice, cracking with the strain of its cursing, her voice dropped several octaves and bellowed in a deep voice that shook the eardrums of everyone in the nave: "I will meet you in hell! This vessel is mine to command now, kneel down before me slaves."

The woman's body shook and seemed to grow in height by several feet, and slowly began to spin. Roger realized there was air beneath her feet; she was spinning above the ground held aloft by an invisible hand. She looked down, smiling at the congregation below her, that was rapidly moving away and towards the door of the church. Only her brother stood firm. He looked around.

"May God have mercy on me," he said, and drew a short sword from underneath his long, fraternity-liveried coat. He stabbed upwards into his sister's body, and red blood came gushing out in a spurt. The woman clutched her belly and laughed. The brother stabbed again. This time his sword went right through her. He twisted and pulled and came away with half her guts wrapped around his blade.

"Die demon!" he shouted. The demon did not die, but the woman did. With a thud she fell to the ground, her entrails and blood spilling around her and staining the floor. The brother now turned to his sister's husband and swiftly cut off his head, killing him in an instant. The long tongue and wings spasmed and vanished.

"No!" shouted a monk, running up to the brother, having broken through the ring of onlookers now frozen in their rush to flee by the man's familial slaughter. But it was too late. He had reversed his sword and thrust it through his own belly while also falling forward so there could be no escape from death. He sobbed as he lay dying. "Father, pray for me," he groaned as his last breaths came.

Only Roger saw the demon that leapt from the dead sister's body. It fluttered and flew to the rafters of the church, and took station behind a stone gargoyle. Roger could see its white fangs grinning at the spectacle below. And then it was gone, hopping from beam to beam, and occasionally flying with slow laboured beats over the rood screen and into the choir. Roger ran to follow it, but before he could two strong arms grabbed his shoulders and dragged him towards the south door of the Abbey Church. Jake was nowhere to be seen, and did not come despite Roger's anguished pleas for help.

CHAPTER 7

Jake looked around for Isabel or his father. If anyone could explain to him what was going on it would be one of these two people. But neither of them was to be seen. When Roger needed calming, Isabel had appeared as if called by a silent message. Just when he thought he would have to knock Roger unconscious or drag him outside, she was there, unruffled, smiling at Jake as if nothing horrible had ever happened between them, pulling out a small bag of something pungent smelling, not a sweet smelling perfume, but yet not an evil smell. And Roger's face muscles relaxed, he stopped babbling and his eyelids flickered for a moment and shut.

Isabel had placed a damp cloth on Roger's brow and gently laid his head on a cushion. Where she had found these items, Jake knew not. "Keep him quiet and in a dark place; too much excitement and noise around him will wake him into a state between the dream and living worlds. If so, he may return to a state of high excitation."

Jake nodded his understanding. Isabel reached out a hand and touched Jake's arm for a moment. Their eyes met and there was a spark of shared knowledge between them, as if to say 'what was once cannot be again, but we are different people now, so let's remember what was good and leave the rest to be forgotten.'

And that was it, no more words passed between them. Isabel rose and walked back to the nave. Jake wondered if Isabel would have said more to him if he had pressed it.

She had told him not to move Roger, but he was overwhelmed by curiosity and there was no way that he was going to leave his master unattended. The surly novice still lingered, not taking part in the service; his only job seemed to be to prowl that section of the transept as if it were his personal hunting ground. Jake wondered that he didn't see the novice lift a leg and piss over each stone column to mark his territory.

"Help me with him," Jake said to him. "I'll get him out of your way." The novice was only too happy to oblige, not shirking physical labour in order to get rid of the two intruders. Perhaps he'd get a lashing for allowing the service to be interrupted, or perhaps, thought Jake, the novice-master would merely sodomise him. A group of men contained on their own and not allowed the company of women, but introduced to young, soft boys, it was no wonder that rumours abounded, and Jake knew that some of them were true.

Jake had pulled his hood back over his head when they entered the nave. He didn't look up, but he was sure that many of the congregation were looking their way, curious about who had caused the earlier uproar. The novice indicated a bench where two clerics sat at the end. They were not monks, but probably belonged to the parish churches in St. Brett's,. They reluctantly moved aside. Even though they were older than the novice, they obeyed, following him back to the transept.

"Wankers," muttered Jake under his breath. An old lady glared at him from under her wimple. He ignored her as he rearranged Roger, whose body, although skinny, had been heavy to move. He adjusted him so that his head

rested against the side of the bench, and found a prayer
cushion to support his head.

And then, when the saint was brought through the
congregation, all hell had broken loose. The man who
killed his sister had been a good friend of his. A baker's
son, he was probably about two years younger than Jake.
They had played football together, drunk together, and
now he had seen the man kill his sister (she'd been a young
tease once), his brother-in-law (a man Jake didn't know)
and himself. He struggled to understand why. He had seen
a man who was sick, writhing on the floor, and the sister
who had said some strange words and then begun to dance
crazily in her madness. Surely they needed help, prayers or
physic or Isabel's pungent herbs, whatever would aid
them, Jake cared not as long as it worked, as long as it
meant enough to those suffering to assist a cure. Perhaps,
as described in Abbot Peter's letter, there was an outbreak
of madness in St. Brett's, but was there devilry in it? He
knew Roger would think so, but he couldn't believe it. He
had seen people who were ill or disturbed by their
thoughts before, but why blame a demon? He had not
seen anything demonic in the church, no ape or bat-like
creatures sitting on their backs, like those portrayed in the
paintings of St. Brett. It was too easy to blame a man's evil
actions upon something else, and what better than a spirit
dedicated to tempt man and to cause him to do evil. It was
the Church's perfect answer to an uncomfortable question:
why did God allow his world to be polluted by evil?

Yet they also said that man had free will to control his
actions. Jake preferred that theory. And now it was his will
to see his father or Isabel, preferably Isabel, and find out
what was happening in his town. He looked through the
crowds. There was crying and shouting and people talking
to each other in anxious tones. The monks tried to usher
people away. He saw a couple of them kneel by the dead
bodies. One man, a monk he did not recognise, with neatly
cut hair around his tonsure and a severe looking face, let

his habit dip into the blood pooling on the stone floor, placing his hand on each of the corpses. Not to bless them in death, Jake realized, but to touch his fingers to their throats. The monk ordered his two assistants (he was evidently a man of some authority in the community by the way he behaved), to take up the bodies and remove them. They were placed on stretchers that the monks had brought and taken away.

"Shouldn't their families take their bodies," wondered Jake aloud.

"They should, but he won't let them," said a honeyed woman's voice that made his skin tingle and his stomach turn. He turned to see Isabel standing right by him.

"I was looking for you," she said. "While you've been gawping, your master has been taken away. Follow me if you want to find him."

"Why has he taken the bodies? What has happened to Roger?"

"I will answer your second question first," she said, taking his hand, and leading him through the crowd in the nave towards the south transept and to the monk's door between the church and the main cloister.

"Where are you taking us? You won't get in there."

"A third question, before I've answered the second? My, you are greedy in your old age." She turned a twinkling look on him. She was still beautiful and looked not a day over twenty, but he knew her to be only a few years younger than he.

"Listen Isabel, you're a woman, they won't let you in."

"Well thank you for reminding me of that. I know some of the monks. And in particular the one you asked about who took the bodies. He's Edmund, the Infirmarer, that's why he took the bodies — for examination after the possessions. He's been taking all the bodies that have been afflicted, trying to establish where the demons are coming from and if they have left any clues as to how they might be defeated. The Abbot and the other Abbey obedientaries are losing their wits over this. Unfortunately they haven't realized that your master is the Roger of Oxford summoned by Abbot Peter to assist them. They think he's either a possible suspect, maybe the necromancer himself come out of hiding, or at least a troublemaker, so the Precentor asked your father to arrest him. He is now under guard in the Chapter House with the Abbot and the obedientaries. I'm sure they'll soon realise their mistake, but I get the feeling that Roger needs you. So come, let us go. Edmund will let me in."

Jake let himself be lead through the church with no more questions, he gripped Isabel's hand tightly and stored away this moment in his memory.

CHAPTER 8

Roger wondered if the Abbot could see the miniature demon and the miniature angel that perched on his opposite shoulders and whispered into each of his ears. Their hushed babble into the Abbot's ears hadn't interrupted the flood of anger and abuse that he had set swirling around Roger's own ears. Roger couldn't tell from what he said whether the angel was winning the argument or the demon. He guessed that probably the demon was. Although the angel did look up with disdain from its perch on the Abbot's shoulder and glared at Roger at one point.

Roger turned his head swiftly to right and left hoping he might catch sight of his own demon and angel secretly giving him advice as well, but with no luck. He must have them; but, if so, why was he not aware of them? Peter Lombard maintained that every man had an angel to guard him from sin, and a demon to tempt him to it, though Roger he had never before read or heard evidence of this actually happening. He wondered why he could only see the Abbot's demon and angel, as no one else in the room seemed to have them. His observation of the Abbot would certainly form part of his opus; it was a most extraordinary occurrence. If only he had the skills of draughtsmanship, he could draw from memory what he was seeing — asking for charcoal and paper now might be impolitic, he thought, given the Abbot's ire.

"So?" said the Abbot.

"Pardon," replied Roger.

"What do you have to say for yourself? Why did you feel the compulsion to disrupt our most important mass of the year? Do you realise the importance of the patrons who attended and had to witness your outburst? Both the Keeper of the Privy Seal and the Warden of the Cinque Ports, and their good lady wives, saw it. And they are very keen, or should I say *were* very keen, on supporting the Benedictines. But who knows, after this perhaps they will turn their attention to some Poor Clares, or Friars Minor instead?"

"Yes I think you mentioned the patrons already. But tell me, Abbot, what about the deaths, the possessions that happened at the end of the mass? I had nothing to do with those."

"We all saw those, and no, I don't think you had anything to do with them. As you know from my letter, these terrible things have been happening more and more often over the last months."

"It's been going on for years," interrupted one of the other monks in the Chapter house. A timid, bent-over man, whose posture made him look older than his fair hair and unwrinkled face suggested.

"No it hasn't," said the Abbot. "Listen," he said to Roger. "If you are to remain here and in my employ ..."

"In the Abbey's employ you should say, not yours, and yes, they have been ..." said the bent-over monk.

"... then you had best act with more discretion. There's enough embarrassment after what happened today. I've had to return Sir Raby's bequest to ensure he keeps quiet, but I can't guarantee nothing will slip out. If you're going to make the situation worse," he glanced at the monk who'd interrupted him for a moment, "then you can leave."

The bent-over monk continued muttering. "... other incidences for years, deaths and more cases of spiritual illness at the hospital of St. Luke"

"Abbot," said Roger. "I need your trust and I need you not to lie to me either. If that makes you uncomfortable, then perhaps I should leave you to it?"

Roger noticed the demon and angel on the Abbot's shoulders pause for thought. The Abbot's brows creased and he stared at Roger.

"How dare you question the honesty of the Abbot!" said a tall, red-faced monk. He stood up from the seat that he had earlier taken in the Chapter house. Roger was wondering if any of the monks besides the timid rambling one were going to be on his side. He had been rushed before the Abbot so fast, and surprised both by the vitriol of his harangue and by the sight of the angel and demon that did spiritual battle on either side of his head, that his surroundings and the occupants of the room had left little impression on him.

The monk with the red-face — weather-beaten and raw like skin that had been scrubbed too hard, rather than red from anger — seemed to expect an answer. He stepped forward further until he was staring down at Roger from a few inches away, and the two servants that had walked him to the Chapter house by gripping his arms and half-dragging him along, grabbed them again and held him steady. The monk wasn't going to hit him was he?

"Do you dare?" Spittle lashed Roger's face, but he dared not wipe it away, or reply lest his mouth betray him with a foolish and witty phrase.

"That's enough," said a man, not a monk, who had accompanied the bailiffs with him. "Perhaps Master Roger should be left to think upon his actions for a while here, and then we can return later to speak with him?"

"Your duties are in the town, not the precincts of this Abbey, Haukwake," snapped the red-faced man.

"Town and abbey, another bloodbath awaits ..." mumbled the bent-over monk.

The Abbot looked thoughtful. "We're all too full of ire and excitation. I think John Haukwake has given us a good idea, it would benefit us all to take a moment to reflect. Hugh," he nodded to the red-faced man, "and all the rest of the obedientaries, I would like to see you in my chamber right now, and send for Edmund."

"He's with the bodies," said one of the monks.

"So? The bodies can wait."

"But you know ..."

"This time he will do as I bid," the Abbot said. "Fetch him."

The monks left the Chapter house, and the layman named John Haukwake followed them.

"Not you John," said the Abbot. "Please do your best to calm your fellows in the church and in the marketplace or wherever they have now gathered."

John didn't look pleased, but nodded his acceptance of the Abbot's command, as they walked through the door. Roger was left in the Chapter house, alone with his two guards.

"Hello," Roger said to them. "I don't suppose you saw any peculiar creatures perched on the Abbot's shoulders just then?"

The two servants looked at each other. Roger looked more closely at them. They were the same men that Jake had chased from the ford.

"Oh," said Roger. A large fist slammed into his face and he fell against a wall, blood dripping hot from his nose.

"Oh dear, it looks like you must have tripped. Now keep quiet until they come back," said the servant who had hit him.

ANOTHER LETTER

*Letter is a copy from an original reputedly found in B.L. MSS.
Caligula folio XX. Date unknown and provenance. Assumed to be
forged.*

To my dearest Uncle, John, Duke of Lancaster,

My first letter to you, so please forgive me my style,
which I know will seem childish to you, who are such a
great general and statesman, and used to getting many
fancy letters, I am sure. My clerk offered to help with the
words, but I told him no, I must learn to conduct my own
affairs in the art of letters, as one day I will be the king, so
must learn these things. So he has just written down my
words, and nothing more.

I did, though, have to punish him for writing in French
when it was my intention to write to you in English, the
language of the people that I will one day rule, after my
grandfather and my father, with all thanks be to God for
his recovery. The lashes across my clerks hand will no
doubt heal soon enough.

May I beg you to keep this letter secret from my
mother? She does not know that I have written to you. If
my clerk tells her, then there will be worse than a whipping
for him, but I gave him one of my favourite brooches to

keep his silence, and I think that his love of money will
hold his tongue.

Let me be frank Uncle, I am very worried about my
father. His illness has grown much worse. We all hoped
and prayed that he would begin to get better with the
move back to England and the care of new physicians,
especially the ones you have recommended to my mother
to tend him. But, I have to tell you, she has sent them all
away, and says that he is ailing worse than ever. He has had
the bloody flux every month, which leaves him very weak,
and for the last week has not left his bed at all, and will not
even see me. My mother tries to hide her tears from me,
but I can see that her cheeks are still wet when she comes
from his chamber. She tries to cosset me as if I were still
an infant with kind words and a smile that I know is only
there to hide the truth from me. My father has always been
a man of strength and vigour, and I still remember him so,
although he has been ill for the last five years. He has not
picked me up and swung me about in his strong arms since
I was three. I hope to emulate his bravery one day, and to
be a proper knight, and also to follow your good example,
of course, Uncle.

Uncle, you are the protector of this realm. My
grandfather is in his dotage, and seems to be more
interested in entertainments and games than I, who am a
child, and certainly, I dread to say it, has less seriousness
about him than I do. And my father, his heir, is dying. If I
were scribing this letter with my own hand you would note
a curling to the paper at, as I cannot hold back my tears. I
sit looking out at the Thames flowing past, knowing that
my father is passing along the painful rapids on his last
journey. I write to you in desperation, as you are the only
man with the authority to act against what afflicts him.

My father's illness is no natural disease, nor do I believe
it is, as some say, punishment for his crimes of war.
Limoges is mentioned when he or my mother cannot hear.
The knights of his chamber whisper about that French city

over their wine before I part for my night's rest. You were there, you saw the horror and cruelty of it, they say. Yet you know my father is a good man, a man of good works, of chivalry. Would he be cursed to such suffering for one failing?

Uncle, my father's illness reaches its zenith every month at the same time, as if his body was pulled by the influence of the moon. At that time he bleeds from many orifices and is left weak. This you know perhaps from my mother or from the knights who wait on my father. But I do not think they tell you what he says, when the bleeding is upon him. He talks of a great beast that comes to him, and imagines that this creature is there in the room. I have seen him in that state with my own eyes, and because he was even crying in fear I looked around in terror expecting to see the beast, but I have seen nothing. He tells me once it has gone that the creature has two aspects. At times it comes to him in the guise of a sage of great power, a wise man, noble and true, and tempts him with knowledge of what has been and what will be, and even the power to know all things on earth. My father admits that he is tempted and claims that he is willing to follow the wise man.

He will then try to rise from his sick bed, and it is all my mother and the nurses she sets around him can do to restrain him, for despite his weakened and fevered state, the nightmare that he experiences is so strong that he feels compelled to rise and to follow the old man. Then my father becomes begins to tremble. He tells my mother, who's fair face becomes racked by weeping, that if he does not follow the wise man, the demon will come.

And then he does.

My father begins to describe how the wise man raises his cloaks and turns around and changes into a horned demon, whose skin has been charred and cracked by the fires of hell. The demon does not have wings and is dressed like a warrior, sometimes like a noble king my father says, but also a leader of the legions of hell. The demon snaps at him with huge canine teeth and growls that it will gouge out his innards with his cruel Moorish scimitar. He orders my father to obey or to suffer cruel punishment. In desperation, my mother falls in with his nightmare and asks him what he must do as she holds his arm and a nurse mops his brow.

"Deny the Christ", he says. "He wants me to deny my religion and turn to the old ways, the ways of the pagan Saexon," he tells them. And with this the dream ends and my father's face appears to become calm. But the true physical suffering is only beginning. Blood wells from his nose, from his ears. It flows from his anus and his penis. I hear the nurses whisper it. It is black and thick, and my father turns pale and is like a ghost, asleep and still in his bed for the whole week following.

Uncle, people name your mistress a witch. Yet I am sure you would not do ill to our family, and so I ask this of you from my heart. Can you help us? Can you ask Mistress Swynbourne to help us? Some evil sorcery afflicts my father, and I am sure, on the faith I have, that he has lived a Godly life that such possession cannot be because of his own sins. There are external forces that mean him ill. Please protect him, and protect the realm. I do not know who would want to attack him. Maybe the French or the Scots have sent spies or assassins? Yet I am sure that all of his household are loyal retainers. But do they not say that the devil covers his tracks well. If anyone can help my father, then it is you, whose perspicacity in so many things is well known.

I realise that I am only a boy. But after my father I am the heir to the throne of England and France, and so I must take on responsibility that is perhaps beyond my normal years. But, Uncle, I don't know what to do. I have spoken to my mother, but she has forbidden me to speak of the nature of father's illness outside our house. If she knew that I wrote to you, I know that you she would be wroth, but you have been so kind to us in the past, and I know my mother respects you. Please, Uncle, I look to you to help us now, with whatever you and your lady can conjure to help us.

Written on this day, the year of our lord, 25th of May, 1376

Richard of Bordeaux at Westminster

CHAPTER 9

The door from the church to the cloister was not locked, although Jake felt sure that this would not have been a problem for Isabel even if it had. She had complete confidence in her ability to pass unmolested to wherever she liked. She had changed since Jake had known her. No, perhaps *changed* was the wrong word. She had always been sure of herself, with an inner belief whose burning flame had attracted Jake to her in the first place. But she had grown into that confidence and taken on all the attributes of the first lady of the town.

They passed into the corner of the cloister and took the enclosed path along the eastern side of the courtyard. Jake looked about him in wonder at the intricacy of the stonework and the stained glass details in the large windows that gave a view of a courtyard where a fountain splashed in the middle of a garden. Gravel pathways led across the courtyard, allowing the monks to wander in peaceful contemplation. Some of the Oxford colleges had impressively large cloisters, and this was smaller than those, but none that he had seen were so richly garlanded with carving and decorative work.

Isabel led the way and Jake followed. She set a fast pace and didn't seem interested in talking to Jake, although they could easily have walked side by side and spoken to each other. She nodded at a small group of monks that they passed. The monks acknowledged her and did not seem to think her presence out of place. They were talking amongst themselves as they walked by, probably gossiping about the events in the church, and Jake could hear sniggering as they walked past. He quickly turned his head to look at them. One of them winked at him and nudged his neighbour.

This wasn't the place for it, but he would have loved to have punched the monk in the face.

At the end of the cloister a door opened and a number of monks came out. Jake recognized Abbot Peter amongst them, along with some others who had been senior obedientaries at the Abbey for several years: the Cellarer, the Sacrist, and the Precentor. They walked in the other direction towards the south side of the cloister. Then another man walked through the door. His father, John Haukwake. He smiled as he saw them.

"Husband, I was looking for you," said Isabel. John's smile broadened. He couldn't have seen him, Jake realized. The look of pleasure had been for his young wife. Jake stopped and turned away. There was an opening in the wall of the cloister leading to the courtyard a few steps away. He walked towards it and into the last rays of sun from the spring evening that bathed the courtyard with light. A shiver went through him as he heard his father and the woman he had loved converse.

"Isabel, you are so good in these situations. Can you come with me to the church and help gather the people together, we must soothe them. Perhaps you can gather your women together — your company of good women."

Jake slowly walked towards the fountain at the centre of the courtyard. Isabel had not realized that he no longer followed her, and that he could overhear them talk together, hear what it was like between them, and hope that what they had together was not love.

"Of course, husband. Has anything happened? What of the man that you took away?"

"He's nothing to do with it; don't be frightened, he's not a necromancer."

"Someone is."

He had heard enough. Jake walked up to the fountain and put his hands in the water. It was cool and he drank from it and bathed his face. He looked at his reflection in the water. Hair unkempt, cheeks jowly with fat and unshaven, halfway between smooth-skinned and bearded. Who could blame the Isabel's of this world — he was somewhere between a youth with prospects and an old man of wealth, but the truth was he had no chance of the latter, and had been deluding himself to think he was ever the former.

"Hey villein, get your hands out of there," shouted a monk who approached from the far side of the cloister. He was old, but walked fast and didn't seem to need the stick that he brandished in the air at Jake.

"Sorry, father, I was just cooling my face."

"This isn't a public washing place, go and join the old crones down by the mill-pond if you want to wash your maggoty skin." The monk held the walking stick up as one might brandish a quarterstaff. Jake shook his hands.

"I'm sorry, I'm just going."

He turned and felt the staff push into his back. "Get on with you, out of here."

He turned round and grabbed the end of the staff. The stubborn monk held onto it, which was worse for him as it allowed Jake to lever him to the floor and then twist the staff from his grip, hurting the monk's wrists as he did so. The man yowled in pain. Jake flung the staff away and sat astride the man as he had seen wrestlers do on saint's days. The monk looked terrified and raised his sore hands to cover his face.

"Murder!" screamed the monk.

"Shut up," whispered Jake and slapped the man's hands aside and clenched his hand over the monk's mouth. He was too feeble to resist and Jake kept slapping the man's hands away in order to keep his other hand firmly over the monk's mouth.

But he couldn't sit astride the monk forever. He was in the middle of the Abbey cloister, there would be other monks and servants passing. He'd better think of something.

And then *boom!* He was knocked sideways off the monk and onto the path, the fall jarring his shoulder, but he didn't have time to think about that as the man who had tackled him rolled over and over and pinned him on his stomach on the ground. Jake was used to these sort of blind-siding tackles from football, but usually the intention wasn't too keep you on the ground after, just to grab the ball off you and carry it away as fast as possible. The man sitting on his back wasn't moving in a hurry.

"He tried to murder me," shouted the monk, coughing. Jake could turn his head enough to see the monk clutching at his throat and gasping.

"I never touched your throat, if I did you'd be dead now!" shouted Jake.

The man on his back pushed his face hard into the gravel and the small pieces of stone dug painfully into his face. Jake closed his eyes and tasted dust and stone in his mouth, which he tried to spit out.

Then he heard Isabel close by, shouting, pleading. "John, get off him, it's your son! There's no murder intended here. It's Jake."

The man sitting on his back stopped pushing him into the gravel and released his hold on him. He felt the man's weight lift from his back.

"Jake?" said his father, now standing above him.

Jake didn't want to turn over. He wished he could just get and up and keep running or find a hole to climb into.

What a way for the prodigal son to return. He hadn't wanted it to be like this.

But he had to move. He sat up into a crouch, dusted himself off and then stood up, still not turning to look at his father. Out of the corner of his vision he saw Isabel whisper into the ear of the belligerent Benedictine, and then, with a worried backward glance at John she supported the monk as they walked away. The monk looked like he was milking it for all he was worth.

His father held up his arms and walked towards him when he did turn round. Jake stood there looking the man who had come to hate in the eyes. There were tears! Had he learnt to act from Isabel as well?

His father tried to embrace him, but Jake shrugged his broad shoulders and stepped aside.

"Do you deny me?" said his father. "I can't believe you have returned, it is my dream come true."

"Don't make me laugh. You wish that I was dead. I am sure my being here is a major inconvenience to you."

"Jake, no. Son, I let us make the kiss of peace and forget the past. Forgive and forget eh?"

"How very convenient for you to forget after all that you did?" said Jake.

"Me? You tried to kill me and your mother."

"My mother! Isabel should have been my wife."

John Haukwake slapped Jake hard across the face. The blow stung, but he stood his ground.

"You're old enough to be her father. Aren't you ashamed of yourself?" No effect. His father stood there. Perhaps he was thinking about hitting Jake again.

"I bet she has a younger lover already father, someone to give her what she needs."

That did it. He father put his head down and charged him like an angry bull. Jake let him knock him to the ground, but he let himself be pushed further and rolled over as he landed. He jumped to his feet and kicked out at his father nearly connecting with his ribs, but the old man managed to get his arms in the way, and Jake's boot hit his forearms instead.

"What's going?" someone shouted. Jake circled round his father who was still on the ground clutching his sore arm. There had been a definite hard cracking sound when Jake's boot had gone in, maybe he had broken the old bastard's bone. He wouldn't be putting it around Isabel in a hurry.

He could see two men, not monks, perhaps servants or townspeople, walk into the courtyard. They were armed with bills. It was two of the men from the ford.

"It's you, the caitiff from this afternoon." Jake felt for his sword, but Roger had made him take it off when they entered the church. The two men saw him search in vain for it and smiled.

"Not so brave now?"

"I hope you don't come quietly, my bill would love to chop you up, you fucking cunt."

Jake felt a lump in his throat.

"Put down your weapons, lads." John had risen from the ground and still clutched his arm, but he spoke with authority to the two thugs. "This man deserves a good beating, but only the sort of punishment that a child would get, he's not man enough for a real fight. Take him to his master in the Chapterhouse."

John Haukwake turned to his son. "I hope you are done fighting. I don't want to see you hurt, but these men will hurt you if I command it. We'll speak again when you stop acting like a baby." Haukwake turned and strode from the cloister.

CHAPTER 10

Roger looked up at the open door of the Chapterhouse, and for a moment thought about leaving. His entrance into St. Brett's had been ignominious by any standards, but he never expected to be imprisoned for it.

"I only reacted to what I saw," he said to himself.

"The truth is not universal. It depends upon the view from where you stand." The voice was familiar enough. Ashenden!

"Where are you?" Roger looked around but couldn't see his tutor's ghost.

"Oh, I took the liberty of floating up here, so as not to disturb you, young sir. I've been watching you all day."

Roger looked up and saw the ethereal shade of Ashenden with one arm wrapped around a saint's statue high in the arched roof of the Chapterhouse.

"You've been with me all day?"

"Well since you arrived in St. Brett's. The Abbot was a good friend and I find the Abbey most welcoming. It was good of you to invite me along."

"I invited you?"

"In a manner of speaking. I'm sure you said it would be useful to have my advice in the future didn't you? So here I am."

·

"I don't remember saying that," said Roger. "Look here comes Jake and those horrid guards, probably come to beat me up again."

"The pen is mightier than the sword," said the ghost of Ashenden.

"Shut up. Don't make me say something stupid like you did with the warden. This lot will probably kill me."

"Alright then, quiet as a mouse," whispered Ashenden in what to Roger sound like a very sarcastic tone.

Jake entered, but the guards didn't. They shut the door with a slam, and Roger heard a key turning in the door.

"Well another fine mess we're in, and even deeper in the shit than I thought," said Jake. Roger didn't like the way his servant was looking at him.

"It's not all my fault you know," he said to Jake.

"Well it is really, because if you hadn't reacted like that in the church you wouldn't have been accused of some sort of sorcery, and we wouldn't be locked up in here."

"What was that hue and cry outside? You look injured, what happened?"

Jake's lower lip jutted out and he folded his arms. "Nothing," he said.

"What happened? Did you get into a fight with those guards? They were from the ford. I wouldn't be surprised if they wanted to even the score. You cause trouble for us by starting fights against the odds. They weren't outlaws. They're servants of the Abbey, paid to guard and protect the Abbey's property. They had every right to stop those serfs running off."

"What because people are property, too? So you're sticking with your own kind, the lords who live off the misery of others, when it comes down to it."

"He's touchy isn't he?" whispered Ashenden from above very loudly.

Roger looked up and glared, but resisted the temptation to bite on the ghost's bait.

"I heard a woman's voice outside talking to the man you said was your father, John Haukwake. Was that ...?"

"Yes." Jake walked over and sat on one of the stone seats that lined the wall of the Chapterhouse. It was indented in the wall and he lifted up his legs and braced himself in the enclosure. He closed his eyes. *Pretending to be asleep*, thought Roger. *He doesn't want to talk to me anymore, he thought. Perhaps best if I don't tell him that she came in here then.*

She had come after the guards had rushed to investigate the noise of fighting from the cloister. Roger had seen her walk past with an elderly monk a few moments before and she had glanced in. When the guards left, she returned alone.

"Master Roger, isn't it? How are you feeling now?" she had asked.

"Uh, much better," he had said, not knowing what else to say. He actually felt awful. His head was throbbing and his sinuses felt like a wire brush was scraping through them, but somehow he didn't think that was the right thing to say to this beautiful woman.

She came over and sat next to him and laid her hand on his, turned it over, looked at the palm and then into his eyes, and touched his brow with her other hand, leaving it pressed against his forehead for several seconds. "Yes, I can feel that you are much eased."

"Um, thank you for helping me earlier, I'm not sure what came over me," said Roger. He couldn't draw his eyes from her face. Her skin was a perfect white like ivory carved to perfection by an Italian sculptor, yet her lips were too protuberant for an Italian painter's ideal of feminine beauty: they were red and full and jutted forward from her face as if swollen with blood.

He longed to kiss those lips.

And he longed to explore her hair with his hands, deep chestnut with rivulets of gold running through it. Were they coloured that way or natural he wondered? He had never seen anything like it.

But what he would remember always were her eyes. Large, with clearly defined whites that seemed to match the ivory of her skin except they were divided from her face by elegant arches of coal black (make-up no doubt), and in the centre, lapping the deep black of her pupils were wide irises of dark rich green, not muddied or streaked with other shades, but solid thick rings of colour the shade of an evergreen leaf.

"I'm glad you are feeling better. I must go," she announced. And with that she was gone, quick steps took her through the door, seemingly not restricted by the long dress she wore, or the demands on most women of gentle birth to walk with grace and meekness. She dressed as a noble might, with rich silks, furs, and jewels, but, Roger realized, she was a commoner, the wife of a burgess only and not even on the lowest rank of gentleness.

His uncles wouldn't approve, would they? 'Diluting the blood' they would call it. Although half of them had their doxies from among the common servants, that was well known, but he didn't like that. They used those women and then threw them away. That wasn't right. Besides, this woman was married, and she was older than him, so what were the chances? She didn't seem that much older, but Jake, in his mid-thirties, was nearly middle-aged, and had told him that she was his same age.

Yet if he did marry a commoner then that would destroy his uncles' plans for him twofold. He would be ineligible for the priesthood and it would annoy them that he had gone against their will. The future could be brighter for him than he thought. He could marry Isabel and then when he published his work based on his findings in St. Brett's, there would be no lack of rich patrons clamouring to fund him. Maybe he wouldn't find them in England, but perhaps in Italy? The Duke of Milan was said to be very interested in the occult.

It was getting dark. Not much light came through the stained glass windows of the Chapterhouse, and they had been left without any other means of light. Roger started to drift asleep. A hand shaking his shoulder woke him.

"Where?" muttered Roger.

Jake stood over him. "The Abbot wants to see you; he sent a novice to fetch us," he said jerking his thumb over his shoulder to where a young boy dressed in a monk's habit and with tonsured hair stood waiting by the door. "I guess that means we're not a threat anymore."

Roger saw dampness glisten on Jake's face below red-rimmed eyes. He raised his hand to touch Jake's face, and began to speak: "Have you been ...?"

"No," Jake turned away before Roger could touch his face. Guilt flooded Roger's belly as he remembered the thoughts he had harboured for Isabel. What sort of person coveted his friend's lady?

The Abbot was staring out of his solar window when they entered, looking out into the darkness of late evening. Roger could glimpse stars above in the night sky. On a clear night like this he should be out observing.

"Master Roger," said the Abbot. "Please accept my apologies for earlier. Your rather unconventional entrance to the Abbey together with the highly excitable state of some of our Brotherhood was perhaps a bad combination."

"So you're not angry with me?" asked Roger. He heard Jake click his tongue. Had he said something wrong?

The Abbot was all smiles and strode over to embrace Roger warmly. "You must forgive me. Of all the monks, I perhaps am the most agitated. The events that have necessitated your coming have been hard for me."

"Stopped the flow of pilgrims, patrons and money," said the voice of Ashenden from above Roger's head. *"Poor Peter. You were my friend, but you did love money — and for its own sake — most of the time."*

Roger resisted reacting to the ghost's words, yet he did not doubt them to be accurate. The Abbot himself wore a rich, fur-lined cloak to protect against the evening chill, and Roger noticed some fine rings on his fingers. His solar, one of his many private apartments in the self-contained Abbot's house, was furnished with finely worked furniture, magnificent tapestries portraying hunting scenes, and finely woven carpets to keep the chill from one's feet.

"It's better that we speak alone, without all of the obedientaries here. The shadow of suspicion has fallen on some of them and clouded their judgement," said the Abbot. "That's why you received a less than courteous welcome."

"We noticed that," said Jake.

The Abbot glared at Jake. "You can send your servant to prepare your room in the guesthouse, perhaps, or check on your horses," he said.

"My servant?" said Roger, feeling a bit lost.

"He means me," said Jake, who tugged his hood further down to hide his face.

The Abbot now glared at Roger; perhaps his pleasant manner was to be only short-lived. Had he done something else wrong? "Jake can stay here with me. We have very few things to unpack, and besides, he helps me to remember things. I'm always forgetting the odd detail you know. His mind is like a sponge, never loses a drop of memory."

The Abbot didn't laugh at his attempted joke. "So he's your clerk then? I thought he was a bodyguard, or perhaps a stable-hand."

"Jake fills multiple roles," said Roger. "I have a cook at my rooms in Oxford, but otherwise Jake tends to do just about everything."

The Abbot fidgeted with a cup and jug and drank deeply for a moment. He looked again at Jake. "I really don't know how you manage with just the one, but I suppose the College takes care of some things as well." To Jake he said, "Do I know you?"

"No, you don't," said Jake.

"You look like someone I used to know though," said the Abbot, stroking his chin.

"Memories come slowly to the Abbot," remarked Ashenden's ghost from on high.

"Somebody's son, perhaps. I would swear you're an older version of some boy I taught when I ran the grammar school here? Here, take off your hood, let me have a look at you."

"I would rather not," said Jake. "I have scars from the pox you see, and …"

"I would like to get started tonight with a few questions for some of the monks who might have experienced the possessions," Roger interrupted. He was worried that the Abbot's memories were about to make the situation more uncomfortable for Jake. "You mentioned in your letter that the Abbey has tried to exorcise the demons from those afflicted. Could I speak to the priest who carried out the exorcisms?"

"Oh, yes, of course. I'm anxious for you to start right away," said the Abbot. "But where to begin?"

"What about with today's events. That was quite a remarkable introduction to the problems that you have here. I have never seen anything of the like before," said Roger.

"I would like to be able to say the same thing, but we have become all too used to such occurrences in the last months."

"He looks older than his years," said Ashenden's ghost, which had now floated down next to the Abbot and laid a spectral hand in sympathy on Abbot Peter's shoulder. The Abbot shivered.

"It's cold in here. Let us sit by the fire." Abbot Peter pointed Roger to a chair by the fire, and seated himself opposite. There wasn't a seat for Jake. "There is a bench by that table. Do you mind?" asked the Abbot. Jake nodded and fetched the bench and sat next to and slightly behind where Roger sat, perhaps not wanting to draw too much attention to himself again, Roger thought.

The Abbot did look weary. The fire in his belly from earlier had died. They sat quietly for a while as the Abbot warmed his hands in front of the fire. It was a cold evening outside, but in the Abbot's comfortable rooms it was as hot as hell. Roger was sweating from the heat. Ashenden's ghost had gone for the moment, Roger realized. It was a distraction that he could do without.

"So," said Roger, breaking the silence. "What happened today is not an unusual occurrence in St. Brett's, then?"

The Abbot scowled. Roger's heart sunk, had he awoken the man's ire again? "Yes, very astute of you, we are indeed beset by demons and witches. For some reason my town and Abbey have become the most Godforsaken nest of witches and demons in England, if not all Christendom."

"Perhaps, a little harsh ..."

"No, that's just what the Abbot of Westminster wrote in his last letter to me. Now the pilgrims don't even stop here, they just carry straight onto Westminster. Very fortunate for the, isn't it."

"Do you think the monks of Westminster are to blame?" asked Jake.

Roger's heart leapt to his throat, but the Abbot no longer seemed to care whether or not Jake's involvement in the conversation of his social betters was impertinent or not.

"No, no. I don't believe my brothers in Christ would unleash witches and evil spirits upon us, but I think they are happy to see the rumours begin to quietly spread that our masses are not the safest place for the salvation of souls. The secret is out, and I fear that by midsummer all will know. I have already received letters from the King and John of Gaunt questioning my lack of attendance at Parliament. They want as many lords temporal and spiritual in attendance as possible, I understand. But how can I leave with the Abbey in this state?"

"Can you tell us more about what has happened? In your letter you state that the possessions began at the opening of the year."

"That's how it seemed to me, although the Sacrist will swear that there had been possessions before then."

"He was the monk who kept trying to interrupt you when we spoke earlier?"

"Was he? I didn't really notice, although for a sacrist he's hardly able to project his voice very well. One of my predecessors was fond of mechanics. Perhaps he should have created a voice-trumpet or some such marvellous device that could project his voice better in the church?"

"Shouldn't be the sacrist then if he can't lead you prayer, should he?" asked Jake. Roger turned to look at Jake and raised an eyebrow.

"The position's paid for, and he does know his scripture very well. He gives a very thoughtful presentation of psalms and readings I always think."

Jake shook his head. "Typical," he whispered.

"So what did you notice first?" asked Roger.

"Looking back on it now, I noticed that on the day of Christ's mass that things were not quite right. There was a lack of goodwill in the air. Too many arguments and bad blood. There was even blood spilt. Someone had opened their shop and was trading. Not just food or ale, which would be acceptable, but best woollens. Another trader didn't like it, thought it was unfair, and they came to sharp words and sharper blades followed. The victim was buried the next day, and the murderer is in our gaol awaiting the oyer and terminer judge to come."

"That doesn't sound too devilish," said Roger.

"Especially, between the burgesses of this place," said Jake under his breath.

"You've had some dealings with them then?" said the Abbot, addressing Jake. "You'll know, then, how quick they are to dispute and eager to take up weapons either amongst each other, or their rightful lord."

"Only by reputation," said Jake, nodding.

"On its own it doesn't sound too strange, but these two men who came to blows had been the best of friends before, never a cross word spoken; then suddenly they were worst enemies. The one who did the murder, the one who opened his shop, was most God-fearing. I was very surprised that he even contemplated doing such a thing."

"What was his name?" asked Jake. Roger thought about giving Jake his chair, he seemed to be leading the enquiry now.

"You need the commoner to aid you, young Sotil, so don't be jealous of his insights," said Ashenden, looking solemnly at Roger from where he had now appeared floating beside the Abbot. Roger bit his lip and bowed his head, wringing his hands.

"Yes, tell us his name, would you Abbot. A full list of those involved is imperative," said Roger. He wouldn't be outdone by his servant. Perhaps the Abbot was right and Jake should be seeing to his room and making sure their horses were fed and watered, rather than sitting here as if he was their equal.

"Yes, of course, he was a draper by the name of Thomas Merys. The name of the man killed was Michael Bradshawe."

"Thank you," said Roger, feeling more in control of proceedings. "You said that Christmas was the start of things, what did it lead to?"

"The main occurrences occurred on New Year's Eve," said the Abbot. "There was the usual revelry amongst the people of the town, feasting, too much drinking, dancing, as you might expect, but — and I only have the word of others for this..."

"Who?" asked Jake.

"Reputable persons. Our bailiff John Haukwake and his wife Isabel gave the most detailed reports to me the next morning, but there were others, too. The cellarer had been present, and some of the novices."

"Oh really, did your monks enjoy the dancing and the drinking?" asked Jake.

"The discipline of my monks and their activities has nothing to do with this question, and is not something for you or your master to concern yourselves upon. Be assured, though, that the matter was dealt with properly."

Roger turned and glared at Jake. What was he doing?

"Although perhaps their debauchery was a sign of sinfulness brought on by demons, Maybe some of the monks are infected by these possessions," said Jake.

"I don't think so," said the Abbot. "Only those of weaker spirit would be affected. None of my brothers have been possessed, I can guarantee that."

"In which cases have you thought that these possessions might not be real?" said Jake. "What if the burgesses are playing you? I wouldn't put it past the likes of Haukwake, or the others, to come up with some such plan to improve their position."

"Haukwake? He's loyal to the Abbey."

"That's what you think," said Jake. "He plays both sides, but he's only out for himself."

"You said something happened on New Year's Eve," Roger interjected.

"A brave attempt, but much too late to take control of the situation," said Ashenden's ghost.

The Abbot rose from his chair and walked over to Jake. "I thought I recognized you and now I remember the insolent manner of speaking that had Haukwake's boy expelled after only a term."

"I can't deny it. I am John Haukwake's son. No doubt it's been told already how I came to a disagreement with my father earlier in your cloister, so I'll not try to hide it. I have no connection to him now, but I do know what he is. And I know, from my own experience, that he is only interested in what will gain him advantage. So I warn you: beware."

"Nevertheless, young Haukwake …" said the Abbot, and was about to continue but Jake rudely interrupted him.

"Don't call me Haukwake. That name is nothing to me now. My name is Jake Savage, and that's all."

"Jake, perhaps it would be best if you went now," said Roger.

"He should stay, Master Sotil," said the Abbot. "I can see that you work as a pair. Sotil and Savage, how very apt. Your man here is astute. I remember that from when he was my pupil. He could have studied, made something of himself — a priest or lawyer perhaps — or followed in his father's steps as a merchant. But there was ever a wild side to you, Jake, too governed by your feelings rather than your soul or any rational mind. I had heard that you had returned and that your welcome for your father was less than familial."

"I didn't want to come back," said Jake, "and I didn't want to fight with my father. I don't want to see him again."

"I care nothing for you and your father's relationship, as long as it does not hinder the mission of your Master and the finding of a solution to our problem. Keep out of the way of Haukwake is my advice. And the rest of his household. It would be unwise to let temptation lead you into more foolishness."

"Yes Abbot," said Jake bowing his head, sounding meek for the first time that Roger could remember.

"Let us talk of more important things. I will tell you what happened after Christmas."

CHAPTER 11

There was the usual mummery, starting off with feasting in
the various taverns and amongst friends. The frivolity
started after lunch with processions of those mummers
wearing masks travelling around the principal streets of the
town, delivering their presents and playing games with
their hosts, who were bound to give presents in return.

We monks of course had sung our masses as usual and
asked God for his blessing in the coming year. We
celebrated St. Sylvester, and there was perhaps a slightly
richer array of food available in the refectory that day, and
some wine, but we made no special celebration for New
Year's Eve. We had to prepare ourselves for the Feast of
the Circumcision of our Lord on the first of January, while
the revelry in the town and all over this country went on.

I'm sure you, Jake, were celebrating that night, from the
grimace you just made. I remember that you were always
one for a drink and a fight if the mood caught you.

Now you'd best calm yourself during the tale I tell you,
because some of it you won't like, I know that already, so
don't interject or I'll never get through it. You will keep
quiet? Good. I don't order you, even though I should, but
even though you're this man's servant, you will never

know your rightful station. You weren't born to be anyone's servant, were you? I'll not question that now, although Roger, I counsel you to think hard on it and take heed of how you govern your household.

I have been accused of governing either with a rod of iron or with too much kindness by all of the obedientaries of St. Brett's since I began my guidance of our community. Yet until this year, I believe, the town and the Abbey have been in relative peace and we have had prosperity. Your father, Jake, has been responsible for much of this. His counsel is measured amongst his fellows and responsive to the wants of both I as his lord, and those he must police and live amongst and do business with.

Put away your judgment, young Haukwake. I don't expect you to agree.

Yet the same cannot be said of your father's wife, Isabel. She produced mixed emotions amongst the townspeople. Among some of the women she was revered. She helped them with cures and the sort of make-believe that women delight in — love potions and the like. But the men always distrusted her, not I think for the magic that they think she practices, but because she taught their wives how to talk back. For these women, it was as if God's natural order was turned on its head. Isabel encouraged them to look for freedom and even to rule within their households. Yet I never saw Isabel order John around, so I did often wonder whether Isabel was trying to stir up trouble. Though apart from some mutterings amongst the husbands, I must admit that no evil seemed to come from her teachings.

That night was a terrible one for her. It started when one of Haukwake's servants came to me and requested that I attend to John. The servant would not tell me where we went, but lead me to a lane in the shambles. A fire burnt there, but not a normal bonfire of celebration. On top of the flames was a figure draped with a dress and fabric that was meant to be hair. Around about it stood men and some women, all masked. They chanted "Burn the witch, burn the Good Woman!" They could only mean Isabel. I wanted to summon men from the Abbey to stop this, but the servant tugged on my sleeve and took me to a storehouse off the main street. That is where I found John and Isabel and the rest of their household, hiding. Isabel was in tears and John was burning with anger. He told me that a child had been found murdered and that the people who burnt the effigy of Isabel had accused her of the crime. I was outraged, but there was little we could do.

I had John, Isabel and their servants taken to the Abbey for protection and I sent my servants out to try to calm the rioters. But to little avail. The town seemed to go mad that night. Several shops were burnt down in the chaos, and I count ourselves lucky that no attempt was made to attack the Abbey. But it seemed that the townsfolk were more intent on a madness directed at themselves and each other. There was anger at the death, as was understandable, but it had turned to a frenzy. I only have the evidence of what I saw from the gatehouse and what some of my servants observed. Many of the people kept their animal masks on, and they acted much like animals. Some bounded along on all fours and made animal sounds, others chased each other and fought, wrestling on the ground. Others, who appeared to have some sort of contrived wings on their backs, were even seen to leap from upper windows of houses in the imitation of birds, but they screeched high-pitched as if they were bats. I know not of what happened to them, but no deaths were reported the next day apart from the child's.

My servants say that they thought demons possessed the people. They saw tails under their coats and real wings sprouted from their backs. I did not see this, but my servants swear to it, so what can I believe? It was more than drink and anger that turned the town to madness that night.

The next day I was much afeared for the safety of
Haukwake and his family. I sent servants out to gauge the
feeling in the town, but the deputy bailiff Lovell reported
that those who had accused Isabel had been spoken to and
accepted that Isabel could not have done it. She had been
seen elsewhere at a feast the whole time. There was
sadness and anger simmering underneath, and a veiled
suspicion, but little else, so John and Isabel went back to
their home.

We looked into the murder of the child, but we were
unable to find much more about it. The records are in the
court files if you wish to look at them.

I hoped that would be the end of it.

But the murders continued. A child taken from one of
the town's families and no apparent culprit to blame. Each
time there was ritual involved in the killing. A circle had
been drawn around the body and strange marks made on
the flesh of the child in ash and blood.

I see that you grimace, and yes, that has been the most
horrible part of it. But what concerns me are the episodes
of madness amongst the townsfolk. There are whispers of
witches being amongst them. Many a night we hear
shouting and howling on the wind. But when we send men
to investigate there is nothing there. And there have been
cases of people falling down and in fits as if possessed.
And then there will be evidence of possession and the very
destruction of the person by the demon inside it, as you
saw today. There have only been a few cases as bad as that
one, but when they happen the whole town is thrown into
alarm. I fear we cannot contain tales of these things for
much longer.

CHAPTER 12

Roger glanced over at Jake, who sat there shaking his head. He surely had to believe in demons now, after what the Abbot had just told them? But Jake was Jake, and as stubborn sometimes as a mule asked to carry a knight in armour on the Sabbath. He would dig his heels in and refuse to budge from his position until he had seen something with his own eyes.

Be that as it may, now he, Roger, had a proper breakout of demons to observe, record, and investigate. The Abbot expected him somehow to stop these creatures of hell. He doubted he was capable of that, but hoped that if they were properly catalogued, it could help with some sort of resolution. If there was fire, then there was usually a cause; someone with a match had started the thing, and if they could find them then they could stop this. Roger didn't think common burgesses could have thought all this up. There had to be a necromancer at work somewhere bringing these spirits into being. But who? It would have to be an educated man, and that surely meant a monk in this small market town, where the concerns of the population seemed to consist solely of making money and getting drunk.

The townspeople, in their ignorance, had turned their suspicions on the beautiful Isabel; but if she was engaged in magic then surely it was only of the natural kind, the finding of remedies for illnesses for example — the home-spun cures that had always been the proper realm of peasant women all over England. Yet would it be so impossible to believe that she might be capable of more dangerous enchantments? She seemed to have cast a spell over Jake and his father both.

Roger was worried about Jake. This was his town, and these were his people, and it seemed that both his father and his ex-lover were mixed up in this mess. But would he step in to help them? Roger doubted it, especially if he denied the presence of the evil spirits in the first place. He had heard him snorting and huffing with incredulity all through the Abbot's tale. Yet he had been interested in pursuing the enquiry earlier, and indeed had interfered too much in Roger's discussions with the Abbot. He must find a way to use Jake to his best effect in the coming days and weeks that this investigation would surely take.

The Abbot had concluded his tale and offered them both more wine. A servant came and poured and Jake accepted a cup. Roger waved the servant away.

"Lord Abbot, thank you for sharing your experiences. I have a number of ideas of how to progress this investigation."

"That's good, that's why you're here. I hope I have chosen the right person."

"Probably not," commented Ashenden's ghost from above.

"Well yes, of course you have. There are a number of things that I would like to do. Firstly, and in no particular order, I would need to speak to those possessed."

"Yes of course, that can be arranged; the ones that are still alive, anyway."

"And the ones who are dead? I saw that one of the monks ordered the removal of the bodies from the church this morning. What was that for?"

"Our Infirmarer, Edmund, has been examining all those afflicted before their remains are buried in their parishes."

"Is he a surgeon?" asked Roger. "Has he conducted a full autopsy?"

"I don't follow what you say. I am no student of Galen, but I believe he has been looking for certain marks on their bodies. Any evidence of tampering by a necromancer or signs that might indicate that the way of the devil was eased in entering them."

"That's interesting. I had never considered the medical aspect of possessions before. Perhaps it is possible that some people are more physically prone to letting in demons, as you say, than others."

"More prone to madness and fancies, mayhaps," muttered Jake.

"As I say, I don't know the details of his work, and from what I hear, he has not uncovered conclusive evidence. He, like you, fancies himself a new Aristotle it seems, and insists on the further collection of data."

"Aristotle be damned. Listen to me young Sotil what the Abbot needs now is quick action not navel gazing," said Ashenden's ghost.

"A compromise," Roger sneered at the ghost.

"Compromise?" asked the Abbot, somewhat puzzled. "I want answers, you can both collect more data and evidence afterwards once these demons have gone away for good."

"Well, I will need to speak to the Infirmarer," said Roger. "But who else? You mentioned the Precentor had been leading the attempts to exorcise the demons from those hosts still alive."

"Maybe those who suffer and live should be treated by the Infirmarer. Don't they need healing as well?" asked Jake.

"Suffer?" said the Abbot. "Yes they do suffer, but they cannot be healed until the demon is out. Would you give succour to the devil, young Haukwake?"

Jake was hardly young, thought Roger.

"So what happens to those who live?" asked Jake.

"Well," the Abbot looked uncomfortable like he was about to pass wind. "It's difficult to know who they are sometimes, but if they are caught and can be detained, and are not masked..."

"Masked?" Roger asked.

"Like on New Year's Eve, the witches wear grotesque masks, the heads of animals, skins, and skulls covered in cloth to hide their faces when the gather for their rites. If they can be detained, or perhaps if their family alerts us, or if, by some miracle, they come to us of their free will, then the Precentor is our exorcist and he has been trying his best."

"To little effect no doubt," said Jake.

"He's not had any success, I agree. He tries hard and can put together a good service, but I suspect his soul is not strong enough to counter the forces of darkness. He is a timid man," said the Abbot. "I would look for someone else to replace him, but a good exorcist is hard to find in my experience, so that is why I rely on you Master Sotil — at least you profess to openly study the subject."

"Perhaps there are no good exorcists out there because these sorts of possessions, no matter what the Church says, just don't happen. It's just another way of keeping people in their place," said Jake.

"You will keep attacking the Church won't you!" said the Abbot. "I thought once your father was a Lollard until he helped start the Brotherhood, but perhaps I confused the father with the infant. I am getting sick of your abuse, young Haukwake."

"Lord Abbot," Roger interrupted with a sharp look at Jake, "my servant will keep quiet from now on. He meant nothing by it. Look on it as merely the ranting of the common man. One hears it more and more in these times of hardship. But I would like to return to his question, because he raises a good point: why are there no similar occurrences? Why are these things happening in England alone?"

The Abbot scowled, but then shrugged. "Very well then, I will let it lie with regards to your servant." Jake crossed his arms, but said nothing. "Just make sure he is quiet in my presence from now on," the Abbot continued. "And as to why there no other reports of demons reported in England? Well isn't that obvious? Who would want it known? I suspect other prelates, less lenient than I, simply have the afflicted people murdered or imprisoned. They say only the saintly can cast out a devil, but how many saints do we have in these days of sin? None, I think. Our only hope is to ask for help from the saints we do have, such as our own St. Brett."

The meeting with the Abbot ended. There was nothing more to say, and Roger was grateful to be getting Jake out of the monk's presence. As they were led away from the Abbot's chambers by a novice monk to their quarters in the guesthouse, Roger thought to admonish Jake.

"Can't you keep quiet?"

"Me, keep quiet? If you had kept your mouth shut in the church in the first place we wouldn't have had all these problems this afternoon."

Quid pro quo.

They walked on in silence until they reached the guesthouse. They were both tired and didn't feel much like talking, but when they got to their rooms, Jake stretched and turned to Roger.

"I'll let you take a look at the bodies if you like while I clean up in here," he said. The room was tidy and basic from what Roger could tell.

"I suppose, or perhaps I will search out the Precentor first."

"Don't fancy poking round in the innards of witches then?" said Jake.

"Not particularly. You don't want to come?"

"No. Once I'm finished here, I'll be doing what all commoners do."

"What?"

"Getting drunk."

Roger frowned. He didn't relish the thought of looking at dead bodies. That was one of the reasons he had shied away from the prospect of studying medicine. Seeking out the Precentor did seem the better option. The timid monk had rather differing opinions on matters than the Abbot, so perhaps a new perspective might be useful.

"Where will I find you if I need you?" he asked Jake.

"Either getting drunk in the New Inn, or getting really drunk and into a fight in the Pilgrim's Rest."

"What's the difference?"

"The New Inn used to be my tavern, so I'll at least respect the furnishings and probably just get a bit sentimental; but the Pilgrim's Rest is my father's place, so anything might happen."

Roger shook his head sadly and went on his way.

CHAPTER 13

The Abbot hadn't told Roger that he had the freedom to roam the Abbey precinct at will, but he assumed that must be the case, otherwise how else might he be able to carry out his investigations? He would just go about his business and if anyone challenged him then he would remind them that he was on the Abbot's business. He wished though that Jake was coming with him, but he had left their room in the guesthouse and gone straight to the tavern.

He had never imagined as part of his vocation of scientific discovery that he would be engaged in what was, in effect, a criminal investigation. Or was this covered by canon law? Probably both, he reflected, as he left his room having gathered up a slate for making notes and also a lens in case the heavens above were clear for investigation and he could perhaps squeeze in an hour of observing the skies in the cloister's garden. Human interaction was not something that he felt very comfortable with. Jake was different, he didn't feel awkward around him, but no one else understood him. He always felt stilted and ill at ease when talking to others about his theories and his latest sightings. Some of the other academics at Oxford showed interest in the scholars he mentioned, but it was obvious that, even if they had read Ptolemy or Adelard of Bath, they had not thought deeply on those matters. He was at present the only Master dedicated to the study of Astronomy at Oxford, and the role was a lonely one. He had to bite his lip every time he heard that another Master had lectured to the undergraduates in the Arts Faculty on the orbit of the moon or the Alfonsine tables, for he knew that the lecturing would be cursory at best.

But hardly anyone attended his lectures. According to Jake, who had been good enough to sit in one of them, it had something to do with his delivery. He tended to go off at tangents he told him, not stick to the point, and too often became involved in the minutiae of things. The students just wanted to get the degrees that would give them access to a well-paid job, usually in the clergy.

So how was he to investigate the doings of people rather than the perambulation of stars? And, even worse how would he learn to put somebody to the question? That sounded more like a job for a lawyer or judge than an academic, or one of the Church's inquisitors in Italy, France and Spain. Never in his short academic career had he had the chance of conducting an examination with a student, as none of them had stayed long enough in his lectures to qualify for him to ask them questions. Ashenden and Jake were perhaps the only people he had ever spoken to at length since he had left home, and he felt there must be something rather special about both of them to put up with him — one of them being a ghost and the other a drunk couldn't be the only reason? How was he to eke the truth out of people he didn't even know, people who would also be averse to answering his questions and might well question his authority to ask in the first place?

Perhaps the best way was to not think on it. Besides the Precentor had seemed like a mild-mannered enough man when they had met in the Chapterhouse earlier, and even willing to help. Hadn't he been openly questioning the Abbot's version of events? He had implied that things were worse than the Abbot had said. Surely he'd be happy to speak to Roger?

Roger didn't know whether to knock when he reached the door of the library. The porter at the guesthouse had informed him that the Precentor habitually worked in the library until late, and if he was not there then he would be asleep. The porter turned out to be the same servant that had guarded the gate to the Abbey on their arrival that afternoon, and Roger had nervously looked around for the giant toad that had earlier hung from his neck, but was relieved not to spy it. Had he been dreaming, or was this man no longer possessed?

The Abbey was quiet as the evening drew to a close. Roger wondered if, in fact, he would find that the Precentor had gone to sleep. After all, the monks had to get up early for their next service at Lauds, so it wasn't as if they could afford the late nights of study that Roger was used to Oxford. What a life, regulated to the very hour, day and night. Is that what was required to control sin?

No one came when he knocked, so he tried the handle and the door opened to reveal a steep flight of wooden stairs that led up into the library. Rather than the wide chamber that Roger was used to at Oxford, the monastic library was long and thin being situated above the northern flank of St. Brett's main cloister. Luckily the stairs were lit well enough for Roger to navigate them, with additional light coming from up above. There must be someone studying still; hopefully it was the Precentor.

He reached the top of the stairs where a door stood ajar. He stood in the shadows of the doorway and looked in, and was glad that he had not rushed to enter the room or called out a greeting. He had always been the quiet one of the family.

From his place in the shadows, Roger could see two occupants of the library, but they weren't studying. Sitting opposite each other at a table in the middle of the stacks were the timid Precentor and a large, winged demon, its long jaw of dripping fangs moving from side to side as if chewing as the two of them conversed in hushed voices.

CHAPTER 14

Isabel looked around, hoping no one had seen her fall. She had banged her knee on the stone flags, and her palms and wrists hurt from her attempt to break her fall. She leant against the wall and used it to lever herself into a standing position. She looked at the uneven floor of the cloister and whispered a curse against the hasty masons the Abbey had employed when this floor was laid. The flagstone at fault jutted an inch or two above its fellows.

She brushed down her skirt and straightened her red silken hood. Thank St. Brett no one had witnessed her mishap. From what she could hear, there were still a number of people in the Abbey Church, which was where she had been headed. She would go there, as John had asked, and see if she might be of some use to reassure people that everything was under control.

She stepped away from the wall, and felt her body sway. Her head felt like it was floating, detached from her body. She leant back against the wall and made herself breathe slow and deep. She knew that John had been shaken by the encounter with his son, yet she had not shown her own alarm. Was that what it was? Was that the cause of her faint and the distraction that had lead to her fall?

Jake had told her, when he caught her in bed with his father, that woman had caused the fall of man. He had used many rough words that she cared not to remember now. With Jake, she thought, the man had not needed much of a shove.

He appeared to have come back unchanged. Stouter and softer around the face, it looked like he had a comfortable life, or a life lived in taverns at least as a customer rather than a landlord. John told her (on the few occasions that she could get him to speak on the subject) that Jake must have gone abroad. He'd not heard of him in England, and, from what Isabel guessed but he had not admitted, he must have asked his trading contacts to look for his son and only surviving child. A soldier he supposed or a thief. Not a sailor, he said. Jake never liked the water, wouldn't even swim in the mill pond on a summer's day for fear of it, despite John's coaxing. John had spoken with sad tenderness on those few occasions. He wanted him back, despite what he had threatened. But this afternoon she had seen the same fire of hatred in Jake's eye that she had seen when he had once come within a sheet's thickness of killing his father and putting an end to her life, too.

The door to the Abbey Church opened and Deputy Bailiff Lovell walked out. He noticed Isabel there, just outside the door. "Oh, Isabel, there you are. Do you know where I can find John?"

She shook her head, but then remembered. "I'm sorry. I do know where he is. He is in conclave with the Abbot. They are discussing what happened this afternoon."

"Are you all right?" Lovell stepped forward and placed a hand on her shoulder. She didn't like him touching her, although it seemed he always took every opportunity to. "You look pale."

"No. I am quite all right. Thank you." She moved his hand off her shoulder and stepped away from the wall, gaining some space to breathe. The garlic and sausage smell of Lovell's breath was enough to make her stomach begin to heave, but avoiding it gave her the impetus to move again, and break out of her faint-headed stupor.

"What did you want him for?" she asked, doing her best to look at Lovell normally. But the way he stared at her when she did so always made her feel uncomfortable. Yet he was John's trusted deputy and John always had a good word to say about him. He'd once been John's servant, quiet, but trusted, nothing special. But after Jake left in a squall of rage, Lovell had risen like a new sun.

"People are asking about him. They want answers; they want to know what's been done about things. There's lots of scared folk still in the church, too scared to go home, although a fair few have gone and no doubt bolted themselves up inside. There's some that say that even the Church is not free of the hand of Satan."

"John asked me to come and see if I could speak to the people in his stead. I will give them reassurance that he and the Abbot have this in hand," said Isabel.

Lovell shook his head. "With due respect madam, I don't think you can provide that. There's great outrage amongst the townspeople. They are scared, they don't know who is going to be next."

"Then perhaps they should keep away from witches," snapped Isabel.

"Right," replied Lovell, "I'll let you get on with it then." He turned on his heel and strode down the cloister.

"Where are you going?" asked Isabel.

"Too look for Bailiff Haukwake."

Isabel watched Lovell shuffle down the cloister. In his long robes he looked more like a clerk than an officer of the law. He probably spent more time in his shop reckoning balance sheets and lists of supplies for the Abbey and for the purveyance writs he received from

London than chasing down criminals. John had found his book-keeping skills a great aid to his business, and despite his responsibilities in law-keeping and his own trade, Lovell still managed John's accounts. She had no reason to dislike the man apart from his obvious attraction to her, which if it came from a less ugly man might have been more flattering, so she did not complain to John, but still she dreaded his regular visits to their house.

She was surprised by the noise inside the church. In the middle of the nave near where Margaret Stokke had been possessed and died, a group of perhaps a dozen women knelt and offered loud and wailing prayers to God and all the saints, but mostly to the martyr, St. Brett, who had fought against demons and the pagans while he lived and was killed for his efforts. They beat their chests and waved their hands in the air toward a space towards the top of the rood screen. *Was that where they thought Goa lived?* wondered Isabel. They knelt and shuffled around in the blood and entrails that had poured out of Margaret, their fine silk dresses reddening at the knees. A group of the Abbey's servants under the direction of the Almoner, the elderly monk who Jake had attacked earlier, stood by, watching the women's display of grieving.

"That's enough," said the old monk. "We need to clean up this mess."

The servants moved forward carrying mops, buckets and brooms and waved them in the direction of the grieving women. They didn't notice or didn't want to notice.

"Give me that," said the old monk as he grabbed a mop from one of the servants. He swung it over the heads of the nearest praying figure, it was Anne Vernon, the middle-aged and quite respectable wife of William Vernon, the richest draper in St. Brett's. "Out of here, now!" he shouted. Anne raised her head from prayer just as the Almoner swung again and she got a face full of water and cloth as the mop squelched into her face. Anne stared at the Almoner in shock, but the other women were on their feet now and screaming at the monk, raising fists and threatening violence.

Isabel approached. "Stop this! There's no need for violence." No one heard her. She rushed up to Emma Dewent who had pulled the mop out of the Almoner's hands and was waving it towards his head. Isabel grabbed her arm just as she was about to swing it down on the monk's tonsured skull. A servant came up and put his body betwixt Emma and the monk as she did so and wrenched the mop away from her. But Emma was pulling against Isabel's grip and trying to attack the monk again.

Isabel slapped her hard in the face. "Stop! Emma! You're behaving like an animal, stop this." Emma gazed at Isabel as if she didn't know who she was. Her pupils were huge. The other women had scared the servants off towards the rood screen where they were regrouping, one of them half-carrying the elderly Almoner. Two attacks in one afternoon, thought Isabel, his heart walls will probably split. At the far end of the nave stood a group of men, Anne and Emma's husbands amongst them. They glanced up occasionally but paid the disturbance little heed. What were they talking about?

She would need to deal with the men next.

"Ladies of St. Brett's listen to me," Isabel shouted. The women at last paid her heed. She waved them around her and they gathered to her in a semblance of a circle. As she walked she noticed the stickiness of the stone beneath. She was walking on the blood and entrails of Margaret Stokke.

"Is this any way to honour your friend Margaret?"

No response from the women.

"By all means pray for her soul. Remember her. But do not behave like fishwives. You are the women of St. Brett's. Many of you are wives of members of the Charnel Brotherhood. You have position, status and power within this town."

A flickering of an eyelash. A nod of a head here and there.

"Margaret will be honoured, but not here and not now. This bloody mess below my feet is not Margaret. Let us take the memory of Margaret away with us. Let us pray for her in her own parish church, St. Peter's, where she loved to make worship to the Lord."

Firmer nods and from more than one.

"If you do this thing for me now, and walk in peace from here, I will take word of it to Abbot Peter. I myself will pay for prayers for her soul, and through the Brotherhood I know you and your husbands will ensure her way through Purgatory is eased."

There were glows of agreement from their faces. Like that first time, the Company of Good Women realized what they could do as women on their own. Like the first time they believed in her. Trusted and respected her. She felt as if angels were lifting her up.

"Now I wish all of you to gather your husbands and your children if they are still here and come with me to the Pilgrim's Rest. John and I have tasked the cook there to make ready his best food and ale. Do you like roast suckling pig?"

"Food is a great healer," said Anne Vernon. "But my husband looks to be in deep conclave with his fellows." The men, perhaps a dozen, most of them the husbands of these women, were still in their huddle, low voices jabbering away with purpose.

"They will follow if you mention ale and pork," said Matilda Porter, wife of Hugh the dyer. Hugh was a wealthy man, but not a member of the Brotherhood. John had intended to gather members of the Brotherhood to the Pilgrim's Rest to gauge their mood and provide them with his hospitality, as he should as their unofficial but de facto lord. Yet Isabel realized now that she would have to invite all comers, if necessary. To refuse the Porters would only make a bad thing worse.

"I will work on them," said Isabel.

"Work your magic, eh?" said Anne. Isabel only raised an eyebrow by way of answer.

"Go now, ladies, and I think your men will follow. I will tell them that the ale and pig is limited to first comers and they will rush like the sea after you."

"They know our love of food after all," said Emma Dewent slapping her not-small belly as she laughed. And so, walking off as happy as if there was no dead friend to mourn, the principal women of St. Brett's and several others left for the Pilgrim's Rest and the pleasure that resides in good food and drink.

As the women left the servants advanced again. "Can witch's blood harm you?" muttered one.

"Only if you let it flow and don't finish the job," said another.

"They should burn the body," snapped the old monk. "Hers and all the other bodies should be burnt."

Isabel turned away in disgust and walked towards the group of husbands. She had promised the women that the Abbot would respect the dead body of Margaret and fall in with their wishes to see her honoured almost as a saint. This clearly would not happen. Had she lain in store more trouble for herself for the future?

She caught site of the metallic flash of a drawn sword as she approached the men.

"Are you going to search each house?" she heard one of them say. She thought that it was Hugh Porter who spoke?

"We must find these witches," said William Vernon. "What would you do, wait until they come knocking on your door, bringing the devil in to sit down to break your fast with you?"

"Burn them, I say," said George Dewent, who stood next to William. He was the man holding the sword, a wicked, broad-bladed falchion, the blade of which he patted one palm as if he was prepared to use it at any moment.

"Mistress Haukwake," said William nodding to her in almost a bow as she approached. She acknowledged his courtesy with a smile. "Put that blade away George," said William, "you'll chop your own fingers off before you lay it 'gainst any witch's throat."

Dewent didn't look pleased. "I would be grateful if you put it away, Master Dewent" said Isabel. "I am sure you will not need it in this house of God."

Dewent sighed but agreed. "I just think we ought to be doing something."

"You're right, but we need clear heads and proper counsel. John has invited you all to sup at the Pilgrim's Rest this evening. He has offered free food and ale to all of you. Your wives are already on their way."

"Some of us are minded to stay here and talk things through and come to some sort of plan of action now," replied Henry Goolde, a mercer and member of the Brotherhood. "Thank you ever so much for your invitation, but I will stay here."

"I am of the same mind," replied Thomas Jackson, another mercer and member of the Brotherhood. The two men turned their backs and walked off in discussion. After a moment a few other men walked with them.

"Do any of you men have loyalty to John?" asked Isabel.

"Please, it's not a question of loyalty," replied Dewent. "Jackson and Goolde have their own thoughts and worries. They wonder what will happen with the big fairs coming up, whether to leave St. Brett's and take their trade elsewhere. But those of us here who make our livings from St. Brett's rather than trade solely of commodities from who knows where, I think we have more care for the town. We want to do something now and not continually put off tomorrow."

Isabel was about to talk, but Vernon interjected. "Now George I think you are being unfair. John Haukwake is our chief officer of the peace that is not a monk, and as you know he is bound by what the Abbot and the monks decide. Also, until now, one could argue that this has been a matter for the religious not for the secular."

"Is murder of children a religious matter?" said Porter. "If we were free, like a proper borough, this would not be an issue. We could decide our own fates."

"And pay handsomely to the king for the privilege. We know you never took our side, Hugh, but one can't run before one can walk," said Vernon.

Isabel walked between the two men who were glowering at each other she offered them both her hand, which they took, reluctant to break off their argument. "I think, gentlemen of the Brotherhood, and Hugh, if you will join us, this topic is best discussed over some fine ale, or perhaps some Malmsley. John has some fresh in from London. Will you not come now with me and join your wives?"

Reluctantly, the men agreed to Isabel's plan and followed her to the Pilgrim's Rest.

§

Isabel felt a glow of triumph as she surveyed the families of half the members of the Brotherhood assembled in the dining room of the Pilgrim's Rest. John, she knew, had doubted that she could manage it, but of those still in the Abbey Church when she had returned, only Goolde and Jackson had refused. She had watched as they left together, a few other burgesses in their wake. These others were men of wealth, but not members of the town's Brotherhood, and therefore not important in John's eyes: Thomas Braserton, goldsmith, Nicholas Hook, tailor, big John Cotton, builder were all men that he could do without flattering by offering membership to the exclusive club, but could still tantalize with its prospect if they did not cross him. Members of the gentry had even begun to join — indeed there had been two landholding gentlemen present that afternoon, and John even dreamed of bringing members of the nobility into the fold. After all, the Brotherhood was founded by the Abbot as the foremost lay organization dedicated to veneration of the shrine of St. Brett's, a favourite site of pilgrimage for any nobles on their way to and from London and the north. She had even once seen John of Gaunt, the King's second eldest son, and it was said, the most powerful man in England bar none, being warmly greeted by the Abbot at the gates of the Abbey's precinct.

Isabel thought well of John's ambitions, they were part of the reason she had chosen him for her husband. But in her heart she yearned for more. London was her goal. She believed that John had enough capital to invest in a London warehouse, and she encouraged him to think beyond their provincial satellite town. He had always listened to her suggestions, but had told her to remember his age. To start anew would take time. He reminded her how long it had taken him to build his own coterie of suppliers and customers. Those who owed him enough to support his ambitions. That was why three of the men who were now sitting with Vernon and Dewent in the Pilgrim's Rest that night were men of lesser means: John Staunton, Richard Nasshe, and Thomas Coverley, fullers all. Finishing the cloth so it was ready for dying was one of the most time-consuming parts of the whole process, and one that foreigners, whether from London, Suffolk or Flanders, paid the mercers of St. Brett's good money for. John's relationships with these men and his reliance on their production had ensured his wealth, and he had repaid them handsomely with a gift greater than gold: the illusion of power.

And there, in the midst of them, sat the cuckoo of the night's nest: Hugh Porter and that jealous shrew his wife Matilda.

Isabel took the platter bearing the roast suckling pig from the hands of the serving girl and brought it to the table herself.

"Well this is just like the old days," said William Vernon as Isabel carved the meat and distributed to each of the trenchers around the table. "You do us proud Isabel, just as John did when we were all rebels against the Abbey. There wasn't a night in those times when he didn't host us here in this very room and provide us with the filling for us to stomach our fight against injustice."

Isabel bowed her head in acknowledgment.

"The Pilgrim's Rest was like our guildhall then," said George Dewent.

Hugh Porter shook his head. "And what guildhall do you frequent now George Dewent? And you William Vernon?" Hugh paused to see if there would be any response. "Nothing to say? It doesn't surprise me. Only John Haukwake and Abbot Peter hold conference together, not even the monks have much to discuss in their Chapterhouse these days. We are ruled by a tyranny of two."

"Look," said William, turning red in the face, "I know you're no member of the Brotherhood, so perhaps you don't understand, but there is no constitution for us to form a guild while we are tenants of the Abbey and that won't change while there is still an Abbey." His wife Anne put a warning hand on his arm. "What you don't reckon, Hugh Porter, is how power truly works. And now because you've excluded yourself from the Brotherhood — and everyone knows it's because of your own contrariness — you don't see it. But even you are a richer man than before, are you not?"

"Richer from my own toil, that is true. Yet I am shackled firmer than I was before. Men of our degree can only fight against power if we join as one and become united. But John and Abbot Peter have you where they want you, separate, in this so called Brotherhood. You're like those girls who with some empty flattery your head is turned. And now, when things aren't as easy and cosy as they once were..."

"You call dealing with plague and the demands of purveyance for the King's wars easy?" snuffled William.

"The Lords used them as excuses to raise taxes where they had been lightened before," said Hugh. "But if anything, war and plague have benefited our town — Lovell and the other purveyors make money supplying the army, and plague has put our rivals out of profit. But now that there is a challenge from the Devil only knows where, they don't know what to do. Since Christmas have any of you had a month in profit?"

Isabel walked hurriedly to the kitchens. "Bring the malmsley now," she ordered.

"But Master John..." said the cook.

"Now is the time." Isabel took the tray of bottles from the serving girl and again presented this new wonder to the men and their wives. Talk of profits and fraternities soon liquefied into toasts to the health of each person around the table, and to Master Haukwake and his beautiful wife Isabel.

Isabel sat at the corner of the table and sipped the sweet red wine, making small talk when put upon and smiling at the happy, forgetful band. Malmsley, soaked with one or two choice herbs that she had mixed in, dissipated ill-will after only a few sips.

She drank her own wine, a lighter red without any herbs, and chatted occasionally with her fellow diners. At a polite moment she excused herself from the table. It had been a long day and she hadn't had the chance to respond to any calls of nature.

On her return from relieving herself in the Rest's gardcrobe in the back yard, she encountered Anne Vernon.

"I do not need to piss, Mistress Haukwake, but I would have a few words with you."

"Speak on," said Isabel.

"Somewhere private and not overheard," said Anne. They left the passageway that had an opening to the smoky kitchen and walked into the stable yard feet away from the stinking cess-pit over which Isabel had sat moments ago.

"Do you enjoy the revels?" asked Isabel.

"Oh yes, Mistress Haukwake." Anne addressed Isabel as if she were by far her senior, but Anne must be another life in age older than she. "You and John are most generous as always."

"And what of Hugh's earlier words?" pressed Isabel.

"Words? I remember them not? I am sure I cannot remember one toast to good health from another, but I am sure his words were nobly said."

"Yes, good. They were. Think nothing more of it," said Isabel, touching Anne's forehead for a moment as she held her gaze.

"I quite forget why I had asked you here," said Anne.

"It will come to you in a moment."

Anne steadied herself against the wall. Although older than Isabel, her hair was fairer and not a grey one was to be found in it, yet time or cures had not been as kind to her broadening figure. She bounced slowly off the wall and stood upright again.

"Now it has come to me. You gave me certain cures to help with bedtime adventures. Now for these I was most grateful, and so was my man, but I have found in recent weeks the old sluggishness returning. And since the meetings of the Company have all but ended it is most difficult to discuss these things with you. What can I do?"

Isabel had been amazed that what she had given Anne had worked at all. She had found the recipe in one of Edmund Hope's books, and its ingredients were so bizarre that she thought it must be fraud. It was Anne's own fault though, if she had not the nerve to come to her house to ask for more.

"I could double the dose of certain parts of the cure and prepare you a new mixture, but I would counsel you to not overexert yourself, or your man, at his age."

Anne bowed her head and gave her a greedy look, and grinned with her mouth half empty of teeth that age and rot had removed. She looked like a pig ready to gobble up some slops. "My man is not as old as you think, and he would be happy for more exertions. Please Mistress, give me an extra dose."

Sighing, Isabel agreed and sent Anne back to the dining room to enjoy the food and wine. If Anne was happy then William was happy and William was one of John's closest allies in the Brotherhood. But she couldn't imagine the old draper as an energetic god of love. Did Anne have a younger lover perhaps? She left the tavern by a side-door and hurried home. She would make Anne Vernon a double-dose of the cure tonight — it would not take her long.

John was not yet home and the servants had not seen her. He must still be in discussion with the Abbot, Lovell and the constables. She wished he had time to come to the tavern. He would be proud of her. She mixed the cure for Anne and left.

But when she returned to the Pilgrim's Rest there were no sounds of merrymaking and the windows were darkening. She could see that candles were being snuffed out. She knocked loudly as the door was bolted. The serving-girl opened the door not trying to hold in a yawn. They had all gone she told Isabel. Henry Lovell had arrived and had words with them and fairly soon afterwards the party had broken up. They hadn't eaten all the food. The dogs would have the bones and a good amount of meat too.

The serving-girl didn't know what message Lovell had given and she didn't much care either. "It was like they realized they had to be somewhere else," said the girl. "Don't blame them, it's late and there's work to be done in the morning."

Isabel realized that she was tired and went home. John had still not returned, but even so she decided to go to sleep without him.

She felt like she hadn't slept at all when she jerked her head up from her pillow and looked around. What was that? She had heard something. Laughing and shouting from many voices. As her eyes adjusted to the darkness she saw that John was lying next to her. His eyes were open.

"I'm sorry," he said. "I should have sent word. I hope I didn't wake you. The Abbot and his blasted obedientiaries kept on with their speculations. We got no work done. They were too busy with their complaints. And then I looked for Lovell and couldn't find him, so I took the new watchmen on their rounds."

"That sound. It wasn't you?" whispered Isabel. "Did you hear that?" The laughter and shouting came again as if blown on the wind, becoming louder and then fading again. She got out of bed and went towards the window and opened the shutters. Light from the stars poured into the room, brightly basking her and their bed even though there was no moon. She strained to listen to the commotion but could hear no better for being by the window.

"You can't hear that?" she asked again.

"No," groaned John.

"Can't you sleep?" asked Isabel. "Is it the noise keeping you awake?"

"No, I can't hear it. Your younger ears are more sensitive perhaps? I don't know what the matter is, but come back to bed, today has been long enough as it is?"

The noises outside seemed to fade so she closed the shutters and climbed back into bed, snuggling close to John. "Are you alright?" she asked him.

"I don't know. It's been a strange day with Jake coming back, Margaret Stokke and her brother, and then the grilling by the Abbot and his monks. They doubt me, you know, and I begin to doubt myself. Perhaps we should move?"

"To London? Would you? You know Henry Lovell had no faith in me either. He said I couldn't bring order to the people in the church, but I did. The Brotherhood were very grateful."

"That's good. You did well."

"Did Lovell find you?"

"No, no. I never saw him." John rolled over and hunkered down into the mattress to get more comfortable. "Spent an hour at least looking for him," he said quietly as he closed his eyes and settled his head on the pillow. Isabel wondered about telling him that Lovell had come with a message to the tavern. A message that had drawn away the whole gathering it seemed. But he started snoring so she gave it up and lay down next to him.

The laughing and shouting came louder again. She could hear it very clearly now. And was that a name they called? It was a name, but she couldn't distinguish what it was. And then a long drawn out scream pierced the air. She sat up, cold sweat trickling down her back. John lay fast asleep. He must need his rest.

She got up and pulled on a coat over her nightdress and some soft deerskin boots and walked as quietly as she could downstairs. She didn't need a light to walk by. The fires of the watch illuminated the market place well enough. But the sounds seemed to be coming from Romeland, the area of common ground behind their house where the annual fairs were held.

Voices, male and female, came on the wind. She could not make out the words, but they had the rhythm and earnestness of chanting. She walked down the alley around the back of the butchers. She stumbled once or twice and saw the stream that separated the alley from the common ground like a deep cut across the blue grass of the night. There was a plank bridge near here somewhere but she didn't know if she could find in the dark despite the blue starlight. Could she jump it? Whoever's voices she could hear it wasn't worth twisting an ankle for or worse. Instead she walked down the back of the houses along the grassy bank of the stream. She looked over towards the common land which stretched out flat over the top of the hill on which the town sat, thinking she should see some fire light or movement, but there was nothing. Just the voices, the chanting and again a scream. A man this time, guttural like an animal slain.

The night seemed airless. It was May and the sky was clear of cloud, but it wasn't cold. Isabel felt sweat pour down her thighs which rubbed together as she walked. The sounds came and went. If there is no wind then what is happening? Was her hearing going? She stopped a moment and took another breath. Perhaps she was pregnant? If only, please God, if only she could have a child. Laughter mingled with the shouts, and a low drumming sound, music and frivolity. The bastards. She cast the idle fantasy of motherhood from her mind and carried on along the stream.

When she reached the main bridge and the entrance to Pikepond Lane she paused again. Now it sounded as if the noises were coming from down the hill. Down by the river perhaps and not from the common of Romeland at all. She started walking. It was dark down here, the houses crowded round her, and it was difficult to see were her feet were going. She tripped and nearly fell. That was twice in the same day, but this time she kept her feet.

She turned round as she couldn't be sure now where the sounds were coming from. They seemed to be getting quieter again and had swung round to somewhere behind her. Was she going mad? She retraced her steps and again passed along the back yards of the row of houses that faced onto the market. She didn't relish the questions of the watch who enforced the curfew just at the moment. John wouldn't be happy that she broke his own orders.

She passed the backyard of their house, and thought perhaps she should just go back inside and up to bed. But what was that? If she had just looked this way before she would have seen it. Firelight casting a warm aura over the north of the town, just past the tower of St. Peter's church. The noises were no louder but she knew this must be it. Should she call for help? No, she wanted to make sure first. She rejoined the main road as it went towards St. Peter's church. The parish priest lived here, and there was an almshouse and a hospital maintained by the monks across the street. It would be strange if the inhabitants hadn't heard the commotion or seen the firelight as well. She walked past the priest's house and saw that a light was lit inside. The priest was awake hunched over a book reading. He should have been able to hear surely? Wouldn't he be worried if fire threatened his church?

Perhaps she was mistaken. Perhaps the priest knew about the fire and there was some reasonable explanation, such as a farmer burning some waste of some sort.

"So glad you could join us," said a woman's voice from behind Isabel. She swung round to see a grotesque face leering at her. It was a mask; whether a real hog's head or made to appear like it she could not tell, but the effect was gross enough. From the look of her, the woman was not pretty or young. Through torn linen of her skimpy dress, plump blotchy flesh showed, and underneath her mask a sizeable dewlap hung. The woman turned with a girlish giggle and ran towards the church. Isabel began to run after her but paused. On the woman's back rode a hairy ape-like animal, with short bat's wings attached. It clung to the woman's back as an infant might be given a piggyback ride.

When Isabel didn't follow, the woman stopped.

"Don't be afraid, there're plenty of masks," she said. "No one need know who you are."

"But you have seen my face," replied Isabel.

The woman cocked her head on one side. "Oh and I suppose you think I should show you mine?"

"Tell me what is going on here."

"Come and find out for yourself," said the woman, who skipped away down the road towards the church.

There was no other choice but to follow her.

The meadow to the north of the church was a pleasant place to go in springtime. It lay next to a stream that fed the river Varn. The monks claimed it as part of their hunting land as it adjoined an area of parkland outside the town, so no cows or sheep cropped its grasses and wild flowers or defecated across it. Families would gather there on Sunday afternoons to eat and play.

Tonight, smoke drifted across the meadow coming from a large bonfire that must have been built around some sort of wooden construction that had now collapsed in the flames. The woman that had greeted Isabel had joined one of the many small groups of people that danced around the fire singing and chanting. The words sounded like Latin, but they were some barbarous perversion of the language: *sathanix, haruspexis, domineus, canis maximus sacerdotus, daemonicus.* Nonsense, thought Isabel, but she had seen words like them in some of the books she had borrowed.

For the most part, none of the people dancing around the bonfire wore any clothes, although they all wore masks of some animal or other. Dogs, pigs, sheep, and goats were popular for the men, and one fat lady wore what looked like an owl mask across her broad face. Some held hands or took each other's arms in some sort of chaotic dance, and they screeched and chanted to the fire. Every time they seemed to do a full circuit they stopped and raised their hands up into the air above the bonfire with a great shout of a word that Isabel couldn't make out. The dancing must have been exhausting if they had been going at it since Isabel first heard the screaming earlier in the night. She watched as some of the revellers fell to the ground in a heap. But they were not still for long. Instead of resting they dragged their bodies together and began love-marking in the grass, grunting and bellowing with pleasure.

So these must be the witches.

What should she do? They made no sign that they had noticed her. The woman with the pig's mask was dancing arm in arm with a tall pot-bellied man with goats-head mask. But they hadn't noticed Isabel standing at the edge of the field. She could slip away and fetch the watch, perhaps, and wake John? But by that time would they still be here? Could she use the moment to unmask some of them and find out who these people were?

But what about that creature on the woman's back? She could see firelight reflecting off the woman's sweat-slicked flesh now, nothing was clinging to her. And then she noticed them. It was like hearing wind through tall grass, but there was no wind. Around the masked people dancing around the glowing fire, something else whirred and circled through the grass. A black wave of creatures too short to reach your knee, but full of points and angles, teeth and claws and bats wings flapping. A dance of demons mirrored the dance of the witches. Were these the demons that each one of these witches was possessed by? She would have to get past them to get to the witches. Trying not to open her mouth lest she never could shut it again, Isabel, turned and ran. She must not scream, she must not scream.

Then, running next to her was the woman in the pig's face. She was fat and old but she kept pace with Isabel, the ape on her back grinning at Isabel. "Isabel join us, your Company of Good Women is dead, join us," she said. Isabel looked away and kept on running. By the time she reached the stream she looked back again and the woman had gone.

She had difficulty waking John, but when he heard what was wrong, he hurried and fetched the watchmen on duty to follow him. They were only a half-dozen, but armed with bills, swords and clubs.

Her heart sank when she saw that the sky no longer glowed with fire over St. Peter's. By the time they reached the field she knew it was too late. Some charred remains of the bonfire scarred the field, and you could see where the grass had been trampled down. Some bottles lay here and there.

"Drunken serfs from the Luetdell perhaps?" suggested one of the watchmen. Isabel didn't even try to gainsay him. What could she prove, and if they believed her what did it matter?

CHAPTER 15

Another pint and he would leave. Yes he would leave and go looking for her. Another pint. Leave. look for her and then talk to her.

Talk to her. And then she would.

And then she would...

"Fuck me."

"Pardon?"

"I said "Fuck me, Jake Haukwake," said a young woman with nice breasts, and what looked like a pretty smile, and all of her teeth, but it was hard to tell in this light.

And particularly after ten pints of Old Brett's Breath. He'd bequeathed the recipe for that particular brew to old Bill Haly who took over the New Inn after he ran out of money, and although Haly didn't brew it as well as he had, it was still the strongest, tastiest ale he'd ever had. Jake was pleased to find that it was still brewed, and that piece of good news had even inspired him to come up with a plan. Never mind Roger and his demons, he needed to talk to Isabel and end this foolishness. She should, and she would, come back to him.

And now it seemed that the Breath had made him remarkably attractive to any young women who came within his domain. If this young hussy wanted him, he was sure that the more mature, although more beautiful and now supposedly more classy Isabel would also fall at his knees, although he doubted she would be so immediately forthcoming as this young woman.

"So you know me?" said Jake.

"I would that you would know me better. I'm hungry for you, I want you inside me," said the woman, hitching up her skirts and flashing her bare thighs at him.

He felt a stiffening in his hose.

The woman came and sat on Jake's lap. He was sitting in the corner of the tavern. The New Inn was mostly empty at this hour. Old Haly hadn't had much more success running the place than he had,. He had been happy to see him back, even letting him have his first drink free, although things were obviously not going well, as Haly made sure he paid up front for each of his drinks thereafter. He hadn't noticed the young woman in the tavern before, although there were a couple of groups of men — some traders from the market, and others travellers stopping for the night, and a few women among them drinking with their men. But this woman seemed to be on her own.

She wrapped her thighs around him and pulled down the low-cut front of her dress so that Jake could see the full teats of her breasts before him.

"Have me, Jake Haukwake, take me now."

"Here?" Jake chuckled. "I think Old Haly wouldn't like that, might put his customers off their ale."

"We don't care about him. I'm a woman, free to do what I want. God has spoken to me and he said go forth and be fruitful, so I am."

"What's your name, do I know you?"

She sat forward until her breasts were up against his mouth, pushing into it as he opened it to speak. He pulled his head back and looked around the bar, worried about what the other drinkers and Haly especially must be thinking. He'd get thrown out at best, and hauled before the Abbey's court at worst. And what if this young woman's father found out? He could get a whipping.

Fear had a sobering effect.

But no one in the rest of the tavern was even looking. Maybe it was darker in this corner than he thought.

"I don't think this is a good ..."

"Idea?

"I have somewhere to be."

"Someone to be with? Listen," she said pulling him to her, until he could not help but start sucking on her full nipples and placing his hands on her hips to pull her onto him. She started untying his hose for him as she ground her hips over his stiffening cock. "Isabel isn't in love with you anymore. She only has one lover."

Jake stopped kissing her and looked up at her face. "Lover?"

The woman smiled. "Yes, her lover is the great deceiver. She's a witch. She taught me everything I know — and the other women of the Company, too — until she betrayed us. She's only in love with Satan, not you."

Jake felt like he was going to be sick. He blinked. He looked at the woman's face as she tried to undo his hose. He did know her. She must be twenty years younger than him. The last time he had seen her she must have been a toddler, just learning to talk to adults. It had been at the Summer Fair. He had sold her father a barrel of apples.

He stood suddenly, pushing her off him so that she landed on the floor. She leapt up with a hiss. Jake ran out of the tavern, with all the tavern's patrons and Haly and his potboy staring at him as he went.

CHAPTER 16

"You're late," said the Precentor.

"Were you expecting me?" Roger replied.

"No, I meant the hour is late. I thought that you might want to speak to some of us, but I am surprised that you have come tonight."

"Do you have time now?"

"Yes some." The Precentor pointed to the chair opposite him, indicating that Roger should sit there. Sit where moments ago a large winged demon had sat according to the evidence of Roger's eyes. Roger looked around. Had the demon simply vanished? Or had it sped to a far corner or rafter of the roof and now watched him with hungry eyes?

Roger rubbed his tired eyes.

"I am here tomorrow morning if you would rather put your questions to me then?" said the Precentor.

Roger lowered himself into the seat opposite the Precentor. Nothing horrible happened. "Let us speak now."

They sat for a few moments in silence. Roger wondered how to begin.

The Precentor was looking at the table before him, hunched over it, but not by choice Roger thought, remembering his bent over appearance when he stood earlier in the Chapterhouse.

"Would you like to pray with me?" said the Precentor.

"Pray?" Roger couldn't remember the last time he had prayed. He thought himself a religious man, well in theory anyway, but whenever he attended the College Church at Merton, he always found his mind filled with speculations and vast maps of the heavens rather than the prayer chosen by the priest that day. Somehow he could never keep his mind to the words pronounced by another to praise God.

"Never mind, you don't have to, you just seemed nervous. I thought it might help," said the Precentor. "I have been praying a lot recently; praying for the salvation of us all. It helps to calm me."

"The exorcisms have not worked?"

The Precentor looked up at Roger (he spoke to the table mostly because of the curve of his back). "Do you think I, a humble mortal, could really have the power to cast out a demon?"

Roger thought of what he had seen moments ago, and of what he had seen on the Abbot's shoulders during their first meeting in the Chapterhouse. "Perhaps the struggle with one's own demons obstructs?"

"Isidore says that a devil and an angel do battle for the soul of every man, but if that were the case, then those who have cast out demons from others would need to overcome their own demon to do so. Perhaps that is the nature of a saint, but not of this mortal man you see before you."

"So none of your exorcisms have had any effect?"

"No, but then again what is the point of only treating the symptoms of the disease, if you do not also try to strike at its origin as well?"

"It's origin? Aren't these demonic possessions the sign of sinfulness amongst those afflicted?"

"That's what one might think, and that is what we are told. But if that were the case then half the monks would be possessed by demons, including your new patron."

"The Abbot?"

"A man who loves pleasure and sin, and uses his office to puff his own pride."

"Is there any pattern discernible in who is possessed?" asked Roger.

"Pattern? Does ill fortune have a pattern? Physically, I can't tell if there is any difference. Edmund Hope, our Infirmarer, has taken the bodies to study, but he has not revealed any of his findings to anyone except the Abbot. I don't know what he has to hide, but I suspect there is something. He is a very secretive man, and one not to cross, so be careful."

"For a man who seems so quiet, you seem brave."

"I am not proud enough to say that I am courageous, but when one has given up hope then why not? I have nothing to lose now."

"You shouldn't take it personally," said Roger. "I don't believe that the exorcism liturgy has any positive effect at all. Why should a mere collection of words have power over the angels of hell?"

"'Angels of hell,' that's an interesting term! So you don't think words have power?"

"Not on their own, no, not without thought, reason, or belief, call it what you will."

"Again, I am no saint, I grant you." The Precentor pushed his chair away from the table, and supporting his weight with both hands, lifted himself up. He was a young man, only a little older than Roger, but moved as if he was eighty.

"I did not mean to offend." Roger moved to help the other man stand up, but he was waved away.

"The truth does not offend me. It saddens me, that is all. I wish to show you something, please follow."

They walked down the long room of the library, past empty booths set into every window on the South side, where desks and benches were placed — the work desks for monks. On the north side were row upon row of cabinets. Their doors were shut; but, Roger imagined, these must hold books.

"You keep your books locked away?"

"They are our livelihood, so yes, we guard them. Illuminations and copying bring us more money than all our lands together. I expect you yourself must have sat to read a volume produced here. We sell many volumes to the booksellers of Oxford."

"But what about books that the monks may wish to read?"

"Books of psalms, missals and so on are located on the far wall." He indicated open shelves that could dimly be seen away from the candlelight that he held in his hand. They were the only people in the library, Roger supposed, so no other lights were lit except at the table where they had sat, and the Precentor had taken that light with him. Roger shivered. He hoped the light didn't go out.

They came to the end of the long room — more like a wide corridor above the lower cloister. There was another door. The Precentor withdrew a key and passed it to Roger."

"Through that door are the legal records of the Hundred court of St. Brett's, as well as copies of the Abbey's deeds and other legal records. I will show you where the Hundred court records are for this year and last, that should be enough. I will wait for you at the door to the library, where we sat earlier. Find me when you are finished and I will lock up."

"What am I looking for in the court records?"

"Coroner's reports. Read about the deaths, and there, I think, you will see the pattern that you seek."

CHAPTER 17

A dark street in the vill of St. Brett's, Nigh-time. 28th of May, St. Brett's day and the early morning hours of 29th of May.

A voice, intent yet slurred, is heard.

"They said she was a witch and I did not believe them. They were backbiters all, so why should I pay them heed? But why else would my father be so entrapped by her to deny his own son? I blame him, but the cause lies in her province."

Enter Jake Haukwake, debating with himself.

"The woman from whom I fled from must have been mad or drunk. What faith should I have in her words?"

Here come three Watchmen conscripted from the town to guard the night against evil spirits and sorcerers. They proceed without light, using the moon only to see their way.

"I just trod in something foul," reports the first Watchman.

"Your foot was in your mouth again then?" enquires the second Watchman.

"No, in your wife. The lack of a lantern is fortuitous as it prevents me from seeing her ugly face underneath my shoe."

"Why you ...!" exclaims the second Watchman.

"Be quiet the both of you," interjects the third Watchman. "If any sorcerer be abroad tonight, they will hear us coming. Do not forget that we are supposed to be secret, to ambush them about their business."

Jake has not yet seen the Watchmen and continues to debate out loud what he should do.

"I know Isabel. I know she would not work any evil, and anyone who says she does slanders her. So, should I go to her? She must surely realise that being with my father is a mistake? Now that I am back she will see things differently."

"What's that sound?" asks the third Watchman.

"The devil farting," replies the first Watchman.

"If he farts words, then maybe, but to me that sounds like a man speaking," says the second Watchman.

"A sorcerer?" asks the third Watchman.

"No look, see it's that man, who lurches side to side and holds onto walls to support himself," says the second Watchman.

"Drunk," says the first.

"Possessed by devils?" asks the third.

"Possessed by St. Brett's Breath if you ask me," replies the second.

Jake stumbles and falls over a low barrel that has been left in the middle of the narrow street. He lies there for a moment. Long enough for the Watchmen to approach him.

One of them pokes him with the wooden butt of his polearm, a long glaive that was once a ploughshare.

"Dead?" asks the third

"Dead drunk," says the second. "Come let us lift him and put in the monks' gaol until he is sober."

"Here, let us load him into a wheelbarrow, he looks stout and my back is sore," says the first.

"Sore? From what?" enquires the third.

"From humping your mother!"

The Watchmen cackle at the joke and proceed to load the heavy weight of the drunken Jake into a wheelbarrow that is more used to carrying marrows and turnips than Haukwakes or Savages.

"You push him then," says the first.

"Me?" says the second. "Why?"

"Because you can give me a ride too," says the first, jumping onto the moving wheelbarrow onto the slumbering Jake. The wheelbarrow begins to pick up speed.

"Hold!" cries the third.

The second Watchman lets go of the wheelbarrow's handles in surprise and looks around for danger. "Where? Is the devil upon us?"

The wheelbarrow crashes into the solid wooden frame of a market stall and spills the first Watchman onto the ground. As he is awake, he jumps away without injury, although he protests loudly to his fellows.

Jake Savage, or Jacob Haukwake as his mother named him, is not so lucky. Unconscious still when the wheelbarrow hits the solid wooden post holding up the market stall, he wakes with a mighty shock and a great pain in his shoulder where the market stall hits it. But his soldiering instincts have not left him. Used to waking at a moment's notice to counter a possible infiltration by the enemy into a camp, or escalade of a castle wall when on duty (usually spent drunk and asleep), he is all action in just under a bat's blink. A sharp dagger is in his hand, and he stands briefly and turns around before hitting his head on a pot left hanging by the careless cook who owned the stall. A pot not worth taking home, but heavy enough to cause damage to anyone's head, even the drink-soaked head of Jake Savage.

"That's foul language," says the third Watchman. "And in the presence of a lady. Can you not see this woman is in mourning?" He stands over Jake as he rubs his sore head and clutches his arm, whispering furiously for him to curtail his dirty tongue.

Jake looks and sees a woman walk past. She wears a wimple and a veil covers her face. She is dressed in black so dark that it stands out in the darkness against the drab brown of the buildings. She holds a bunch of white flowers before her.

"Who is she?" he asks.

"Someone who deserves your pity," says the first Watchman.

"Unhand me, won't you," demands Jake.

"Do you not know that Bailiff Haukwake has forbidden any to walk around at night? There is a curfew; you should be in your bed or back in the tavern from whence you came," says the second.

"I don't know it, and if it be true then where does that lady go unmolested by your attentions?"

"She has a right, for she mourns her daughter every night at this hour," says the first.

"What happened to her daughter?"

"She died."

"What? Of course, but ..." Jake pauses as the Watchman glares at him. "How? Tell me the tale?"

"Well it happened over a month past now that they found the body of the young girl staked out ..."

"Don't tell him!" says the second.

"But why not?" says the first.

"He's right," agrees the third. "This man is a vagabond, and a foreigner from another shire or London perhaps. The tale will be known soon enough in many places if you tell more, be still your tongue."

Jake shrugs. He wants to see Isabel, and yet his eyes and those of the Watchmen follow the lady as she walks through the shambles and in the direction of his father's house at the North end of the market. The three Watchmen take off their caps and bow their heads as they watch the lady walk through the bright torchlight of the market, fires blazing to ward off evil and scare away sorcerers. Jake does not bow his head. The third Watchman has let go his arm, so he takes a step backwards out of their sight and then walks slowly but steadily away. There is a side alley that will take him to the end of the market, past his father's house, yet across the path of the mourning mother.

"Where are you going," calls out the first, noticing his departure.

"Back to the tavern as you told me," Jake replies.

"Right you are. Be on your way then, and don't let us catch you out here again," says the first. "Come on boys, I have some dice and you have some pennies for me to win before the next sorcerer comes our way."

CHAPTER 18

Roger poured through the Coroner's reports, looking for patterns, making note of anything he thought might be useful.

Margery Hegate, 8 years old, found by the Constable Will Penny in Pikepond Lane, dead from wounds. Throat was cut by a sharp blade and the blood emptied from her body. Five candles were found in a circle around her, knocked over and extinguished. There was paint on her limbs, but any letters or symbols written there were blurred by the rain that had fallen that evening.

13th May (Moon full, rising in Aries), wrote Roger.

Simon Saddler, 7 years of age, found by his elder sister, Mary, 12 years old, in the woods by the River Varn, 50 yards downstream from the North Mill. Decapitated. His head found in a pit, partly eaten by woodland creatures.

14th April (Moon full, rising in Pisces), he added.

Phylis Strong, 5 years old, found floating in the stream by the Grange bridge, the grate blocking the path to the Abbey having stopped her corpse floating away. No signs of wounding, but her face was a strange yellow colour, bile leaking according to the Abbey's Infirmarian Edmund Hope, who inspected the body.

15th March (full moon again, but in which sign? He would have to consult his astrolabe)

Other deaths of children: Peter, John, Mary (not Simon's sister), Katherine. Less detail about their deaths, but each had died either violently or perhaps accidentally rather than of any sickness. All died away from their homes, and were found either the night they died or the next day after a search by their parents. A month between each. Nearly. A lunar month not a calendar month. Some gaps between these deaths though. Older people died. Some violent, but they were usually due to fights, or people witnessed their deaths — a mason killed when a stone block from the Abbey Church fell on him. Tragic, but not unusual.

What about the gaps? What could explain them? Children from outside? Travellers? Roger flicked through the other court records. Here was one in June of 1375 — a month when there were no violent deaths of children recorded in the St. Brett's coroners book. A plea to the Hundred Court to look for a child, lost by a family of wool merchants on their way home from London. They had stopped at the shrine of St. Brett's for the day to pray and make an offering. They stayed that night in the Abbey's guesthouse, and their young son, only four years of age, had played with some of the Abbey servants in the yard while his parents were shown the shrine and the collection box. The servants, stupidly, had left the boy alone, playing. They had left him with a small brush and he had played at sweeping the steps outside the church. No one saw him after that. The court promised to look for him, but nothing was heard after that and there was no record of what the parents did either. Their names were given, but not the name of their town or village. There would be no way of finding them again, or their child.

The pattern that the Precentor had spoken of was obvious. Deaths of children, each a lunar month apart. So why had no one else commented on the timings before? There was scant description of the circumstances before the start of this year. Had the Abbot's concerns about the apparent celebration of witchcraft in the town at the New Year highlighted a problem, which the coroner responded to by providing more detail after each death? Had the witches been to blame for these deaths? And if so, why had none of the ritual aspects been noticed before this year? Perhaps no one had looked for them, or maybe whoever was killing these children in this way had simply become careless and over-confident.

The descriptions of the bodies did not provide enough information for Roger about the rituals used. Any searching through a book about magic would be pointless. But perhaps if he could speak to someone who had found the bodies? The full moon must also be significant. He wondered if the library had any books on astrology. A good copy of Ptolemy might help, or a tome of natural science might do as well — to see if there was any link between the moon and certain occult practices.

His candle was almost burnt down; he had best get back to the Precentor. He would ask him if the library had a copy of Ptolemy. Roger sighed. He began to gather up the pile of coroners rolls scattered over the table in the records room where he had been working. It was difficult to sort the rolls of paper without reading each of the items carefully again to determine their date.

"Hello, what's this?" said Roger. He spoke to no one but himself, and his voice seemed louder than he had expected. He looked through the door wondering if the Precentor would think it odd that he spoke to himself. Jake hardly noticed anymore when he did.

No one came, so Roger returned his attention to the piece of parchment that had caught his eye. It was on the back of a court roll, a piece of parchment probably taken from another book that had been taken apart to supply paper stock for the court records. A book that the monks didn't need any more, or at least didn't value. There was an illumination, faded now, but once well drawn and coloured. It depicted a king with an axe, but rather than sitting on a throne, he was under it, and floating above the throne was a tonsured priest, making the sign to ward off evil. Next to the illumination were a few fragments of Latin verse, but the rest had been obscured by a stain of some sort, perhaps glue where the page had once been bound to another book to strengthen it.

Or perhaps to hide it?

Roger sat down and looked at the fragments of the lines. They were written in a good hand, better than the script he often saw in his own times. Where had he seen script like this before? A copy of King Alfred's translation of Boethius at Winchester, he thought. That had been written before the conquest in the time of the Old English kings.

He got out his own slate and made a note of the words he could discern.

King of the Britons slain...
Great Brett Wea...
Christian Man never was he, upon his death the pagans wept
And upon that man the devil did...
Mighty Bifrons of two faces he ...

The rest was lost.

Roger stared at his notes and read the words again out loud to himself. Was this poem written by one of the first monks of the Abbey?

A voice came from over his shoulder. "According to legend, St. Brett was an early English king murdered for his Christian beliefs."

Roger yelped. He had no idea that the Precentor was behind him watching him. "Where did you ...?"

"I did not mean to scare you, but it is late and I must lock the library and take a few hours sleep before Matins prayers. You found what you needed I trust? You found a pattern, something to investigate?"

"Yes, I think so. The children, one a month. One every lunar month that is."

"That's right." The Precentor groaned.

"You're tired, let us go, my candle is about to go out anyway."

"Not tired, but I have a throbbing pain that won't go."

"You should see the Infirmarian perhaps?" said Roger.

"Oh I rather think that would do more harm than good."

"Excuse me?"

"No matter. Those words you were saying when I entered, where did you find them?"

"Oh, those. On the back of a court roll. Do you know what they are about? You said something about the legend of St. Brett."

"Yes, a Christian King, murdered by his brother, a pagan, but then St. Brett inspired the first priest of our Church to stand up to the pagan. *Bryth* was the name of the pagan brother, I think, in Welsh. The first Abbot of St. Brett's banished him to the Welsh borders."

"You're Welsh?"

"Yes, partly anyway, from Monmouth. We knew him as Bryth, it has a similar meaning to Brett actually: Briton. Bret Wealdan is the name of the over-king of Britain. They say that was King Arthur's title. But that's all myth and legend isn't it?"

"Don't let the monks of Glastonbury hear you saying that."

The Precentor laughed, but then winced again. "Ah my neck, this pain is getting worse. Now I really must go. Please," he said not kindly as before, "please, let us go, now."

Roger nodded, not wishing to argue and let the Precentor hurry him down the long library room and down the steps into the cloister.

"You know your way to the guestrooms?" asked the Precentor at the door.

"Yes I can get there."

"Good." The Precentor looked around the cloister as Roger turned to go and retreating back into the entrance to the library steps shut the heavy oak door.

Roger stared at the door for a moment in puzzlement. "I thought you wanted your bed," Roger said under his breath. He certainly needed his.

CHAPTER 19

Jake had planned to visit Isabel, but now he was more interested in this woman, the mother of a dead girl, who kept the memorial of her death every night. He might be drunk, but, he promised himself, he would not call out to her, just watch and see what she did. Watching someone pray, that was not something he had done before. But perhaps he and Roger should talk to this woman, tomorrow, when they had both slept. He would follow her to find out where she lived, and hope that the Watch, and the woman, did not realize what he was doing.

As he thought, he must be drunk. This was a stupid plan.

But at least he was not as stupid as the Watch. Their guarding of the town was abysmal, any necromancers, sorcerers, witches, why, even the King of France himself and all his army, could probably march through St. Brett's on their way to London and those three buffoons would not notice. His father really must be desperate if he had had to take on volunteers of that calibre.

The town was quiet as he walked the last part of the alley that would take him to the north end of the market, and past his father's large house that faced onto widest section of the market place, just by the Eleanor Cross. So perhaps the Watch had some effect after all. *Then again, maybe it's just very late,* he thought as he stifled a yawned.

There was a loud yowl and Jake jumped in surprise. Yellow eyes glared at him and he heard a cat's hiss. He saw a large black cat run away into the market place and then vanish. Now if he were superstitious he'd probably think, "No witches? There goes one now."

If it was a witch then it had taken no notice of the woman kneeling before the Eleanor Cross. Her head was bowed and Jake could see her lips moving by the light of the torches that lined the market. There was a danger of fire from those if the wind picked up. They were placed well away from the houses, but still. His father really had lost it if he thought that were a good plan.

But they did cast a powerful light over the public spaces at the centre of the town. The praying woman would be able to see him if her head was not bowed in her prayer, her eyes closed, he hoped. He had best hide himself.

He stepped to the wall of a house that ran along the north side of the alley. The shadows were deep here and he shouldn't be seen. He wondered if the woman was anyone he might know, but at that distance and with the veil and wimple that she wore, he couldn't make out her features. Perhaps he should have asked the Watchmen before he had fled?

She had placed her flowers at the foot of the Eleanor Cross, and he could see that they sat on top of a whole pile of other bunches of flowers, brought by her on other nights he supposed. The Cross was right in the middle of the widest part of the market street which formed a triangle with its widest side here at the north end and then tapering into a narrower street near the Abbey precinct to the south and a warren of small streets and alleys which held numerous shops.

The houses at the north end where he watched were larger. Grander like their occupants. Right across the way was his father's house. A large, three-story house that towered above its neighbours, which were of two stories only. Part of the ground floor was stone now, where before it had only been wattle and daub like nearly all the other houses of the town. That had been a change since he was last here. Things must be going well for his father.

As Jake studied the house in the light of the torches that lined the market, he saw a light appear in a window on the second story. He shaded his eyes to cut out the glare of the torchlight from the market and thought he could make out the silhouette of a woman. Isabel?

The woman at the Eleanor Cross came to the end of her prayers. She stood and made the sign of the cross across her own breast, then turned and looked at the Haukwake house. Jake thought she was looking at that window with the light. After a moment the silhouette in the window disappeared and a few moments later the front door of the house was opened. Isabel rushed out. Her hair was loose and uncovered in contrast to the sober appearance of the woman who had been praying, and her shawl was carelessly wrapped around her, barely covering her bare shoulders showing some of the flesh of her breasts. His father, if he had any shame, shouldn't let her go onto the street looking like that, thought Jake.

"Margery, won't you come in a while. We have a fire and there is wine if you would like some," said Isabel, speaking gently to the grieving mother.

The woman shook her head. "I curse the day that I ever accepted your hospitality, Isabel Haukwake. From that day, my little girl was doomed. That's why you wanted me and the others weren't it? We had children, children you could murder."

"Margery, that's not true. I had nothing to do with your daughter's death. Why do you listen to those idiots who say so?"

"You taught us remedies, but I should have known there was something ungodly about it, devilish."

"Margery, please, you and all the others were only helped by what I taught you. Half the time it was other women of the Company who taught all of us new things, all sharing treatments and tricks to make the hard lot of women easier to bear. Do you call your fellows witches as well?"

"Maybe some have fallen into the clutches of demons, yes. What about old Margaret who died in the church at the hands of her own brother?"

Isabel bowed her head and after a moment said, "She was one of the ones who expelled me from the Company, don't you remember?"

The woman snorted. "Because she knew what you were, and then you put a demon inside her in revenge. You killed her — and you killed my daughter too!"

"Margery, must you always listen to backbiters? You know in your heart that isn't true."

"They say you bewitched Master Haukwake, younger as well as elder, for your benefit."

True. Too true, thought Jake.

"Do you deny it?"

"Of course I deny it," said Isabel shaking her head.

"You told us about using caraway and how to mix it with garlic, I remember hearing you whisper to old Margaret how it had won you the love of both a father and a son, taverners both. Deny it."

"I do not, though such was never my intention, Margery. But you must see that making an aphrodisiac is not the same as planning sorcery that involves human sacrifice, now is it?"

"Not the same, no, but I think it shows something about you. I never had to win a man through trickery. I was never so desperate for control and power over others as you are. That's what it's about isn't it. You came from the gutter—"

My doorstep, one November morning, thought Jake,

"—and now you wear silks and furs, and sit at the front of the church like a lady. I hear you want to turn old John into a gentleman and join the Corporation of London one day. I hope you rot in hell, before you do." Margery spat in the ground again.

"I have had enough of your insults, Margery Hegate. Why don't you go home now?"

"Why? More murders of innocents to conjure?"

"If you slander me one more time Margery ..."

"You'll what? Oh I wish I had not sent Peter away. I mean to send word to wherever he has fled and when he hears he will come back here and beat you black and blue the way he did me, but he won't stop until your brain pan is crushed and ..."

"Madam, are you in need of assistance?" A male voice, a young man who stood in the doorway of John Haukwake's house behind her, stepped into view, placing a hand on her shoulder. *A lover, or a servant, or both,* wondered Jake. Others had heard the argument raging outside the Haukwake's door. Jake could see windows and shutters ajar with heads poking out to listen. Here and there candles flickered into life inside houses nearby.

"No, I am sure Margery is about to leave us," said Isabel to the young man.

"Simon, does she have you bedazzled too? Why don't you put an end to the witch, help me end our town's nightmare." Margery stepped forward, her hand out imploring.

"Shall I fetch the Master, Madam?" said Simon.

"Just remember my little girl, won't you, and what you have taken from me." Jake could hear tears in Margery's voice as she spoke. And then she turned and strode away from the Haukwake's house.

Jake followed her through the market place. Before she reached the open space in front of the Abbey gatehouse where the three Watchmen "stood guard," Jake ran up to her and called out to her to stop.

She was alarmed, but not scared, more ready to defend herself and fight than run away, thought Jake.

"I mean you no harm, I want to help you," he said, keeping a respectful distance, so not to frighten her further. "My Master and I have been summoned to St. Brett's by the Abbot to solve these crimes of sorcery."

Her eyes narrowed and she grunted acknowledgment. She stood waiting to see what he had to say.

She told him how her daughter was found at the foot of the Eleanor Cross. She had been laid out with five candles around her, and strange symbols marked on her body. Her throat had been cut and the blood drained from her body. "They used a sharp blade the Infirmarian told me, you could see that by the way the flesh had been parted, so maybe she didn't suffer too much eh?" And there was no blood on the ground around her, the blood had been taken.

Jake stepped closer and took the woman in his arms as she began to cry. "We'll get them, whoever it was."

"We gave her my name. I thought I would die after the childbirth, I was near death. My husband said we should name her Margery so that my beauty would live on in the world. He is a charming bastard when he wants to be. What's your name sir?"

"Jake."

"There was a Jake Haukwake wasn't there, son of John." She stepped back a pace and looked around her.

"There was," he agreed.

"Why do you speak to me here, at night in the dark? Do you mean to slay me? You're Isabel's lover still, aren't you?"

"No I'm not. I admit to you I am John's son, and I did once have a place in my heart for Isabel, but do you think I have any love for her now? A woman who cast me aside for ... for ..."

"Perhaps she promises you things. The Jake I knew of was a passionate man, passionate enough to kill to get what he wanted. I will have no dealings with her. Swear that you do not love her and that you are against her, or I will call the Watch."

The Watch mustered under the purview of John Haukwake, the husband of the woman you hate so much, thought Jake. But he could see that the woman was scared and so she should be. It was not wise to walk alone at night with a man that she knew not.

"I was fooled by her witchery. You are right I am a violent passionate man. I tried to kill my father and her, too, as they shared the same shameful bed. I left blood on the sheets but they lived."

"Renounce your love for her on this cross," she held out a wooden cross that hung as a necklace from her throat, "and mayhap I will believe you. Otherwise be gone."

"I only want to help you," pleaded Jake. What was wrong with him, how could he be so weak? "I will come again another day with my master. He is a Master of Oxford, a wise and worthy man."

"You are an honest man, Jake Haukwake."

"Savage is my name now." He turned and walked, and then ran once he reached the corner and was out of her sight.

CHAPTER 20

The last thing Roger remembered was his head hitting the pillow and the next moment his eyes opened and bright sunshine beamed through cracks in the room's shutters. He felt warm and cozy. The straw mattress and the down pillow were more comfortable than his own bed in Oxford, and for once he did not feel an anxiety to leap up and be about his work. He hated to admit to anyone, but some nights he barely slept at all, his repose consisting of lying down, closing his eyes, and pretending to sleep for a few hours while calculations, measurements, and theorems painted themselves on the back of his eyelids and rushed through his brain like maniacal chariots. But this morning he felt truly rested and content and he was happy to laze for a while, perhaps the rest of the morning if he wanted to. His mind was a blank. He couldn't remember thinking of anything while he tried to sleep, or even of dreaming. A perfect, uneventful night.

It would be so much easier, he realized, to simply lie here than to go and face the task in hand. He could pretend that the Abbey didn't exist outside these walls, that there wasn't a town scared out of its wits by a series of child murders and demons possessing its folk. Returning to his study to pore over charts of the heavens or a Greek text was a pleasure that he could not indulge in. Here he was expected to solve the unsolvable, to put the world back in order, and the demons back in their hells.

A loud snore ripped through the air like a bullock's fart, leaving Roger's ears reverberating for painful seconds as the air waves adjusted.

"What the devil ..." gasped Roger.

He leant over the side of the bed to see that Jake was curled on a rug with a blanket half-wrapped around his body, which lay at a diagonal angle across the floor as if the door had been opened with him lying across like a draft break but had then been pushed aside. Perhaps it had? Roger remembered that the door being rather difficult to move last night when he came in.

Or had someone else been in their room?

Roger gulped. The mist was clearing from his cobwebbed brain. He remembered a creaking sound and the cadaver of that woman who had exploded with a demon bursting her entrails all over the church floor. Her corpse! He had seen it walk into his room last night. She had peered across his bed, her fingers wet and sticky with the slimy stuff that wasn't quite blood that came from her guts, where the demon had emerged. And then, and then...

Yet had he woken up and remembered nothing? And had he felt contented and forgotten everything for a moment, perhaps in the knowledge that at least he was alive and that thing had not taken him? And yet perhaps it had not been real at all?

But the image of her burst body wouldn't leave him. That carcass had looked real enough. He had seen right through her rib-cage, seen her lungs moving, the wet slap of her torn heart beating, and then moonlight shining right through from her spine to her ribs. Thank God he couldn't remember her face.

Roger jumped out of bed and pulled his breeches on and tugged a robe over his nightshirt. He must see that body and then he would know it was not still alive. He had seen the Precentor last night, and he had said that he should ask the Infirmarian about the bodies and about the care of those possessed. So he would do that. Yes, he would get out of this place where his night had been marred by her presence and he would prove that she was dead.

A thought jumped into his mind. Perhaps the Infirmarian would know of *De Corpus* by Herophilos on anatomy? The book was legendary. None knew of it at Oxford, but he had heard of it in Italy and acquired a small pocket-book that purported to give summary of the Greek's lore. Symbols, sigils, letters, and digits began to revolve in his head blocking out the memory of decayed fingers and Margaret Stokke's ripped-open body. If he had been conscious of it, Roger Sotil would have breathed a sigh of relief. Now with his task obvious before him, and the prospect of enquiring after new knowledge enticing him, he slipped on his shoes and stepped over Jake to open the door. There was an indistinct murmur from Jake, but nothing more. Roger looked for a moment at the face of his man. The mouth was pursed open and the cheeks sagged out like a child's. Roger smiled and left the room.

The Abbey precinct was quiet, some servants went about their duty but Roger realized that there were no monks to be seen. He could smell meat in rich spices cooking. Was it that late? Roger looked up at the sky. Indeed the sun was just past the zenith of its daily journey cross the heavens. He walked briskly to the refectory, his stomach feeling cavernous as it contemplated its hunger. Inside, the forty of so monks of the Abbey sat whispering to each other while a bored-looking brother, standing at a pulpit situated above them halfway down a gallery, droned quietly in Latin from a large missal laid before him. *How good of him to not disturb their conversation,* thought Roger.

The monks were tucking into a good meal of well-spiced stewed lamb and pottage, and supped wine from plain white but finely turned pottery cups. Roger did not see Edmund there. Roger approached a servant who loitered by the door.

"You can find food at the guest-house or one of the taverns in town if you're hungry," said the servant before Roger got the chance to speak. Were those insect legs poking out of his ear, or just particularly bristly ear-hair? They seemed to move with every word the servant spoke.

"I was actually looking for ..."

"Gone hunting and will be back later this afternoon."

"With the Infirmarian?"

"No? Why do you ask?"

"Because that is who I am looking for. I thought he might be here eating."

"There's a place for him at the high table, but he rarely takes advantage of it," said the servant indicating the table on the dais where the Precentor and a couple of other monks sat, each apart from the other and avoiding conversation. He tried to catch the eye of the Precentor, and watched as his head nodded — falling asleep. That was no wonder as he stayed up later than even Roger. He wondered if the Precentor had visited the Infirmarian as he suggested or not. What had he said? Something about a cure doing more harm than good?

"If you'll be wanting him he'll be in the infirmary, I ne'er seen him eat much though, so no doubt he'll be mixing his 'pothecaries or reading something."

"Not tending the sick?"

"Too close to the sin of human flesh, I expect, for his liking," said the servant, who stood resolutely in the doorway of the hall, arms folded. "Now if that is all?"

Roger understood, nodded and left. He walked through the bright spring sunshine towards the infirmary cloister with its small cluster of single-story, red-roofed buildings. A small chimney in one of them puffed wood-smoke into the sky. Perhaps Edmund or some of his assistants were hungry after all?

He entered the small cloister that sat at the heart of the infirmary buildings. The garden at the centre was pleasant enough and the day was warm. It would be nice to sit there for a while and relax. Although for some reason the quiet stone walls of the place repelled him and he felt disinclined to go further. Strange, he was never one to idle, yet here he was contemplating sloth. Perhaps, if the Infirmarian wasn't there, he could rest, and perhaps some useful thought would come to him about what to do next. The door to the dormitory was shut, but not locked, and he went in, expecting to be greeted by coughing and foul smells of sickness and disease. He hated hospitals and covered his nose as he entered, for Galen said that contagion's first port of entry was by the nose, so if he could he would guard against entry from that extremity first. He had once entered a plague ward in Italy by mistake, and there the doctors wore masks over their faces to protect from the death's breath. Perhaps, he pondered, demons came like a plague, too, and could infect a town or Abbey through their foul vapours?

But his hand need not have worried about its work as a shield. Inside there were a dozen beds lined up, their grey woollen blankets undisturbed by the bodies of the ill. Except for one. At the far end of the dormitory lay a tall monk — well whether he was tall or not, Roger couldn't actually say as he was lying down, but unless the bed he lay upon was intended for a child then he must be tall as his head lay on the pillow and his feet jutted over the edge despite his long legs being bent to form what looked like a perfectly symmetrical triangle.

He didn't look ill though. Perhaps one of the monks had found a place for a sleep after lunch. Monks were said to be an idle bunch, not even bothering with their duty of prayer unless pressed to it. Roger was about to turn and leave when the lying monk spoke.

"He has been expecting you," said the reclining monk, who did not stir, but Roger realized that the man's eyes had not been shut in sleep at all. "If you go to the centre of the garden and wait by the pond I will fetch him."

Roger was surprised that the Infirmarian knew he was coming, but tried to keep his composure. "There is no need to fetch him. Perhaps if you show me to his chamber?"

"I don't think he will like that. Just do as I say. I won't be long. I have nearly counted all of the imperfections on these beams."

"Pardon?" said Roger.

"It is my punishment. You think I am idling don't you? Well I wish I were, but Master Edmund has seen fit to punish me for my mistakes and has commanded me to count the mistakes of nature in the wood that forms the beams of our infirmary. I was nearly finished when you came in, and now I must check which beams I have examined and which are still to do and then fix those in my memory."

Roger shook his head in astonishment. "I will go. I would not wish to prolong your punishment." The monk made no answer, so Roger left and went back to the garden. At least he could sit in the sunshine and soak up the warmth for a while. He looked around, but there were no benches or seats. That was strange for an infirmary garden, he thought, where it would surely be good for the ill to sit and receive the warmth of the sun or the vitality of the sweet air from the garden's flowers and herbs. The pond that the monk had mentioned was very little to speak of and stank from neglect. The water was covered with a slime of green growth, and he doubted if any fish deigned to live in it. With not a little effort, Roger found a section of its stone rim not overgrown with moss and weeds and sat down, placing his copy of the Paracelsus summary on his lap, and opened it for a moment to glance at the badly drawn but enticing illustrations of the human body.

He did not have to endure the discomfort of his seat for long. From the east side of the cloister, opposite the infirmary dormitory, entered a monk who must be the Infirmarian. This man had striking black hair, well-cut except for a small, yet perfectly circular tonsure. The small patch of bald head glistened in the sunshine. The face below was gaunt and deeply lined and appeared as if it did not belong to the hair. It was an old face on the a body of a young man who stood erect and poised.

Roger stood up as the man approached and did not know how to greet this person, should he bow or extend his hand in friendship? The monk looked at him hard, but said nothing. Roger was forced to say the first word.

"Thank you for seeing me, I have come with some questions. I would like to see the bodies of those who died yesterday in the church."

"That is not possible," said the Infirmarian.

"But the Abbot has given me permission to see and know all that I must to solve this crime. Please do not be difficult about this."

"Can the Abbot put ashes back together again? Or maybe you have that power. In which case you are welcome."

"You burnt them? But why?"

"The bodies of sinners were deemed not to require a burial. The stuff upon them was too disgusting to be called human anymore."

"Did you find anything of interest before the bodies were burnt?"

"Of interest? No, nothing at all. Blood, guts, the stuff of life on display. God's rich pageant for us all to see — no wonder it is hidden away. It is disgusting stuff."

"But it's your trade, is it not?"

"My trade? My vocation is to serve God. I see you carry a book?" said the Infirmarian pointing to the volume Roger clutched in his hands.

"Yes. A gloss of texts that includes mention of Paracelsus. His opus sounds interesting, but I have not heard of a library with a copy."

"You don't need his anatomy to know how to heal. Good health and bad, it is God's will. Prayer is what I recommend."

"And only prayer? What about the teachings of the Fathers of the Church? Of the many scholars that have followed after them?"

"An Oxford man, aren't you?"

"You have a library here as fit as any at Oxford; you live and work in a place of learning, yet you seem to reject it."

"If I were Abbot, then perhaps things would be different. Learning is a means to an end, a shortcut, and should not be loved for its own sake. In that regard it is as dangerous as money, diverting man from the narrow path. Why read and learn when one could act?"

"You have no medical texts then?"

"As I said, there is merit in learning if the end deserves it, but no more. I have what is sufficient for my needs."

"And Paracelsus is not sufficient for your ends? You must have knowledge of the book."

"No, Paracelsus and the anatomy of the human body is not something that I need read about. I have seen a copy, but one glance was enough."

"Where?"

"You are hungry for knowledge are you not, Master Sotil? Hungrier to learn than to solve the puzzle that the Abbot has set you."

"If you would answer my question, I would be about my business; but, yes, I do find that the expansion of knowledge is like the picking of fruit: one must take what is ripe and within reach while it is the season."

"A very clever metaphor, you should be a preacher and turn your words to more fearful purposes. The fear of God is not bound by season. Hellfire and the pit do not wax and wane depending upon the warmth of the sun. I will tell you. It was in Egypt. There, are you satisfied? It will not avail you much, as the library that contained the volume is now as much cinder as the bodies of the late demon-infused Margaret Stokke and her brother."

"Egypt? Much other scholarship comes from Egypt. Hermes? Solomon's texts I hear were also written down there."

"I know nothing of these books. I was there on crusade, a failed crusade full of misery and death, but a fitting sacrifice to Our Lord. You seek information, but I think you seek it in the wrong place. It is about time you looked outside the Abbey. I would look at the town. It is not only monks who can read Latin in these end times."

"How did you come to be a monk at St. Brett's?" asked Roger. "Your English is strange to my ear."

"Look, I have told you all I know. Go to the town, look for someone who hates children, someone who hates them enough to kill them."

"What kind of person would do that?"

"A person beyond the grace of God, of course."

"St. Brett's is a small town; most of the people must be known to the monks. Is there no suspect, someone beyond God's grace as you say, who you suspect?"

"God gave man and woman free will. Yet some choose to use their free will to subvert His commands, to place themselves above the natural order of things, to use foul arts to bring themselves power. Look for such a person and I am sure you will find such a suspect. Someone who came from nothing and now exults herself above all others, too good for God's grace."

He suspects a woman then? And one who knows Latin and is high in status. There can't be many such people in a town of only a thousand souls, thought Roger. "It sounds as if you have a specific person in mind?"

"Master Roger, your Oxford learning was money well spent, for I think you can draw conclusions that I cannot see. Perhaps you have a gift for inquest that you did not realise?"

"You think so?"

"More than think, I know it, for the Lord has spoken it to me."

Roger felt something prickle around his chest and neck. Was his hair standing on end or was it something else? He felt hot and sweaty and wanted to leave the infirmary immediately.

"Well thank you for your help, Brother Edmund, you have been most... umm..."

"Helpful?"

"Uh ... that might be it. Yes?" Roger found himself backing towards the door, not willing to turn his back on Edmund for some reason, like a cornered prey-animal keeping its attacker in sight.

Edmund reached towards him and Roger instinctively raised an arm to block him, but the monk was stronger and casually brushed Roger's block away, leaning past him to open the door and let him through into the cool, refreshing sunshine outside the infirmary.

"Goodbye, then," said Roger, nodding for some reason at the impassive face of the Infirmarian. He turned and walked briskly away from the infirmary cloister, not daring to look back in case that face was still watching him. The burning prickling sensation of heat did not leave him and neither did the Infirmarian's words: "end-times." Millennialism to be sure, but "sacrifice"? What did he mean by that?

CHAPTER 21

He plunged the knife into her again and again and again and finally she fell back into the bed, to land, laughing, in the arms of that disgusting old man. Jake woke and blinked, something sticky covering his eyes. He wiped it away, then looked at his hand expecting to see blood and entrails, but found just the yellow pus of sleepy eyes. He shivered despite the warmth of the sun beating through the half-open shutters of the guest-room. How had he gotten here? Did he speak to Roger last night and tell him about the mother of the murdered girl? He should do that, but then she might remind him of his promise. His promise to renounce the woman that he loved. The woman that he had murdered just now in his dreams.

Even drinking yourself fucking stupid doesn't help forgetting now! Damn it. Where had he got that grog? He didn't remember anything about where or what he had drunk, although by the taste on his tongue it was fairly cheap Bordeaux red. Despite that and his hangover, he remembered vividly the encounter last night between the mother and Isabel, and the promise he made to that grief-stricken woman. He looked at his hands. That could sometimes give him a clue of what had happened the night before. They were stained red with wine and he saw a splinter of wood that needed pulling out, but nothing else. He looked around the room. Roger was gone, and there were no jugs of half-finished drink. Nothing to line his stomach with. Roger wasn't one to do his own housework, so if the jugs weren't here he must have drunk them somewhere else and then somehow staggered back to their room.

He lifted himself to the windowsill and opened the shutters. The bright spring sunshine dazzled him. It was low in the west already. Late afternoon. He had slept nearly the whole day and still felt awful. He stifled a yawn that nearly made his head split with pain. Must remember not to open his mouth too wide or move his neck too much for a few hours yet. Or maybe not even until tomorrow.

He sat down heavily on Roger's bed. The sheets were a mess so he must have slept there.

Time passed and Jake looked up. The shadows in the room had moved and he had just been sitting there like an imbecile. His stomach let out a roar. It was time to fill it and then start drinking again. Perhaps he would see Roger later.

He got up and walked more steadily to the door than he expected, and continued cautiously down the steps.

"Fucking arsehole!" shouted someone in the courtyard. As Jake walked down the steps he could hear more swearing and someone sweeping something and banging around with furniture and cupboards.

"Keep it down!" hissed Jake. The racket was coming from the kitchen that provided food for those lodging at the Abbey's guesthouse. He needed food and hoped the cook could provide it if he wasn't still angry. Jake looked in through the open doorway. "Any food going?"

A sweating and fat Abbey servant, dressed in an apron and pushing around a broom, turned and glared at him. "Not until eventide now. Lunch was over hours ago. Where have you been?"

"Nevermind. What happened here?"

"The lazy fuckers who would have given you your lunch couldn't be bothered to clear up this mess," said the cook, indicating a heap of broken crockery and sticky red liquid that had partly dried on the floor next to a broken-up pantry door. "This was the wine store. But I guess that lazy tart, Kerwyn, who does lunch couldn't be bothered to sort it out."

"Oh, I see, bad luck for you," said Jake. He smiled and felt his stomach lurch a bit. He had wondered where he'd found and drunk that red wine last night. Perhaps this was the answer? "I'll head into town and find a tavern, then."

The cook looked him up and down and sniffed. "All right then, as you wish."

Why was this place so full of dick heads? wondered Jake.

The late afternoon sunshine gave the town of St. Brett's a wash of gold slashed with dark shadows. *Hides much of the grime,* thought Jake. *You could almost be happy to live here on a day like this.* But like many days, Jake had not see many of its daylight hours.

He left the Abbey by the large gatehouse that opened onto the top of Pikepond Lane to the west of the market. There were a couple of taverns on the far side of the market he could try, or stop at one of the cook-shops where he could get a pie and a pint of home brew for just a few pennies. His purse felt light without Roger around.

Stallholders in the market were packing up their wares and folding up awnings. Jake turned up his collar and hunched down. Still he found it hard to weave through the groups of busy traders and the few buyers loitering for a late bargain. "Pardon," he said as he bumped into a woman stacking boxes of vegetables. She shook her head, but didn't reply. "My fault," he said as his shoulder caught a roll of linen being carried to a cart and spun round its porter. "Watch where you're going," said the man. "Get back to your pot where you belong," he added as Jake shuffled on. The warren of stalls and wooden shops seemed never-ending despite the small area covered by the market. There were more than there used to be, he felt sure of it.

He wished he wasn't in this stupid town. The abbot, Isabel, his father, they could all go to hell. Even Roger. It was his master's fault he was here at all. If only he didn't owe him for Hampton.

A man was sweeping up outside his shop down one of the narrow shambles as Jake approached, hoping to take a short cut across to the far side of the market. This time the collision was no accident. Jake didn't try to squeeze past but launched his shoulder into him, only bracing against his broom handle stopped the man from being knocked to the ground.

"What are you looking at?" said Jake. He walked on. The man shouted something.

"What did you call me?" Jake shouted back, rushing up to the man and gripping him by his shirt. Jake's powerful arms easily lifted the man off the ground. He ignored the man's wailing and flung him onto the dusty street. A woman opened a window shutter and looked out from a house across the street. Jake glared at her, and she quickly slammed the shutter closed.

She hadn't seen anything had she? And if she had, then so what? Jake strode down the shadowy alley. He kept his eyes focused on a growing pool of light that marked the end of the alley, yet his legs fought against him and sent him lurching from side to side. But he kept on going. There were taverns on that street. And salvation perhaps.

§

William Hoode stood on the steps of the Dog and Duck and swore under his breath. He was a God-fearing man and there were children just inside the threshold of his establishment, or he would have shouted his foul curse for all to hear. He looked over to where the tower of St.

Brett's loomed over the buildings of the shambles opposite and bowed his head. Even a thought was a sin, he knew. But even so, if their trade did not pick up soon, he would not be able to afford the rent of the tavern any longer, and then where would they be? Certainly not aspiring to membership of the Brotherhood, like John Haukwake had suggested. That man was more cunning than a fox, William knew, but he surely had enough money stashed away to allow another tavern to trade on equal terms next to his own. Enough travellers and pilgrims came to St. Brett's to fill the bar and the beds above, yet the Dog and Duck was only ever half full at best.

What did that friar say who preached at the Isabel Cross last Whitsuntide? "Blessed be the meek for they shall inherit the earth" William smiled as he heard his children's laughter behind him. At least he had them and his beautiful wife.

"Get away from here," shouted Old Maud from the Wilted Sparrow next door, one of Haukwake's places. She was shooing a beggar away from the inn's door. *Just the sort of patron to drive other paying customers away, and unlikely to have coin of his own,* William thought. And now the man was stumbling this way. He had a thick brown beard, hair that looked a dog and cat had fought in it, and there were stains on his breeches that looked like piss. William crossed his arms and stood resolute in the doorway of the Dog and Duck. The beggar wouldn't be getting into his place, either.

But where was the charity in that? William sighed. The Good Samaritan would help any man, even a beggar and a stranger. And this one looked like he needed some help.

"Molly," he called to the eldest of the children, still not in her teens, but old enough to serve in the tavern when they had guests. "Warm some water will you, we have a patron who needs a bath."

§

"Take just a sip of it. There that's enough." Jake did as William bid. He felt better now. The brew had some sort of medicinal herbs that had cured him of his headache and stripped some of the webs away from his thoughts. The sleep had helped, too.

"Who would have thought it?" said William, smiling across the table at Jake, was slowly devouring a large roast dinner. "I thought I was helping a poor stranger, doing a good deed like the Samaritan, and instead I find that beneath the grime and the shrubbery it's my childhood friend."

"You still did a kindness. There's many in this town who would rather pretend that they had never known me."

William's wife, Kate, brought over another jug. "This time it's milk. No ale today for you." William had always told Jake that he would have the pick of the girls, but he had found himself a pretty one in Kate — curls of blonde hair snuck from under her hood, and her eyes twinkled at Jake, despite his foul state.

"A bit of ale might settle things down, though," said Jake, kicking himself inside. What a drunkard he must sound.

"Not in here," Kate was kind, but firm. "I won't have you leading my William astray."

"What's an astray, Mother?" enquired their son Hugh, no more than five years of age, but helping to sweep the floor at the other end of the bar. Sharp ears picked up everything at that age.

The three adults laughed. They were the only ones in the tavern besides a bored-looking potboy who polished some tankards behind the bar. The Hoode's couldn't afford any more staff, and had to do much of the work themselves. In a busy little town like this it shouldn't be that way.

"No customers this evening?" asked Jake.

William's smile drained from his face. "No, not tonight, a bit slow."

"You remember, before I left, I owned my own tavern in St. Brett's. Those were hard times."

"Yes, I remember — you were pining after Isabel. To tell you the truth, you let that place go."

William got up and looked around, and gestured to his children and wife as they busied themselves around the empty tavern. "If you work hard then things will come right in the end."

"I was struggling from the beginning, William. This place was alright in those days, half-full at least during the busy times, and full on holy days. I remember watching people coming and going with envy. Your father didn't make the mistake of disobeying John Haukwake. So how did you cross him?"

William frowned. His wife stood watching from the kitchen door. She wanted to hear this.

"I spoke my mind that was all. Just said what was right and just, that a man who was charged with assessing weights and measures or ale and bread should not be the same man that owned the largest taverns in St. Brett's."

"And where did you say it?" asked his wife, steel in her words. She knew the answer.

"In the Hundred Court, beneath the old Ash tree," William said, sticking out his chin in defiance as he spoke and looking Jake in the eye as his wife glared at him. But that was only for a moment. And then she came to Jake's table wringing her hands.

"Would you be able to say something to your father, Jake? Something to help us? William is a good man, too good. He didn't mean anything by it. He knows it was wrong."

William looked like he was about to say something, but then thought better of it.

Jake would have laughed if the woman wasn't on the verge of tears. "I can't. You see I'm the last person you want as a friend if John Haukwake is your enemy. I loathe the man more than any on God's earth."

"Because of Isabel?" asked William.

"You should forget about that painted whore," said William's wife. "She has caused nothing but trouble."

"Not what you used to say," said William.

"I don't need her to tell me what a woman is capable of," she replied. Jake could well believe her.

"Yes, I suppose that's part of it," said Jake. "But he never wanted me to succeed on my own. He always wanted to rule me, and that's where I went wrong with my own inn. He didn't like it when I tried to do things my own way. He helped me get set-up with money and everything, but then he kept loading me with his plans. Like he was starting out again himself and wanted to do it all over, but not make the same mistakes."

"So did you come back because you heard about his sickness a while back?" asked William.

Jake shook his head and felt a shiver run through him. "Sick? That tough old goat? He thinks he's twenty-one every day. If he was sick it was some ploy, I'll wager you."

"No, I saw him, Jake," said William. "He collapsed in the market one day. He had just left his house, and then he came over all pale as if the blood had been suddenly drained out of him, and he fell to the ground. Isabel was there in an instant, and his servant, and they carried him inside. He didn't emerge for two weeks. Fever they say, although they didn't say much about it, tried to keep it quiet, I think. Molly heard it from one of the maids that he had sweated blood through his skin."

"But he's better now isn't he?"

"I suppose ..."

"When was this?"

"A month ago, it was ..."

"And nothing more than this one instance?"

"Yes, that's right. Have you seen him?"

Jake winced. "I've seen him, but it's not why I came to St. Brett's. I followed my Master, the fool that I am. He's in the employ of the Abbot. Here to solve the mystery of your so-called demons, and the death of the young..."

William kicked him hard under the table and Jake looked around at the children's faces watching him.

"Well that's why I'm here, but it's a pretty sorry effort. I don't think my Master has a clue. He's no inquisitor."

"I've heard about this Oxford Master, some say he's a sorcerer, too, come to catch one of his own kind. Takes one to know one they say."

"He's no such thing. Spends too much time with his head in the clouds rather than his feet on the ground, but he'd never do anything like sorcery. And if you ask me, anyone who does is a damn fool. There's no such thing as demons and magic. Life's what it is and that's that."

"But what about the miracles of our Lord and the Saints? How do you explain those?"

"Well you'd better not be calling them magic, that's a start."

"Oh I didn't realize. Have I blasphemed?" said William crossing himself.

"Maybe just a little bit. There's differences in meaning and subtleties. If a wondrous thing is done by God or in God's name, it's not magic they say. Although I've never seen any such wondrous things and know no man I trust who has, so what credit you give that I don't know."

William smiled at him. "Despite it all, though, you have done alright for yourself, you know. Your dad got you educated at least, you know your scripture a bit from your time at the Grammar School, and now here you are manservant to a man of law."

"Well I've had some scrapes with the law in the past, and my master is no judge or lawyer, so I'm hardly a man of law."

"Well there is one coming, should be here in the next few days. The Abbey haven't said nothing, but a merchant returned from London heard that the Lord Chief Justice himself was coming to St. Brett's."

"Lord Chief Justice? You mean Cavendish?" asked Jake.

"Yes, quite sure. They mentioned his reputation. Likes to hang 'em first and not ask any questions afterwards." Jake didn't laugh at William's weak joke. Would Cavendish remember him? Bound to, he thought, the man didn't like it if anyone got away from his justice, and Roger had swooped Jake out of the hangman's noose with some style. He had to put as many miles between himself and Cavendish as soon as possible. But could he abandon Roger, the man who had saved his life from certain death at Cavendish's hands?

"Are you all right?" asked William. "You look like you've a fever. You're shivering. Hey, Molly get Master Haukwake a blanket."

"Don't use that name!" snapped Jake.

Jake saw Molly look at him with fear. He blushed. So he was scaring children now, too. He should be ashamed of himself, but he wasn't.

"Leave the blanket," he said. "Look, I'm sorry for shouting." Turning to the girl, Molly, he said, "Please forgive me."

"I do so sir, of course."

"You have a good family, William, and it's best if I'm not around here to make things worse for you. I'll take my leave of you now and thank you for your kindness. This may be the last time I see you, as I'm going to leave later today, go back to Oxford probably. I don't have any coin on me, but I'll send something from Oxford for the clothes, or I could give them back to you later today. You've been very kind to me. More than I deserve."

"Don't be foolish Jake. Why are you going? Are you scared of the Justice? Has he a warrant for you?"

"More cause than a warrant, I fear. This is a small town …"

"No one here will give you up. Besides, your father's the Bailiff, and he'd have to arrest you most like and bring you before the Justice before any judgment be served."

Jake reached over the table and grasped both of William's hands. "The last time I was in St. Brett's I tried to kill my father and Isabel, and yesterday I think I nearly tried to do it again. Do you not agree he would rather see me imprisoned or, better yet, on the end of a rope?"

"He's your father! He won't want to see you swing!"

"You think he has the will to protect me from Justice Cavendish? The Justice won't let me slip through his fingers again. I'm one of his few failures. He'd welcome the chance to clear my name from that short tally."

"Jake, we need a man like you here. And I think even your father needs you. I don't know if any of the rumours about you and Isabel and your father are true, but let bygones be bygones and stay. Listen, you know I don't think much of the man, but I am sure he'd want you to stay."

Jake shook his head and stood up to leave. "I'm sorry. I'm going to make my report to Master Roger and then leave this afternoon."

"Hugh, Molly, come here and say God be with you to Master Hau.., to Jake, to Jake?"

"Savage. I'm called Jake Savage now."

"To Master Savage then." William smiled. The two fair-haired children, each no higher than Jake's belt, beamed at him and came up to their father shyly giggling as they came.

"It would mean a lot to me, and to my wife, if you could stop whoever's doing these terrible things in our town."

Jake ruffled the hair of the two children. "You keep your father out of trouble, you hear!" He grasped his friend's arm for a moment, then headed to the door.

"We need you Jake," said William.

Jake shook his head. "I wish I had never walked into your pub, William Hoode."

CHAPTER 22

A little before dusk, Isabel walked through the un-tilled water meadows along the River Varn. This was the perfect time for finding cowbane and angelica. Cowbane could be harmful to animals, but used in the right amounts, Isabel could use it as a powerful pain-killer. And, together with angelica, its properties for defending against witchcraft were well known. If she could find enough of these two herbs, then perhaps she could mix something that would protect her and John.

As she wandered the meadows, Isabel enjoyed the heat of the late afternoon sun on her face. May was one of her favourite months. There were beautiful sunny days like this one and enough rain showers to prompt the earth into life. The summer months could sometimes be drab by comparison, not living up to the promise of their forerunner.

She knelt in a patch of sunshine at the edge of the meadow near the trees that marked the edge of the Abbot's hunting domain. Here the townspeople could walk through to the Abbot's mill, but were forbidden to take game or timber. A few flowers and roots, though, would not hurt, and there was a great array of them on the edge of the meadow beneath the trees where the cows and sheep were prevented from roaming by a low fence. She started filling her basket and hummed a tune that her mother had once taught her.

> *Spring has come with love to town,*
> *With blossoms and with birds round,*
> *Which all this bliss bringeth;*
> *Daisies in these dales,*
> *Notes sweet of nightingales;*

She wished she could just stay here, away from the town and its backbiters. Perhaps she would wait until it was nearly dark to walk back and avoid the accusing gazes along Pikepond Lane. Why did the path between her and these beautiful fields have to be the poorest street in St. Brett's?

"Damnation," she cursed. Now that her worries had intruded and broken the spell, perhaps it was best just to go. She would have to collect more flowers and roots tomorrow, for somehow her heart was not in it today. She stood up and decided to walk through the wood instead of round the edge of the meadow. The way was somewhat obstructed by banks and roots, but it was quicker than going around the side.

As she walked up a slight slope covered in bluebells beneath the shadows of the beech trees, she thought she could hear buzzing. The noise became stronger, and she recognized the sound of flies. There was a stink of carrion, and she could see on top of the slope a patch of ground where the bluebells had been flattened and smashed aside and bloody pieces of meat lay strewn around. Some predator had made a big kill, she thought. A deer perhaps? But what had killed it? A wolf so near the town? But what else? Neither the Abbot or a poacher would have left any game to rot away like this.

Isabel thought about walking past and avoiding the dead animal, but curiosity won over her sensibility. The smell was awful, and she soon realized that this was no animal. There was no fur; instead, the torn pieces of black fabric indicated clothes, and the pieces of bloody flesh were flanked by human flesh. Here and there, she saw a finger or other piece of human anatomy. Was that a nose, perhaps? A piece of jawbone lined with blood and attached to a partly consumed flap of lip and severed tongue sat on a bread trencher. Someone had literally made a meal of this person. She must have been in shock, because her stomach did not heave immediately, and she found herself walking through the mess, the bottom of her skirt dragging across the bloody body parts and picking up some of the blood. She knelt down and inspected a pile of guts that had been cut up like sausages and arranged on another bread trencher, the body's penis in a place of pride in the centre of the pile. A knife lay nearby which must have been used to cut up the intestines. It was a delicate, but sharp dining knife. Not powerful enough to dismember this man.

That was when her stomach finally rebelled, and she ran for a tree to support her with one arm while she stood bent over projecting her stomach into the bluebells at her feet.

She stood for a while, recovering her composure. Her basket had toppled over and lay amongst the man's bloody flesh, the contents ruined. She didn't care. What was the meaning of this? Who had killed the man and then taken the trouble to mock his body in this way? Had they followed through on the sick joke of a feast and actually began eating his body? The flies were numerous and the body was beginning to decay, so they must have left it a while ago rather than being scared off by her arrival. She hoped that was a reassuring sign. But if they hadn't run, then perhaps they were watching and waiting to come after her as well.

Was it the witches?

"Hulloo, Mistress Haukwake. How fare yee?"

Isabel jerked her head up in surprise. It was Samuel, the miller's son, leading a mule. His father, Edward, walked behind, deep in conversation with Jake. The two other men looked up as Samuel spoke. She looked down at her hands and dress and realized that this might not look too good. She hoped that they would remember where their loyalties lay and not jump to accuse her. The miller and his son were practically retainers of her husband's. The son, in particular, was kind to her, and she suspected that he had somewhat of an adolescent crush upon her. The father, while always mannered was colder. His wife had taken up the Company of Good Women with eagerness, and she suspected had tried to change things around her household, much to Edward's displeasure.

And Jake? Well Jake hated her, and he was here to uncover the secrets of St. Brett's. But it was too late to run. The three men were walking through the sparse woodland towards her, and would see where she stood very soon.

"Mistress Haukwake," said Samuel as he approached. "Master Savage here is looking for the Precentor of the Abbey on behalf of his master, would you know where he is? He was spotted walking down the hills to the river early this morning."

Isabel looked down at the pieces of human carcass strewn about and wondered. The scraps of torn cloth were black like those of a monk's, but nothing else seemed to be recognizable. "Come and see," she said to them as they came nearer. They still hadn't seen. But she could see Edward's face screw up at the smell of carrion. Jake avoided looking at her, and his face was set in a mask of what must only be rage. He looked flushed as if he had taken on too much ale already that day. *Same old Jake.*

Samuel smiled. "What is it Mistress? What have you found?"

"Maybe the Precentor; I don't know. I think he was a monk, anyway."

Samuel stood in shock as he realized that he was now treading on lumps of meat and bone and gut and skin. He dropped the reins to the mule, which kicked out and decided it wanted to be elsewhere.

"Samuel!" snapped his father, and the boy stood stock still and then looked at his irate father and ran after the animal.

Edward picked his way through the carnage towards Isabel. "What happened here? Was this once a man? Master Savage, I think your master and the Abbot should see this, look at her hands they are covered in blood, and her dress."

"You think I did this?"

"I think we should fetch the Abbot and his servants," said Edward, ignoring her reply.

"I found the body like this," she said. "How could I have done so much damage and ripped this body apart like this?"

Edward knelt down and stared in horror at the trencher and its foul contents. "Someone who hates men did this. This is what comes of witchcraft and women gathering together to turn wives against husbands."

"When John hears what you've said, you'll regret it!"

Jake stepped forward between them. "I'll make sure she doesn't get away. Why don't you hurry after your son and that errant mule and then go and tell my master, I'll bring her back."

"You don't want any help? What if she tries to bewitch you? Whatever demon she summoned ripped this man to shreds. We should bind her and tie to the mule to make sure she can't escape."

"No," said Jake. Looking at her she saw him wink. "She may have minions in the town. We don't want to alert them and allow them chance to flee. I'll bring her to the abbey alone so as not to cause any alarm to the other witches. My master can question her there."

He walked up to her and grabbed her arm. His grip pinched, his whole hand enclosed the flesh and bone of her upper arm like a vice. "Now will you come willingly or will I have to use force."

It gave her great satisfaction to spit in his face. But she got a back-handed slap for her trouble, and Jake didn't fake that. "You fucking cunt!" she shouted at him as she strained against his grip that tightened on her arm.

"Calm down, or they'll be more of that," said Jake. There was something frightening about the way he looked at her. As if he was enjoying this too much. Had he intended to hurt her all along if he got the opportunity? That night when he left, when he drew a knife in their bed chamber... He had meant to use it on both of them.

Jake turned to Edward. "As you can see, It's going to take some time to tame her. I'll make sure she's ready for questioning, might see if I can get a confession out of her now."

"I understand," said Edward and he winked at Jake now. "Give her everything she deserves. But I wish I could help." The miller trotted off calling out for Samuel.

As soon as Edward was out of sight, Jake let go of her arm.

"You scare me Jake Haukwake. You should be trying to find whoever tried to do this, not planting false hopes in the head of a woman-hater like Edward Miller."

"What else could I do?" he replied.

She shook her head and picked up her basket and walked carefully through the bloody corpse. Her dress was ruined, but in the half light perhaps no one would notice the blood stains.

"Where are you going?" shouted Jake.

"Back home."

"If I were you, I would leave town."

"I'm not like you, I don't run away. John will protect me, the Abbot is his friend and everyone else relies upon John for their wealth. This rumour will pass, but I would appreciate it if you and your master could catch whoever did this." She strode on, ignoring Jake as he called something else after her.

As she walked up the road through the woods towards the town, she came across Roger Sotil walking the other way, holding an unlit lantern. He would need it soon as the gloom of evening came on.

"Have you seen the Precentor of the Abbey?" he asked. "I urgently need to speak with him."

"I have seen him — all too much of him — but you won't get any sense out of him now." She described what she had found but left out the details of Jake's rough treatment of her, just saying that he would find most likely find Jake at the scene now.

"But you say the miller suspects this of you?" said Roger. "Is he mad? It is most obviously the work of a demon controlled by some foul necromancer. We will catch him, my lady I promise you that." Roger bowed awkwardly to her and then went on his way to where the body lay in pieces.

The master at least was a gentleman. And although shy and awkward, not unhandsome, she thought.

CHAPTER 23

Laid out in a table in the infirmary, the lumps of flesh began to resemble a human body again. The only thing was that they seemed to lack any bones. The long muscles of the arms and legs had been expertly filleted (a butcher couldn't have done better). The layers of skin and thin sheets of muscle were all that remained of the torso, and the foul-smelling innards had been piled in a copper bowl at one end of the table. Jake had made the obvious observation about the lack of bones when they arrived, but Roger had pedantically observed that there were, according to Paracletus, over two hundred bones in the human body, and it was unlikely that they had all been removed.

"They have all been removed," said the Infirmarian.

"Really, are you sure? Have you checked?"

"Oh yes I have. No doubt they will be used in some sort of devilish magic." If he knew how to, the Infirmarian might have smiled, but his expression was more like the fixed grin of a skull. "Your servant, although he appears common, has more wit than you in this matter. And no doubt in other matters."

If the Abbot hadn't arrived at that moment, Jake would have thought about either leaving or hitting the monk. But now it was the Abbot's chance to show his anger. The Infirmarian bowed as the Abbot entered. "Lord Abbot, I trust you have my report on the body? May I be excused? I have an urgent matter to attend to."

"Yes of course. Thank you for the use of the infirmary for this …" He winced as he looked at the body laid out. "…matter."

It's your Abbey thought Jake, why the deference?

"Did he tell you anything useful before he died?" the Abbot asked Roger. "The name of the necromancer perhaps?"

"Well no, not quite. We did have a very interesting discussion, though, and the night before he showed me papers that point to a ritualistic killing of the young children. There is definitely a sorcerous motive behind the killings."

"That's all? What are you hiding from me? One of the most senior monks is brutally destroyed by who-knows-what and we are no closer finding out who did it? We don't have much time!" growled the Abbot, slamming his fist into his meaty palm. He glared at Roger.

"Perhaps the Precentor was about to reveal the necromancer's identity?" suggested Jake. "He had sent my master a message that he wished to speak to him again."

"And I am sure he can speak for himself," snapped the Abbot.

"Well, um, I did mean to ask you about something the Precentor said. But that can wait. I think he may have been possessed so maybe he was made to do something against his will…"

"What!" exclaimed the abbot. "Why do you say this?"

"My master thinks that there're demons everywhere," said Jake.

"The Precentor was conversing with a demon when I first entered the library, before he realized I was there. Sometimes demons can only use the senses of humans they possess so perhaps that explains why he did not sense me immediately."

"Or perhaps you were seeing things again," said Jake.

Roger paused, as if listening to some silent voice, then his mouth opened in an "O" of remembrance. "Of course, that's right," he said to no one in particular. "Well then Abbot," he said, "what about the reports on the bodies? The Precentor told me before he died that no one but you were granted access to the Infirmarian's reports about the dead bodies. And the Infirmarian gave me no further information despite the license you granted me to investigate." Roger paused and folded his arms in what looked like smug satisfaction. "What do you say to that?"

The Abbot's face glowed red; then the man thankfully took a breath to speak and the colour dispersed. "I say nothing to that. If the information was of any use, I would have told you; but all you need to know is that the bodies were marked with some foul necromantic symbols. That is all."

"Necromantic symbols!" said Jake. "So exactly what do you think my master is an expert on then?"

"Watch what you say," said the abbot. "There's a Justice coming to town, as you may have heard, and I wouldn't be surprised if you have reason to keep on my good side while he's around, or things could go badly for you."

"How did you know...?"

"A guess informed by my knowledge of your history, Jake, and one that I see was spot on," said the Abbot."

Roger interrupted. "But those symbols — tell me are you saying no one transcribed them?"

"Of course not? None of us are knowledgeable in those things are we? I assume that your servant was confused when he said you were. I know you are well studied in the lore of astrology, but I would hope that the signs of the zodiac are completely different from those marks that appear on the corpses?"

"Well actually not necess..."

Roger paused and didn't finish that sentence. "Oh," he said to the empty air somewhere above and to one side, "I see what you mean." And then to the Abbot. "No, you're right, they're not the same at all."

"But there's someone who might know about such things," said Jake. "If the rumours are true."

"Who?" asked Roger.

"You mean you don't know? The story is rife all over town. It's my father's wife. Isabel."

"Isabel? Absolutely not. She is a fine, beautiful woman, of a kind heart and generous nature."

"You don't know her like I do. A beautiful face hides a cruel heart. She will do whatever it takes to get what she wants. And that may well include dabbling in the foulest of dark arts. There's folk that say she bewitched my father."

"I don't suppose you would stand witness on that account before the Justice?" said the Abbot. "If so, perhaps a pardon can be arranged?"

"My Lord Abbot," said Roger. "You surely can't believe that such gross rumours about her to be true?"

"There has to be some explanation for why the culprit has not been found." The Abbot paused for a moment and looked away as he spoke to them, staring out of the window of the infirmary into the cloistered garden. "Perhaps they are protected in some way. If it is her, then John Haukwake will have some explaining to do. It does appear that the evidence against her is mounting."

Roger bit his lip and looked away. *Foolish boy,* thought Jake. *She's got you turned too. Let's hope for your sake it does not last.*

Jake thought he would have felt happier to hear that the Abbot intended to press on with the accusations against Isabel. But instead he felt like a man who had been looking forward to eating a feast the whole day and then found, when he was at table, that his appetite had left him.

A monk entered. "My Lord there is a party of villeins here to see you lead by John Haukwake." *Villeins! That prejudice did not wane easily.*

"Haukwake!" said the Abbot. "Come to plead his wife's innocence, has he? Master Roger, I would like you and your man to attend me. I think you will find this audience interesting."

§

Jake could tell that this wasn't his father's idea. Goolde and Jackson had never been John Haukwake's allies, yet here they stood to either side of him as if they had physically dragged him into the Abbot's hall.

He also noticed that John refused to look at him. He'd never seen his father in a moment of such weakness, and it seemed that his father didn't want to acknowledge his presence if he could help it. Well Jake didn't owe him anything, so that was fine by him. But his father's enemies amongst the burgesses were enjoying this, and Jake hated to see those bastards gloat.

Goolde came right out with it. "Lord Abbot, we want you to arrest Isabel Haukwake forthwith. We represent the wishes of the burgesses and the whole town."

"The whole town?" said the Abbot, looking at John as he spoke.

John said nothing, but looked at the floor. What could he do?

Hugh Porter stepped forward from the back of the small group. Come to twist the knife further into John, Jake supposed.

"Not all of us want to see that woman lynched for something that hasn't been proven," said Hugh. "By all means she should be questioned, but I do not see how it could be her."

"You idiot," said Jackson, spitting as he spoke. John looked at the man with disgust, as if he wanted to punch him. "She is in league with the devil. She calls demons to do her will. Some great beast of hell ripped the Precentor limb from limb."

"You honestly think she could hurt children?" said Hugh. "What woman could do that?"

George Dewent pushed past Hugh and turned to address the group, his sword springing from its scabbard and waving into the air. The Abbot flinched at this. "There can be no doubt that she is a witch. She seduced the Haukwake's, father and son, and yet she has born no children. She tries to turn the thoughts of our own women with ideas about living in the same way as men, living off their own work, and not worrying about raising a family. She failed with that and now calls upon Satan to aid her in her revenge. It's clear as day!"

John tried to speak but his words were all but drowned out in the clamouring for Isabel's arrest, trial, and speedy execution. "She has always wanted children," or some such were the words he said, Jake believed.

"So where is she then?" asked Jackson of the Abbot. "I hear one of your retainers was bringing her in for questioning. That's right isn't it Edward?" The miller, standing in the crowd behind Jackson, nodded. "Do you hold her in a cell in the Abbey? We would like proof that she will not be a danger to our little ones anymore."

"That is news to me?" said the Abbot. "Master Roger? Jake? Where is she?"

"Let me explain," said Roger. His words were met with cries of derision.

"Master, perhaps it's better if I do," said Jake. "I was there. With Edward I found her at the site of the bloody murder of the Precentor."

"And where is she now?" asked the Abbot.

"She got away," said Jake.

"You let her escape?" said Dewent. "You fool!"

"Perhaps he helped her," said Goolde. "Remember, before the father, the son was seduced by her."

Jake could see that they were all suspicious of him. Even John looked up at him, acknowledging his presence for the first time.

"She did not seduce me. But, Edward after you left, I don't know what happened. One moment I was talking to her, and the next I was waking up on the ground and it was getting dark."

Jake was lucky. Dewent seized on this further evidence of Isabel's witchcraft. "See, she used magic again to get away. She knows she's guilty. Jake felt hollow inside.

"Or," said Hugh Porter, "she knew she would be wrongly accused and wafted some drug below Jake's nostrils. She is skilled in remedies of all sorts, and I hear that she counsels the women of her company to carry such medicines that will help ward off the attentions of a molester."

"I want to redeem myself in your eyes," said Jake. "And you know I have no love for my father or his whore. I will set out to find her this very night."

"And we'll come with you to make sure she you do not let her run," said Jackson.

John Haukwake shrugged off the arms of Goolde and Jackson and walked from the room. He was followed by Roger, whose look at Jake was full of rage. The others remained to plan the hunt.

CHAPTER 24

"Forgive me," *Jake had said to her as he let go her arm.* Isabel looked back over her shoulder as she walked away, wondering about this man Jake. Perhaps she had loved him once. He could be kind, but he had a funny way of showing it. Each time she looked behind her, he was still standing there, watching as she went. *He still loves me,* she thought. But his way of showing it wasn't so funny.

What was she going to do now? It would be dark in an hour or so. The evening, despite the bright sunshine of the day, was darkening already, and John would be expecting her home. Not to cook his dinner, he was immune to such foolishness, and besides they had servants enough to perform such duties. John valued her for her company. She knew that if she had stayed with Jake all those years ago, she would have been little more than a bitter housewife by now, tired of his drinking, and complaining of the scrubbing and cooking she had to do. She looked at her bloodied hands. These were the hands of a gentlewoman, not used to physical labour. She had chosen well when she abandoned the boy for the man.

John would know what to do. She would go back to their house and tell him everything. He would speak to the

Abbot and ensure that no taint of this evil was placed at her feet. She stumbled down the bank that was the main lane from the mills to the town. The high banks and hedges loomed above her and all but blocked out the light, but she was happy to be on the way back to her husband.

Edward the miller had been so certain that she had done the murder. And it couldn't have looked good, her standing there, covered in blood. But really, what did he expect of her? That she could summon Satan himself? Some of Edmund's books had alluded to what was called necromancy, the summoning of evil spirits or demons. But she had no interest in that. It seemed too much like the infantile wish fulfilment of silly boys. *Summon a demon to do your bidding and you can have everything you want: power over others, the woman you desire will fall in love with you, the demon would even tell you the future.* Ridiculous! Yet something supernatural must have done that to the Precentor. Surely no human — or humans — could be capable of it?

As she climbed the hill, a beat of wings to the left of the lane caught her attention. Something heavy landed in an alder tree just ahead of her. It was no bird. She could see burning red eyes staring at her from the tree and a thin body as dark as the darkest night flanked by two huge bat like wings. She blinked her eyes and shook her head. Was it a trick of the light? She looked again, and this time she could see those great bat's wings were bearing the creature aloft. The beast circled to the right and flew across the lane, momentarily blocking out the sky above the trees.

Isabel had never been one for day-dreams and fancies, and she didn't believe she had started imaging things now, at this time in her life. This was real. She watched as the creature flew slowly from tree to tree, all the time its red eyes marking its presence as it moved through the dim of dusk and then looked back at her. It was going away from her. And then suddenly it was moving faster away from the lane, towards the south of the town, back towards the meadow where she had gone to pick angelica. Back towards where the Precentor's body lay in pieces. Was Jake still there?

Sweat fled from the pores in her skin as fear overtook her. If that thing could rip apart the body of the Precentor, then it might do the same to Jake. Isabel dragged herself up the grassy bank of the lane, and used her pruning knife to cut a way through a fox's gap in the hedge. Even so, the elm's branches scratched and tore at her. She cursed as she felt a strip of linen being torn from her skirts. She dropped her basket and lifted up her skirts and began running through the trees to the south.

She hardly had to look up to follow the creature as it went through the trees. The sound of its heavy wings was loud enough, and it did not fly far before it would land, each time with a crash of branches and leaves high in a tree above her. It would pause and wait for her to catch up, staring down with those red eyes that shone like beacons of evil through the darkening eve. The thing wanted her to follow it.

The wood was getting thicker, too. They were moving away from the trees where the townspeople gathered fuel and deeper into forest that was not even hunted on by the Abbot. They must have crossed the river, but she could not determine where or how, as the Varn now lay on her right hand side — or had they somehow started going in another direction? Wherever they were, she did not recognize the area. Here there were brambles and thick undergrowth that made progress more difficult, the trees were larger and had thick trunks and large roots that rose out of the ground like giant's fingers ready to grasp her or trip her unwary legs.

She looked up. The demon looked down on her from high up in the canopy of the forest, and she could only just make out its red eyes. Did this thing kill the Precentor? Was she wise to be following it? She stopped and sat on one of the large protruding tree roots that half emerged from a mossy bank. The moisture of the moss seeped through into her clothes, cooling her for a moment. She was hot and sweaty and her hair stuck to her face. She had a sudden thought. When had she last bled? Her time should have been at least a week ago shouldn't it? No! Two weeks ago. She was pregnant. She must tell John. He would be so happy.

"Going somewhere?" hissed a voice at her shoulder. She actually thought she jumped out of her skin at that moment — she found herself on her knees in the soft loamy earth, and then she was scrambling to get up and face whatever had said those words. The demon was not as close as she had feared. It clung easily to the thick trunk of the tree next to which she had been sitting. Isabel's heart beat as she weighed up her options and met the gaze of the beast.

She had come this far, she had to learn something from it. "Why have you brought me here? Did you kill the Precentor?"

"To die!" shrieked the beast and it swooped down towards her from the tree, its wings spread wide, blocking out the sky. Isabel screamed, and put her hands to her face. She felt hot sulphurous breath on her face and a vibration of the air from the demon's wings.

She looked up and found herself staring into the thing's grinning face. It hovered just above and in front of her as if waiting for something, its wings buzzing fast with an action like a fly's rather than a bat or bird's. At this close distance she could see the creature's features, not just a black absence of colour with red mouth and eyes set into it. The contours of the face showed an ape-like visage, like the paintings she had seen in the Abbey church. *How did the artist get it so right?* she wondered. And what a funny thing to think of when she knew she was about to die, she realized. But it wasn't just her death that she need worry about now. The thing was waiting. Perhaps she still had time to escape. She bent down and flung dirt in its face. *A demon does not agree well with the earth upon which man or woman tread.* While the thing spat and shook the earth from its face, Isabel ran to hide behind the trunk of a broad oak.

What next? She was no exorcist of the Church, she did not know the correct Latin — and that knowledge had not helped the Precentor to purge the souls of the possessed before they died or to save his own life, so what chance did she have, who was surely a heretic in her beliefs?

She didn't have much chance to ponder her next move. The demon appeared suddenly in front of her, this time walking on the ground. "A puny trick, human, but now that I have tasted your land, I can walk upon it. Now it is time for your blood to soak that earth. Prepare to die!"

Isabel could do no more than lash out with her fists, which made contact with the creatures smooth hard body, but did not stop it from grabbing her in its taloned hands. Its razor sharp teeth were inches from her face as it opened its mouth wide.

"Domine Sanctus," she began mumbling a prayer. "Lord protect me." She was going to die, she knew it now. She closed her eyes and could feel the demon's hot breath move nearer. But then suddenly it was like a fresh breeze had come and the demon was no longer holding her, she fell to the ground like a sack of straw and opened her eyes. The demon had fled half way up the tree and was snarling at a newcomer who stood not ten yards away from them.

The newcomer was Edmund, the Infirmarer. He carried a staff to help him with walking, and pointed it towards the demon while with the other hand made the sign of the cross. "In the name of the Father, and of the Son, and of the Holy Spirit, amen. I abjure you, Spirit to leave this wood. Thou shalt do no harm to this woman." He said the words with a stern authority and a sort of booming power that Isabel had never heard from him before. She even shuddered. The demon hissed and climbed further up the tree. Edmund continued with his speech: "Foul demon, I command you to be gone, in the name of the Lord," Edmund made the sign of the cross again and Isabel could see the demon flinch with what looked like pain.

"A," said Edmund and again made the sign of the cross and the demon shuddered as if hit by a hammer.

"G," another cross.

What were the letters Edmund spoke? Isabel had never heard God's name spelled out in such a way before. Was this magic, or just an exorcism liturgy she knew nothing of?

"L," spoke Edmund, and crossed himself again.

"A," and a final crossing. "Whose name is blessed unto all ages, that you should not harm nor do or inflict anything evil against his servant of God, whether sleeping of waking."

By this point, Isabel could barely see the demon anymore, it was as if he was ascending up into the heavens. She could still make out the creature's red eyes, now like stars that glowed through the forest's canopy. But shouldn't it be driven into the ground back to hell?

But the Infirmarer hadn't finished.

"Christ conquers," cross.

"Christ reigns," cross; each word was like a hammer blow.

"Christ commands," cross.

"May Christ bless us," cross, "and defend us from all evil," cross.

"Amen."

Isabel could see the demon's eyes no longer. The sky seemed to brighten somewhat, as if the darkness of evil had been driven from it. Isabel realized that she was on her knees. She was exhausted and couldn't stand. Edmund walked to her and placed a hand on her shoulder. But was it to comfort her, or to acknowledge her submission to him?

"Rise," he commanded. And she obeyed. He turned and she followed him into a clearing nearby that she had not seen before. Above them it seemed that night had

221

come on swiftly. The sky was dark except for the thousands of stars that circled in the firmament. She gazed up in wonder as she could actually see them moving on their night's circuit through the heavens.

"What is this place?" she asked.

"You ask for more knowledge? I thought you told me that you'd had enough," Edmund replied. He raised the hood of his monk's habit over his head and he looked taller and menacing.

"I have. I want nothing more to do with magic. All the terrible things that are happening in this town are being laid at my feet."

"How unfortunate," said Edmund. "The witches, whoever they may be, have become more powerful — or, I should say weaker, in that they allow the demons to rule their passions and to become so destructive. You have heard of the Precentor's murder?"

"The miller Edward found me when I had just stumbled upon the remains. He thinks I did it, and by now perhaps the whole town will think it, too."

"And John won't save you?"

"Of course he will. I have nothing to fear from my husband."

"But can he control the ravening masses? They want answers. Their children are being taken now, not just vagrants and strays. This can't go on much longer," said Edmund.

"That demon?"

"Yes."

"I think it led me here. If you hadn't turned up when you did, my soul would be who knows where by now?"

"Purgatory, if you listen to those fools in Rome or Avignon," said Edmund. She had never heard him speak like this before. Wasn't it heresy to deny the existence of Purgatory?

"Well, I wanted to thank you, but you know it changes nothing between us," she said.

"I don't know what you are talking about," said Edmund. "I was merely taking an evening walk, I heard sounds, and came to investigate, that is all. You should not feel that you owe me any debt."

"And I don't," she replied. "I thanked you for the loan of the books and I returned them, but in the end I did not find them that helpful."

Edmund's lips trembled. "You gave me the kiss you promised happily enough."

"I gave it because it was the only payment that you would accept."

"I can make things go much better for you. You should remember that."

Isabel shuddered. "It's only the cold," she said stepping away half a pace as Edmund reached towards her.

Edmund cocked his head to one side. "Do you hear that?"

"I don't hear anything," she said.

"It's a search party come looking for you. I suppose you would like me to help you, to tell them what happened. That a demon was trying to kill you and that therefore you must be innocent, too? Is that right?"

"I don't believe you, I can't hear anything. Besides how would they find us in the dark?"

"Over here!" shouted Edmund to the ears of the forest. He turned back to Isabel. "Easily enough I would think, if I keep shouting."

"Over here!" he shouted again, cupping his hands to project the sound.

"I'll make my own way back. I'll be under John's roof before they find me." Isabel turned to leave. She could just about make out the trees and she thought she could find her way back the way she came. Couldn't she?

Then a light flared behind her. She turned and Edmund was holding a torch. It seemed to have appeared from nowhere and had been lit in an instant. "A light like this would help light your way would it not?" he said.

"How did you do that?" she asked.

"I can do a lot more than that. Those books you dismissed with such disdain are but the first steps into a very wide field of knowledge; one that I will soon be the master of."

With the light from Edmund's torch, Isabel saw the glade in which they stood properly for the first time. Carcasses lay about, animals she hoped, but the ground was matted and the grass beaten down by dried blood. Around Edmund she could clearly see a circle marked out in some sort of white powder, with symbols drawn within it and under his feet, that looked like the ones in his books.

"Isabel, you can join me. Share in my power in this world and the next."

"Never," she hissed.

"I knew that you would deny me to begin with, as Peter denied the Christ, but I have seen a vision. The two of us crowned in heaven with the angels. And on Judgment Day, which is not far away, we will be among the judges of the Lord. Your accusers will perish in lakes of hellfire."

Edmund was the necromancer! Had he brought the children here, to this place, to kill them? To drain the blood from their bodies and then to summon evil spirits to his side? She felt her stomach turn at the thought of it.

"You don't have much time to think," he said. "They have dogs you know."

Then, on the night's breeze she could hear the bark of hunting dogs and the shouts of men.

"I can make this go away for you."

What was that old tale? Between the devil then or the deep blue sea?

CHAPTER 25

I should have stayed out there, thought Jake. But now he was stuck in the Abbey gatehouse watching events unfold through an embrasure, with the Abbot seated in front of him and Roger peering over his shoulder.

"Can't you stand next to another one? There's not enough room," he hissed. Roger looked angry, but moved to another arrow slit further along the chamber.

The gatehouse was also the Abbey's prison, serving to house those awaiting the King's justice on one of the circuit judge's irregular visits. A man could be locked up in here for years just waiting trial and sentence for a simple crime. Sometimes the Abbots got impatient, providing room and board for such extended duration, and served up their own sentence beyond the bounds of their jurisdiction.

But the large gatehouse was also like a small keep, protecting the Abbey from its own serfs. Nearly thirty years ago it had been besieged by many of the men who now formed the Charnel Brotherhood — and who now stood in the front row of precedence at the Abbey church. John Haukwake had been instrumental in mending relations between the town and the Abbey, but old fears ran deep — and now, with a crowd of armed men outside wielding torches despite the rain, the Abbot had ordered the gates shut and barred. A half-dozen or so of the Abbey's servants had taken crossbows out of storage and stood at arrow slits around the gatehouse, ready to fire in case trouble began.

Jake and a small search party had found Isabel in the woods — the dogs had sniffed her out. God alone knew what she was doing there in the middle of the night, with rain coming on. Some of the others said she had fled and that she was in hiding. She had said nothing in her own defence, she simply stared at Jake in silence, but gave nothing away.

Someone had blown a hunting horn to indicate that they had her, and they all the search parties met again near where the Precentor's remains had been found on the road from the town to the mill. That was when Jake knew there was going to be trouble. He had hoped to escort her to the Abbot himself, and place her in his care; and then perhaps he and Roger could find the real murderer and put a stop to this madness. The Abbot was John's ally and it would be safer for Isabel in the Abbey than in the town, Jake's plan hadn't worked out like that.

The crowds of angry townspeople demanded instant justice as the band climbed up Pikepond Lane towards the Abbey. Jake had lost control of Isabel as soon as the mob started heading back towards town. Three or four men pulled her away from him, and she was lifted above their shoulders for the whole crowd to see. The crowd cheered. They didn't carry her for long, though, as a scrum of people pressed in upon them, hands reaching out to try to grab and hurt Isabel. Jackson, Goolde, and Dewent took control of her, and together with serving men of their households, kept the others away. The assistant bailiff, Lovell, was supposed to be in charge, but Jake only saw him once or twice, and nowhere near Isabel was. The mob slowed as they neared the market square and Abbey, with its huge gatehouse that loomed over the houses.

Jackson, Goolde, and Dewent pushed and pulled Isabel through the crowd towards the Hundred Tree, the old tree that stood in the centre of the market place, where from time gone by justice was served at the court of St. Brett's. A circle formed around them.

Jake's words of protest had fallen on deaf ears. He knew there was no chance that he could free Isabel on his own, so he made for the Abbey. But despite his pleadings, there he remained. At the Abbot's order, he now watched — locked up inside the gatehouse — as the mob proceeded to carry out some sort of trial of their own. Jackson and Goolde acted as the judges, calling forward witnesses, many of them women, to testify against Isabel, while Dewent waved his sword around and reminded everyone of the justice that they would show Isabel.

"A noose and a sword to the belly to let her guts fall out to be eaten by dogs," Dewent shouted. He sounded drunk. A madness like drunkenness had overtaken all of them, although Jake could not see anyone drinking. He had seen madness like this in France — a madness that desired murder and blood.

The Abbot was furious. "They subvert my rule. How dare they? They are traitors all." But he would do nothing about it. He was too scared to intervene, as if reminding the mob of the Abbey's existence might divert its anger towards the monks rather than to the woman who now stood on a crate beneath the Hundred Tree, a noose slung over a low branch hanging beside her, ready to take her weight.

"This is so terrible, we must save her," said Roger. He hit the stone wall with his fist and winced in pain.

"We must," Jake murmured in agreement. But how? What could the two of them do against a mob of several hundred? This was going to be the end of Isabel unless he could do something. He looked at the Abbot, who sat calmly enough, but was biting his lip. He would do nothing. Where was his father? Perhaps the mob had him somewhere as well. Goolde and Jackson might have seen this as their chance to seize power in the town and imprisoned him or worst.

"Lord Abbot," said Roger. "Give me permission to leave by the postern gate on St. Mary's street. It's only fair that I warn Isabel's husband of these proceedings."

"No one's opening any of the gates," said the Abbot. "How do we know that there aren't more of them out there waiting to get in?"

"Lord Abbot," said Roger, "you asked us here to see justice done and this is no kind of justice; at least let my man try to save an innocent woman?"

"Innocent? I'm not so sure; all the evidence points to her, after all. If I had some more men, some soldiers, then I would crush this mob and their jumped-up rebellion . But as your father, Jake, knows, it is best to be patient and play politics. Goolde and Jackson appear to be the new power in town and I will allow them their way in this, but tomorrow they will have to pay a price for today's concessions."

Jake bared his teeth. He knew better than to shout at the Abbot — his old school-teacher could give as good as he got and was capable of meting out harsh punishments for insolence. He would have to be clever. Perhaps he could sneak out or bribe the gatekeeper?

"Your concession may not be needed," said Roger. "Look, here comes another party of men."

Roger moved aside to let Jake peer through the arrow-slit nearest to him. Sure enough another group of people had arrived in the square. He could see that they were armed as well, some bore shields or pieces of armour, some wore helmets, all clutched weapons: bills, halberds, glaives, and swords. His father led them alongside Hugh Porter. Hugh Porter? What was he doing there? He was one of his father's sternest critics, yet here he was at the head of the group, smaller in comparison to the mob, but still perhaps fifty strong, well-armed, and standing shoulder to shoulder; a force to be reckoned with. Jake watched as the mob parted, not wishing to get in the way as the new force marched from the north of the market towards the Hundred Tree. In response, Dewent began running to and fro shouting commands, gathering their adherents together, Jackson kept a firm hold of Isabel, but Goolde joined Dewent, and drew his sword in readiness.

The rain was coming on harder now and some of the torches began to flicker. Many of the townspeople didn't want to be involved in whatever confrontation might happen, but neither did they wish to miss it. Like a sea washing out with the tide they retreated back down Pikepond Lane, or towards the safety of the shambles, leaving space for the two parties — the fifty or so of Haukwake and Porter against the more than a hundred men of Jackson, Goolde, and Dewent's affinity, less well-armed on the whole but more numerous — to face off each other across the market square.

"At last my bailiff makes his appearance. I trust he will restore order," said the Abbot.

"I thought you had given up on him," said Jake sourly.

"Your father's rarely beaten so easily, but it will be instructive to watch the outcome of this."

But it was Porter who took a step forward to address the mob. "We have come to restore order in the name of your Lord, the Abbey of St. Brett's. You are to release your prisoner into our hands so that justice can be done at the Abbot's will."

"Well put," said the Abbot.

"Why doesn't your father speak?" said Roger to Jake.

"The crowd will know his partiality," Jake replied. "The fact that Hugh Porter has joined him gains him much."

"Although where are his normal allies?" asked the Abbot. "I have not seen the men who would normally be at his side at church or feast at his house or inn. They seem to have deserted him now. To me he looks rather desperate and weak, not to speak out himself."

"My father is not weak," said Jake.

There was much shouting coming from the market in front of them. Those who held Isabel had refused to let her go. And now Hugh was stepping forward with others at his shoulder brandishing weapons. He again commanded them to release Isabel.

But they refused.

Jake already knew what was going to happen. You couldn't have so many armed men in proximity and such overt conflict, without at some point a sword being drawn in anger or someone taking a pot-shot from a bow. Hadn't been so long ago that fighting in Oxford had left many dead on both sides, gown and town. Jake had seen it happen countless times in France — the routiers, some band of mixed English, Gascons, and others, him usually amongst them, threatening a town or local French lord. Either one side backed down and left the field, or there were blows.

But still he watched in horrified anticipation of what was going to happen. It was like watching at Mystery Play at the time of the Passion or Saint's day festivity; but instead of watching actors pretending with ill-made costume, this performance was very real and deadly.

It started happened all at once. There was a flash of sword being drawn by one of Porter's men, and then someone was charging Porter himself with a pole-axe swung high above his head. A shield came up and deflected the blow. There was a clack and burr of arrows being fired, but the press of bodies was too close for much archery to be wanted. The clash of metal against metal, men's cries of anger, fear and excitement filled the air so that Jake could not hear what Roger was shouting to him. It didn't matter anyway; there was only one place where he was going. He could see his father down there in the middle of it all. He had a mace and a shield and was swinging his way through the crowd towards Isabel. But Jackson had a knife to her throat, and Dewent was pointing at John Haukwake with his sword.

"Get him! Get the witch's bastard!" Dewent shouted. A group of five or more thugs, stocky workers clad in thick leather hauberks and wielding bills and axes, made a dash for his father. Porter and his men were fighting their own battles, and of Haukwake's men and retainers, none had been as passionate as he to charge into that crowd. He was alone.

The gatekeeper had left his halberd leaning against the gate while he watched through an open shuttered grill in the Abbey gate. He'd swiftly opened the gate at Jake's command. The foot long halberd spike at his throat meant he needed little convincing, but he slammed it shut again as soon as Jake was through. He thought he heard Roger shouting again from the other side, the fool had followed him down the stairs of the gatehouse. But this was a fighting man's work now; what good could Roger's astronomy do here?

For that matter, what good could Jake do? Separating him from where his father had been fighting, and where Jackson held Isabel near the Hundred Tree, were a mass of people, some watching, waving fizzing torches around in the rain, and others, compatriots of the rebels against John Haukwake's authority, trying to join the fight. This was like a football match on one of the more popular festival days, everyone wanting to become a player and join in the chance to grab or at least see the ball. He'd heard that this was what a big battle had looked like as well, but he'd never found out. His involvement in Gaunt's French campaign of '73 had consisted of skirmishes and small sieges, and he'd mostly stood to the rear or the flanks with his bow, not joined any scrum of men-at-arms. But this was a scrum of bakers, fullers, carters and victuallers, not armour plated soldiers. And he needed to get through the press of bodies.

"A demon, a devil!" he called out. The rabble of armed craftsmen and labourers in front of him turned as he shouted and screamed. "A beast of Satan this way comes, make way!" The crowd didn't really know what was happening — and neither did he — but they looked at him with fear in their eyes as if he were possessed, and perhaps he was. And so they moved out of his way. That and his bulk and the fact that he waved his halberd in the air above his head, quickly cleared a path for him to where the action was taking place.

He pushed past the last few combatants, men actually fighting each other who had been far too busy to pay attention to any rabid shouting to their rear. And then he was in an open space, the killing zone, that sort of gap that might open between two battle lines as men withdraw from blows for a moment and weigh up their next attack. To the right, moving towards the Hundred Tree, he could see Porter and a couple of men fighting with Dewent and his servants, swords clanged against other swords and shields. They had the power and anger to cause damage if they hit something, but not the wit and training of a knight or sergeant-at-arms to find a way quickly past an enemy's defence. That was a good thing. Jake could not see much blood on the ground, or anyone obviously dead or dying.

But where was his father?

A man pushed past him to charge a man crouching by a fallen body. The crouching man was knocked aside, and Jake saw the flash of a dagger and blood, black in the torchlight jet into the air. Shadows played like demon spirits all around, but more of the rebels were pushing past him, pressing forward their attack with cries of "he's down, Haukwake's down!" and "he's captured, slit his throat!"

Jake moved forward. He jabbed the spike of his halberd into a man's back and the man wailed, but moved aside, not dead just bleeding a little. He poked and slashed using the pole of the halberd to batter a way through. The crouching man had been one of Haukwake's servants Jake saw, but now his life-blood had emptied into the mud of the market, leaving the ground sticky around him as Jake moved forward. The man who had killed him had put aside his shield and crouched over a man lying on his side who was dressed in half-armour, with sheets of plate protecting his arms and a padded brigandine protecting his body, but his helmet had rolled away and Jake could make out a patch of blackness in the fold of grey-white hair that belonged to his father's head.

"Is he dead?" someone shouted from behind.

"Not yet," replied the man who crouched over Haukwake's body.

"Then give us the traitor witch's head!" another screamed.

A hand tugged at Jake's shoulder. "Let me through, or I'll stick you with this knife," someone claimed. "You've no right over any other to see the traitor die."

Jake slammed back his elbow into the man's face. He heard the bone break in the man's nose, a pity it wasn't his jaw too, and felt the body slide to the ground behind him, the press of men had pushed everyone so close together.

There was a flash of a blade in front of him. There was no time to waste. Jake wasn't used to wielding a halberd like this, but the head of it was shaped like an axe, so couldn't be too different from chopping a piece of wood. He lifted the pole-arm high in the air and brought it down hard on the man's back, using the momentum of the weapon's fall to add power to the strike.

The body seemed to split down the back to one side of the man's spine, shearing through ribs where they joined the back-bone, and sending blood spraying into Jake's face. He didn't worry about pulling the halberd from the man's back, it would take too long. He pushed the falling, already dead, body aside and crouched by his father.

The rebels were too stunned to react quickly, and some of Haukwake's men took the advantage and found the courage to press forward the attack, so that for a moment at least Jake and Haukwake were out of danger as men moved past them to press home any advantage the dramatic killing of Jake's assailant had brought them. Jake knelt by his father, whose eyes were closed and body still. He put his hand to his father's mouth, he could feel breathing at least.

His father looked frail and thin inside his armour. The plates did not fit him well and the heavy padded coat seemed to sag to the ground as if there were nothing to hold them up. Jake touched the damp patch on the hair. Just a small cut he thought. His father's hair was soft and wispy at his touch, the skin crinkled and soft. The man was getting old. What was he doing running around like this with a sword and shield playing champion?

Despite the weight of the armour, Jake found that he was easily able to lift and carry his father's body. Haukwake's men opened up a path for him through the crush of bodies trying to get into the fight. They found a bench near a market stall that had been smashed up during the commotion. A woman ran over. "Is the master going to be all right?"

"Nan?" said Jake.

"Yes it's me Jakey. Oh how we've missed you. This foolishness is too much to bear. Let me take a look." Together he and Nan Wyth, the woman who had been his father's housekeeper and chief servant for as long as he could remember, laid down the old man and looked at his wound. "We'll need a poultice on that," she said indicating the cut. "The mistress would know something good for it."

"Isabel?" the old man spoke and his eyes flickered open.

"Quiet, you need to rest," said Nan.

"You need to get him back to the house. Are there servants that can help you carry him? Perhaps make a litter?" said Jake.

"I'll get some," said Nan and picked her skirts up she started looking around for help.

The fighting had died down, and Jake noticed that things were quieter. He could hear his heart thudding against his ribs. He hadn't paid attention to how the battle was going — for that was what it was now rather than a street scuffle, since he had raised the stakes and almost chopped one of his father's enemies in half. He turned now and looked. Torches bobbed up and down erratically across the plaza. Near the Hundred Tree he could make out Dewent holding Isabel close to him, a glint of metal held at her throat, a knife to slice it with.

"Release her!" shouted a voice. Jake stood on tiptoe and saw another man with a prisoner. It was Hugh Porter, holding Goolde with a knife to his throat and two other men at his side to make sure he couldn't escape.

"She's a witch and deserves this. If you kill him, that is murder and you'll swing for it," shouted Dewent.

"They are going to kill her?" said his father from behind him. The old man had woken and risen shakily from the bench while Jake was watching the drama unfold.

"She should be tried by the Justice, not by your lynch-mob," shouted Porter. "Goolde is our prisoner and a breaker of the peace, as are all of you. Sheath your weapons and go home now and we'll not arrest you."

"You make me laugh!" said Dewent. "We hold the witch and we have right on our side. It's you who should stand down, unless you're witches, too!"

There were hoots and shouts at this, mainly from the crowd of onlookers who'd had no part in the fighting.

"Let me lean on you but don't make it obvious," John Haukwake said softly to Jake. "I'm going to make that fucker Dewent pay for this."

§

Isabel wanted to scream out, but her voice had cracked and dried so badly that all she could do was croak with anger. Besides, if she moved a hairs-breadth, she feared that the dagger might cut her throat. Dewent's ranting voice made her ears ring as he bellowed insults at Hugh Porter. Thank St. Brett that someone had come to her aid! If they hadn't, she would be swinging from the rope that dangled from the tree next to her. She had wanted to see John one last time before she died. She had kept asking her captors about him, but each time she spoke she only earned herself a kick or a punch in the ribs for her trouble.

She had enjoyed a smile, though, when she saw John and his men approaching — and with Hugh Porter, too. Those around her grumbled that Hugh had been bought by John's money, but the man she knew had always had principles, which was why he had never been accepted into the town's inner circle; while the likes of Goolde and Jackson and Dewent, who now threatened to slice her life-blood's away onto the market square, had accepted John's lordship when it suited them, but now turned rebel against his authority. She had still hoped that the Abbot would intervene, but it seemed that the monk was a coward after all, and she would receive no help from that quarter.

She had started to cry when she saw John fall amid the crowd of fighting men, but then from nowhere, Jake had appeared. Where had he got to? He had been the one to capture her, but soon enough he'd gone, too. Happy to collect his coin from the Abbot for a job well done, she had thought at the time. Jackson had laughed at her tears, but then she laughed in return when she saw him taken prisoner after Jake had chopped their fellow almost in half with a halberd.

St. Brett's was turning into a living hell: murder, battle, witchcraft, injustice, and death. A place in Purgatory would be so much sweeter than this. To see her own husband die before her own eyes had been too much, so she wanted to clap her hands and cheer when she saw Jake drag him clear and Nan and he attend upon him — and then like Lazarus he rose again, leaning on Jake. He tried to hide his reliance on him, but it was obvious to her, who knew him so well.

And he had came back to the fray and shouted for her release.

But Dewent's knife came closer to her throat, and his other arm squeezed her tight across her chest. Her legs were bound together and her hands, too, behind her back. She could not wriggle free. Dewent's bony forearm dug painfully into her breasts crushing the breath out of her.

And then an explosion lit up the top of the great Abbey gatehouse. Fighters on both sides were caught by surprise, all looking up in amazement at the burst of flame. On the battlements a large brazier was burning, and Isabel could make out the black shadows of men struggling in the grip of other men. More prisoners!

"Get him!" shouted Porter.

That treacherous bastard Jackson had used the distraction of the flames to get free! Porter's men picked up their pole-arms and surged towards Jackson, but he had been enveloped into a crowd of his own supporters and their pursuit turned into another battle. But they didn't have the heart for it anymore and withdrew as they saw that all their advantage had been lost.

Dewent put his mouth close to her ear and whispered: "Now it's time for you to swing, witch."

Isabel tried to jerk her head back so that it might hit Dewent in the nose, but he was quicker with the palm of his hand and shoved her head hard from the back of the neck. She buckled with the pain.

Everything went black for a moment, and then she could feel the cord around her neck and she was being lifted up, men holding her legs beneath her. She looked around and all she could see were faces grotesquely featured in the flickering light and shadow from torches and the bonfire atop the gatehouse. People she had passed on the street, that she had bought from, had given alms to in only the past few days, shouted at her, laughed at her, and grinned at her torment.

She looked around in panic. Near the back of the crowd stood Jake, with John leaning against him, but there was something wrong with her husband, he looked so thin and pale and she saw him fall so fast that Jake didn't have time to stop him hitting the ground. Jake knelt to help him, but something was wrong. My husband, my husband, she called, or she thought she did, but she did not know if her voice worked anymore.

And then she thought she had been deafened by the mob's hatred, because she could hear nothing.

Into the silence came the voice of Edmund, the Infirmarer. That monotone, accentless English voice that hailed from nowhere in England. His words were clear and carried across the clear night sky through which the stars shone down upon the multitude now fixed to the spot rather than milling in frenzy beneath the Hundred Tree.

And praise be to St. Brett, she was lowered to the ground, not gently, but not roughly, and the noose slipped off her head. No effort was made to loosen the cords that bound her hands and feet, but the men who held her stepped back and allowed Jake through and he picked her up and carried her away to where John sat, next to the clock tower, waiting for her. His face glowed with happiness to see her alive, and once Jake and Nan had sliced through her bonds, they embraced.

"He has the witches," said Nan. "I always knew that they would see reason and catch them what did it."

"Who caught them?" Isabel asked. "Was it your Roger, Jake? Did you have some clue after all?"

Jake looked away. "No clue at all. The monk Edmund told the crowd just now that it was Edward the miller and his son. They found buckets of blood in the mill, and some devilish books and potions."

"Edward can't read!" said Isabel. She looked up over the crowd to the roof of the gatehouse. Edmund had the two prisoners held before him by Abbey servants, and was telling the crowd as if preaching a sermon, of the wickedness of witchcraft and the evil that these men had done.

"And when I put the question of the dead children to them, that's when the demons showed themselves. A small, impish one had taken possession of the boy, but the father... Oh the father was taken with an arch-demon! A guardian of hell's gates! He was of mighty power and cursed me greatly and made the miller to froth and foam. He hated me for finding him out and for trying to expel him. But, listen, I was not strong enough to expel the demon. Only death can do that — the beast is inside this man Edward the miller, even now."

There were shocked gasps and screams from many at this news. The miller and his son were only shadows on top of the gatehouse with the great burning fire behind them, but they seemed to jump and jerk at these words and the men who held them by each arm seemed to have trouble holding them.

Then it was as if both men forgot their fetters and their captors arms were as if air. They pulled easily away from those guarding them. Edward the miller jumped up onto the low battlements and began to scurry on all fours like some sort of giant rat or squirrel who hopped from battlement to battlement, and then he was climbing head first down the wall, and jumped to cling to one of the carven gargoyles that jutted out beneath the gatehouse battlements. His display of agility ended there. Unable to get a grip on the gargoyle he plunged down, screaming as he fell. Isabel couldn't make out the words, but they sounded like those of human fear, sure enough. His son had followed more tentatively, giving the servants under Edmund's orders time to reach out and make a grab for him as he jumped from battlement to battlement, but as he tried to escape their clutches, he too fell, spinning head over heels, a guttural roar escaping his lips until a dull thump met him as he hit the ground.

Both men were dead. And that was it. Isabel and John walked slowly home, unmolested by any adherents of Jackson, Goolde, and Dewent. Jake was gone when she looked around, but Nan walked with them, together with the half-dozen male servants that John had gathered to fight for him. Porter came running up, a grim smile on his face.

"So the Infirmarian saved you in the end, and not our swords," he said. "Who would have thought that a monk would care to solve the mystery?"

Isabel shook her head wearily. "I think it's only just beginning to be solved; if anything, we may be further from the truth."

John frowned. "But you are safe, that's all that matters."

For now, thought Isabel, for now.

CHAPTER 26

The Abbot would be pleased if he saw the market today, thought Isabel. Merchants were coming north from London to buy goods, paying their tolls when they left. And look, there was a cart-load of wool coming in from a Northern town, either to be fulled in the Abbot's mills or to sell on again to a merchant from London, or maybe even Flanders. Her John's hopes were set on establishing a regular deal for such a trade. He had spoken of a letter from a merchant of Bruges. He expected big things to come from it. So it appeared that no one in London, Derby, or Flanders had yet heard the news that St. Brett's was plagued by demons.

Yet she felt like a prisoner as she watched the market trade from her window. She should be down there at the stall in front of their house. But John had told her to stay away. The servants could do the marketing, he said. She suspected that he was quietly glad not to see her haggling and calling her wares like a common cook-wife. He said that he admired her spirit, but she knew that he didn't think it befitting a lady to be engaged in trade.

"Two for a penny? Yes there you go madam," said the maidservant, Alison, to a farmer's wife who had been looking at Isabel's stall for a while. Isabel strained to see what the woman had bought, but it was wrapped now. That sounded like too low a price, whatever it was. She could sometimes catch half a sentence or word from below. Enough to infuriate her.

But at least it kept her mind from wondering to the place where it churned over whether Edmund knew what she knew.

Here they came, at last. Jake leading the way, clearing space for his Master as they moved slowly through the tide of sellers and buyers. That young man was taller than Jake, but he looked so vulnerable, so at odds with the physical world. Perhaps he was one half in the world of spirits?

She couldn't tell them here. She hadn't told John on purpose, and it wouldn't do for him or one of the servants to overhear now and for word to reach him. He would know of course, when they caught Edmund, but she didn't want him to hear about her involvement with that despicable monk, or what he had proposed to her. John felt bad enough about her hawking her wares in the market; he wouldn't be happy to know that an offer had been made for her body, too.

But she couldn't speak to them in the market or in a tavern, either. Too many prying ears. She couldn't know which might belong to a witch.

She summoned George. "Go and tell Alison to stop giving away all my goods. I expect a profit by the end of today." George nodded and started to leave.

"And George, where is Master Haukwake?"

"He's in the yard out back, talking to some Flemings about wool," said George.

"If he asks, tell him I have gone for a walk to collect herbs for his afternoon bath. I am going out."

George was a fine figure of a man, Isabel thought as she watched him go up to Alison outside and pass on her instructions. He was as tall as Roger Sotil, but unlike the scholar, had the muscle to define and align the frame. It was a pity for womankind that he was so stupid. He would do well at the stall —no doubt he would attract a number of the wives who were her main customers — but she feared that he had trouble even counting a few pennies. Was that a smile from Alison? And there, he has placed his hand on her arm while he tells her something. Isabel sighed. There would be baby on the way soon enough and they couldn't support a maid who couldn't work. She would have to tell John.

George was coming back to the house now. Should she question him about Alison? And here, too, were Jake and Roger. *You have let yourself go Jake,* she thought. *Hair looks like a bird is nesting in it and your face is hairier than a bear's. But your Master doesn't look like he need shave at all, poor boy.* Too young for this dangerous knowledge she held perhaps. Too young for his own dangerous gifts as well? Magic, in her experience, was something mastered only by long study and patience. *This boy had best be careful with how he used his gifts, or he might get burnt.*

She watched as Jake tapped George on the shoulder and asked him a question. George pointed up at her window. She gathered her skirts and replaced her slippers with a pair of ankle boots. As the front door was opened she was already trotting down stairs.

George held the door open and introduced the two men to her. She laughed and took a hooded cloak from a hook by the door.

"I know them already, George, they are helping the Abbot. Did you not know?"

George frowned, and stood ready to take the men's cloaks or hats if need be.

"Run along inside, George. These gentlemen won't be coming in." Jake frowned and Roger looked on meekly. "Gentlemen will you accompany me on a pleasant walk to the river?"

"The river?" said Jake. "Why not talk here?"

"I'm sure your Master would not mind a walk, and besides he might want to see where some of the killings happened. Would that be useful Master Sotil?"

"Oh yes, I hadn't considered looking at the scene of the ... of the crime. But yes, please, lead on."

"One of them happened right outside your door, didn't it?" she heard Jake mumble as they walked out into the warmth of a sunny May day. Isabel bit her lip and pulled her hood around her head to cover her face as much as she could.

Despite the crowds, they made quick progress through the market. Jake's natural presence helped plough most people out of their path, but she also thought that people were moving away as they saw her coming. One moment they would be about their business and then would happen to look her way and turn hastily, not wanting to meet her eye, an eye that might bewitch them. She had loved living in St. Brett's, but now it felt like a prison, yet worse, with her accusers always around her.

Roger hung back and walked by her side. At least he didn't shy away from her or accuse her. But what if like his name, he was more subtle than he appeared?

"Master Roger," she said as they walked. "Thank you for attending upon me. I have come into some knowledge that I think may assist you."

Jake looked over his shoulder and said, "You'd best not speak it here then!"

"I don't intend to; that is why we are going to the river."

"Couldn't you tell us in the house?" asked Jake.

Roger tried to interject: "Jake, I am sure there is a good reason for Mistress Haukwake to ..."

"Jake, you know what servants are like," said Isabel talking over Roger. "They would be gossiping if they thought we were talking secretly, and if they heard anything, the news would be all over the township by afternoon."

"Maybe it's because you have something to hide? Do you see these stocks here, Roger?"

"Yes?" said Roger. A drunk grinned toothlessly as they walked past the stock at the southern end of the market, a stone's throw from the Abbey precinct wall.

"Well many people in this town would like to see Isabel in them."

"Are you one of them, Jake?" she asked.

"Why?" said Roger.

She saw the drunk in the stocks wink at her. "This is foolish. Lower your voice, will you Jake," said Isabel. "You should be in those stocks yourself."

Jake laughed. "I'm sorry, the stocks are the wrong place. Where do they usually put up the gallows? Is it on Romeland field? The law says it's a death for a death doesn't it?" said Jake.

Isabel walked on ahead of Jake and Roger and began to turn towards Pikepond Lane that would take them past the Abbey Church, its gatehouse, and down towards the river.

The crowds were thicker as the market narrowed around the entrance to the street. There were carts trying to get past and Isabel had to wait. She felt Jake's presence behind her like the breath of Satan on her back.

"Do you see that church and its fine tower, Isabel?" hissed Jake. She didn't turn round. "Don't you know that magic is a sin? How can you sit in there, and John with his confraternity of the holy bones, or whatever it may be. Does he know what you are?"

There was so much venom in his voice. Where did it come from?

Roger touched her arm and she turned. "You know magic?" asked Roger, his eyes were kind. She shook her head slowly to Roger's question.

"Where have you been?" said Jake raising his voice. "Of course she knows it and she does it, too. The whole town seems to know that — apart from you and my father."

Just humiliate me in public why don't you, thought Isabel. *What do you want? My public hanging right now?* She took hold of Roger's arm. "Please sir, quieten your man or I will return home and take the information I have with me."

Roger nodded and Jake was silent. It was odd, this relationship between them. She could not imagine Jake playing the servant for any man, yet his position with this sensitive academic seemed to work well for him.

They waited for the carts to move on, then moved down the steep and winding way along the narrow Pikepond Lane. As they passed the Abbey Gatehouse that also doubled as the Hundred's prison, the crowds began to thin and only the occasional townsperson passed them. All made sure that they passed on the other side, and none met her gaze or offered her a hello, although she recognized all of them.

"Lady Haukwake," began Roger. He paused as Jake sniggered like a teenage boy. *Pathetic,* thought Isabel.

"You don't have to call me that; my husband is not yet a gentleman," she said, her gaze lingering for a moment on Roger's bashful face. He looked up and smiled. "But thank you for the compliment. One day perhaps you will call me your lady?"

"I feel sick," mumbled Jake.

"Well ... Mistress? Can you tell us anything about the murders?" said Roger.

Isabel looked around at the houses that lined the narrow street, their windows overhanging and nearly blocking the light as the road wound steeply down the hill into the river valley.

"Let us talk when we reach the woods; it will be quieter there."

"We have made scant progress finding anything to solve the mystery," Roger said, heedless of her suggestion. "The monks have been unhelpful and deny any knowledge, while the townsfolk, Jake tells me, won't talk much about the witches — or if they do, they make wild and hasty accusations."

"About me, you mean?" she replied.

"Yes," said Roger.

"They accuse you, and you don't do much to dissuade them of their opinion," said Jake.

"When I came here and married John, I tried to help the other wives of the town, and the young, unmarried ones, too. They, like all women in these days, and maybe ever since Eve, I suppose, have been under the foot of men, made to feel lower than them, that they are somehow to blame." Isabel could feel the blood flow to her cheeks. "All I tried to do was give them the tools to help themselves. Men have their strong arms, their weapons, swords and the law to aid them. Women must use their minds and knowledge of nature if they are to have any chance. I should have known that my efforts were futile. I should have learnt that the last time."

Jake shot her a quizzical glance. She had never told him about her first husband, Isabel realized.

"Do you know something about magic?" Roger asked. That fire in his eyes again. The excitement of youth.

She put her hand on his shoulder and drew his head down to her level. "Shush, that's enough for now" she whispered in his ear.

She noticed the warmth in his face as she let go of his shoulder. Perhaps that had been cruel to Jake, but then he deserved a bit of cruelty just now.

"I'll see you there," said Jake, and he set off at a jog towards down the Lane. Perhaps she had twisted the knife too hard?

They came to the end of the row of houses along Pikepond Lane and followed the road as it went through a few fields kept by those who lived nearby, each divided into small fenced pastures, and reached by a complex series of gates. Troughs and pig pens were dotted throughout, giving the place more the appearance of a workshop than a rural scene. The pigs, chickens and goats were not as shy as their owners had been and regarded them hopefully, wondering if they brought feed. The Abbey did not allow much room here for the townspeople. The monks jealously guarded their hunting rights and this side of the town near the Abbey's mills did not benefit from any common land, all of the fields being rented from the Abbey. So it was a short walk, and after less than twenty yards they entered the narrow stretch of assorted woodland growth where the people were allowed to gather firewood, and then the wood proper: taller, thicker trees, with the undergrowth kept clear to allow huntsmen to ride though. As they walked, they could hear the slow creak of a mill-wheel and the gurgle of water as it flowed over a weir. They would see the mill soon enough if they kept walking.

Jake was waiting for them up ahead. The path widened into a clearing in the place he stood, where a path ran across the main road. The path was used to reach the other mills and also lead to places where fishing nets were set by those licensed by the Abbey to fish the river.

"This is the place," said Isabel.

"Where one of the children was found?" asked Roger.

"Yes, that's right," Isabel replied

"How did he die?" jabbed Jake, not looking at her as he said it.

"I wasn't there!"

Jake shook his head but didn't reply.

"Do you know *why* he died though?" Roger asked.

"I won't lie to you, Master Sotil. I have some knowledge of magic, although magic does not have to be for evil purposes. I know how to calm people who are ill, to ease pains and sometimes to gain some hint of the future. That knowledge, that wisdom, gives me sight of the spirit world sometimes when it seeps into ours. I saw that demon yesterday as well as you."

"God, not you as well," groaned Jake.

"I am an astrologer. I don't know anything of magic," said Roger.

"But you study how the stars are influenced by angels both light and dark, don't you?"

"How did you know about my research? I have only written of it in my notes."

"Your mentor was a friend of the Abbot, I believe that he spoke of what you were studying perhaps in a letter, I don't know, but someone at the Abbey was very interested to hear about your theories, and they told me."

"They told you?" said Jake. "Whispers in bed perhaps, with some monk?"

"Don't be disgusting," said Roger. "Shall I tell him to go away?"

"No. He's angry and hurt, and that's partly my fault. I am thick-skinned to ignore his insults. But perhaps, sir, I could speak with him for a moment?"

Roger nodded and Isabel walked over to Jake.

He glared down at her.

"Jake, let us talk later about what has happened in the past," she said, looking up at him. "May we, please? There is a lot of anger in you. You need to let go of it."

Jake shrugged.

Isabel sighed. "So be it."

Roger was pacing around the clearing looking at the ground as he did so. "So why the murders?" he asked. "There seems to be magic ritual involved?"

"Yes, there is. The monks should have known that, and everyone in the town suspects sorcery or witchcraft, and thus it came back to me."

"I see," replied Roger. His brow wrinkled as if he was thinking hard on what she had just told him. How much could she trust them? She must tell them what was happening, but perhaps they didn't need to know everything. There might be more to this young academic than she thought. Certainly he seemed to listen and respect

Jake, so there was a danger that his thoughts might be poisoned by Jake's bile.

Roger turned to her suddenly. "And what were you going to tell us? You haven't yet told us anything we didn't already know?"

That's right, she thought, but now she must give them something.

"I believe the murders are sacrifices: human sacrifices of a virgin in order to summon a demon. That is bad enough, but the regular occurrence — another one every month — scares me."

"What about the fact that children have been murdered? How do you think the parents feel?" said Jake.

"Terrible of course," said Isabel. "Are you going to listen to me or not?"

"I found you!" her husband's voice called. "Master Sotil, and ... ah ... Jake."

Isabel smiled at her husband as she saw him approach along the path.

"I thought you might be here, Isabel, looking for fresh herbs and roots. She makes a wonderful elixir for my bath, you know, Master Sotil." *Ah, your timing could have been better John,* thought Isabel. *What are you doing here?*

"Husband," said Isabel, "I was showing Master Sotil around the town. He wanted to see the site of the murders. It is sad that this beautiful spot now has tarnished memories for all of us."

John walked towards them, out of the shadows of the wood and into the clearing where they could see him better. Isabel's heart started to pound. Holding onto John's back with arms around his shoulders like a pack was a demon!

Isabel struggled to stay calm. "Husband, why are you here?" she said. He was here for a purpose but not one of his own devising.

"I ... I don't know. I had an urge to see you, I suppose." John looked doubtful and then his face glowed with pleasure. "I have just concluded a fantastic deal with the Flemings. Tonight we will host them for dinner to celebrate the partnership."

The demon grinned at her, too. Sharp yellow teeth shone with some viscous liquid that dripped from their tips and then disappeared before it could land on John.

Roger came to stand next to her. She looked at him. He didn't say anything, but his face was creased with concern. *He must stay quiet*, she thought. He caught her eye and she quickly shook her head . He nodded back and kept his mouth tightly shut.

She looked back at John. The demon on his back whipped out a long muscular arm, hairless and the colour of phlegm. The creature drew a taloned hand in front of John's neck. In response, John scratched at his neck as if he has an itch.

Isabel's heart pounded. The demon smiled and stared at her. The thing's eyes seemed to grow and all sound and vision aside from the demon became a haze. There was a voice, she thought, John's maybe. But she watched the demon. She watched as it put its taloned hand now to its mouth and pursed its jagged cruel lips. *Be quiet, be quiet, don't say a word* it seemed to say. The finger swung lazily from side to side as the demon shushed her.

And then the sound was back to normal and she could hear John speaking. She put up her hand and interrupted him.

"I'll walk back to the house with you," she said.

"And what about dinner tonight? I think we should invite the Abbot don't you?"

"Yes, yes." The demon nodded and smiled to her. *Good girl*, it mouthed.

"Isabel?" said Roger. Isabel looked at him and shook her head. She took John's arm and they turned and walked back to the town. She looked at John, her pulse dancing. The demon was gone.

For now.

Behind them she heard Jake exclaim: "Can someone tell me what the fuck is going on?"

CHAPTER 27

Roger's long, bony frame was not made for small spaces. His kneecaps were in pain from crawling along the low passageway and his elbows seemed to leap out to bash the narrow stone walls at every opportunity. On top of that, he could not see where he was going, Jake had closed the door nearly shut in case any keen pilgrims might show up wanting to get closer to the holy St. Brett. He was not one of the most popular of Saints nowadays, but you never knew, and Isabel said that the crawl-way — or Holy Hole as it was known — was still used on occasion. Jake had called it a sewer and told Roger that he was not going down there. Roger was about to tell him it didn't matter, as Isabel had said she would only have him follow her down the passage underneath the shrine, but thought better of it. There was a fractious aura between those two which scared Roger. He didn't know if Jake was more likely to kill Isabel, or try to make love to her. It was no doubt safer for everyone if Jake didn't come along. "Get back," hissed Isabel. "That's my arse you're groping, not the rotten boney butt of St. Brett, you know."

Roger snapped his hand back and mumbled an apology. He could feel his cheeks burning.

"It's all right, it's dark down here," replied Isabel. "I think if I move a panel we can go up into the shrine."

"With the Saint?" said Roger.

"You have a problem with that?"

No that was fine, thought Roger. Sharing a confined space with a beautiful woman and a box of embalmed bones was all he had ever dreamed of. "After you, my lady," he replied.

He heard Isabel snort and then there was a crack of light from above. It was very dim — just the light that filtered in from the outside of the wooden-and-gilt enclosure that enclosed the Saint's body, and then came down through the gap revealed by the panel into the tunnel below. Normally, the door at the other end of the tunnel would also be open, and pilgrims would be able to see much better, no doubt with a monk encouraging them to make their way as rapidly as possible in order to get more of them through. He had seen something similar at Winchester Cathedral. Roger remembered watching the pilgrims lining up to go down on their hands and knees through the small gap, a monk taking their shilling in payment for the privilege of getting nearer the holy bones of St. Swithen's.

He watched as Isabel pulled her legs up into the small gap and caught a glimpse of the pale smooth skin of her shapely calf. He dragged himself along slowly to give her time to move into the shrine, but when he looked up at the gap in the tunnel ceiling through which Isabel had just disappeared, he found himself looking up at a longer length of ivory skin belonging to Isabel's thigh as she held her skirts to prevent them from catching on the casket. Roger coughed violently, he had forgotten to breath.

"Be quiet," hissed Isabel, who had now found a place in the far corner of the shrine, where she would not be exposed by the windows of the tight enclosure. "I have found somewhere to sit. You'll have to squeeze in on the other side of the casket, away from me."

That was probably a good thing, thought Roger.

Getting through the hole was not too difficult, but finding space inside the small shrine was. The entire shrine was little longer than the height of a man (or saint), and only three feet high. Roger must have been at least a foot taller than Isabel, and had long arms and legs to match, so it wasn't easy to fit them around the casket of the Saint. In fact, he found the best position was to sit with legs either side of the death-mask of the Saint which lay upon the top of the casket.

"What's that made of?" said Roger.

"What?"

"The death-mask. The sculpture on top of the casket."

"It's made of the Saint's flesh," Isabel replied shaking her head. "All of it is the Saint's flesh. There is no sculpture or beaten mask and cape."

Roger leant back. There was a certain smell of the apothecary about the place. Embalming fluids could be potent stuff, he had heard, and they would dye anything they came in contact with a horrible yellow, so it was lucky his robes were so dark.

"That's... that's remarkable. Usually all you get is a finger bone or a nail, or scrap of hair," he said, genuinely impressed.

"Yes, they've really excelled themselves here. Not older than a hundred years, though, if you ask me," she said.

Roger frowned. "Right, that's reassuring. Are there any genuine relics of St. Brett's?"

"I don't know, and frankly I don't care. I only hope that this place is holy enough to ward off any of the necromancer's summonations. Now stop all this blathering. You want my help don't you?"

"Well of course I do, but if you know who did it why don't you just tell me who's responsible?"

"I think you know why. You saw the threat."

Roger paused. Of course she feared her husband's death. That demon's mimicking of cutting John's throat had been clear enough. He sighed. "So you can't tell me anything, and we're no nearer the truth."

"The truth is right in front of you, but you won't open your eyes to look."

"What do you mean?" asked Roger.

"If I spell everything out, it will mean death," said Isabel. There was an edge to her voice. "Let me ask you something, in battle if another man is armed with a sword, do you face him with bare hands?"

"No. You meet him with a sword," came Jake's voice from below them, "or better yet, with a pole-arm."

"What are you doing there? You made me jump," said Roger nursing a bruised head.

"I decided it looked more suspicious if I was hanging around outside, attracting attention, so I came down here," Jake said, pulling himself partway up into the shrine. "Besides I wanted to know what her highness had to say."

"So did you leave the door open on the outside?"

"Um, no. But it's unlocked"

"I hope none of the Abbey watchmen spot it and put the padlock in place," said Roger. "If they do, we're stuck in here."

"Well," said Jake, "we best keep it quick then." He twisted around in the hole to look at Isabel. "Tell us who's been murdering all the children."

"You know I can't do that."

"No, not really," said Jake. "Would you rather be asked these questions by Justice Cavendish?"

"Jake," said Roger, "your father has been threatened with death by the necromancer's demon if Isabel tells us."

"You still believe that?"

"Look, I am trying to tell you what I can," said Isabel. Roger could see her eyes reddening and her lip trembling, "If you don't listen to me, the killings are going to keep happening. Now, listen please: you need to fight like with like."

"What? We need to take the battle to the necromancer's children?" said Jake. "How can we do that when we don't know who he or she is?"

"I'm not going to slaughter innocent children," said Roger appalled.

"Perhaps you two would stand a better chance if you weren't so stupid," said Isabel, on the edge of tears. "How does the necromancer get his power to murder and kill?"

"By summoning demons," said Roger, suddenly feeling quite as stupid as Isabel had named him. "So we need to do battle with the necromancer's demons!"

"No, you don't want to try that. I very much doubt if you could keep control of a bunch of battling demons," said Isabel. "You want to find answers."

"So we ask a demon?" said Roger?

"Ask a demon?" said Jake. "Why would it give you a straight answer?" He chuckled.

"Not what I was thinking of," said Isabel.

"But that's what you said!" said Roger. "Use a demon."

"*Use* a demon, but they are notoriously treacherous and deceitful unless properly bound, and even then I wouldn't trust them."

"Oh you wouldn't, would you," said Jake. "No wonder they called you 'witch' — you know far too much of these sorcerous things."

"And I am saying far too much. So let us keep this quick."

"So who then?" asked Roger.

"Who else was there when the children were murdered?"

Roger paused to think, but Jake spoke first. "The children. But they're dead."

"But," said Isabel, "A demon can help you raise the dead and speak to them. The demon may not answer your questions accurately, but you can compel him to do your bidding if you have the right conjuration."

"I am not going to do any such thing," said Jake. Isabel looked over at Roger.

Did she really expect him to be conjuring demons? The thought of it was ... well disgusting but intriguing too. "Well how do you know this? How do we do it?"

"I have already told you too much. Someone's life is in danger." Isabel turned her head, and wetness glistened in the weak light that shone through the cracks in the side of the shrine.

"You'll have to excuse my master," said Jake. "He's not the brightest and he could use some help."

"The person who has done these things found this knowledge not far from here. You must do the same."

"Oh I see. The library," said Roger. He had been hoping for another excuse to root around in that old chamber, but it was a shame that the Precentor was not still alive to help him in his search.

"Probably not," said Isabel. She bowed her head and began to cry.

"Hey, what's the matter?" asked Jake, reaching over to touch her leg. She didn't move away.

"I'm so afraid for John."

"Come on let's get out of here," said Jake.

"But where Mistress Haukwake?" said Roger. "Where else could these books be?"

She looked at him with tears running down her cheeks as she scooted towards the gap in the floor, her mouth set in a firm line of anguish. "They would have burned me or hung me for trying to do good. All I wanted was to know how to help people, to cure their ailments or make their lives easier, make a marriage work better, and they called that 'witchcraft'."

"So where are the books?" asked Jake.

Isabel looked around. "I daren't tell you anymore, you'll have to find them. Now, please let's go, and please hurry. Master Roger you need to do your job."

Roger gulped. For her he would do anything, but was he capable of it?

CHAPTER 28

"I still say that we should start our research in the library," said Roger as he and Jake walked down the cloister.

"But she was telling us the books weren't there," said Jake. "That would be a waste of time wouldn't it?"

"A review of the available literature in the library will form a good base for further research. It will also help us know what texts we are looking for — references and sources and the like."

"Do you think we have time for that?" said Jake.

"Um, I don't know," said Roger. "I'm sure if we cut a few corners we could get there. Perhaps we don't have to make our notes too exhaustive?"

Jake had fetched Roger's writing equipment from the guest-house. Roger was lucky to have such a literate man-servant. Despite his rough manners and soldierly experience, Jake had been educated to grammar school level by the very Abbot they had just been to see. And although he had been expelled, he seemed to have picked up plenty in a short time and had become invaluable as a scribe to support Roger's research at Oxford. He also had the annoying habit of often speaking more common sense than Roger.

"We haven't got long," said Jake. "I think we need to find these books this morning, and if possible do what we have to do tonight." There were no monks or servants nearby, but Jake was rightly cautious about not saying outright what they planned: to summon a demon.

"But if we jump right in..."

"Master Sotil," Jake said. He only addressed Roger so formally if he was cross with him, Roger knew. "You yourself just told the Abbot that his problem wasn't solved, that those millers weren't his necromancers. Now he wants results, and fast."

The Abbot had not needed much convincing. He must have known that the idea of two barely literate millers being responsible for the possession of several townspeople and the ritual murder of dozens of children just didn't add up. "I don't know what the Infirmarian believes," the Abbot had said. "But I don't harbour much hope that there will not be more killers and demonic interventions. And if anything happens before or during Cavendish's court session... well the consequences don't bear thinking about. I'm relying on you, Sotil."

Roger looked hard at Jake. "He gave us permission to search wherever we needed without warrant — that includes the library which has been closed, and is still closed, since the Precentor's death. I just have the feeling that there is something there that might be useful."

Jake didn't say anything in reply. *He is angry with me,* thought Roger. More pressure to find those books, something that will help them summon a demon. He shivered despite the warm May sunshine. What were they doing? He had no wish to sell his soul to some evil devil, yet Isabel had been adamant that this was the only way.

Jake took out the big ring of keys the Abbot had given him. *"Unlock this mystery,"* he had said. *"I don't want any surprises jumping out when Cavendish is here."* Jake silently unlocked the library and held the door for Roger.

The library was bathed with sunlight at this hour and they had no need of candles. Jake placed the writing equipment in a booth by one of the upper cloister windows and joined Roger, who was already scanning the stacks of books and rolls.

Three hours later they had a good collection of tomes on the reading desks. But they were all volumes that Roger reluctantly admitted that he had read before and which contained little but frivolous references to magic and demons; mostly warnings, and the occasional exorcism or a charm to prevent possession, but certainly not details of how to summon one.

"Well, is any of this useful, do you think?" asked Jake. "Can we set about summoning this bloody demon?"

"There must be other, more useful books somewhere else," he replied.

"Are you sure? You've been down each stack twice and into that room at the back, but it's just court rolls isn't it," said Jake. "God I'm hungry, let's stop to eat."

Roger rarely noticed when his own body was telling him to stop working, but as he heard Jake's words his own stomach gave a loud roar.

"Hah!" laughed Jake. "You too, let's go to the guest-house refectory."

So they proceeded out of the library, locking it as they went. As they walked past the church, they could hear the sound of plainsong. The monks were singing the psalms for sext.

"Jake, you go on. I'm just going to stop in the church for a moment."

"To pray?"

"Uh, I don't know. Maybe."

The door from the cloister to the Abbey Church was unlocked, and as Roger went through he was nearly knocked over by a procession of monks coming the other way, looking forward to their lunch. They shuffled quickly along, each glancing curiously at Roger as they passed.

He waited for them to pass, then entered the now-quiet church. He couldn't blame Isabel for not telling them more. She knew more — he was certain of that — but he had seen the gesture the demon on John's back had made. The intention was clear. Whoever had bound that demon to their will had threatened to kill Isabel's husband if she said anything more. She had been brave to even meet with them, and braver still to give them some clues. It was a pity that Jake wasn't so forgiving. Despite having saved her from the noose not two days ago, he was dismissive of suggestions to her innocence. The grudges he bore her ran deep.

Roger wandered through the church. A couple of pilgrims were kneeling before the shrine of St Brett's in which he had earlier met with Isabel. They looked like farmers or craftsmen by their humble garb, but still they had travelled all the way here to get the saint's blessing. The two men stood and Roger noticed two things about them. They had similar features, brothers at least, or maybe even twins, their faces looked the same, but their hair was cut differently. But one stooped badly and could only walk with the help of both his brother and a stout walking stick. They moved slowly away from the shrine, and dropped coins into the box that a waiting monk pointed towards as they left. A donation for the saint and his monks in the hope that they would benefit from his healing. There were no more pilgrims, and the monk walked away taking the box with him, for safekeeping and no doubt to eat his own lunch. Roger felt slightly faint. He could do with sustenance, but he was too desperate to solve the riddle to eat yet. Where were the books? He glanced around. He was alone. He looked again at the wooden shrine, images of the saint murdered by his own pagan bother carved onto the outside. Perhaps asking for the saint's blessing was worth a try?

Roger walked over and took a candle from the side and lit it from another bigger one. He knelt down and placed the small candle in the rack in front of the shrine. An offering of light for light. He bowed his head. He was not used to this. What should he say? Even when absolutely required to attend mass at Merton College, he hurried through the words of the Lord's prayer, and during the other blessings and prayers he would be thinking only upon his latest research, to such an extent that a neighbour on his pew might need to nudge him to let him know that the service had finished.

Roger closed his eyes and put his hands together in front of his chest. This was what it looked like, but what did one do next? You thought some good thoughts, he supposed. Plead, beg, and wish for good things to happen. What would a holy person, a saint wish for, how would they pray? Would they justify their good works to God and then ask for something in return? Was that how it really worked, a sort of bartering system? Of course Saints acted as a sort of intermediary didn't they between the poor sinner, *id est* Roger Sotil, failed investigator of demonic possessions, and the deity God Almighty.

So then St. Brett, whoever you were, what can you do for me? Children are dying; there's a full moon again in five days, and another innocent child will surely be seized and sacrificed for some demonic purpose. And we're clueless to know what to do.

That was a point. What was the necromancer's plan? He was summoning demons but to what end. To murder people? There were easier ways to do that weren't there. Dip into any chronicle of history of the ancients or the Bible even — especially the Bible — and you could see that people were rather adept at murder and torture and cruelty. Why did you need a demon to help out with that?

So what have you got St. Brett? Or … what was your name before? The Precentor told me something of the origins of the word. What was it? Brett Walden, or Brifren something or other like that. Bifrons? God I'm awful at this, perhaps I should ask one of the monks about how this praying is done.

"No you're doing just fine."

Roger looked up and opened his eyes. He didn't need to look behind him because he knew the words had come from right in front of him, from the shrine itself, where now there seemed to be a shimmer of light, red and then glowing orange to yellow and pure blazing white so fierce that he had to raise a hand to shield his eyes from the glare.

The voice spoke again. A clear male voice not of this world. Was this what angels sounded like? It was too masculine, he thought, to be an angel. The voice of the saint. He was speaking in the saint's voice.

Who?

Roger realized he hadn't been listening. The voice began again. *"Are you a little surprised? Don't worry there is no reason for you not to be alarmed. I would be, too, if I were you."*

"Who... What are you?" Roger managed after several attempts to get the words out of his mouth.

"I am the spirit of this place. You called my name and I came."

"The saint! St. Brett."

"What do you wish? Tell me how I can help."

Roger knelt looking between his finger at the shifting patterns of light, which did not coalesce to form any definite shape, but something definitely taller than it was broad. The shape of a person, perhaps. That could be a head at the top, but then the white glare came back and he had to squint and look away. What did he want to know? He must remember.

"We need some books. Books of necromancy. Can you help us?"

"Books of necromancy? To conjure a demon?"

What was he doing? Asking one of God's saint to help him find such evil things? "Yes that's right. It's to save the children. Just to save the children. That's all."

"Then I think I can help you."

CHAPTER 29

He would have to say something sooner or later. But what? Where do I find elderflower? Is that a mandrake root? For goodness' sake, he had slept with this woman, kissed her, done other stuff with her, which now his father was doing to her. For God's sake...

"I think we'll find most of those roots that you're looking for over here," said Isabel. "And what was the other thing? A salamander's heart?"

"Uh yes," said Jake. "What's a salamander anyway?"

"A type of lizard. There are lizards on the cliffs further upriver, they like the heat on the rocks. I'm sure that will do." Isabel walked alongside him, swinging her basket. She looked happy enough. But then perhaps she would be. She had avoided death against all the odds, and now she had both himself and his master running around doing her bidding without so much as a direct command. Was this all somehow part of her plan? No, surely not even she would do that?

They walked along in silence for a while. Isabel would stop and add something to her basket. "So you'll be needing this, and this."

Jake felt like he needn't have been there, but Isabel had been insistent that he accompany her. "It's your summoning after all, isn't it?" she had said.

They came to the river and Isabel pointed to the low cliffs up in the hills to the north. "That's where they'll be. Where the sun warms those rocks."

"Lucky it's a sunny day," he said.

"And you don't get many of those in England," they both spoke at once and laughed as they realized they were both saying the same thing together. Isabel glowed a smile at Jake. By the Saints how he loved that woman, he always had. He didn't know whether to laugh or cry.

The path up into the hills was steep, and there was no path at all out to where the cliffs rose above the river. They weren't high cliffs, but steep and rocky enough to be difficult to get to. No one bothered to graze sheep up here or plant crops, the land wasn't worth it. "You come here much?" asked Jake.

"Only if I need a salamander's heart," replied Isabel.

"You're a regular then," said Jake.

Isabel turned and smiled. "Give me your hand Jake. It's steep here." He helped her climb up the slope of tough grass broken by rocks until they reached a shelf of grass and rock near the summit. "Thank you," she said. "I'm glad you're here."

"You don't normally need help getting your salamander hearts do you?"

"No, but you see, with everything that's happened, it doesn't feel safe anymore."

"Is that why you wanted me here?" asked Jake.

"Yes. And it is your summoning. I know you don't trust me, I could be here picking any old rubbish couldn't I?"

Jake glanced down at the scrap of paper he held in his hands. Roger's scrawled handwriting scribbled across the page, a list of perhaps twenty items that he had noted down from the books. Roger had been in too much of a rush to tell Jake how he found the books, something about a well?

"We could have checked what you'd brought back. I'm ... we're grateful that you helped us so much."

"You still suspect me and that's the truth," said Isabel coming closer to him until they were almost touching, her face just below his, her jaw set in a firm look of reproach, her body inches from his.

He leant forward and they were kissing, their warm lips crushing each others in a frenzy of movement. Jake put an arm around Isabel's back and moved her closer, he felt her breasts against his chest and her leg moved up around his hip to press herself against him.

Something bit his leg. "Fucking hell," he shouted and clutched his calf in pain. Blood welled through the fabric of his leggings.

Isabel shouted at Jake. "What's the matter? What have I done?" She looked as if she was about to cry or curse him. What had they been doing? Where did that come from?

Something scurried behind a rock. "Something bit me hard. Look at my leg." Jake drew his dagger. "Maybe it's a rat, or maybe it's one of your lizards."

A black creature slithered from under a rock and darted towards them. Jake waved his dagger at it, but missed by a mile. The creature shot past him and went towards Isabel. She didn't run or try to defend herself, just stood there; and Jake thought he saw her lips move, but he could hear nothing. Then the creature froze for a second. Jake stared at it. He had never seen anything like it. It was no bigger than a kitten or a puppy, with black, lizard-like skin, but it's ugly face was like that of an ape or a man's but with jagged white teeth frozen in a savage grimace. On its back were a pair of folded bat's wings.

"What the fuck...?"

Isabel held up a hand for him to be silent, and then she had her wimple off her head and in a spark of movement

268

bundled the creature into it. Immediately it started twisting and turning, trying to get free.

"Demon, I demand you tell me your purpose. Why do you attack us?" Isabel said in a voice of authority.

The thing jumped out of her arms as she said these words, flapping its black wings rapidly like an insect. In a tiny voice rasped a reply. "Your husband-father is paying for your treason, bitch. That is all I have to say."

And with that it was gone, not flying away or slithering between rocks, but disappeared into the air. Isabel was already running down the hill. Jake stopped to pick up her basket and her wimple and followed after her, glancing about for lizards on the way.

CHAPTER 30

"I tried to keep him inside," said the servant. "But he insisted on going out."

"Couldn't you have restrained him somehow," snapped Isabel.

"But he's the master, and besides, that look he gave us. Like a man possessed."

Isabel watched from the shop-front of their house as her husband, the respectable leading burgess of St. Brett's, known for his business acumen and authority, ran around the market square (thank the Saints it wasn't market day) and played tag with whoever passed by — or at least tried to.

"It's not fair, no one will play with me," said the distinguished John Haukwake, in an old man's imitation of a small child. The passersby smiled at him and laughed nervously, pretending that it was some silly game. But Isabel watched them as they hurried past, gossiping amongst themselves. And more worryingly still, people were forming into small groups around that part of the market to watch the performance. An old man in his dotage he looked now, gone mad.

Isabel had seen enough. She strode into the square and took John by the arm. "Mummy," said John in his child's old man voice. "Why won't the naughty people play with me?" There were titters of laughter from those watching, and Isabel caught sight of one or two small boys being sent by their parents to fetch others. This would be worth watching, they thought.

She grabbed his arm and whispered in his ear. "Come inside now please."

"No, I shan't," said John the old man child. Something black and scaly flicked out of John's ear, , brushed Isabel's cheek, and then, was gone again. Isabel could hear laughing, but it wasn't from those onlookers come to mock her husband. It came as if from a deep well, echoing around, but it was from the thing inside John's head and came out through his ear.

"Inside now," hissed Isabel. "I have … I have sweets."

"Oh goody! Sweets! Yum yummy mummy." And John despite his age and his wounds from the battle yesterday began jumping up and down in excitement.

"Quick now," said Isabel. "Or they'll be all gone."

Jake was standing, watching them from inside the doorway of their house. His eyes were wide and he shook his head as she ushered her husband inside.

"What the hell …?" he began. She silenced him with a look.

She managed to get John to the parlour before all hell broke loose. The child-like behaviour had been nothing compared with this. He flung her arm away and snarled viciously at her. "Away from me whore!" he shouted, in a voice that Isabel didn't recognize at all. John had never been angry with her and she had never heard him raise his voice, even when a servant did something wrong. He could show his displeasure in more subtle ways.

"That's no way to speak to her," said Jake.

"You fool, he doesn't understand," said Isabel. "That's not him talking, it's a demon."

One of the cooks who had been watching wide eyed from the door to the kitchen screamed and ran.

"Bullshit," said Jake. "He's just a fucking stupid old man. Just showing you his true colours he is. About time you realized what an asshole he is."

John sat down on a chair with his legs wide apart, eyes glaring at everyone. "Hello little boy," the voice of whatever was inside John said to Jake. "Come and sit on my knee. And I'll give you a god-damned seeing too." John thrust his groin in the air and rubbed himself, and stuck out his tongue to wag it at Jake.

"He's gone mad," said Jake to Isabel. "Should be fucking locked up."

"No. This is my fault, my stupid fault," she replied.

John and the chair he was sitting on began to turn a circle on the floor. "Any of you fucking bitches want to go for a ride," he called.

"How's he doing that," said Jake. "Yesterday he could barely stand unaided."

"I'm trying to tell you, it's the demon. Please Jake, will you fetch your master?"

"Roger?" said Jake. "Yes. I've seen enough of this." Jake walked from the room and Isabel heard him slam the front door on his way out.

John stopped spinning. He looked around the room. His manservant, George, stood next to Isabel, his hand clutching the pommel of his dagger on his belt. And the two cooks peered from the safety of the kitchen, hesitant to show themselves. "All of these out of here," said the voice of the demonic John. "I want counsel with the whore alone." He pointed at Isabel.

The servants hurried away, doors slamming behind them. They were bound to be listening, Isabel knew, and then tale of whatever was said would be over town within minutes.

"Do you really want to speak to me privately?" she said.

"I think that is best don't you?" said whatever was inside John. "But don't worry they won't be able to hear what *I* say at least. In fact, from now on my words will be silent for them and only inside your head." And with that, John's lips opened and closed stupidly like a fish trying to suck in air or filter water through its gills, but did not form words. The voice was inside her head and now it had nothing of John's cadences. It was evil. Pure evil, like liquid bone melted by the hottest flame dripping into her ear. She winced and held the side of her face and pain as the demon laughed.

"See your husband? He's been turned into a jibbering fool hasn't he?"

"Who are you? What do you want?"

"You think you can trick me that easily into telling you my name?" The voice rose in pitch like fingernails drawn across a clay pot. *"It wouldn't do you any good, but I'm not going to tell you. That's not important. What's important is that you listen?"*

"To what?"

"Are you listening?"

"Yes!" She fell to her knees the pain in her ears and her head almost unbearable, she felt like she was about to faint. John sat in his chair in front of her face smiling stupidly, tongue hanging and head lolling from side to side. Isabel could smell something bad then saw the dark stain in John's trousers.

"Now if you don't want him to be like this forever, you're to swear something. Do you understand?"

"Yes."

"Any backsliding and I'll be back and I'll do worse to him and then start with you as well. There's no one else you love is there? Just him? But mostly you love yourself, I think, from what I've seen?"

"There was my mother," she said, tears of pain like hot boiling water springing from her eyes and dropping steaming to the floor.

"You never loved her. But she went to heaven at least, which is a long way above where you'll be going."

"She's in heaven?"

"Maybe? Do you want to find out?"

"Tell me. Is she?"

"We'll see. Keep your mouth shut and we'll see. Now here's what you're to do. No more helping those two investigators. There's mostly useless and hopeless, but my master knows that you're cleverer than the pair of them. So stop what you're doing. You're to not speak to them again. Agreed?"

"I agree. But why don't you just destroy them? They're the problem, not me."

"Because the investigation has to be concluded doesn't it? Do you think my master's stupid like them? He wants them to go away having found that there is no case to answer. You were lucky he didn't let you take the blame."

"You can't get away with this forever."

"We don't need to. Just long enough. The end is coming soon."

"The end of what?" asked Isabel.

"The end of the world."

CHAPTER 31

"This isn't going to work," said Roger, opening the grimoire on the table before him.

"I wish you had said that an hour ago. Would have saved me a lot of trouble." Jake folded his arms and watched Roger leaning over the book. Was this really going to be worth it? Roger didn't seem to know what he was doing. He had spent the whole day looking through these books, mumbling some sort of incantations sitting in his room in the Abbey guest-house, while Jake had gone back and forth finding the last of what they needed and searching out a place for them to carry out the summoning. The mill, now empty since its inhabitants had thrown themselves off the Abbey gatehouse, had been a good choice he thought, but Roger hadn't looked too happy about it. He had muttered something about "less occult power due to the distance from the hub". This was all a fool's errand anyway. If Isabel would just tell them who was responsible, they wouldn't be going through this charade.

"Right. I think we're just about ready to get started," said Roger.

"Oh good, I can't wait," said Jake. He could do with a good sleep once this was over. It wouldn't take long surely to realise that there was no way that Roger could summon a demon.

"Pass me the doll," said Roger. Jake went over to his haversack and retrieved the cloth doll of a little girl and handed it to Roger. Roger said some words that sounded like Latin, but Jake didn't recognize them.

"What are you saying?" said Jake.

"Hush!" said Roger and continued his incantation. Then Roger walked into the circle he had drawn in pale ashes on the flagstone floor to the centre where a solitary candle burnt in a simple silver holder.

He started swinging the toy over the flame, still chanting, and the cloth of the toy began to singe and catch light.

"No, stop!" said Jake. "What are you doing, I was going to take that back later!" Jake stepped towards the circle. He hadn't wanted to break into the dead girl's house anyway. He had protested to Roger that this was too much, but he had been insistent. And now this! It was an outrage.

"Get back!" hissed Roger. Jake stood as if frozen at the very edge of the circle. He raised his foot to move forward, to grab the doll before it burnt to a cinder, but he couldn't. He could lift his leg so far but then it stopped, as if the line of the circle was a barrier.

"This is wrong, and it's not going to work," he shouted at Roger. He turned his back on Roger and strode around the edge of the room. He wanted to do something to make this better. They had to find whoever had killed that little girl, whoever had killed all those other children. The same person that had killed the Precentor, driven the miller and his son so mad that they threw themselves to their deaths, and sent his father mad.

Roger was back outside the circle now. He was ignoring Jake and looked down at his grimoire. "Now we can begin the summoning. Jake, I need you to be quiet for this bit."

"Fine," said Jake. This was pointless. It wasn't going to bring those dead children back or bring them any justice. Isabel was the key. She knew so much more, but when he and Roger had gone to the Haukwake house to see if they could do anything for his father, she hadn't even let them come into the house. "He's better now," she had claimed and just shut the door in their faces.

So now he was here, watching Roger play-act at summoning a demon. Just another pointless exercise, in his opinion.

The torches around the room flickered as a soft breeze filtered in through the cracks in the shutters. They had closed them up tight to stop any light showing through lest someone spot the suspicious glow from the town. Although there shouldn't be anyone wondering around the woods and the river at this time of night.

"I'm going outside," Jake announced. And when Roger, hunched over his books, didn't reply, he opened the door, walked out and shut it carefully behind him. The quicker they could get out of here the better. These woods gave him the shivers. Death and mystery lurked here, and there were far better places he would rather be at gone midnight. A tavern or a whore's bed for instance. And preferably not in St. Brett's. He'd had enough of the place. The woods and road and the wheel of the great mill churning the water were highlighted in pale grey by the light of the night sky. He looked up, the stars shone strongly overhead and there was a nearly full chunk of moon up there. Nearly full. Nearly time for another killing.

Soft orange light shone around the edges and through the cracks in the shutters. If someone passed by they'd surely see something. They'd be gone soon though. He could hear Roger's mumbling and chanting from inside. Reading the gibberish scrawled in those books. Nonsense for gullible idiots written by credulous fools.

277

The light from the cracks in the shutters glowed brighter until it was a blinding white; then vanished suddenly. A throbbing sound came from inside. Jake's heart raced and in a moment before he could think about what he was doing, he was back inside.

Roger was standing there, hand held up as if about to give a blessing. The long pale fingers of his other hand clutched the edge of a scrap of manuscript, torn from a weathered, leather-bound volume he had let drop to floor at his feet. The torches were out, but Jake could see well enough. At the centre of the circle was a low glow of blue light, and a figure was forming out of the shadows. Tall, over six foot of him.

"I think it might have worked," said Roger not turning around to look at Jake.

Jake came and stood next to his master. "Is there time to reverse it? Should we flee?"

Before Jake could say another word or Roger speak in answer, the figure became whole and the torches around the room flared back into life, throwing their dark shadows across the room and illuminating the figure of a tall, distinguished-looking man with a long finely cut white beard. He was dressed in crimson and ermine robes, and stood at the centre of the room. Despite his height, Jake noticed that *he* cast no shadow.

The tall old man frowned. His cheeks creased as if heavily wrinkled. *How old was he?* wondered Jake, suddenly realising that was a completely ridiculous question if this was some sort of ghost or spirit.

"Hǽl ábéodan," said the old man. "gehwilc you. Are you my summoner's master? You do me honour if that is the case." And the man bowed in grudging acknowledgement. "But you look too young to be the man of royal blood. State your case."

"What?" said Jake.

"I don't know," whispered Roger. "This isn't what I expected. Where are the wings? The horns? The blackened leathery skin?"

"Why was he talking funny?" said Jake.

"Speak now, or let me pass back to whence I came," said the white-bearded man. His voice was deep and musical. He could no doubt sing a good ballad. Probably best not ask him for one now though, thought Jake.

"Uh, we ... we wish to speak with the dead," said Roger.

The old man nodded. "Yes, and so that I can do."

"With the ghost of Margery Hegate," said Roger.

"She is buried in the cemetery of St. Peter's Church. Come let us proceed," said the old man.

"Right then, let's pack this stuff up. I don't want to have to walk all the way to the other end of town and then back again to get these torches," said Jake looking around. "Best not to leave any trace is there?" He looked around himself again. "Where has the mill gone?"

A good question. They were now in the middle of a dark cemetery with the black shape of a church looming above them. The flare of the torches had gone as had the walls of the mill. The old man stood to one side, regarding Jake and Roger, and before them was a stone tombstone, freshly cut and small. A family of villeins would not usually afford such a work, but this had been paid for by the Brotherhood. By the light of the moon and stars they could make out the words *Margery Hegate, beloved daughter. 1371-1376.*

Roger plunged to his knees before the old man. "Are we in the presence of an angel or a saint?"

The old man looked down on Roger and beckoned him to rise up again. "I am here to answer, to perform a service for you as required. This is the girl's tomb?"

"Yes, master it is," said Roger.

"Don't call him that. You're his master during the summoning aren't you?" said Jake.

The old man smiled. "Your thegn knows more of the protocol than you, it seems? It is true you have me at your bidding. But tell me, I would request that you answer one question before we proceed?"

"Of course, what is it?" said Roger.

What is it, thought Jake? *Are you an idiot? He could probably try and have our souls bound to the devil forever. Who do you think you're dealing with here? This soft old man is a demon.*

"I would like to know, only if it is not too much trouble," the old man looked at Jake at that point, and he felt a shiver run through him. "Whether my master's servant, who I normally correspond with, has finished with my other duties?"

Jake wished he could take Roger aside at this moment and hammer out a proper response, but in the end Roger's answer was as good as could be expected. "For me to answer that, you would need to be more specific about which of my servants you speak and also the duties performed. I have so many servants, you know ." Roger stood now. Upright and when not hunched over a desk he was nearly as tall as the old man.

"I see," said the old man. "In that case shall we proceed with raising the girl from her grave, and then I will have performed the duty that you requested."

"Don't you want an answer to your question?" asked Jake.

"Not at present," said the old man. "I would like to think upon it more. Your master's answer was an interesting one nevertheless."

Roger and Jake exchanged looks. What was going on here?

The old man stared at the tomb from where he stood behind them. Jake didn't like turning his back on the old man, but he didn't move any closer to the grave. Within seconds the earth in front of the headstone began to move. The earth was newly dug and no grass had taken hold, and as they watched a hand and then a head of thin, fair hair began to emerge from the soil.

Jake felt his own knees hit the earth and he clasped his hands together. "By Mary and all the saints, protect us." When had been the last time he had prayed. But this was so wrong. What were they doing?

Small hands were moving and reaching up to force the soil aside. They could see a face now, pale in the moonlight. Jake didn't want to see any more detail than that. She would be worm-eaten by now. He had seen too many dead bodies rotting in the wars in France. And then the hands stopped moving.

"I cannot," said the old man.

"What?" said Roger.

"There is something wrong," said the old man. "You are not the master who normally summons me at the place of the brother-killing. There are others curious to know who you are. Other thegns of the fire river. I must go back."

"But you are bound to serve me in this!" shouted Roger. "That's what the book said. You cannot go back on this now."

"Why have I not been given the blood of virgin sacrifice to quench my thirst," said the old man, his voice becoming less smooth and taking on a roar like thunder. "Do you offer me that?"

"What would that entail?" said Roger.

"Find me a young child unsullied by intercourse and I will show you," said the old man.

"I don't think we'll be doing that actually," said Roger.

"Well then. I will be gone." And with that he was.

CHAPTER 32

"Listen to me." Roger nudged Jake awake. "How long have you been asleep?"

Jake looked at him with groggy eyes, then regarded the jug of ale at his elbow and the half-eaten sausage and chunk of bread that lay next to it on the board. "Since after I drank that ale." He rested his head back upon his arms.

Roger poked Jake again and passed him the book he had been reading through. It was the *Liber Sacratus*. He had not used it that night, but after reading through a few pages while Jake slept he had realized that it contained lore that would have been useful to them. According to the *Liber Sacratus*, he had been asking all the wrong questions of the spirit they had summoned.

"What am I looking at?" asked Jake.

Roger pointed out a section of smudged inky scratching on the page.

"I'm either too drunk or too tired to read that," he said shoving the book back towards Roger.

"I'll tell you then."

"Yes please do," said Jake into his sleeve as he rested his head once more. A dull grey light was coming in through the windows of the common room now, and Roger wondered if he could rouse the house-keeper for another jug of ale. It might serve to get Jake's attention better than he could. They had been up all night, not sleeping since the old man's spirit vanished in the graveyard.

It had all been for naught, and Roger blamed himself for that. His first conjuration and he got it wrong. He should have read all the books more thoroughly and been prepared. Been prepared to ask the right questions and to somehow get the damned spirit's name. He didn't like to think of what that thing really was. Demon didn't sound like the right word for the old man, dressed much like a scholar of Queen's College Oxford in his crimson and ermine gown. He had a distinguished, academic, yet authoritative look about him. Roger would like to have that aura when he was older. He wanted to rush through the intervening forty years and just get to being highly regarded and distinguished all at once.

He and Jake had spent the whole night since talking about what they had seen. Neither could believe that it had worked, Jake most of all. They had spent some time in the graveyard digging the little girl's grave open so they could push her body back in. And then they remembered the gear that they had left at the mill. So they hurried through the town and down to the river. All the time Jake talked in urgent hushed tones of what they had seen. The raising of the dead was what had impressed and terrified him the most, even more than the appearance of the demon. Roger had been excited to hear Jake talking — he was a believer at last, and there was no going back. The old cynical Jake was gone, he thought. But then Jake had suggested they wake the housekeeper at the guest-house and get some early breakfast. A meal that seemed to consist in Jake's mind mostly of ale. Same old Jake, getting drunk to avoid life's troubles.

Roger explained his ideas to Jake. Jake shook his head. "The trouble with you is that you're just got no sense of perspective."

"What do you mean?" said Roger.

"Well you're suggesting that we summon that spirit again aren't you?"

"Yes of course. Once more, and this time I think we will get what we need from him."

"Well that's another day lost isn't it. And then to succeed you're saying we have to somehow get this demon's name and work out what questions to ask, and it still might not work. Plus on top of that I'm going to have to break into the Hegate's house again and find some other pathetic little possession of hers for you to burn. And that, Master, is where I draw the line. I'm not doing it."

Roger frowned at Jake. But he knew he was right. The book he had read also spoke of how duplicitous demons were and how apt they were to take their summoner's extremely literally. The chances were he would make some mistake and the conjuration wouldn't work. And as Jake said, another theft from the dead girl's house was perhaps taking things too far.

"What are we to do then?" Roger asked.

"Well it's obvious isn't?"

"Wish you would tell me then," said Roger.

"Isabel knows and she's not telling. We have to get it out of her."

Roger shook his head. "That won't work. You didn't see it, but a demon threatened the life of your father right in front of her."

"Bullshit."

"So you don't believe in demons again. What about last night?"

Jake shrugged. "Well ..." How could he deny it any longer. Demons had proven to be real after all – he'd seen the creature on the cliffs and then the spirit they had summoned the night before.

"You're right though," said Roger. "Isabel is our only chance, but she can't tell us the truth. Something's happened."

"Something to do with my bloody father. He's gone mad and she's scared. Stupid old fool."

"Mad — or more likely possessed as punishment for helping us," said Roger. Was it true? Had he just pointed something out to Jake that they both should have realized?

Jake hiccupped. "Enough's enough. I'm going to talk to her and that father of mine. They've got to come forward. They'll have to take sanctuary in the Abbey if they're scared."

Jake stood up and shivered. "Are you in any state to do this?" said Roger.

"No," said Jake. "I'm not. But I'd rather go alone. I've got a few things to say to that pair." Jake strode to the door and out into the morning gloom.

CHAPTER 33

Jake walked out of the entrance to the guest-house and ploughed right into a man coming the other way.

"Fuck's sake," said Jake, feeling his shoulder.

The other man was busy picking up the bridle that he had dropped, and some rags to polish the leather. "I'm sorry, sir," said the man. A servant, to look at him, thought Jake.

"Beg pardon myself for my language," said Jake. "You gave me a fright." The man was liveried, Jake noticed, a badge on the arm of his riding jerkin. Three hart heads argent on a field sable. Cavendish's arms. When had he arrived? During the night maybe, while Roger and he were preparing things at the mill. The justice would be looking for someone to hang. Jake nodded to the man, with whom he had now made his peace and hurried on through the Abbey precinct. At the gatehouse he asked the sleepy gate-keep to open a door for him and out into the marketplace.

There were few people about. Some of the townsfolk herded cattle to their houses to be milked or carried tools out to their fields outside the town. Some of the cooks were setting up stalls, getting ready for the morning trade. Jake could smell hot pie and was tempted to stop. That sausage in the guest-house had been cold and full of gristle.

The servant who answered the door came back with the message that his mistress would not speak to him. "What about your master then?" asked Jake. The servant went away, and it was Isabel who came to the door.

"Inside quickly," she said. They went through to the parlour, scene of his father's madness yesterday.

"Not going to offer me a drink or bite to eat?" said Jake.

"What do you want?" asked Isabel. She looked tired. Her hair had been shoved helter-skelter under a wimple and there were dark semi-circles beneath her eyes. *I wonder how long it takes her to make herself look younger every morning,* thought Jake.

"I know something has happened," said Jake. "You've stopped helping us. But you have to. You have to tell us what you know."

Isabel shook her head.

"My father's been sent mad because of this hasn't he?"

"He's alright now," she said. "He is just taking time to rest after the recent events."

"So he's better now then? Is that the reward for you to keep quiet? Who are you scared of?"

Isabel didn't even shake her head. She just glared at Jake. He walked up to her and took her by the shoulders. She shrugged off his hands. He put them back on her shoulders with more force and made her look at him. "This can't go on. Justice Cavendish is here. He won't leave until he has someone swinging for these crimes, and if some other child is murdered while he's here, fingers will point to you again."

"I am innocent. The millers did it, everyone knows that now."

"Cavendish will know of the accusations against you soon enough, and he's not stupid. He'll know that a couple of oafish millers aren't behind all of this."

There was a knock at the door. *Was it Cavendish already?* thought Jake. The servant looked in at the parlour door to enquire of Isabel whether he should answer. He raised his eyebrows when he saw Jake's hands on Isabel, and she shrugged them off. "Answer it please."

Roger bustled into the parlour. "Have you heard — Justice Cavendish is here?"

"We were just discussing it," said Jake.

"Listen, Isabel," said Roger full of wide-eyed enthusiasm. "If you would come with us and put the story before the Justice, I'm sure they will protect you and your husband. The perpetrator can be arrested straight away and put under Royal guard."

"Royal guards?" sneered Isabel. "Haven't you learned anything? What good do you think guards and swords and shields can do?"

"What then? Perhaps you would like to sit next to the Abbot all day? He must, by definition, be the holiest man in the town?" said Jake.

"Don't joke about this," said Isabel. "It's far from funny. Now get out of my house, the pair of you, and make your own way to solving this."

The door to the parlour opened and John Haukwake came through it wearing a long night shirt with a fur coat thrown over it against the morning chill. His face was sleepy and tired but showed no signs of madness of possession. "We have guests, Isabel? Master Sotil, Jake, welcome. What's this all about?"

"You look well, father," said Jake.

"A few more hours in bed would see me looking much better. But look at Isabel. She looks beautiful whatever the hour." Isabel stared at her feet. "Can I help either of you? It is early to host guests."

"Sir," said Roger. "As you are aware, although the millers were blamed for the crime, so saving your good lady wife, we think they were but scape-goats for another, and that your said wife can help get to the truth."

"You accuse her again? Is that your game? Coming to take her from me to a cell in the Abbey before letting her break her fast." John's voice rose in volume as he spoke. "This your idea Jake? Did you have some sort of mind for revenge?"

"We're not accusing her," said Jake. "For God's sake, we saved her life, and your bloody life, don't forget. You ungrateful old..."

"So you could have another go at killing us again," snapped John. "Make up your mind — do you want us dead or not? Taken you years to decide, it seems. I'd like you to both leave now. Leave us in peace."

"I'm not interested in killing anyone. We just want the killing in your town to stop. How many more of your town's innocents do you want to see dead?"

"None of course," said John. "What do you accuse me of? I'm not hiding anything."

"I think what Jake is trying to say," interrupted Roger. "Is that your wife is hiding something. We know that she knows, but she isn't telling; can't tell, in fact."

"What? Is this true, Isabel?"

Isabel looked up at her husband. "Don't make me talk of this. I love you and I won't see you harmed."

"Harmed? Harmed by what? Are Goolde and Jackson outside with one of their mobs? They're happy enough for now. I'll make it worth their while come the next fair."

"Master Haukwake," said Roger. "She's not lying to you. You are in danger. I saw it with my own eyes. A demon threatening to kill you, to slit your throat." Isabel winced.

"If what?" said John.

"If Isabel helped us anymore with our enquiries. She knows who the necromancer is but she can't tell us," said Roger.

"I don't know anything," said Isabel. "These men are desperate John, can't you see that?"

"Sounds like you're trying to hide something," said Jake.

"She's got nothing to hide," said John. He walked over to his wife and put an arm around her shoulders. Jake swallowed. "Come don't be afraid," he said to her. "If there is something to tell then so be it. Why do you think someone will harm me? Has someone threatened you?"

Tears welled in Isabel's eyes and she nodded to John. He held her head on his shoulder and let her cry there for a moment. "But," she sobbed. "If I say anything, they'll kill you. A demon ... a demon will come and it will kill you."

John laughed. "Me? A demon? You've been reading too much again, my dear. There's no such thing. There's people with strong imaginations about and someone intent on murdering children with the belief that they can summon some spirit. But I don't see any demons walking about. Do you?"

Roger and Isabel both nodded. John shook his head. "Son, what's going on? Have they all gone mad?"

"It's possible," said Jake. "But if they have, then I reckon so have I. Roger summoned something last night. He came in the form of a man, but he was able to do things that no man could do."

John rolled his eyes. "Come on! What nonsense! Isabel, tell us who is behind this if you know, and don't worry about me. We'll all go to the Justice this morning and tell him. He can arrest the man and there will be no danger."

"I fear that may be no protection."

"It would take several hours surely for the necromancer to summon another demon," said Roger. "I think if we acted swiftly the case will be closed."

Isabel looked at them all and sighed heavily. "I won't tell you here," she said, her shoulders sagging. "Let us go now to the Justice and I will tell you in his presence."

"I have another idea," said Jake. "What if you told us now and we go and find this man and take him before the Justice? That would be safer. We don't want the man at large, escaping, and then conjuring some revenge against my father."

"Your concern is touching, Jake," said John. "Let's make ready to go. Isabel, lead us to where the man is to be found, and if he is there, tell us who he is."

John and Isabel went upstairs to dress properly, while Jake and Roger waited in the parlour.

§

Hiding amid the beams of the Haukwake parlour, a small imp watched, out of sight of the humans below. When there was no more to be heard, it scrambled along a beam and found a small crack in the plaster in the corner of the room, crept through, and out to the floor above.

There it found a window ajar and launched itself into the morning air, looking much like any small bird, except for its sharp, cruel teeth and dog-like face.

CHAPTER 34

Isabel knew that, somehow, this was all going to go wrong. But what could she do? Refuse to tell even her own husband? Still, she had not expected him to be as angry as he was.

"So he's a monk that much is clear, and we're in the infirmary, but there are no monks here, so I suppose we're looking for the Infirmarian, are we? Edmund is his name, is it?" said John. "The man is from Flanders originally, but I know little of him. And you know him how?"

They were all watching her. "He leant me some books... some books to help with my remedies."

"Is that all?" said John.

"What are you suggesting?" said Isabel. What did he take her for?

"What did he take in return?" said John.

"How dare you," she said. "He was kind to me, that was all. He made me feel uneasy sometimes, but he wanted no payment or favour for the books he leant me. Besides I handed them back." She turned her back on John. She heard him sigh.

"So what now?" said Jake. "You're going to the Justice, and meanwhile this man, Edmund, has gone. Could he be at prayer? He could be somewhere else in the Abbey. I could root him out," he said starting to draw his sword.

"Why don't we go to the Justice," Isabel said. "He has men. He can organize a search." She walked off in the direction of the Abbot's house, which would surely be where an important guest such as the Justice would be hosted.

"I think she's angry with you," she heard Jake say to his father. They shared some sort of stupid male joke about that. Idiots. She smiled. At least they were talking to each other, even if it was at her expense.

At the Abbot's house she knocked on the massive front door and waited. Jake was edging backwards. "Tell you what," he said. "I'll wait for you over by the stables."

"Got something to hide?" said his father.

"It's a long story."

A servant opened the door to them. He looked rather surprised to see them, but immediately showed them into the Abbot's hall, which was concealed from sight of the door by a wall that held a minstrel's gallery above it.

Inside the hall, where morning light came through pretty stained-glass windows that ran the length of the room, pictures of Saints and previous Abbots adorning each one, stood three men conversing: the Abbot, a man with a forked beard and a lawyers cap upon his head, who must be the Justice and the Infirmarer, Edmund Hope.

"The witch has come to us, my Lords," said Edmund. "Seize her before she can conjure any demons to protect her!"

At a nod from the man in the lawyer's hat, his guards moved forward, each taking one of Isabel's arms. John grabbed one of the men's shoulders trying to pull him back as they yanked Isabel towards the group of three men, but he was easily brushed aside.

"What the hell are you doing?" said John.

"We've come to arrest the Infirmarian," said Roger. "He's the guilty one here."

Edmund smiled with smug satisfaction at Isabel as she was brought before the Abbot and the lawyer. They ignored the protests of her husband and Roger. "Be quiet in my hall," snapped the Abbot. "All will be explained. Justice," said the Abbot turning to the lawyer. "This is the woman Edmund spoke of."

The Justice regarded her. "A witch then? This will be a first for me, and I believe a rarity in the history of English justice, we don't get to hang many witches."

"*Burn* you mean, surely?" said Edmund.

"In this country, hanging is the prescribed punishment for sorcery and witchcraft. No cases of it that I know of, though. So Isabel, it seems that you will be making legal history." The Justice smiled a cold smile. "You can take her to the cell. In the gatehouse was it?"

"Yes Justice Cavendish," replied the Abbot. "Quite secure I assure you."

"Set a double guard," said Edmund. "This woman is dangerous. Allow her no visitors."

"Edmund, thank you for your assistance. That will be all."

"No," said John. "This man should stay, and face his accusers. *He* is your witch, not my wife."

"A young wife, and an old husband," said the Justice. "Do you wear horns, is that it?"

"She tried to seduce me," said Edmund. "And when that failed, she put the devil in me."

"She did no such thing," said Roger. "You threatened to have her husband killed unless she kept quiet about what you were doing."

"A convenient story," said the Justice. "What is she hiding? I hear the opinion in the town was that she was a witch, and that she was only saved by the actions of this monk. Why would he then threaten her so? It sounds like he was trying to help her, but was foiled by her into only capturing her accomplices, the miller and his son. There is evidence that both men were her consorts in the bedchamber and in devilry."

"What nonsense," said John. "What proof do you have?"

"She sent a demon to possess me," said Edmund. "And both of these men witnessed it admitting that Isabel was its master. In fact the Abbot was the one to exorcise it from my body. It was there when I accused the miller, it has been pulling the strings on Isabel's behalf all along."

The Justice narrowed his eyes. "So you see there is proof from a witness so to speak, although I doubt we can make that creature appear in court, or would want to. Yet I have heard its testimony already so it is admissible."

"But we have no chance to mount a defence against such a witness," said Roger. "How will I cross-examine such a thing?"

"You'll defend me?" asked Isabel.

Roger nodded.

The Justice smiled at Roger. "We know each other already, don't we? Yes, I thought so. Is your man here?" Roger looked away. "Hmm. A lawyer and a scholar are you? Well, good luck. Now take her away, I'll argue this no more here. She'll have her day in court. The session will take place tomorrow. Abbot, would you be so kind as to organize the building of a proper gallows, to be ready by tomorrow evening?"

Isabel was led from the room. She could see John turning red in the face with rage. he was so angry that he was unable to speak at first, but she heard his shouts as she was taken through a back door of the Abbot's house and towards the Abbey gatehouse to her cell. He would fight for her, she knew. But what hope did they have? A young scholar with, she guessed, no legal experience to defend her, and the case already decided in the Justice's mind.

CHAPTER 35

Jake was sitting with his back to the wall of stable, waiting for them to come from the Abbot's house. He would have to keep low until they found Edmund, but then what? Back to Oxford with Roger he supposed. Or stay out of sight until Edmund was tried and hung and then think about staying in St. Brett's? Could he do that? An hour ago he'd called John Haukwake 'father' for the first time in years. It had been a thrill to see that old fire back in his eyes. The desire to put things right, to save, to protect. That easy dismissal of foolishness, and commitment to decisive action. But what of Isabel, was he over her? Could he accept that she would never be his? Perhaps it was the better part of valour to accept that his father had bested him in that and let it be?

A couple of men walked past. They wore Cavendish's badge and Jake bowed his head, just in case. If they had been present at Southampton three years ago, would they still recognize him? Best not take the chance. He didn't want to be on that scaffold next to Edmund.

Why had Edmund done it, he wondered? A monk with too much time on his hands? And the access to privacy with his role as an Infirmarian. Medicine didn't seem too far away from such dark magical arts in many ways. Potions, charms, the study of old knowledge. Perhaps that explained Isabel's interest. That's all it was, she claimed. Edmund had leant her some books to assist her, but then he had made advances on her. He thought that his father's apparent lack of concern showed partly jealous and partly satisfaction that his young wife could elicit such desire. But Isabel had form. One could say that she seduced son and then the father, and had she now turned her attentions to the monk (the holy ghost) when she wanted something he had? But for what ends? She always wanted more, more power; had magic been an easy route to these ends?

Jake looked up and saw his father and Roger coming out of the Abbot's house. They were without Isabel, and their faces were downcast. Jake leapt to his feet and hurried over, unconcerned about who might see him.

"What's wrong?" he asked.

"They've arrested Isabel," said his father. "The bloody idiots have got it all wrong. That monk accused her."

"What! How could they?"

"Edmund accused her of bewitching him," said Roger. "Made it sound very convincing."

"What was their evidence?" said Jake.

"Why do you believe them?" said his father. "Ready to be convinced by them are you? I thought you were on our side finally."

His father stormed off towards the gatehouse. "Where are you going?" said Jake.

"Back home to fix this."

Jake hurried after him and Roger followed behind, picking up his scholars robes to jump over a pile of fresh horse dung.

"We'll help," said Roger. "Jake, I offered to defend her in the trial."

"That's good," said Jake. "What are you planning, father?"

"We can't wait for a trial," said John. "We'll have to sort this the old way. Like back in "69." That had been the year the townspeople besieged the Abbey to extract better terms out of their overlords. His father had not fought amongst his fellow townspeople, but in reality his cool head had been the power behind the decisions of the town council. "I hope you've sharpened your sword, Jake."

They passed through the gatehouse. Outside they were surprised to see quite a gathering. Half of the Charnel Brotherhood was there. Goolde, Jackson and Dewent all stood in a group near the Hundred Tree and watched as they walked through into the market place.

"But father, what if they're right? Had you considered that?" said Jake.

John stopped walking and said in a voice loud enough for everyone to hear. "Are you with me or are you with the fucking monks? They're covering up for one of their own. They don't give a shit if any of our children are killed, or if our people are turned mad by their doings. We're like ants to them." John looked around, spittle flying from his mouth as he spoke. He waved his arms wide and his face was red with anger. "Enough is enough, I say; are you with me, son, or not?"

Jake could feel the crowd stepping closer, waiting to see what would happen. It was as if half the town had been waiting for them to come out. They were all waiting to hear his answer.

"I'm with you," he said, and clasped his father's hand. And then everything happened much too quickly. Later he would wonder if there was anything he could have done. Could he have spotted Edmund standing there under the gatehouse, watching them with a cruel smile on his face? Could he have calmed his father, not doubted him and Isabel? It was his fault. His fault. Although at the time he had blamed Roger. "Why can't we bring him back?" he'd begged. "Why didn't you stop Edmund?"

It was all in vain. As soon as he clasped his father's hand, a grin of pride had crossed the old man's face; then he suddenly withdrew his hand again to clutch his chest and his knees were buckling and he was on the ground, his face bright red and then purple, his eyes bulging and saliva bubbling on his lips.

He was dead in moments. Gone forever.

CHAPTER 36

She had been through the passage of the Abbey gatehouse enough times, but had never actually been inside. She never thought she would. A glance or a nod to the guard yawning as he sat on his stool by the doors that nearly always stood open during the day time, was all the thought she'd given the place. Until that night when Edmund had appeared on its crenulated roof and accused the miller and his son of the crime she might be hung for. It was an ugly building. Like a loaf of bread with jagged teeth on top of it, not elegant rounded towers like a proper castle. And it was thrown together from brick and a hodge of cut stone and rocks in mortar. But it did its job. It kept unwanted people out and accused people in.

They led her up the spiral staircase at the back of the gatehouse. She was taken straight up, not stopping until the third story, a low-ceilinged floor beneath the roof and the battlements. Here was where the Abbey kept its prisoners. Felons accused before the Hundred Court or simple miscreants needing a night in the cells to quieten them down and let the drink drain from their blood, all treated with an equal lack of hospitality in the Abbey cells.

The cell she was placed into was one of eight in a straight row all along the back of the gatehouse. There were no windows in her cell; the only light came through a grill at eye level in the door, and even this was second-hand light, finding its way from narrow arrow-slits that had been built into the corridor. This place was a mixture of prison and defence, the monks not being concerned about separating the two.

She'd been given a wooden cup of small beer and a dry crust of bread, but no one had spoken to her since they'd locked her in. There was not much to do except sit or stand. The only furniture was a pile of straw on the floor with an old ragged blanket draped over it. It didn't smell like it had been cleaned since the last inhabitant had been there. And there was a earthen chamber pot in the corner. No one had come when she asked for it to be emptied, so when Roger visited, she was relieved to have someone to talk to, but also ashamed at the stench of her cell.

She felt wretched when Roger told her of John's death. It had happened just outside the gatehouse where she was imprisoned, but she had heard nothing. No sounds off the market or street seemed to penetrate these walls. She hoped that her wailing could not get out. Roger had offered to leave her in peace, but she had demanded that he stay.

"I'm sorry, Master Sotil, for my state. I'm sorry for knocking that pot of filth over and flinging my mattress at the wall and for..."

"You do not need to apologize," said Roger. "Please, I understand."

Isabel looked at Roger. He was so young. What could he understand? But she'd had enough of shouting and ranting. "It was Edmund wasn't it?"

"I think so," said Roger, his face downcast. "But I heard some muttering in the crowd. Some of them accused you of it."

"Oh that's sweet! Now I am the killer of my own husband. That bastard, Edmund, has some nerve."

Roger shook his head. "I don't know what to say. He can't get away with it and you can't stay in here any longer."

"I'm sure I won't. I reckon that fucking monk will accuse me in the Justice's court tomorrow, and that will be that."

Roger shook his head again more violently. "I won't let happen. I plan to see justice done for you and for your husband and for all the dead that monster has foisted upon this town."

"Someone has got to stop him, but I can't see you overturning the judgement that has already happened. You heard the Justice; he's already preparing the gallows from which I'll swing."

"But we know it was Edmund. He confessed it to you, didn't he?"

"And you think the Justice wants to believe my word?"

"No, but if we ask for trial by jury then you have a chance — a group of men who will hear your story as well, and if we can find witnesses and evidence to disprove the accusation..."

"A group of men! Exactly the problem!" Isabel exclaimed. "And where do you think these men will come from? St. Brett's of course. The same men that were ready to have me hung but two days ago will now get their wish with all the force of the law at their backs and comfortable in the knowledge that they do no wrong."

"It would be a great wrong, my lady, if they did that," said Roger. His blue eyes gazed at her in earnest. He was a passionate young man, and not unhandsome. She threw such thoughts from her mind. John's blood was barely cold in his veins and she was thinking like this. What was wrong with her?

"I have no chance," she said, tears springing to her eyes. Were they for his benefit? "My word will be drowned by their accusations."

"That is why you need someone to speak for you. I have told the Justice that I will defend you. I hope that you will allow it?"

She smiled. "You're more a fool than I thought you were. What can it gain you except an enemy in the Justice, in Edmund, and the Abbot? You had best be careful that Edmund does not come after you next."

"If we can make the jury and the Justice believe our tale, then it will be Edmund who will have to be afraid."

She shook her head. Didn't Roger realize that Edmund's powers set the physical strength of men at naught?

"But," Roger continued, "if I am to plead your case, you must tell me everything about this man and your involvement with him. Any dealings you have had with magic of whatever form, for they will throw as much ... er ..."

"Shit at me?"

"As many lies," he said, "as they can."

So she told him everything. She told him how she had watched as Edmund commanded the demon that pursued her in the woods, how he had threatened her unless she joined him, how he had lusted after her and demanded a kiss from her for the loan of his books of magic. The books were not what she was after. She had been looking for advice on remedies for healing, for easing bleeding pains and for making women fertile after a long time fallow. There had been some reference to such things, but much of what she saw but did not read contained rules for summoning spirits, for binding said spirits to one's will and commanding them to tell you of the future or to harm one's enemies or to acquire for oneself the love of a woman or the death of a man. So she had returned the books to Edmund.

Roger scratched notes on a piece of paper as she spoke, blank pages bound into a leather cover, a book without words until Roger created them. She had never seen such a thing before. Roger was full of surprises. Was there a chance for her? Could Roger out-talk Edmund in court? Then the thought came to her.

"You should attack him where it will hurt him most, turn the tables on him," she said.

Roger looked quizzically at her.

"The Abbot has protected him, but I have even heard the other monks grumble about Edmund Hope's strange views. I think you could easily accuse him of heresy. He has spoken to me of how he believes the end of days are coming and that it has been brought upon by the corruption of the Church and the lay powers. Find some way to attack him on this. If you can draw him out so he speaks his true thoughts on the Church, then he will condemn himself. The Abbot and the Justice will not want to protect him then."

"But what if he has a point?" said Roger.

"A point?"

"About the corruption of the Church, I mean, and the government. Should we condemn him for such opinions, when his crime is murder and necromancy?"

Isabel leaned forward to Roger and looked him in the eyes. "Roger Sotil, what do you want from this world? Do you want to defend me and the people of this town against evil or argue about how many angels can dance on the head of a pin? If the latter, then you are no use to me and I suggest you leave. I will defend myself."

CHAPTER 37

No use crying. Your tears won't wash away your sin.

That's what his father used to say. And his mother? She had died so long ago, when Jake was but a small child. But he remembered her as kind, compared to his father. He had always meant to ask his father to tell him more about her. The mother he had hardly known but loved and longed after. But now it was too late, and now his father was dead as well.

Jake felt angry with himself. He was forced to leave his father's body in the care of the Haukwake's household servants. He couldn't bear to be there a moment longer. He had to run away and he did. Straight back into the Abbey precinct.

His thoughts hadn't been on revenge. Edmund had gone again as quickly as he appeared. Jake just needed to find somewhere to be alone. Inside the Abbey there were too many monks and others, servants, pilgrims, men from Cavendish's retinue, milling about or hurrying to see what the commotion was in the market outside the gatehouse. He had run through the cloister avoiding the looks of the monks as he went past. What use were they? Could their prayers help his father?

He found the door to the Church of St. Brett's wide open, but inside it was empty. At last he was on his own and he could cry.

Huge hot stinging tears as salty as the sea flooded out of his eyes and he let out a coughing choking sound as his face screwed itself into a grotesque imitation of a man's face. But he was no man, was he? Just a blubbing child. What was wrong with him? He'd hated his father. He'd never wanted to see him again, never wanted to come to St. Brett's just so he could be humiliated. But here he was, and it was worse than he had ever thought possible. All the old emotions, and ones he'd never known he had, came rushing to the surface.

He found himself near the altar of the church on his knees, his tears soaking into the stone slabs of the floor making a puddle of salty water at his knees soaking into the linen of his hose. He didn't deserve to live. Why should he? He had brought this upon his father. He had ruined everything all over again, but this time there was no going back. And what had it all been for? For nothing. Edmund was free and Isabel would die next.

"I wish it was me in the gaol," he mumbled. He found that he was clasping his hands together as if in prayer. And why not? He was in a church. If ever God should listen then it was at a time like this. And couldn't God be vengeful and angry? Shouldn't he strike down with supreme vengeance on those who did evil? "I wish that Edmund should be punished. Punish me and punish him. He deserves to die."

A hand touched his shoulder and he looked up and saw an old man touching him. "Peace be with you, I know of your troubles," said the old man. He had a soft long white beard and was dressed in dark crimson robes. A circle of gold shimmered above his head.

"Are you an angel?" said Jake, his lip trembling as he spoke.

"You could say so. I am the spirit bound to this place."

"You are St. Brett? So am I dead or am I gone mad?"

"Neither, but your passion and your grief brought me here," said the old man. "I have come to provide comfort, but only to those warriors who are brave enough to do what is right. Are you ready to do what is right?"

Jake thought for a moment. He must have been made mad by his grief. This couldn't be happening. It was a vision of his own madness come to torture him. To taunt him. "You know I am not brave," he said brushing the old man's hand aside.

"You are braver than you think," said the old man. "You have the mark of a warrior."

"I am no knight."

"Knight! What does that word even mean? Someone with wealth and status. You have the strength to stand up for what is right, to stand next to your comrades in the shield-wall. You are a warrior, Jake."

"Who are you really?" Jake said looking up at the face. He could see the dark vault of the church through the man's skin. He trembled, but not from cold.

"Do not be afraid, I mean you no harm," the spirit said patiently. "I am the spirit of this place."

"St. Brett?"

"If you like," said the old man, a smile cracking on his lips. "Tell me Jake Savage — a good name that. How would you have me help you?"

"I want to avenge my father's death. I want Edmund Hope caught and his crimes to be made known. I want to kill him."

"Those are three different things. And I can help you. But not yet; you will have to be patient. At the right time I will come again."

"When's the right time?"

"Not today. There is more at stake than you realise. I have seen the crown in flames, princes dead and murdered, their blood boiling with fraternal hate. And this town is at the centre of it. The town of my brother."

"Your brother?"

"The story of my pious brother is long, and not one you have time for now."

"Why not? How long?" Who was he really speaking to? In the legends, St. Brett's brother had been a pagan king who had killed the pious Christian believer.

"You had best be gone before the rage of revenge overtakes you. Listen to me, Jake Savage, *now is not the time. Remain calm if you want to get what you want.*"

And then he was gone. Jake knelt there, but he could feel his neck tingling, the hairs of his head itching, and the hair on his back tingling underneath his woollen shirt.

"Still here?" It was the voice of Edmund. The monk stood watching him. "The Justice doesn't know that you are in St. Brett's. But I could so easily tell him."

Jake stood up. Trying to keep calm, but he didn't know how, he wanted to draw his sword — a sacrilege, to draw a blade in the church — but he kept still and didn't even let his lips move.

"I would suggest that you tell your master to leave," said Edmund, "and that you go with him. Nothing can save Isabel now. She should have listened. And that's the price she's paying now. Do you really want to pay the same price?"

"Your time will come," said Jake.

The monk raised an eyebrow. "And yours, too, but sooner than you think. Remember, Jake, you're an outlaw in the eyes of the law. If anyone knew who you were and of your crimes, they'd have every right to cut off your head."

"I'd like to see them try."

Edmund shook his head. "You're a fool. Listen to my advice: get out of St. Brett's and live, or stay and lose your head." The monk turned and left, not waiting to hear any reply from Jake, which was a good thing, because it might have come in the form of a punch or a stab.

And that wouldn't do, not in this holy place, where angels or demons appeared and spoke to him. Who'd have thought it? His new best friend and guardian was a saint?

CHAPTER 38

Roger didn't feel comfortable about sharing a table for dinner with the Abbot and the Justice while Isabel rotted in a dank cell. The Abbot had sent his chamberlain to request Roger's presence at dinner that evening, and had made it clear that Roger had very little option but to accept. "You will wait on the Lord Abbot tonight, in his chamber, were the smug servant's words." There were just the three of them. He hadn't seen Jake. He guessed that he must be with his father, grief-stricken. Would he go to see Isabel, so that they could comfort each other?

He sampled some of the soup, but the taste was too sweet for his liking. Too honeyed. But his stomach was empty and in need of food, yet he'd rather he had less rich fare and poorer companions to sup with. At least Edmund wasn't there. The Abbot sat in a large wooden chair big enough to be a throne, and the Justice and Roger sat opposite him across the board. He was trying to put them both in their place, Roger guessed. The Justice did not seem happy about it, either. He cast an evil look at Roger as he was shown to his seat by the servants. The Abbot smiled at him, then quickly glanced to see the Justice's reaction.

I'm but a pawn, thought Roger.

The Abbot thanked them both for attending. "We gentle folk should take counsel and comfort from one another in such troubled times."

"Yes?" said the Justice. "So, Master Sotil, as well as being an expert on astrology, and Oxford's new professor of law, tell me, what is your noble heritage? I was unaware that I would be hosting a noble pleader in court tomorrow."

"I am the youngest son of Lord Ufford of Keisley, in Westmorland," Roger said, blushing. If his uncles found out he was crossing swords with the Justice of the King's Bench, their reaction would surely not be good.

"Oh really?" said the Justice. Even the Abbot raised an eyebrow. The conversation proceeded to boring topics of genealogy, claims of title, conveyancing, offices held and forfeited and all the tedious gossip of lordly life that had caused Roger to flee Westmorland. That and the threat to thrust him into a political position in the Church. He looked at the Abbot as he chewed some venison, nodding without listening as the monk held forth on some matter of demesne right and the collection of tithes. If his family had it their way he might be in the Abbot's shoes now, or perhaps an archdeacon or bishop somewhere, working his way up the ecclesiastical ladder of government office-holders. At least he wouldn't have had to suffer the boredom of law, like the Justice. That option was even worse. As a priest he might have been at least able to indulge in some study on the side.

"So what will you plead tomorrow?" asked the Justice.

"Mmm?" Roger wasn't prepared for the direct question. It came out of nowhere and knocked him off balance.

"Well I assume that you are going to plead not-guilty, but on what basis?"

Roger narrowed his eyes and looked at the Justice. "With the greatest respect, my Lord, should the Judge and the pleader for the defendant be discussing such things the night before the trial?"

The Justice shrugged. "As you wish, but sometimes a Judge can provide advice for a young lawyer in his first case, which might be especially useful for yours, perhaps?"

"My case?" said Roger.

"Well, with you having no legal training and pleading for a defendant who the whole town wants hanged against the accusations of a senior obedientary of the Abbey, with the full support," the Justice glanced at the Abbot who blushed, "of the Abbot."

The Abbot's chamberlain entered the hall and whispered in the Abbot's ear. "I am sorry gentlemen, but there is some irritating business that I must attend to. I will not be a moment."

"Oh don't concern yourself, take your time," said the Justice.

As soon as the Abbot was out of the door, the Justice leant over the board to Roger. "Speak quietly if you must speak at all, but mostly just listen to what I have to say; the Abbot won't be long."

"What's going on?" said Roger, not particularly whispering.

"Be quiet I say! If you can't then both you and your client deserve everything you get tomorrow."

Roger nodded and whispered. "All right, what do you wish to tell me?"

"I don't trust the Abbot. There is something fishy here. The Abbot is scared. Edmund has some sort of power over him, and I suspect that it comes from the court?"

"Court? Which court?"

"The only court that is higher than mine own, the King's court, and the King's second-eldest son."

"John of Gaunt?"

"Hush! Gaunt is a great benefactor of the Benedictine abbeys, including this one. St. Brett's is on his usual itinerary to his castles in the north. I am sure the monks are lined up to sing hundreds of masses for his soul upon his death. You had best tread carefully tomorrow."

"But what can I do? Why are you telling me this, do you want me to give it up?"

The Justice smiled. "I am no friend of Gaunt's."

The Justice leant back in his chair just as the Abbot entered the hall. "I'm sorry, some idiot wasting my time, pretending to have a message for me from London about the Parliament."

"What news from Westminster?" asked the Justice.

"None," said the Abbot. "The messenger gave me a scroll informing me that nothing had happened. Now what a waste of time is that? Anyway I would think you would be better acquainted with events."

"No not I. I am not asked to attend, being merely a humble servant of the King's justice; it would not be my place to make the law as well as to see it carried out."

"You jest with me, Lord Justice Cavendish? Why, you are one of the King's most trusted servants, are you not?"

"In name and title, perhaps, but the King does little ruling nowadays and spends more time playing at the role of lover, despite his age. I think you know that his son, the healthy one, not the ill, rules England in his name. Have you had no word from Gaunt? I hear that he addressed the Parliament in the King's name?"

"No word," said the Abbot. And that was it. They ate in silence, through another course, a fruit salad, berries, and apples from the Abbey's own orchards, in a sweet honeyed sauce with sour cream to give a tangy contrast of flavours.

"That was delightful, my Lord Abbot," said the Justice. "But tomorrow will be a busy day and I have to consult with my staff before retiring, so I will bid you good night."

"Oh that's a shame. I was going to ask my musicians to play for you. Are you sure you won't stay for one more cup of wine."

"No, but perhaps our new lawyer here will. I doubt that any preparation can save his client on the morrow."

Roger was left sitting glumly at the table across from the Abbot. "I must be going, too. Although the Justice is no doubt right of the hopelessness of Isabel's case, still I am tired and need my rest." He had to get out of there. He felt suffocated by the last two hours stuck between these two men.

"As you wish. I think we are all tired after the last few days. But can I give you one word of advice?"

"Yes?"

"Give it up for your own sake," said the Abbot.

"My own sake? What about Isabel?"

"She is doomed, whatever happens, but for you to try to defend an impossible cause is of no benefit to you. I have asked the Justice already if there even needs be a trial, but he insists. None of this looks good, and it will look worse if recorded in the court rolls of King's Bench. Remember why I brought you here? You have a duty to the Abbey and the reputation of St. Brett's."

"I will consider it," said Roger, and hurried as fast he could from the Abbot's hall. For St. Brett's and for the cause of truth he was ready to defend Isabel to the utmost.

CHAPTER 39

From the battlements of a blood-red keep high on the banks of the river Phlegethon, where blood churned around the heads of those sent to hell for violent sin, Bifrons gazed out and watched. His black-scaled body dripped with blood from the cauldron that he had vacated, an iron cup lay dashed on the floor, its bloody contents spilled on the flagstone paving. He felt the steam coming off his body as his rage thrummed greater with every beat of the drum, with every stamp of taloned foot or cloven hoof along the rocks of the blood-river's shore. A few lone centaurs remained stationed along the river's cliff-tops, their arrows darting in the water at the bobbing heads that occasionally emerged above the torrent of the bloody rapids. A paltry force, not big enough to perform their duty, thought Bifrons. Even now he could see some figures on the far side of the river, dragging their pink naked bodies onto a low shelf of rock, and attempting to climb up the far side. Their ability to escape the river unharmed was intolerable.

He turned and regarded one of his thegns: a snake-headed demon with long reptilian arms dressed in bronze breastplate. "So are you marching as well?"

"Yes dominus, we have received our orders." The creature's tongue darted in and out. The vile thing. Bifrons felt like stamping on it and spearing its foul snake's head with his sword.

"I am overlord of the western Phlegethon and these are my legions, yet I have seen no order to march."

"A statement of fact and one that cannot be denied," hissed the snake-demon. "A mistake surely that someone somewhere forget to tell you."

Bifrons growled, and the snake-demon cringed back, its forked tongue darting out in defiance. A mistake? No mistakes were made here. There was one thing you could say about being in Hell, and that was that the errors and human frailties of mankind were well behind him.

"Who does the order come from?" said Bifrons. He unsheathed his dark curved scimitar and waved his war baton in the face of the snake-demon. He would have the head off this demon if it did not tell him.

"From the highest authorities, dominus. Now shouldn't you be back in your cauldron? We're all sinners here, and I haven't seen you drink any blood since last bell."

Bifrons let out a roar that shook the very battlements and projected a wind of hot gas straight at the snake-demon, who lost his footing and went spinning into the air and tumbling over the side of the blood-keep. The drums and marching feet paused for a moment and Bifrons glared at the demons as they marched past.

"No one marches except on my orders!" he roared, his voice booming across the entire valley, bursting the ear-drums of sinners and demons alike. "Back to your barracks, and be ready for inspection at seventh bell." Bifrons grinned a toothy, bloody grin. "I will decimate you and eat alive the flesh of those chosen."

The demon legions came to a clashing halt, pieces of armour, claw, and talon smashing against each other like some foul mechanical engine grinding to a halt. The demons looked up at the top the red keep. Some squirmed in fear of Bifrons, while others hissed and scowled their rebellion.

"Dare you defy your war-chief? I have seen you, scurrying off in ones or twos abandoning your duty. What calls you? Some sinner from the world above? Shame on you!" Bifrons roared, bloody spittle showering from his mouth over the battlements.

Then there was a hum in the smoky air, a vibration that seemed to pin everyone to the ground and all but knock the demons to the ground. And then the tension was released and a disembodied head, twice the size of Bifrons' frame, appeared in front of the keep, suspended above the ground, man's massive face, grinning cruelly at him, A band of flaming gold circled the head, pressing into the burning flesh.

Bifrons knelt on the floor without hesitation. "Woden, my Lord."

"We must talk. Inside," the voice from that massive, disembodied head commanded. With nothing more than a thought, the two appeared in an inner room of the red keep. Woden stood whole, cloaked and hunched, with a traveller's broad-brimmed hat sloping across his face. He stood, regarding the scene outside from a narrow aperture. He seemed small and old, but though he appeared as an old man, he was strong enough. He rarely saw the need to clothe himself in the fearful might of demonic strength. His ways with sinners was more subtle.

Bifrons sat in the bubbling, hot blood of his bath-like cauldron —not at his own wish, but because Woden's command had placed him there. He winced as the burning liquid scolded his sides. He hardly noticed the pain after so many centuries, but the degree seemed more intense. It felt like Woden was punishing him.

"I have told your legions to continue their marching," said Woden, hunching under his cloak as if in need for warmth, although the keep's chamber was as hot as molten iron. "Do you wish to defy my order?"

"No my Lord," said Bifrons. He dared to look up at Woden's face, but turned away again as Woden glared at him with his evil eye. The eye that could terrorise mortals to death. Bifrons shivered despite the heat of the room.

"My Lord, I feel that you are displeased with me. I only want to have my share of the glory that my legions march towards."

"In your day, Bifrons," said Woden, "you were a great war-leader and a ferocious man-slayer. You brought many raven-pickings to hang upon my tree. But you are not needed for your strength alone. You have cunning, too, and affinity with royalty. Nobleness mixed with cruelty flowed in your mortal blood. We cannot complete this destiny without you. Your deeds towards this end must continue."

"That is a great honour, my Lord," replied Bifrons. "But, I would know where my legions march."

"Bifrons, you are too eager to worry yourself over concerns that would trouble a mortal." Woden walked up to Bifrons and, taking his arm, ushered him to his feet. "The time of man is soon to end. Material cares and honours will soon be of no matter. You need to learn to dismiss these from your mind. Think only of this. Together you and I will be at the right hand of the Bright Star in the greatest battle at the end of time. What more can you wish for?"

Bifrons felt the fiery blood in his veins pounding. There was so much he wanted to ask, but instead he gritted his teeth. "Nothing more master," he replied.

CHAPTER 40

Roger's collar itched. One of Cavendish's servants had brought it to him early that morning, just after the break of dawn. For once, Roger had not been awake for hours. He had planned to stay up all night rehearsing the case for the defence. He'd made copious notes, had paced back and forth thinking over numerous points of evidence. Perhaps he should have looked in the Abbey library for legal texts, for Bracton or Raley. But it was too late for that. Instead he decided that he must go over his speech. A fine speech appealing to the mercy of the judge and jury, that was what was needed. He'd never been to anything grander than a manor court in England. But where he had studied for a while, in Avignon, home of the Papal See, he'd visited many courts and appeals at the request of his master, who found those unlucky in law perfect clients for a remedy most unnatural. Those cases always seemed to be won by the most eloquent lawyer with the quickest way with words. So he, too, would do the same.

But what to say? He had laid down on his bed to think it over, and the next moment he opened his eyes at a loud banging on his doors. Dull light came through the open shutters of his window. He shivered and thought about putting on some clothes, but found that he was fully dressed. The case! His speech! What about Isabel? How would his eloquent oratory save her if he knew not what to say? The banging continued, and he heard a voice say: "Look, I'm just going to leave it here, compliments of the Justice."

Cavendish had left him a robe and collar usually worn by a sergeant-at-law at one of the Inns of Court in London. He was honoured. He would be dressed correctly at least, even if he did not know what to say.

The trial was to be held in the Abbey's Chapter house, and it seemed to Roger that he was the last one to enter. The room was not huge, and it was already packed with perhaps twenty monks sitting in alcoves along the wall. Between these rows sat the Justice, with the Abbot sitting on his right side and two tables arranged before them where the court's notaries would record proceedings. On rows of benches facing the judge, the Abbot, and his officials, sat perhaps a hundred townspeople, male and female of all ages and professions. The place was noisy. Cavendish was busy consulting one of his clerks. The Abbot and the monks sat in silence, regarding with horror the intrusion of the laity into their Chapter house.

Roger pulled on the collar to loosen it. He could feel the heat rising in his neck and spreading like a glowing coal across his face.

He was glad, though, that the room was noisy and busy, as no one looked his way or seemed to notice his confusion. He made his way through the rows of benches, thinking to make his way somehow to near the front of the impromptu courtroom. All these people would be watching him. He froze. He hadn't prepared his speech. He had nothing to say! And all these people would be watching him stammer and stutter over his defence of Isabel and then surely that would be that and she'd be convicted, sentenced, and dead. What had he done?

A friendly face looked up at him. The Justice waved him forward and said with a clear voice that cut across the hubbub of the room, "Come Master Roger, your bench is here," he said pointing at the side of the table that faced him. Opposite sat a dour-faced clerk, who only looked up to sneer as he took his seat.

Roger nodded his thanks to the Justice, but he was already occupied, this time in a conversation with the Abbot at his side.

"Excuse me," he said to the clerk opposite him. The man looked up from his roll of parchment and frowned at him. Roger took the plunge, wanting really to ask the Justice some questions, questions he should have thought to ask him or someone last night. Answers to which any lawyer with more than a moment's experience would know. "Can you tell me where the accused is?"

The clerk shook his head, but answered anyway. "Coming. Soon." He went back to his roll. It was a very long roll and he was scanning down it and making little ticks and crosses on it and occasionally grinned to himself when he found something particularly good to tick.

"And just one more thing," said Roger. The clerk looked up, but slammed his quill onto the table in irritation.

"Yes?" he hissed, in a "I haven't got all day" tone of voice.

"Uh, do you know who will act for the prosecution?" The man smiled. "I am."

There was a commotion at the door behind him. Roger turned. Isabel, her arms weighed by chains and held by an armed guard on either side, was led through the rows of benches. Hisses and murmurs greeted her, and the general level of noise plummeted. This was what they had all come to see. The entertainment had arrived.

Two rows of arched pillars lined the Chapter house chamber, and it was to one of these that Isabel was chained. Roger rose to protest, but was waved away by

Justice Cavendish. Roger glanced over at Isabel to see how she was taking all this. She seemed to look right through him. Indeed, she was looking right past him, her eyes searching for a face in the crowd. Had she forgotten that John was dead, or was she looking for Jake? Jake was probably gone now, Roger reflected. In his obsessive haste to work on the case last night, he had completely forgotten about the whereabouts of his manservant. But he wouldn't abandon Isabel would he?

Roger had little time to reflect on Jake's doings. The court began. First the Justice began laying down the rules of the court. And then one of his clerks read out the charges against Isabel, each one being met by hisses and intakes of breath from the assembled townspeople.

The prosecutor that shared Roger's table was allowed to go first, much to Roger's relief. He began reading from the top of his long roll of parchment. He called his first witness, Edmund Hope, Infirmarian of the Abbey.

"She attempted to seduce me," Edmund told the court. "She wanted to use her body to extract books from the library, books that I knew nothing of, but which she claimed were magical. But my flesh was not weak, thank St. Brett, so she tried magic on me, and only my ring, given to me in the Holy Land, protected me from the love-potions that she tried to make me drink."

"She tried to seduce my husband, too," said the next witness, Anne Vernon. "She drew us women into her coven, tried to turn us into witches, claiming that we could have more power than men, who she said were craven fools." There was some chuckling at this from the crowd, and nods of agreement from the women-folk. "And she liked to use potions, brewed with magic ingredients."

"My Gilbert was as randy as a goat after I tried one of her potions on him," said old Mistress Alington, next up to be questioned. Roger fidgeted with hands. He didn't even have any papers to look through, that might calm his nerves. "So sore I couldn't walk for days."

"But it wasn't just love she was after, she wanted power, too," another woman, Mistress Stokes, said. "She told us that we could have whatever we wanted in life, but that we'd have to really want it, do things that we may be scared of. That's when I reckon she turned to killing the young 'uns to get blood for her demons."

Why was it so damnably hot in here wondered Roger, and why was Isabel staring at him? He avoided her gaze and regarded the next witness — the prosecutor had only got part way down his list. How many would there be, wondered Roger? It was already two hours into the proceedings.

"She told us that we must look for new husbands, ones that were strong in spirit," said Mistress Stokes.

"And what did you take her to mean by 'strong in spirit,'" enquired the prosecutor. The lucky lawyer didn't have to do much leading of the witnesses, but this was a bit much, thought Roger. Perhaps he should remonstrate with the Justice? He stood up, but the prosecutor pointed at him and said, "A man like him for instance?" That brought a guffaw from the benches and a twinkling smile from Mistress Stokes, all her broken and yellow teeth gleaming in the spring light that shone through the stained glass windows upon her.

"Oh no, I don't think she meant a fine young man like him. She was all for us taking power to ourselves and that could only mean one thing I reckon."

"Marrying yourselves to a devilish spirit?"

"Fornicating with demons? Aye, I reckon that's what she meant."

A bell tolled. It was the hour of sext and the monks would need to go and pray. "We'll adjourn here until after the seventh hour," stated the Justice.

He had some time at least to construct a case to save Isabel. Roger leapt from his seat and waited anxiously to speak to his client.

CHAPTER 41

Jake watched as a crowd of townspeople poured out of the Abbey gate. Was the trial over? His heart beat faster. Perhaps Isabel would be free soon? He gulped down his flagon of ale, and left his half-groat on the table. As he strode towards the crowd, people looked up at him and parted like the sea before Moses in the Bible. They didn't want to meet his eye, let alone speak to him. Jake shrugged and walked slowly back to the tavern. He would hear soon enough what the latest news was from the court. He sat in his recently-vacated chair and turned his head to the window, avoiding any glance his way from those who came in after him. Several of them had been avoiding him in the square.

"Open and shut if you ask me," said one of the men.

"Plenty more witnesses to come against her though," said a woman.

"Plenty of bloody talking, too; you womenfolk can't shut up," said the man again.

"Aye, but there's plenty to be said against her."

"Are you going to be saying anything?" asked the pot girl. It sounded like she wanted to be part of the excitement of the court ,too.

"Not me, I never had anything to do with that witch," the woman spat on the floor.

There was more like this, but Jake let it wash over him. Whatever had happened, it wasn't over yet. It sounded like the tedium of the court proceedings was only just beginning, but the inevitable end wouldn't be far off. Then he spotted it. The sign. She was already considered guilty it seemed. Workmen with carts were laying out thick timbers in the widest part of the market, shouting at stall-holders to clear their pitches away. It wasn't a market day, but still their stalls were up or folded away in the middle of the market place. Two men walked towards the workmen and their carts. It was the Justice and Edmund. So the Justice was in on it too, thought Jake. That bastard Cavendish, he should have known.

And what was he going to do? Sit here and get drunk? Or help Roger? But that was impossible, if he showed his face in court he'd be arrested in no time and find himself swinging next to Isabel.

He threw down another half-groat. He should go back to the guest-house at least and get his things. He'd only a small purse on him and no travelling coat. The saint, or whoever it was at the altar, had told him to have faith, had assured him that if he was brave it would all work out. But he was no knight. He had nothing but a dagger in his belt. There was no way he could free Isabel from the clutches of her guards.

But if he didn't do something then what was there worth living for? He'd seen his father cut down by Edmund, and now thanks to the Justice and that fucking monk, the love of his life was going to go the same way, but this time wriggling from the end of a rope.

He walked out into the spring sunshine. Just at that moment Edmund looked up from his conversation with the Justice and spotted him straight away. Worst luck!

Edmund immediately nudged the Justice and pointed at Jake. But Jake was already running. He knew the streets and alleys of St. Brett's better than anywhere. If he just kept going then there was no way they would catch him.

But just how long was he going to keep running?

CHAPTER 42

As Roger walked in to the cell Isabel clapped her hands. Slowly.

Roger started stammering, but Isabel didn't even let him begin.

"What a performance! You've excelled this morning. I should be paying you a king's ransom, but you're kind enough to help sign my death sentence free of charge."

"But that's why I'm here. I haven't had a chance to build a proper defence for you yet, but you can help me with that."

"Perhaps it would be better if I just spoke for myself? At the moment you're not even challenging any of their witnesses. What's it called when you do that?"

"Oh, you mean a cross-examination. I will get to that, you know. I am preparing a very good speech as well. I am sure it will sway the jury to your side."

"Do you know who the jury are?"

"Ah! Actually I hadn't thought about that. There will be a selection of the townspeople. I'm sure some of John's allies will be part of it, so you shouldn't worry there. And did you know? The Justice I think is on our side. He told me himself."

"That's interesting because I know for a fact that the jury is completely made up of monks. The Abbot insisted on it. So whatever the Justice's views are, they're going to be outweighed by whatever the Abbot wants, and believe me he will want no taint of this to stain his monks."

Roger looked at her. He didn't know what to say. He wanted to cry, but knew that probably wouldn't encourage her. Although the cell was filthy and stank, she still looked immaculate. You could make out shining wires of her copper hair sneaking underneath her wimple, black as befitted a woman in mourning. Her dress was black and clung to her, showing her curves. Yet a large silver cross hung round her neck reminding those court onlookers of her piety.

"How about we go over the evidence," said Roger. "Maybe we can call back some of those witnesses."

She smiled, and for the first time he saw a tear drop down her cheek. "The tragedy is that, apart from Edmund, they are all telling the truth: I did make potions for them to help with their love lives, but more often for illnesses. I did encourage them not to put up with the shit their husbands give them. I wanted them to be more like me, but now they attack me."

"Then we need to get at Edmund."

"As well as the Abbot and the monks. You seem to forget that he has the legions of hell at his disposal."

Roger winced. The legions of hell? That was a frightening prospect, but she was right. What hope did they have against such power.

"We'll think of something."

"You had better think fast," she said, wiping moisture from her face. She paused, looked up. "Where is Jake?"

"I don't know. Gone or in hiding, I guess. The Justice knows him. He was outlawed by Cavendish. That's how we met. I helped him escape."

She gripped his arm, and whispered through gritted teeth wet with salty tears. "Then you need to help me escape."

CHAPTER 43

Jake tumbled to the ground behind an earthen bank that held up a line of trees. Here he would be out of sight for a moment but able to watch the road through the woods in case they sent men after him. If they sent dogs, then he would worry. Only a horse would save him, and a fast one at that. The sooner he could get out of the vicinity of St Brett's, the better. His breath came harsh and fast, his gasping burned his throat. He hadn't run so far in years. Last time would have been in France, running to evade a French cavalry charge. There was that other time in Hampton escaping Cavendish's men the first time. This time he hadn't seen or heard any pursuers, but he could not believe that they weren't right behind him. He should still be running, he thought. Perhaps wading the river to throw off any scent for the dogs. But his body wouldn't let him.

His heart thumped hard. He felt his chest. That was funny. It didn't sound right. Funny beat to it. Then he realized it was hoof beats he could hear.

"Shit!" he hissed. They were right after him and he was sitting here day dreaming. He shuffled along the bank and peered through a clump of brambles at the road. But the hoof beats weren't coming from St. Bretts, but from the direction of London. A single rider was urging his horse on up the hill towards St. Brett's. Here was a fast horse, perhaps a little tired if the rider had come all the way from London, but a horse with four legs, nonetheless.

In a few seconds the horse and rider would be level with Jake. It was going at a good canter, so when Jake appeared shouting from behind the earthen bank the beast tried to veer round him rather than ride over him. But the rider, a young man, and very much surprised to see Jake, wasn't ready for the sudden change of direction, and came tumbling from his saddle, but still kept hold of the reins long enough to slow the horse down and forced it to stop and rear-up. The horse had been about to climb the earthen bank on the other side of the road and now that it was pulled back, it lost its footing and fell down the bank in an awkward heap.

Jake was the only one still on his feet. But the young man was scrambling to get up again and trying to free a sword from the scabbard at his belt. Jake could draw his dagger much quicker; he had the advantage, and he used it. He lashed at the youngster's sword arm, cutting it above the bicep. The boy winced in pain, giving Jake time to gain more advantage. He kicked the lad in the face, stunning him, and knocking a tooth out of his mouth.

Jake rolled the boy onto his stomach and twisted his arms until they were locked behind his back, then lay heavily on top of him, preventing him from moving. Although the boy wriggled, there was no way his slender frame could free itself from under Jake's bulk. The boy turned his head sideways and gasped, "I'm not a good fuck, you son of Sodom, and I have no money to speak of, so let me go."

Jane recognized that face. It had been only a week ago, but he recognized the boy as one of the three horsemen he'd encountered in Abingdon. He noticed then on the boy's collar the entwined SSs of Gaunt's livery.

The boy couldn't see him very well and didn't seem to have recognized Jake. Jake wasn't sure why he did it, but he eased himself up off the boys back. "Go on. Get lost. It's your horse I want, not your money or your skinny bottom."

The boy sprang to his feet, lithe as a wildcat, grasping his bleeding shoulder. "You're a stupid robber aren't you?" And with that the sword at his side was in his hand. His weaker left hand, Jake hoped, but he seemed to hold it well enough. In comparison, Jake's shorter dagger now left him at a disadvantage.

"You're that old bastard from Abingdon. We should have killed you before. Who sent you? Was it Burley?"

Jake didn't know who Burley was, but the fact that the boy now recognized him decided his own fate. He'd learnt the trick of a Genoese routier in France, and while the boy stared at his face and waved his sword threateningly in his direction, Jake changed the grip of his dagger.

"You might as well tell me who you're working for. If you cooperate, maybe they'll be a place for you with us. The Duke pays well —"

Apart from a gurgle, those were the last words the young lad spoke. He was some mother's son once, although he'd hardly been bred to kindness. Now he writhed on the ground in his death throes. Jake did the decent thing and removed the dagger from his throat and let the boy's last breath out of his body, along with a ghastly death rattle.

He had to let the horse out of its suffering, too. It had made little fuss. Just lying there moving its head off the ground to try to work out what the matter was. But its leg was broken and it would have laid there in quiet pain until someone else came, or worse: animals or birds arrived to feed.

No horse and a boy dead. But what he had said was intriguing. Why had one of Gaunt's men come here? There was no horse to take, but maybe the boy had money, and his sword would be useful. It looked like a fine blade. Jake strapped the scabbard to his own belt and looked through the lad's things. He had been travelling light. Probably coming for the day and then returning to London. There was a purse, but it only contained a few shillings and pence, enough for a couple of meals and a jug of wine and any tolls a traveller might need to pay, but little else. The horse yielded more. A single saddle bag was strapped to it. And inside a single book.

It was *De Vegetabilibus* by Albertus Magnus.

The boy had come in such haste to deliver a book?

Jake threw it down and shook his head. But then he noticed a piece of paper jut out. It was new paper, not part of the book's binding. And there was what looked like fresh writing on it. He picked it up and read it. It was written in Latin, well every other word was, but the non-Latin words looked like nonsense to him. There was a word in Latin at the very beginning, though, that caught his eye: Infirmarian. The piece of writing had something to do with Edmund! It must be some sort of message for him. Roger knew things about languages he didn't. He would need to see this.

With a sigh, Jake slipped the saddle-bag over his shoulder. He was headed back to St. Brett's.

CHAPTER 44

The tower was empty. All of his minions had gone it seemed; only a few guards stood sentry at the gates of the sinner's cages. For this one day of eternity, they would be lucky and would not suffer any especial torture for their crimes on earth.

Bifrons felt like one of those sinners. Woden had refused to tell him more about what was happening. Apparently Bifrons, the arch-demon of the seventh circle did not need to know where his demon legions were going. The demons had donned war-gear. Even the pathetic, scrawny, bat-like creatures who he'd never liked had strapped armour plate to their bodies and helmets to their heads. The Centaurs who shot arrows into the river of blood had, with the help of the eel-demons, cast great nets into the river and scooped up the swimmers consigned to its depths and loaded them into a locked barge, ready for when they return.

Even the demons whose task it was to remind him of his own sin by soaking him in boiling blood had left their posts. He pulled on the chains. Without anyone to watch him ... He pulled again and the chains snapped from the walls. Woden and Satan had endowed him with great strength and it was easy enough to break the chains from the wall, but not so easy to take them from his wrists. So he wrapped them around his hands instead until his fists were encased in gloves made of iron.

"That could come in useful," he muttered. He stomped through the tower, down the steps and outside. A wyrm moved its head as he came to the bottom step.

"You're supposed to stay!" it screeched at him. Hot vapour wheeshed towards him from its open maw.

"I want to go with the others," Bifrons replied. "They are my carls."

"Your carls don't want you with them. Woden says you're not trusted anymore. He's got a plan for you." The wyrm laughed as much as wyrms can.

"Has he now?" said Bifrons, drawing himself up to his full height above the wyrm. The beast was halfway through laughing at him when he brought the chain-clad first smashing into its nose, snapping and smashing its teeth out of their places. His other first smashed down onto the creature's horns and ripped them from its head.

"If you don't want more pain, then you'll tell me where they march."

"Alright, alright. It's to that town you were so fond of visiting, the one you've been banned from. Sounds like things are kicking off in a big way, now that you're out of the picture. Satan is going to get his Armageddon at last, and it's no thanks to you."

"How are they getting through?"

"The normal way the sinners come in of course. You can just follow the marching feet."

Bifrons slew the beast anyway. He had no belief in honouring promises made to such foul scum as wyrms. He turned to the Minotaur's gate and marched.

CHAPTER 45

"So you read Greek?" asked the Justice. Jake could have sworn that he'd already asked Roger that question a hundred times.

"Yes," replied Roger. "But not on a regular basis."

"Well that would be hard, wouldn't it; not many Greeks around Westmorland or Oxford, even."

"But I have read it enough to know what these words mean. Actually they're not Greek words, the person who transcribed it has merely used the Greek alphabet and swapped Greek letters for Roman script."

"So the words are in English?" said the Justice, sounding puzzled. Jake crossed his fingers where he stood outside the door. He wore a hood in case any of the Judge's servants saw him and knew him, but luckily the Justice had sent them all far away when Roger told him the contents of the letter. He didn't know that he, Roger's servant, remained behind.

"No they're in Latin. The whole letter is in Latin if you change the Greek letters to Latin — well, except where there's not an equivalent in Latin. In that case what the writer has done ... it's quite interesting actually..."

"No, no, that's fine. I'll take your word for it for now."

"But what about if you have to present the evidence in a court of law?"

Jake heard a pause. Had they made the right decision? Roger seemed certain that Justice Cavendish was an enemy of Gaunt's and would be happy to see him brought low by events at the Abbey, but he seemed hesitant now that they had actually found evidence to demonstrate the Duke's involvement.

"There's no way that I am going to present this evidence in court," said the Justice. I'm not sure what we can do with this. The ramifications of it are ... well let's just say I'm not sure if I would be executed for treason if I revealed it, or if the Duke of Lancaster, the king's own son, would be laying his head on the executioner's block."

"But what about Isabel? You're not going to let Edmund get away with this?"

"Oh no, of course not. We'll arrest Edmund straight away and then release Isabel. Edmund will be put on trial, but I think it might be best to hold him in custody first. I need to consult with some of the other lords on how to handle this. But we'll keep Edmund safely locked up. Lord Percy has some strong castles up North. We'll send him to one of those — keep him away from Gaunt, too. But that's not for you to worry about."

"I am glad to hear that my Lord. And you remember what I said about my manservant?"

"Oh yes, you said that there was something that you'd like me to discuss on that count?"

"Jake, will you come in?" Jake hesitated. Could Cavendish really be trusted? He pushed open the door and entered. Cavendish looked up curiously.

"Well I can't see him because of that damn hood. What is he? A leper or something? There's nothing I can do if he has leprosy."

"Something worse," Jake said, pulling the hood back to reveal his face.

"Outlaw," said Jake and Cavendish together.

"You brought this letter?" said Cavendish.

Jake nodded.

"And the man who carried it was Gaunt's man?"

Jake nodded.

"And what happened to him?"

"Dead. And his horse."

"You didn't have to kill his horse too..."

"That was an accident, believe me. I would dearly liked to have kept that horse alive."

"Uh well, I see." Cavendish paused.

"You're a traitor, too," said the Justice. "That's why I imprisoned you; and you became an outlaw when you escaped from justice. I would like to know someday just how you did that, although I suspect you won't want to tell me, and besides now is not the time."

Cavendish stood up and walked to the door. "Come on then let's get that fucking monk."

"But am I ..." said Jake.

"Of course you are bloody pardoned; now hurry up, we haven't got all day."

CHAPTER 46

Isabel rubbed her wrists. She was grateful to be free, but the exhaustion of the last few days was finally getting to her. She felt so tired. She couldn't believe what the Justice had told her when he came to her cell. Outside in the broad sunlight, Roger and Jake stood, looking equally tired, yet smiling as she came out. She felt like she was going to weep and wanted to go and hug them both, and laugh and dance; but then she remembered John, cold in his grave and that Edmund was still on the loose, and her blood boiled for revenge. The Justice had two armed guards with him, relieved from their duty in the gatehouse now that she was free. In a few minutes they would be returning with Edmund under their protection instead of her.

"He's at prayer," a monk told them when they enquired as to Edmund's whereabouts. In the church where the horrors had been orchestrated just a few days ago. A fitting place to put an end to Edmund's crimes.

The group moved swiftly through the cloister and entered the church. There were a number of monks in the nave and hanging around the choir, although there was no service taking place. There in front of the shrine of St.

Brett's knelt Edmund and next to him the Abbot, bowing their heads in prayer.

"Do you smell something unusual in here?" asked Roger as they walked towards the shrine.

"Nothing. But then again I haven't washed in so long that my nostrils have given up in protest," commented Jake. Isabel smiled at Jake's crude joke. She wondered how bad she must smell. A bath would be welcome once she had seen Edmund locked up.

A monk tried to usher Cavendish away, but the Justice brushed him aside. "I won't have him escape justice a minute more, prayer or no prayer. He'll have plenty of time to beg for God's forgiveness where he's going."

Edmund stood up without any further bidding, but the Abbot remained knelt in prayer beside him. "Can I help you Justice Cavendish?"

"Come quietly with me, you have charges to answer before the King's Bench and before God."

"Oh, I think you're too late for that," Edmund said, smiling. From beside him the figure of the Abbot rose, standing to his full height, but he kept on rising, and then wings pierced through the back of his habit and a flame appeared from his mouth. The figure that had been the Abbot turned, engulfing the monk's clothes in flames as it flapped, hissing heat and flame all around. Only Edmund did not wince from the sight and the searing heat.

The Justice's last words were engulfed by a fiery trident that appeared in the flame demon's hand and plunged straight through him. His body exploded in a fireball of flesh and cinder that knocked the stunned party off its feet. The guards that had accompanied the Justice were now fighting off other demons, luckily not of the burning variety, but vicious nevertheless that had erupted from the bodies of the numerous monks that had closed in on them while they watched Edmund and the Abbot.

Isabel had stepped back like the others. Next to her, Jake had drawn a sword and was looking around wondering where they could go.

"How extraordinary," said Roger, who seemed to stand there calmer than any of them.

"You can run if you like, but you won't escape," shouted Edmund.

"Let's run then!" said Jake and he grabbed her arm. She shrugged him off. She could do her own running. They scampered towards the side-door that led from the cloister, but that way was barred by two demons, man-sized, ape-like creatures with the wings of bats and the jaws of dogs. The beasts carried cruelly curved swords and black plate armour strapped to their limbs. Jake made a rush at them with his sword and was able to batter them back, giving Isabel and Roger a chance to get to the door.

But then the roof of the church came crashing in. A piece of masonry hit the floor next to Isabel and a falling beam knocked her off her feet, but most of the rood screen did not fall inwards into the church, it was simply smashed up and dispersed in a cloud of dust. A huge demon swooped down, its outstretched wings longer than a man's span on each side, and grabbed her in its talons. The creature did not travel far, but dropped her in a painful heap next to Edmund where two more ape-like demons threw weighted nets over her and prodded her into stillness.

§

Jake fought bravely, but Roger couldn't see how he could outfight the more than twenty demons that crowded the church. Both of the Justice's guards now lay dead, but Jake seemed determined to kill all these beasts of hell and rescue Isabel. While he battled the man-sized ape demons, the fire-demon still flapped its wings high above the nave of the church, singeing the roof-beams off what was left of the roof, while the evil looking giant-vulture perched with wings folded next to Edmund and the imprisoned Isabel.

Roger did the only thing he could think of, and began reciting the conjuration that had summoned the demon Bifrons to them before. It was time to fight fire with fire.

He knelt down and closed his eyes. Within what seemed only seconds he felt a hot breath on the back of his neck, and suddenly a strong arm was around his waist and had lifted him off the ground. He looked up to see a face of horror, tusked and dog-like, the visage huger and more terrifying than the demons that Jake had been fighting. Then he saw that there in the beast's other arm was Jake, wildly trying to swing his sword at the creature. The beast's huge bat-like wings flapped and carried them directly upwards, through the broken roof and out of the church. Down below the giant reptile-vulture took off and flew up towards them.

Roger closed his eyes. Perhaps if he continued his conjuration Bifrons would come and save them. "Domine ihesu christe miserere hominis istius ..."

"I am here you fool," snarled the demon that gripped them both. "Jake, will you kindly stop striking me with that toy. I know you are a great warrior, but you will not hurt me or any demon with that thing."

"Bifrons?" said Jake.

"You've met him before?" said Roger.

"You both know me but maybe in different guises."

"But Isabel... we must save her and you're taking us away from her," said Jake.

"And just in time. If I hadn't arrived now — with a little help from Master Sotil's words, thank you — then you would both be dead. Do you know who that fire-demon is?"

"Umm," said Roger.

"No I don't think you do. It is Adramelech, one of Woden's henchmen. And he is most feared. Even an arch-demon like myself is no match for that hazard."

"But what will they do with Isabel?"

"As she's not dead yet, I suspect that the necromancer, Edmund Hope, has other plans for her. But now let us think about getting you two to safety. That vulture can pick up some speed once it gets going. I will drop you in a safe place and then turn to defeat it."

"But where's safe?" said Roger looking down. The whole town looked like it was in flames. The streets were choked with people and creatures fighting each other. It was as if each person had turned on their neighbour and picked up any weapon or item that could do damage and attacked with it. Some fled. Some stood in the path of the demons and tried to fight them. The scene was one of chaos.

"I am minded to take you many miles from here. But do you have any suggestions?"

"I think the answer lies in London, let us go there," said Jake.

"Yes where Gaunt is," said Roger. "The necromancer's master."

"Gaunt?" said Bifrons. "I like the name not, it does not conjure to me a picture of a generous lord in the mead-hall. So to London it is."

Roger glanced at Jake. His heart hurt with worry. "We must save Isabel."

"First things first," roared Bifrons.

The vulture was right behind them now, but Bifrons halted in mid-air hovering, so that the huge reptilian flying wing swept past them and vainly tried to turn back towards them. But it was too late. It did not see what was coming. Out of Bifrons mouth flame leapt and smothered the vulture in fire, burning up its wings as it plunged to the earth.

Jake turned to Roger and smiled. "See, things are looking up already," said Jake.

THE END

TO BE CONTINUED IN BOOK 2 OF *THE SOTIL AND SAVAGE ADVENTURES*

ABOUT THE AUTHOR

Mark Lord is a UK based writer, living in the southeast of England. He mostly writes historical fiction and fantasy, although he has been known to write a bit of Science Fiction now and again.

Mark's favourite authors include Gene Wolfe, Ursula le Guin and Iain Banks, and he is currently getting into Dan Simmons and Neal Stephenson. Outside SF&F he enjoys the thrillers of Robert Harris and loves Tolstoy's War and Peace.

Mark is also the Editor of Alt Hist, the new magazine of Historical Fiction and Alternate History, see http://althistfiction.com for more details.

You can find out more about Mark's writing at http://marklord.info.

Printed in Great Britain
by Amazon